The Big House of Inver

The Big House of Inver

by

E. Œ. Somerville

and

Martin Ross

J. S. Sanders & Company
Nashville

First published in 1925 by
William Heinemann, London

First J. S. Sanders & Company edition 1999

Introduction © 1999 Gifford Lewis
Notes © 1999 A. & A. Farmar

ISBN: 978-1-879941-47-2

Published in the United States by
J. S. Sanders & Company, Inc.
Post Office Box 50331
Nashville, Tennessee 37205
In association with
A. & A. Farmar, Dublin

Printed in the Republic of Ireland

1 3 5 4 2

Contents

Author's Note

An established Firm does not change its style and title when, for any reason, one of its partners may be compelled to leave it.

The partner who shared all things with me has left me, but the Firm has not yet put up the shutters, and I feel I am justified in permitting myself the pleasure of still linking the name of Martin Ross with that of

E. Œ. Somerville
June 1925

To our intention
1912–1925

Introduction

The authors Edith Somerville (1858–1949) and Violet Martin (1862–1915)—whose pen name was 'Martin Ross'—were cousins. They were born into the Anglo-Irish gentry just at the time when that class's social, political and financial influence was waning rapidly. As a result, their dominant political experience was the melancholy, long withdrawing of power, privilege and a sense of belonging, from the old colonialist families. Edith, who died in her nineties, lived just long enough to see southern Ireland freed from British rule and declared a republic, and her brother brutally murdered by men claiming to represent the interests of the new state.

The Martins of Ross, Oughterard, County Galway, were bankrupted by the Famine of 1845–48, long before the Somervilles of Drishane, Castletownshend, County Cork, began to feel the pinch during the Land War of 1879–82. When Mrs Martin and her daughter first went to their cousins in Cork they were taken for 'sponges', parasites living off their richer relations. Many such families struggled to preserve the Big Houses built in more opulent times. Just as impoverished aristocrats in England looked to American heiresses to save the family fortunes it was all-important for the Anglo-Irish heir to marry money if the old place was to be kept up. Spare sons could be placed in the Army or the Navy, but daughters were a handicap. The cousins were therefore faced with social and financial constraints which obliged them either to marry or live off their parents, who had male children to educate and a shortage of money. In this they were not so very different from others of their class in England. What was different was the with-holding, as they were to see it, of the loyalty of both the native Irish among whom they lived and of the English establishment which cast them adrift. The Anglo-Irish were 'the middle nation': in good times belonging both to Ireland and to England, but in times of trouble disowned by both.

Violet Martin was the last of the long line of daughters of James Martin of Ross who died when she was ten years old in 1872. Something of the emotional chill of Martin's upbringing strikes us in a letter by her sister Edith Dawson when she described the birth of Violet in June 1862: *She was the eleventh daughter that had been born to the house, and she received a cold welcome. 'I am glad the Mistress is well' said old Thady Connor the steward; 'but I am sorry for the other news' . . . she was the prettiest child I ever saw . . . a dear little child, but quite unnoticed in the nursery . . . I think the unnoticed childhood had its effect. She lived her own life apart.* Soon after James Martin's death the great house of Ross was shut up, the eldest son, Robert, moved to London and Mrs Martin and her remaining family moved to Dublin. There they lived in the gloomy Martin town house, and Violet attended Alexandra College. With her reserved personality and her thorough education Violet Martin was a contrast to her slap-dash, gregarious cousin Edith, who was brought up in the village of Casteltownshend in West Cork, surrounded by a community of outgoing Coghill cousins and Somerville siblings.

With her 'twin', Ethel Coghill, she was deeply immersed in dancing, music, light literature and flirtation. Her mother, Adelaide Coghill, was the opposite of the absent-minded Mrs Martin. Edith was Adelaide's first born, and though she shamelessly favoured her sons, Edith came in for all her critical attention with a devouring obsession. At the same time, to her mother's distress, a twist was put in Edith's character by her grandfather, who adored her, taught her to ride and hunt and generally planted the seeds that led her very early to claim for women equality with men.

Just as noticeably as they chart the undoing of the Big House the novels of Somerville and Ross chart the slow liberation of women from Victorian strictures. Edith wrote: *Probably when the history is written of how The Woman's place in the world came to include 'All out-doors' (as they say in America) . . . it will be acknowledged that sport, Lawn Tennis, Bicycling, and Hunting, played quite as large a part as education in the emancipation that has culminated in the Representation of the People Bill. The playing fields of Eton did not as surely win Waterloo as the hunting-fields and tennis grounds of the kingdom won the vote for women.* With the goal of independence for women, political and financial, a suffragist of the time thought of sex and marriage as the end of freedom and pleasure, not the beginning of it. This thought took some time to crystallise in Edith for in her late teens and early twenties she showed a straightforwardly vigorous sexual interest and made three connections with young men. One of these, Barry Yelverton, died of enteric fever in 1885; he may be safely identified as the subject of love poetry composed by Edith, later criticised by Martin in 1886. The other two, Hewitt Poole and Sydney Vernon, both of them her cousins and impecunious, were sent packing by her mother. It is possible that Adelaide Somerville simply could not bear the thought of losing her daughter. Her intrusion into Edith's life, vivid in her letters, is complete and inescapable. Martin had no known loves, but she had a weakness for the *Punch* humourist Warham St Leger, whose zany humour was a twin to hers, but nothing came of their relationship.

Edith always relied on 'playfellows' to bear her company, and these might be male or female. Ethel Coghill's brothers Egerton, her painting partner, and Claude (Joe), her dancing partner, were always close to her. As they reached their middle twenties and married one by one, Edith mourned their loss. She complained that Joe had lost all his 'wild freshness' to domesticity. But this came later: when Martin came to Castletownshend in January of 1886 it was at first difficult for her to make any special connection with Edith as the crowd around her was so great.

Before they met, when Edith was twenty-eight and Martin ws twenty-four, both cousins had tried earning their own livings independently, Martin by journalism, Edith by graphic art. By selling paintings and drawings, Edith had earned enough to pay for her own art training. Martin arrived on the scene at a pivotal point, just as Edith was establishing roots among a group of Irish and American women artists who studied in Paris for part of the year, and who made an income out of portraits, land-

xi

scapes, graphics and book illustration. Had she remained in this grouping her destiny would not have been literary but as a commercial artist.

Martin underwent a thorough makeover of her character in Castletownshend, greatly helped by Edith's younger sister Hildegarde. She took part in charades and theatricals, played piano accompaniments to order, and made herself a playfellow fit for the vacancy left by Ethel's marriage. She had extraordinarily quick intuition and sympathy despite very poor sight. Although this hardly appears in photographs, Martin had personal magnetism, a quality often withheld from beautiful people. Like her brother Robert, who effortlessly dominated any stage, she had that attractiveness that rendered whoever else was present into a grey area. Her charm worked on all ages; Mrs Somerville succumbed and was tractable, thus making the career of letters much less difficult for Somerville and Ross than it might have been. Somervilles at Drishane who knew her when they were small children remembered into their old age the hypnotic influence of Martin's voice, that became the living voice of each new person as she told a story. A dumbstruck and shy Diana Somerville met Martin for the first time when she was eight, coming down late to the breakfast table. Mercifully there was a distraction before she was exposed to the horror of formal introductions: she was subtly drawn into a fast-moving hunt for Martin's escaped pet mouse on the breakfast table. It was finally trapped in the toast rack and the frantic escapee was revealed to be nothing more than Martin's napkin, cleverly folded and held in her hand.

In 1888 Edith and Martin joined forces to create the literary firm of Somerville and Ross, producing their first novel, *An Irish Cousin,* in 1889. After three more novels, including their masterpiece, *The Real Charlotte,* they achieved a decent income and lasting international acclaim with their stories *Some Experiences of an Irish R.M.* in 1899. There was nothing unusual about collaborating in artistic endeavour, nor about women writing for money. When Ethel and Edith wrote gothic horror stories together they were deliberately emulating an aunt: their Aunt

Louisa had written, with another cousin the playwright Willy Wills, a 'Shilling Shocker'. Ireland was not short of women novelists who visited Cork frequently enough for their income to become known, like Mrs Hungerford with her £1,000 a year.

The literary partnership between Martin and Edith was born out of expediency. They found 'another way'—an alternative to marriage or maiden aunthood in a brother's household. Happily they scored a hit with their first novel *An Irish Cousin* and settled on writing as their joint profession. In interviews with literary journalists they described their job-sharing in quite matter-of-fact terms. However, when Martin died, on 21 December 1915, and Edith was temporarily *hors de combat*, her brother Cameron took it upon himself to supply a description of their writing together to Charlie Graves and E. V. Lucas, which was widely quoted. Edith wrote to Cameron from Lismore on 6 January 1916:

I am afraid you didn't get it quite right. It is impossible to apportion general responsibility in our writings but even to have said 'hardly a paragraph, a phrase etc. etc. was written singlehanded by either of us' would have been an exaggeration—even in the quotations which Mr Lucas gave some were hers, some were mine—If I ever said those words—which I hardly think possible—I was making far too sweeping a statement, and I should be grateful if you would not continue to quote them. Whether Cameron, who had preternatural sense in some quarters while being senseless in others, realised that a mystery would be good for business or simply romanticised the partnership we will never know, but it was Cameron who set the ball rolling. Despite her efforts, Cameron's words put in Edith's mouth were out in the public domain and have been there, repeated over and over again by later writers, ever since. Literary inspiration was a subject of popular interest and discussion. Some creative writers noticed the resemblance of their inspired writing, where they were not conscious of what was impelling them to write and had no memory of what they had written, to automatic writing. Edith was describing the writing of *The Real Charlotte* when she wrote: 'of all the company of more or less tangible shadows who were fated to declare themselves by our pens . . .' as if the disembodied personalities of their creations had possessed the writing instruments.

After Martin died, J. B. Pinker, the literary agent for Somerville and Ross, who hardly wanted to lose a sure-fire source of income, encouraged Edith to compile a memoir of Martin and their life together. He hoped thereby to persuade Edith to keep writing. The memoir *Irish Memories* (1917) is a most fascinating mélange of quotations, taken from anywhere in the chronological layers of their papers, and made to fit the story. Fictitious interludes were added to fill out bare patches. An invented scene at Whitehall, to the west of Castletownshend, is introduced to explain the impulse that inspired their first novel. Edith falsely claims to have marked Martin out as a collaborator at once, whereas it was only after her return from Paris (some months after they first met) that they worked in the studio at a communal effort—a mock-learned dictionary of the family catch phrases—with Herbert Greene, Edith's faithful suitor, and yet another cousin. All this culminated in a romantic, and fabricated, account of their early relationship.

Pinker must have been pleased at the overall effect. *Irish Memories* sold well, (and unexpectedly) was taken by the sophisticated as a chronicle of lesbian love, and Edith's loneliness was banished when the musician Ethel Smythe charged into her life like a crusading sex therapist. However, a relationship built on such foundations could never survive, let alone become the great and passionate love affair that Ethel hoped for. Their brilliant letters to each other, now at Queen's University Belfast, show two clever women at purposes that became so cross that the frustrated Ethel charged off in disgust in another direction.But the object of convincing Edith that a continued career in writing was possible, and financially the best option, was achieved. After the death of Martin Edith wrote a further fourteen books under their joint names, though there were to be no more 'Irish R.M.' stories. Undoubtedly the best of the new work was *The Big House of Inver*, published in 1925. This takes the analysis of the decline of the colonialist families a step further and presents a bleak picture that is only implicit in *The Real Charlotte*.

The post-1915 novels are fascinating to analyse as the products of a conversational technique: a conversation that had been from 1888–1915 uttered aloud, and that was from 1915 until 1949 channelled into an internal dialogue. This latter was a feat achieved through love, intensely detailed memory and thought transference. Whichever, the reading public had an appetite for the style.

The Big House of Inver is dominated by Shibby Pindy, born out of wedlock to a Catholic girl by a gentry father. Her Christian name has mutated as it descends in caste from Isabella to Ishbel to Shibby, and her surname from Prendeville to Prendy to Pindy. She is a woman trying to hold together the remains of Prendeville lands, and the family great house, for her object of devotion: the heir, her legitimate half-brother, Kit. She is the housekeeper of her worthless father. The action of *The Big House of Inver* arises from the attempts of this very powerful, strong-minded woman to reverse the circumstances of generations. Her struggle is that of her old family, of which she is an illegitimate offshoot, but spiritually and genetically a descendant of the proudest and grandest of them. But despite her strength, Shibby Pindy is doomed to failure, defeated by the new rich on both the Irish and the English sides. An important theme of the novel is how the traits and inheritances of history play out in the present; the layers of the struggle run not only between the *present* Irish, English and Anglo-Irish, but the ancestors as well.

Like W. B. Yeats, as a writer Edith Somerville was indebted to spirit guidance; unlike him she had grown up in a family circle where Spiritualism was an accepted and important conduit of human communication with the dead. The Coghill family had a deep interest in Spiritualism, Sir Joscelyn Coghill—Edith's uncle—was one of the first vice-presidents of the Society for Psychical Research founded in 1882, on the initiative of William Barrett FRS, then Professor of Physics at the Royal College of Science, Dublin. Sir Joscelyn's brother Kendal, though initially sceptical, had been converted to belief by what was for him incontrovertible evidence. The brothers had attended the seances of the remarkable physical medium D. D. Home (1833–86). Much experimentation took place in Castletownshend both at The Point and Glen Barrahane.

Kendal Coghill used to investigate the means of spirit communication called automatic writing, whereby a gifted person, with a pen resting on the hand, not gripped, fell into a light trance and an unbroken line of writing, without punctuation or word breaks, streamed from the pen. Kendal found that Edith and her brother Cameron were both gifted in this way, and they recalled, in their mid-to-late teens, their puzzled curiosity at the screeds produced through no volition of their own. From the 1880s onwards this gift was put aside by Edith, but when, at the prompting of the medium J. E. M. Barlow, she went back to automatic writing after the death of Martin, the gift—which had lain fallow for more than thirty years—was still with her.

It was the most natural thing in the world to the Coghills that spirits both existed and should wish to communicate. Edith used to be perplexed by the negative attitude of her Church to Spiritualism, expostulating that the Church was organised on the basis of spiritual communication with a being whose existence was not proven, whereas Spiritualism was merely communication with beings who had but recently existed; the leap of faith required of the believer being so much shorter Spiritualism did not seem to Edith to be at all irrational. The Society for Psychical Research had published that fascinating and unnerving survey *Phantasms of the Living* in 1886. Under Mrs Sidgwick and the Balfours the Society's investigations were minutely scientific and careful. One of the Society's earliest successes was the rigorous work by the investigator that unmasked Madame Blavatsky in the use of props. (This questioning rigour eventually repelled 'believers' from the society, most famously Sir Arthur Conan Doyle, who resigned in 1930.) Martin died during the First World War, in the course of which abundant evidence was recorded by the Society of spirit manifestations by the war dead at the point of death. Perhaps it was because of the widespread atmosphere of interest and acceptance caused by this that Edith's resolution to carry on writing with Martin as a spirit guide seemed not particularly odd at the time. Yeats was in communication with spirits from spheres and time zones that make Martin's seem positively run-of-the-mill.

The Big House of Inver is dedicated 'To our intention 1912–1925'. On 18 March 1912 Martin wrote to Edith from Kilcornan, Oranmore describing a visit to the 'wonderful wreck' of the St George's Tyrone House: 'there rioted three or four generations of St Georges—living with countrywomen, occasionally marrying them—all illegitimate four times over. . . . Yesterday as we left, an old Miss St George daughter of the last owner was at the door in a donkey trap . . . She was a strange mixture of distinction and commoness, like her breeding, and it was very sad to see her at the door of that great house—if we dare to write up that subject!'

As it happens, Martin had somewhat misconstrued the real circumstances, as Mark Bence-Jones points out: *Tyrone House, the magnificent 18th-century mansion of the once-powerful St Georges, on the shores of Galway Bay, had been abandoned in 1905 after the death of the 96-year old Honoria, widow of Christopher St George, though two of her daughters continued to own it jointly. Christopher St George had married very much beneath him; moreover Honoria was a Catholic and he a Protestant and in the days when mixed marriages were legally invalid unless performed by a Protestant clergyman they had been married by a Catholic priest. A Protestant marriage had followed but not until after the birth of ten of their twelve children who were consequently illegitimate in the eyes of the law.*

The family's decline was not quite as complete as Martin thought: 'They were,' she wrote: 'all illegitimate four times over' having heard some garbled account of the invalid marriage. And she was under the impression that they had for several generations been in the habit of marrying village girls, whereas before Honoria's time their wives had been consistently grand.

Martin's letter was marked later by Edith with 'a possible subject for a book'. When Martin died Edith was left with a mass of notebooks and letters. Having mined them successfully for *Irish Memories*, it was but a short step to the completion of novels they had discussed and plotted. In the Preface to *Mount Music* of 1919 Edith states: 'This book was planned some years ago by Martin Ross and myself. A few portions of it were written, and it was then put aside for other work. Without her help and inspiration, it would not have been begun, and could not have been completed. I feel, therefore, that to join her name with mine on the title page is my duty, as well as my pleasure.' It was published on Martin's birthday, a gift of which Edith was convinced Martin was conscious.

The Big House of Inver was similar: the central action of the book is clearly placed in 1912, the year of Martin's letter (and the year the Home Rule Bill was introduced, only to be overtaken by events). In cultivating what the psychical researchers referred to as a 'secondary personality' Edith invested great mental energy. She wrote with Martin every evening between seven and eight. Both for companionship and as a means of keeping the motor of Somerville and Ross running it was a success, and Pinker, the agent, and Longmans and William Heinemann, the publishers, accepted the validity of the continued existence of Martin as a writer through the medium of her partner.

Many of the themes in this novel are rehearsed in Edith's letters to her sister Hildegarde regarding the failings of her brothers. The roof of the old house in Castletownshend, Drishane, which the Somerville family had lived in since the eighteenth century, had started to go in the summer that *The Big House of Inver* was published. Edith had tried to persuade Cameron to give up the maintenance of the house in 1921, when to both Somerville sisters it seemed the most economical measure was for them to live together in a smaller house. But Cameron persuaded Edith to hold on to the dream that they both had: to leave the family home to a Somerville heir. This was well-intentioned but impractical; in effect, Cameron retired from the Army to live in Drishane with his sister while the family seat fell into disrepair around them. An old friend of the family, Mrs Anstey, wrote to Rose Cameron Bingham in 1934 describing Drishane during her recent visit: *Somehow the Somervilles seem to weather the storms in a wonderful way. I don't think they notice very much! Cameron, dear fellow, never sees what is under his nose and Edith is too pre-occupied and too unaccustomed to keeping her eyes open except as regards the people (the peasants) of whom she can write. Otherwise the whole dining-room might be festooned with cobwebs and she would never give them a glance! I long to clean and tidy things . . . I loathe dust and neglect . . . Those curtains only hang together by films of dust! . . . if a leg of a table is broken, it is not mended and then a strange leg is thrust underneath, the original one having meanwhile been used to light the fire! That is true! I am sure they will be able to stick to Drishane if only Cameron shows a little common sense.* The theme of *The Big House at Inver*—in its Shibby/Kit relationship—quite clearly echoes its author's helpless emotional predicament in the favouritism she showed throughout her life first to her brother Aylmer, who was as well the favourite of his mother, and to Aylmer's son Desmond, whom Edith called 'My boy'. It seems that Edith, despite all her feminism, was fated to repeat her mother's failings of over-indulgence and special pleading for her elected male god. In the triumph of the Weldon family, originally servants of the Prendevilles now become masters of the Prendeville house and lands, we find a drama that was repeated in many forms in the wake of the 1903 Wyndham Land Act when for the landlord the only way out was to sell up. The Big House and all its human dependencies, still functioning in *The Real Charlotte*, have by 1912 been swept up and reshaped under new owners to whom the lands were significant, but not the houses.

As Edith wrote later about the novel 'this is the history of one of those minor dynasties that in Ireland, have risen, and ruled, and rioted and have at last crashed in ruins. They had their great days of power and plenty, and built fine homes that now stand empty. Their very names are sunk in squalor, mis-spelt, mispronounced, surviving only illegitimately.'

Gifford Lewis
Oxford 1999

Chapter 1

The Big House of Inver stood high on the central ridge of the promontory of Ross Inver, and faced unflinching the western ocean.

It might seem that a wish for the sight of the sea and sunsets had been its builder's reason for traversing the usual practice of his country, and sacrificing shelter and bodily comfort, to scenery, and the lust of the eye, but one may be reasonably sure that Mr Robert Prendeville, who built the Big House during the last years of the reign of Queen Anne, had not much thought for the beauty that lay, most literally, at his feet. (And yet it cannot be gainsaid that he was a man of taste and built a fine house.) The probabilities, almost—judging by the family character—one may say the certainties, are that he set his house midway on the long headland because thence, on the one hand, he could see the coming of the vessels that brought claret from Bordeaux to Western Ireland, and on the other, could take note of the Queen's ships that were nearly as interested as he in the destination of the red wine.

This was, to be sure, the chief reason why Mr Prendeville left the old house, back among the trees of the Demesne of Inver, where there was indeed good shelter, but a man should walk an up-hill half-mile to see the blue water. Perhaps, also, he was attracted by the thought that high on Ross Inver stood the tower, tall and square, that, since the time of his Norman ancestor who built it, had guarded the Prendevilles from those whom they and their companion adventurers, called, with soldierly arrogance, The Wild Irish—as who, in later days, should say The Gorillas.

The impartial chronicler of the history of Ireland (if the future achieves such a prodigy) regarding the many thousand acres acquired by the Prendevilles, and remembering that the verb to acquire is non-committal as to methods, might think that protection was rather required by the Wild Irish (or Gorillas) than by their Norman invaders. But this is a point that need not now be dis-

1

cussed; and as to the question of the claret, it must not be supposed that Mr Robert Prendeville was a common smuggler, breaking the laws for mere money. He was, on the contrary, a very great personage, who owned the better part of the Barony of Iveragh, and to outwit the King, and specially a newish King, of a breed Robert Prendeville thought little of, was an affair that knocked no feather off a gentleman's dignity. Moreover, the claret was of the best.

Ross Inver struck out due north from the mainland into the sea, facing, across the harbour at Cloonabinnia, the lesser promontory of Ingard Head. It was like nothing so much as a carpenter's long saw, with serrated rocks, like teeth, on its western side, and a smooth stretch of sandy shore on the east, facing up the wide Bay of Monarde, as it might be the back of the saw. At the head of Cloonabinnia Harbour, between Inver and the village of Cloon, a quiet river, the Fiddaun, came sliding out of the rich plain of Moyroe, giving the reason for the name Ross Inver, the Point of the River-mouth. The Prendeville Demesne went inland from the root of the promontory, spreading both ways with the sweeping curve of a peacock's tail, five hundred acres of grass and woodland, with a ten-foot stone-wall round all, built boldy in the brave days when a skilled mason's wage was something less than fourpence.

Inver house embodied one of those large gestures of the minds of the earlier Irish architects, some of which still stand to justify Ireland's claim to be considered a civilised country. It was a big, solemn, square house of three stories, built of cut stone, grandly planned, facing west in two immense sweeping curves, with a high pillared portico between them and stone balustrades round the roof, and enormous carved stone urns wherever such could suitably be placed. Robert Prendeville gave his architect a free hand, and was not the man to stint his ship of a ha'porth of tar. A wide and deep area went round three sides of the house; the back was guarded by the high walls of the stable yard. In front was an immense semi-circular gravel sweep, surrounded by a low cut-stone wall, with iron railings and high wrought-iron gates, with ample room for a coach and four horses to wheel and turn inside it. A flight of limestone steps led to the hall-door, and under the balustrades on either side of them Robert had had inset the 'marriage-stones' that he had taken from

2

the elder house among the Demesne trees, big blocks of limestone, carved with the names, very arbitrarily spelt, and the coats-of-arms, of his ancestors and their wives, and over the door he had built in a grey slab, with the family crest, a mailed hand, and the family motto, 'Je Prends,' carved on it.

Robert's son, Christopher, whose nickname in the county was Beauty Kit, had installed a specially important marriage-stone that recorded his alliance with the noble house of Breffny. Beauty Kit was a bad boy, dissolute and drunken, but his looks and his fortune were as good as his morals were bad, and, as the Lady Isabella's father, the Marquis of Breffny, said, it is unreasonable to expect everything in a young man. The Lady Isabella Devannes was a match in beauty for Beauty Kit, and more than a match for him in most other ways, specially those of society. She took him to Dublin and pushed him through a season at the Viceregal Court, well pleased with the sensation made by so rich and handsome a young couple as she and Kit. In a new coach, with four blood horses, she drove him back to Inver House, followed by a post-chaise-ful of Italian workmen, brought from Dublin to bring the decorations of the house up-to-date. Kit's friends in the county gazed in awe at the splendours of the dining-room ceiling (when they were not regarding the reverse side of the dinner-table) and swore that Kit was a lucky dog. He was made High Sheriff of the county the same year, and Lady Isabella and he drove in state in the new coach into Monarde, the county town, and there, in the stern old Prendeville town house, with its narrow windows, and its stone coats-of-arms built into its grey walls, Lady Isabella entertained very magnificently the County Quality, while she made no secret of her opinion that they were very small beer indeed. Kit's friends, whose views as to their own vintage did not coincide with those of his wife, began to think that perhaps he was not so much to be envied after all. Kit's own views on the subject had not very much time to form, as, after five years of rather exacting matrimony (whose rigours were, however, mitigated by unofficial consolations) he died of small-pox at the age of twenty-eight, and in so dying was saved a life of mortification, as the illness, not content with taking his life, had first taken

3

also his beauty, and it was said (by Kit's friends) that Lady Isabella on sight of him had uttered a cry of horror, and without a word had rushed from the great bedroom at Inver House in which he lay dying, when they brought her to bid him farewell.

Yet it would seem that, after all, Kit was the only man in the world for her. After his death, she shut herself up in the Big House, and there lived for long, lonely years, refusing, in arrogance, to know, or to let her children know, her neighbours, freezing herself into, as it were, an iceberg of pride, living to see, at last, her only son, Nicholas, marry the daughter of one of the Inver gamekeepers, and her two daughters, Isabella and Nesta, go off with two of her own grooms.

The glories and the greatness of Inver therewith suffered downfall. Five successive generations of mainly half-bred and wholly profligate Prendevilles rioted out their short lives in the Big House, living with country women, fighting, drinking, gambling.

The legitimacy of the succession was secured by means and stratagems that need not be recorded. Somehow out of the mire an heir would be evolved and acclaimed, and the process of drinking and dicing away the lands of Inver would be carried on with all the hereditary zest proper to a lawful inheritor.

The seventh in descent from Robert the Builder was Jasper Christopher, with whose birth in the month of June, 1824, this record may be said to open. Ireland is a friendly, and an informal country, in which pet names, and nicknames, and abbreviated names, are bestowed early and are seldom outlived. There had been a Prendeville whose mother's affection had taken the unfortunate form of addressing him as her Pigeon, with the consequence that as 'Pidgy Prendy' he was known until he died. Similar instances are many, therefore, Jasper Christopher may be regarded as having had luck in being known simply as 'Jas.' Jas succeeded to what remained of the family estates at an unusually early age, as a matter of fact, just a month after his birth, because his father, Christopher FitzRobert, was killed in a duel on the day on which his son and heir was christened.

Christopher FitzRobert had sown the usual family crop of

wild oats early, and had to some extent restored the family credit by marrying a woman of good birth, Miss Susan Moore, of Gurtha. On the whole, as Prendevilles went, Christopher Fitzrobert seems to have been meritorious. As to the duel, in which he lost his life, it was not of his own seeking. His wife, the young Madam Prendeville, was naturally put out when she heard that the day, and even the hour, fixed for the combat was that on which her first-born was to be received into the company of all good Christian people. But this was not Kit's fault. The coincidence was conceivably due to the fact that the seconds in the affair had, as it happened, been cast for the part of the baby's god-fathers. The Long Strand of Ingard was the place chosen for the fight, and, since Cloon church was within half a mile of the Long Strand, it was obvious to the gentlemen who were doubling two such important parts that two birds might be conveniently killed with one stone.

This arrangement, admirable though it was from the point of view of Messrs. Frank Moore (Mr Prendeville's brother-in-law) and Nick D'Arcy (brother of Kit's opponent) came near to spoiling the whole affair, so most people said, since the coming double event gave rise to much talk, and the police somehow got wind of what was going to happen. The situation was only just saved by the principals and their seconds hurrying from the church to the sands, and, wading far out into the sea, there exchanging shots, with the consequence to Kit Prendeville that has already been mentioned.

A grand sight it was, and a great day altogether for the Parish of Ross Inver! Everyone was delighted. Four of the finest young gentlemen in the country walking out to their middles in the water for all the world to see, and they in their Sunday clothes, with their tall hats on them! No four finer young men in the Globe of Ireland! Well, and isn't it a shame for the like o' them to be shooting at one another? Oh pity! Beat on the donkey, Mickel Paudyeen! Let ye be hirrying before we'll be late! What call have we coming here at all and we to be late?

Thus, and much more, the onlookers, who had gathered in hundreds from the four corners of Ross Inver to the Long Strand, the bells of Cloon Church having warned them that the young heir was being christened, and that there was no time to be lost

5

if they wanted to the fun that was to follow.

One wonders if anywhere, save in Western Ireland, could such a sight have been paralleled. The four young bloods waist-deep in the shining sea, with the blue sky of June above them, and the seagulls squealing over their heads, and young Madam Prendeville, with the newly christened Jasper and his retinue of nurses, sitting in her yellow chariot by the edge of the tide. The sands, right and left of her, were thronged with the people of three parishes; fish-women and fishermen from the near-by village of Cloon, and wild men, Prendeville tenants, from back in the bogs of Iveragh and Moyroe, all gabbling in Irish their views as to the merits of the combatants, betting on the result, enjoying to ecstasy such nerve-strain as they were capable of feeling. It was, indeed, later, hinted by some of the Iveragh men that since their landlord was over six feet high, and his enemy, Peter D'Arcy of Milltown, but a little fellow, nearly a foot less than Kit, there was too much of the one and not enough of the other above water. But the general opinion of the crowd on the sands, and of the priest of the parish, as well as of the parson (who, being himself a man of the D'Arcys, had made haste with the service, being naturally anxious to see that all things were done decently and in order,) was that the fight had been carried through handsomely and creditably.

At the subsequent Enquiry it was agreed that the 'Peelers,' having arrived too late to do more than shout disapproval from the shore, could not then have been expected to risk a ducking, or worse, by wading out to the fighters, all of them being young gentlemen of known spirit. Peter D'Arcy got away to France in a fishing-smack that was hanging on and off the land to see what was to be seen, and Christopher FitzRobert joined the very shady shades of his ancestors by a route which they, no doubt, thought becoming. So, as the Reverend Harry D'Arcy said, all ended well and pleasantly. Kit had a great and grand funeral, out to the ancient graveyard on Deer Island, followed by all the country in boats and *coraghs* of all sorts and sizes, and mourned with *caioneing* that wailed far along the blue water and scared the seabirds out in Monarde Bay.

6

Young Madam Prendeville put up a handsome stone cross to her husband's memory, and placed it as near the scene of his death as was possible. Then she addressed herself to life at Inver, and to the care of the property, as Regent for little Jasper Christopher, and, by the time that he was short-coated, she had found that widowhood at the Big House was not a condition easily to be dealt with. According to the hiving custom of her husband's family, (which was also pretty generally that of the time and country) the Prendeville relatives and collaterals, from the late Christopher's grandmother, the old Madam Prendeville, (who had been no more than one Joanna Halloran, daughter of a tenant) down to his half-aunts, and several indefinite cousins, were all established as determined inmates of the Big House. It did not take long for the young Madam to realise her powerlessness in the face of so many and firmly-vested interests, and, being a young woman of character and intelligence, she lost no time in packing up the silver and her wardrobe, and betaking herself and the baby to Monarde, and there establishing herself in the family town-house.

It was no more than three years after this that the old Madam died, and so fierce were the battles waged over her effects, and so incessant the rows and the ructions which their partition involved, that the police had once more to interfere in the Prendeville affairs. This time they met with more success. Authorised by the young Madam (by letter, from Monarde) and supported by the Prendeville bailiff, old Mick Weldon, the 'Peelers' made a sweep that could hardly have been called clean, but was indubitably thorough, of the Big House and its inmates, who scattered to various outlying footholds of the family, each bearing with him or her—as was not an unusual feature in the dispersion of such a hive—such spoil of furniture, pictures and china, as could conveniently be abstracted. The young Madam had done well to take the silver with her to Monarde.

The routing of the squatters being thus effected, Madam Prendeville, with her father, James Moore of Gurtha, drove out the twenty miles from Monarde to Inver in the yellow chariot, and having taken over the Big House, empty for the first time since it was built, she left it in Mick Weldon's hands, to be let as

7

soon as a reliable tenant could be found. It happened just at that time that Tithe riots broke out in the parish, the Reverend Harry D'Arcy being a stickler for his legal rights, and indisposed to regard the question from any point of view save that of the law, and before things had settled down—(not without the rather rigorous peacemaking of the Military from Monarde)—the Rectory was burned to the ground. Madam Prendeville's representative, Mick Weldon, found his opportunity in this misfortune. Inver House was let to the Church, and the Reverend Harry D'Arcy established himself there until such time as the ecclesiastical authorities chose to rebuild the Rectory. This effort was not made for some years, and time therefore was ample for fallings-out between the tenant and the representatives of the landlord, that is to say young Jas, now a spoilt and naughty little boy at a day-school in Monarde. It is probable that the original trouble which had brought about the duel, persisted, as troubles will, in lonely places where distractions are few. At all events it is certain that the Reverend Harry was not an improving tenant, nor can the company he kept be said to have been of an improving nature. He was a bachelor and a sportsman, and he filled the Big House with his sporting friends, among whom was young Lord Ballyfaill, that dashing blade of whom it was said:

> *'No dog with a tinkettle tied to his tail,*
> *Made half such a racket as Lord Ballyfaill!'*

The Reverend Harry and his young friends seem to have made a very considerable racket in the Big House, one of the party even, with a regrettable lack of originality, dragging a favourite hunter up the hall-doorsteps, riding him, slipping and clattering, across the marble-paved hall into the great dining-room, and there setting him to jump the dinner-table, with the result that the horse broke several legs of the table and one of his own, so that he had to be shot where he fell. The rider, who was drunk, escaped uninjured. The moral of this incident is obscure, but its immediate result was that the Reverend Harry received a notice to quit, and being, as he considered, ill-treated and insulted, he was, before he left Inver, at the pains to pull off a considerable portion of its roof. Thus he let the weather into

8

the house, and so departed, somewhat comforted.

It may be supposed, given the climate of the West of Ireland, that the first step to have been taken by the owner of the house was the repair of the hole in the roof. The month was October, and Mick Weldon told his employer that there was as much water coming down the front stairs on a wet day as would carry up a good salmon. Madam Prendeville and Jas, who was by this time fifteen, and more spoilt than ever, took the mail-car to Cloon, and recognised that the case of the front stairs had not been greatly overstated. None the less, in the opinion of young Jas, family self-respect could not sanction any steps, save legal ones, to be taken in the matter of the hole. Accordingly mother and son loosed the law on Mr D'Arcy, and established themselves in the old Tower of Inver in order to guard the Big House against further attack.

By the time that the Prendevilles had won their case, their lawyers had pocketed the better part of the compensation. Madam Prendeville, disregarding the expostulations of her brother-in-law, Mr Robert Prendeville (who was next after young Jas in the succession) mended the roof with a make-shift patching of thatch, and deposited what remained of the compensation money in the Bank, against the time when money would be wanted to buy a commission in the Army for Jas, who, since his mother refused to sanction the Navy, refused, in his turn, to consider any other career.

After this Madam Prendeville and her son continued to live in the Tower of Inver. Jas decided for himself that he had had enough of schooling, and from his decisions there was no appeal. He found occupation and instruction enough in riding the tenants' horses, and shooting over the wide acres of the property, and—and this pleased him best of all—sailing a little one-ton yacht that had been his father's, up and down the coast, in all weathers, keeping his mother's nerves on the rack by his disregard alike of advice or danger. Since the day that she had seen Christopher fall in the bright water, Madam Prendeville had hated the sea.

Three years later, when Jas was eighteen, he went to India, a cornet in an Irish Dragoon regiment. This was in the year 1842, the year following on that of the disaster in the Khyber Pass, and

Jas, who had smelt powder at his christening, received a further baptism of fire in the ensuing war, that ended with Sir Charles Napier's famous despatch, 'Peccavi' 'I have Scinde!'

Jas came back from India in 1849, a Captain (at a price), a horseman, with a well-earned reputation as a good fighter in a tight place, as well as the character of being able to carry more liquor for his age than any other man in a hard-drinking regiment; fully qualified, in fact, to take first rank as hero in contemporary military romance.

Chapter 2

That Madam Prendeville was not among those who received and welcomed her son is explainable on one hypothesis only, and that, as it happens, coincides with the facts—which is not invariable with hypotheses, especially in Ireland. She, or to be more accurate, that which had worn too frail and thin to house any longer her tired soul, was lying beside her husband in the prehistoric graveyard on Deer Island, on one of the slabs of the Prendeville family vault.

While young Jas had been fighting in India, his mother had also had a fight in hand. In the end the enemy had been too strong for her, but her fight had been a gallant one, and it was fought against heavier odds than her son had had to face. Until those whose bodies lie in the desolate crowded graveyards of the south and west of Ireland can tell the poor histories of their lives and deaths, what things were suffered by the people of all classes during the years of the famine of 1845, and onwards, can never be known.

> *That flow strewed wrecks about the grass,*
> *That ebbe swept out the flocks to sea,*
> *A fatal ebbe and flow, alas!*
> *To manye more than myne and me.*

Many an ancient property foundered and sank in that storm, drawing down with it—as a great ship in her sinking sucks down those that trusted in her protection—not alone its owners, but also the swarming families of the people who, in those semi-feudal times, looked to the Big Houses for help. The martyrdoms, and the heroisms, and the devotion, have passed into oblivion, and better so, perhaps, when it is remembered how a not extravagant exercise of political foresight might have saved the martyrdoms. As for the other matters, it might only intensify the embittering of a now outcast class to be reminded of what things it suffered and sacrificed in doing what it held to be its duty.

But in those dark years there was no bitterness in the relation

11

between Madam Prendeville and the helpless host of starving creatures that surrounded her. The estate, already deeply mortgaged, went down deeper still into the trough of debt. Like many others of his class, Kit Prendeville, when he died, had—as a recent historian of Ireland says of that régime of landlords— 'an estate heavily burdened with charges . . . little margin and few reserves.' Yet during the famine 'some men distinguished themselves by a self-sacrificing devotion, one of them flinging all that was left of his fortune and health into an effort to save his poor, and died in the effort.'*

Madam Prendeville, with the same sense of duty, somehow laboured on through those desperate years. How could rents be paid by starving people whose fields were as though they had been poisoned, and with the food that they trusted to turned to black slime in the furrows? She set up a soup-kitchen in the great marble-paved hall of the Big House, and the dying people came creeping in from the lonely Iveragh country to get what they could of her. Not much indeed she had for them, but she did what she could. She killed her bullocks and her sheep for the big pot that was boiling day and night in the hall of Inver. She wrote begging letters to England and America. It was through her efforts that an American meal-ship came to Cloonabinnia Harbour, sailing right up to the fish-quay by reason of a marvellous high tide, and unloading there the cargo of golden maize that was more precious than much fine gold. It was like a miracle to the stricken people, and so also was the still more miraculous flood of small fishes, sprats or whitebait, which came rushing up the harbour, urged by what compulsion no man knew, to cast themselves ashore on the Long Strand of Ingard, in myriads beyond computation. How many lives they may have saved will never be known, but that they came at the hungriest hour of that hungry time is sure enough.

Madam Prendeville wrote a long letter to Jas telling him all about the miracle, and how Mr D'Arcy had preached a sermon about it, taking the story of the Manna and the Quails as his text. She came of a generation inured to long sermons, and, being a fair-minded

---

* Richard Martin, of Ballynahinch, Connemara. *The Story of Ireland* Stephen Gwynn

woman, she did not permit the family feud to bias her into thinking an hour and fifty minutes too much of a good thing. In fact it was with disapproval—(even though she wanted to make her letter pleasant to him)—that she told Jas of the behaviour of the Rev. Harry's brother, the Admiral, who had sat with his big gold repeater watch on his knee, and after the first hour of the discourse had caused it to ring the time every five minutes.

'I told Harry I'd give him a suv'rin if he'd stop at the hour,' the Admiral had said, 'but that he should owe me a sixpence for every five minutes outside it; and begad, before he had done prating, I'll be shot if the dam' feller didn't owe me a crown over the job!'

'But this!,' as Madam Prendeville wrote, 'was no more than was to be looked for from one of the D'Arcys. What can you expect from a cob but a kick?'

When Jas came home with his regiment in 1849, the famine had passed and gone, and his mother had gone too. In the end of the trouble, when the storm had to some extent died down and the shadow was lifting a little, she, who had come safe through the worst of the bad times, went down with the famine-fever that still loitered on in 'backwards places.' A beggar-woman brought it in her rags to Inver, and Madam Prendeville died of it, with the tears wet on her cheeks for the son whom she would not see again.

Jas had been fond of his mother, who had served him well, and had always indulged him with the assiduity that was, in her time, considered to have been the meed of male offspring, and appears not to have been inconsistent with common-sense in other matters. But in the excitement of home-coming he soon ceased to miss her. He had not even her grave to visit, since she had been absorbed by the discouraging family vault, and Jas, who, thanks to her instructions, was accustomed to think first of himself, found it more agreeable to dismiss the thought of her from his mind.

In the primitive Ireland of mid-Victorian times a welcome-home seldom failed to a son of a ruling house, especially if, as in Jas's case, he was returning as the heir to his inheritance. The Prendeville tenants, the fisherpeople of Cloon, and the neighbours of all sorts and degrees, turned out to receive the young landlord with suitable rejoicing. Tar-barrels and bonfires blazed, and the public houses of the village ran dry before the welcome was exhausted. Old, now very old, Mick Weldon poured forth on Jas a flood of blessings that would have done credit to the repertory of any Hebrew patriarch, and then sang his *Nunc Dimittis*, and signified his intention of retiring (on a suitable pension), indicating at the same time his son John as his most reliable, not to say inevitable, successor.

Old Mick and Madam Prendeville had done well for Jas in their stewardship of what still remained of the once far-reaching Prendeville property. They had somehow dragged it through the famine without failing in mercy and charity to those whom in those long-past times they held in the hollow of their hands. Now, in spite of the heavy mortgages, both old and new, it was still bringing in a fairly steady fifteen hundred pounds a year. Jas found a useful sum standing to his credit at his bank, and proceeded to spend it with the dash appropriate to a handsome young captain of Irish Dragoons and a man of family. The proposition of John Weldon, his new bailiff, that some of the money should be devoted to re-roofing Inver House, seemed to Jas extremely dull and quite unremunerative. He declared that he preferred to live, as he and his mother had done, in the old Tower. Time enough, he said, when he had left the Service and married and heiress, as he intended to do some day, to waste good, hard cash on a house as big and bare as a d——d barracks. John Weldon was but four years older than his young employer, but in all practical matters he was many centuries his superior. He was, in fact, a young man of unusual perspicacity, with the advantageous endowment of a jovial temperament and a crafty brain. He did not fail to perceive the unwisdom of beginning his career on so unsound a basis as that of putting his employer's interests before his own, and since these latter were, naturally, to establish himself securely in the position of sympathetic Grand Vizier to a spoilt and wilful young Caliph, he agreed that the roof might—in all senses of the phrase—hold on for a while, and advocated, alternatively, the buying of a nice brace of young horses ('belonging to a cousin of me own,' John said) that would make into hunters for him, if his leave lasted into the winter.

The Prendeville relations of every degree of consanguinity, from respectable Uncle Robert, who had borrowed his late sister-in-law's pony-phaeton, and wished to keep it, down to disreputable fourth-cousin Tom Pindy, whose rent was heavily in arrears, all buzzed hungrily round young Jas, with the persistence of horseflies round a plump young colt, just turned out to grass on a hot June day. Uncle Robert kept the pony-carriage, and Jas could do no better than 'forgive' Tom Pindy his arrears in view of his relationship. (Pindy, or Prendy, it should be explained, were local variants of the Prendeville name, and Pindy, the more common form of the two, had, as a matter of convenience, gradually been accepted as a mode of distinguishing those of the family who were entitled to bear a bar-sinister on their scutcheons, from those on whom this distinction was not entailed.)

But the most persistent of the horseflies of Cloon was the Widow Hynes, who had been Christopher Prendeville's foster-sister, and the bar most sinister of all to the young Head of the Family, was that of her public-house. In virtue of the link of foster-relationship Mrs Hynes claimed Jas as her especial prey.

'Is it you to pay me, my lovely Captain? Me that was your own Dadda's foster-sister! If I could run down gold in a cup I'd give it t'ye—an' more than that! An' why wouldn't I? Arrah, what's gold t'ye?'

To this inquiry, and its accompanying libation, Jas was wont to respond with a piece of that metal of which Mrs Hynes thought so little. What, indeed, was a guinea here or there to a young landlord with a fat balance at his bank and what he felt to be a long—even an endless—rent-roll?

The widow did not confine the tokens of her allegiance and affection to those allurements that the State had licensed her to dispense. It had not taken her long to discover that Jas was vulnerable at more points of approach than the one obviously weak spot. The Prendeville motto, *'Je Prends,'* had in Iveragh and Cloon received the sanction of centuries, and the Widow Hynes was sufficiently mediæval to enable her to accept with composure a certain *Droit de Seigneur* that was, as a rule, based rather on might than on right. So it was that when she poured libations to her young lord, she did so, more often than not, by the hand of her good-looking daughter, Margaret, and resented not at all that Jas should in his acknowledgements, include a kiss to the cup-bearer. Jas had never heard of the *Droit de Seigneur*, and he was equally unaware of possessing Mr Wordsworth's authority for asserting that they should take who have the power. Jas was a child of nature, as well as being the son of his father, and when he wanted anything he obeyed, quite simply, the family motto, and took.

So he carried off the handsome Margaret to the old Tower of Inver, and kept her there in defiance of priest and parson; and Margaret's mother seconded the denunciations of the Church with very tepid remonstrance. Many a Prendeville before Jas had done the same thing.

'And why wouldn't the like o' them plaze theirsels?' said the Widow Hynes, with the half-admiring, half-cynical indulgence of the Irish peasant woman of her time for the misdoings of males of a higher class than her own, 'and mostly, in the latter end, they'll marry the girl!'

It is indeed probable that Jas would thus have made his peace with all concerned, but he was caught away from Inver, at a moment's notice, by a summons to rejoin his regiment, which was to start immediately for the Cape.

The 'latter end' that was, according to the optimistic Mrs Hynes, to regularise everything, being thus frustrated, the conclusion of the whole matter, as far as poor, good-looking Margaret was concerned, came with the birth of a daughter. The old woman with 'a lucky hand,' whose ministrations on such occasions were considered indispensable, brought, in that lucky hand, the fever that had already taken its toll of too many of her patients. Margaret slipped quietly out of a world that she had known for no more than nineteen years. Perhaps, after all, the hand had brought her luck.

By the time, which in those days was many months, that the news reached Jas in South Africa, the episode had passed into the background of his mind, and—since there are few things less certain than that absence makes the heart grow fonder—it must be admitted that Margaret's death affected him less disagreeably than

16

the necessity of writing to John Weldon and directing that a solatium was to be bestowed on Margaret's mother, and some provision made for Margaret's child. Unwanted and superfluous though it undoubtedly was, Jas felt—and was conscious of magnanimity in so feeling—that he could not entirely ignore the existence of this latest recruit to the ranks of the Pindys.

Chapter 3

It was about two years later that Jas came back again to Inver. This time no flags flew, nor bonfires blazed. Jas was not anxious for demonstrations. He advised John Weldon of this, and also of the fact that he had left the army; this latter determination—so he wished it to be understood—because he found that soldiering in peace-time bored him, and the South African climate did not agree with him.

At the County Club in Monarde, there was a whisper that the disagreement was rather with Jas's Colonel than with the climate of the Cape. The whisper gradually strengthened, becoming definite in the process. Jas drank; he had got drunk at Mess and had pulled the Adjutant's nose. The whisper went from strength to strength; Jas had run *amok* through the Sergeants' quarters at midnight. In his night-shirt. He had knocked down the Sergeant Major. There was no mistake about it. Young D'Arcy, who was in the same station, had written it all home to his people. 'The Colonel let him send in his papers,' young D'Arcy wrote, 'which was more than he deserved.'

Of Ross Inver in the month of May it might very truly be said that the lot had fallen to its owner in a fair ground. The headland of Inver was clad in the delicious jade-green of new grass, and lighted with the whiteness of hawthorn bushes and the yellow flames of furze brakes. In the shrubberies round the Big House the thrush and the cuckoo and the wood-pigeon were calling with the strong and tender voices of spring. Laburnums, with their drip of gold, gleamed among the laurels; dandelions shone like little suns in the rough grass in front of the Tower. In the demesne the old oaks and beeches had made themselves young again with little frivolous leaves that seemed quite unsuited to their venerable limbs. In shady hollows the April flood of primroses still lingered, bathing the feet of the slender birch trees that sheltered them, thronging in thousands round the grey limestone boulders. The keen smell of seaweed came up on the west wind from the harbour, a smell that has something

18

alien and unfamiliar in it, a breath from a foreign world; and here and there, where the young leaves were thin on the branches, the surrounding sea filled in the spaces with turquoises that it had borrowed from the high skies.

Nevertheless, goodly though Jas's heritage assuredly was, after not many weeks of freedom from regimental rule and routine, he began to find the splendid isolation of Inver as dull as soldiering in peace time. He had given no date for his arrival at the Tower, yet, on his arrival he had found all things prepared handsomely for his reception, with a fine piece of beef roasting on the spit in the kitchen, and a bottle of whisky on the table in the sitting-room. Jas had spent a couple of days in Monarde, and the driver of the mail-car was sister's son to the Widow Hynes' brother-in-law, which indirectly accounts for the fact that on the day before the Captain's homecoming, Mrs Hynes had transferred herself to the Tower to keep house for him, and with her had gone that superfluous little Pindy whose existence the Captain had been unable entirely to ignore.

The widow was a good cook, and made existence at the Tower comfortable enough, in a rough, untidy, abundant way. Jas did not mind the roughness, but he was bored. The wide-spread Prendeville property had kept at a distance from neighbours of his own class. He had been too long away to be able as yet to enter with much interest into local affairs, fishing, fairs, fights, marriages, and the solace of village society was somewhat tempered by the fact that it was always, very deferentially, left to him to pay for the whisky necessary to stimulate the flow of soul. Jas was open-minded enough, but he resented compulsion in any form, and he had a deep-rooted objection to doing what was expected of him.

June was passing, July was near. The weather was still and foggy. Tom Pindy and his fellows delighted Jas not; the Widow Hynes, with her proprietary affection and her complacent assumption of their common interest in the superfluous little Pindy, was becoming a nuisance. He wandered moodily in the demesne one close, quiet afternoon, with eyes and soul shut to its beauty, scowling as he passed a little barefoot, curly-haired child, that sat among the daisies in the grass in front of the Big House, playing with a black

19

kitten. She made him think of Margaret, which was not exhilarating. In fact, the thought of Margaret filled him with resentment. She would have been an alleviation. He hadn't felt lonely, like this, the last time he was at home. And, since she had chosen to die in this inconsiderate way, why couldn't she have taken the child with her? Jas did not formulate these sentiments in quite so crude a fashion as this. There are thoughts, like colours, or scents, that do not materialise in words.

The end of it was that Jas took the mail-car into Monarde one fine day, and established himself in the well-remembered 'town-house,' where he had lived with his mother, the ancient house in which the Lady Isabella had held high state, and had terrorised Grand Juries, and Judges, and Monarde society generally. Jas was a fine young man, well equipped with the traditional height and good looks of the Prendevilles, as well as with the assurance that generally accompanies such inheritance. In the tall hat, the gorgeous waistcoat, the tight plaid trousers, and the neatly curled whiskers of the bucks of his day, Jas walked into the County Club next morning, and there met a few men who had known him as a boy. They did not seem as glad to see him as he had expected. He offered them, casually, some of his reasons for having left the Army, and told them how ill the climate of the Cape had suited him. Their lack of sympathy, even of comment, seemed to him marked. But they were dull old dogs; it made no difference to him, he decided, whether they were silent or no.

The wives and daughters of the dull old dogs were quite a different affair, as Jas presently found. The town and the surrounding country-houses were full for the Monarde Summer Week of Horse Show, and Cattle Show, and Flower Show, which would be followed by the Race Week. Young Captain Prendeville was agreeable and good-looking, he had a pretty tenor voice, and would sing when he was asked, and his name was high on the Grand Jury list as an owner—even if only an owner in name—of many acres. The wives and daughters shut their ears to the whispers from the Club, and Jas had more invitations than he knew what to do with. Now and then a young lady might hint that Captain Jas was not a very safe partner after supper; or a matron would murmur to her companion at a dinner-party that it was a pity that that young Prendeville—— To which the companion—who would be, no doubt, one of the dull old dogs—would look humorous and knowing, and would probably raise and tilt a little finger and would respond:

'Takes his whack, they say!'

In those days that a man should take his whack, more or less, was considered no more than was natural and genial; but it gradually came to be thought that the practice of Jas in the matter of whacks was excessive. Invitations began to slacken. Whacks were all very well in their proper time and place, but even the least straight-laced of the Monarde hostesses considered that a young man should be able to keep sober at a dance until after supper, when, of course, 'nice, tourney rules' might be set aside. And then the end came. Jas was asked to a dinner and a dance at a big country-house, on the last night of the Race Week, and found himself one of a large and lively party of young men and women. The host, and the elder men were in no hurry to leave the table after dinner.

Jas sat with them, and dancing had begun before the last bottle of port was finished. It was nearing the hour of supper when Jas's absence was noticed, and some of the young men were sent in search of him. They found him asleep in an arm-chair in the dining-room. The candles on the dinner table had nearly burned out and were flaring in the draught from the open windows. The cork of that final bottle of port lay on the host's desert plate, amid the ashes of his cigar.

When, a little past midnight, Captain Prendeville awoke, and pulled himself together, and strolled into the ballroom, he was still a little sleepy and confused, but not so much so as not to be able to recognise the sensation caused by his entrance. The ladies shrieked, the gentlemen guffawed. It was after supper; many were wearing head-dresses of coloured paper, out of the crackers, all were rather riotously ready to be amused. Jas stood still and blinked at them, bewildered.

'I suppose something's dam' funny,' he said, 'but I can't see the

21

joke.'

One of the sons of the house was standing near. 'No, my boy, I daresay you can't,' he said, with a shout of laughter. 'But you shall!'

He caught Jas from behind by his elbows and ran him across the room to a mirror.

The last of the corks and the last of the candles had been used with good effect, and the artist who had combined them had made the most of his opportunities. A huge black moustache and eyebrows, and a great pair of spectacles decorated Jas's furious face.

Jas stared at his own ridiculous image, with, for background, the nightmare ranks of red, grinning faces under maniac hoods and bonnets and fool's caps. Then he turned on the lad who was holding him, and wanted to fight him then and there.

But, as Napoleon says, you cannot strike where there is neither fear or resistance. Also he could not fight all the young men, and the more he raged the more they laughed. It was the west of Ireland, seventy and more years ago, and, as has already been said, the time was after supper in a hospitable house, where the motto for such moments was 'The night's young, and drink's plenty!'

So Jas went home to bed, and washed his face, and the next morning (or rather, that same morning) putting his nose in the air, and mounting his highest horse, he went back to the Tower of Inver, telling himself that he would never again set foot among the men who had made a mock of him.

Chapter 4

It has been said, often enough to ensure credence—since repetition will generally convince if it does not exasperate—that the climate of Ireland is destructive of energy and breeds inertia and lethargy. Whether or no this is true (and it is certainly open to argument), Jas Prendeville's resolve to live at Inver and do nothing, was taken as a proof of it by the few who still counted themselves among his friends; while those who were not in that category were accustomed to ascribe his determined self-isolation to what they euphemistically called his liking for turning up his little finger.

Yet it was hardly fair to lay all the blame on either his little finger, or on the climate, even on that soft western climate that soothes and discourages in almost equal degree. In sinking at the age of twenty-seven into existence at Inver, Jas was following the line for him of least resistance. He loved the sea. That was not strange in one whose fathers had for centuries lived on Ross Inver, with deep water on both sides of them. He bought a big fishing-smack, and took a crew from among his tenants, and spent most of his days and nights out in the wide Bay of Monarde, beyond the headlands of Inver and Ingard, thrashing up and down the coast, setting trammel nets, and trawling, and keeping half the women of Cloon supplied with fish, not so much out of charity as because it was a well-recognised fact that a gentleman could not sell fish, (save fish at large, in the waters of his own river).

The invisible, invincible webs of heredity spun themselves round Jas. The fascination of the sea, that had held his fathers before him, now held him fast. The strain of peasant blood in him, inured through long ages to monotony, asserted itself, teaching him to accept with composure the life of a village; and it, possibly, was also responsible for the enjoyment, that gradually grew in him, of the position of king of his company. (One may be sure that in the Kingdom of the Blind the One-eyed is happy in his pre-eminence.) Half-educated, vain, comfortably assured of his supremacy at home,

Jas told himself that he was not going away again to be bullied and insulted and made a fool of! He had had enough of that game. First the Regiment, then those snobs at Monarde! Damn them all! . . . He might go to London for a while. He was a man of the world. None of your dirty little Irish towns for him . . . Jas was magnificently cosmopolitan, especially when, sitting on the counter of Fourth Cousin Tom Pindy's public house, he talked of India and Africa to an admiring and thirsty circle of fishermen.

But he remained at the Tower of Inver.

And at the Tower, or on board his boat, Jas continued to live his life, a life that slowly lengthened beyond the usual span. Into its details it is unnecessary to enter. There were episodes from which Captain Jas was extricated only by the watchful intelligence of John Weldon; adventures that came easily to a young man in the disastrous position of King of his Company. Many were discreditable, none would repay investigation. It is enough to say that Jas lived on at Inver, attended by the Widow Hynes and her grandchild; always talking of going away 'for a while,' and not going. Each year sinking down a little nearer to the level of his companions, with narrowing ambitions and a lower standard as to the amenities of life. Drinking, not to excess, yet ever too deeply; resenting less that the name of Prendeville should be inscribed by an ambitious Pindy on the signboard of a public house that had bloomed into a hotel; even patronising the bar of that particular Pindy on the accepted fact of his kinship with him as Head of the Family.

The years of the Land League, and the Famine of 1882, bore heavily on Captain Jas's resources. His tenants, adopting the convenient Plan of Campaign, held up their rents. His cattle, running on the demesne lands, were 'driven,' or mutilated, or stolen. John Weldon, who, having started from his father's shoulders, had continued to ascend the social ladder in singularly direct relation to his employer's descent, had been obliged, at, as he said, a good share of trouble to himself, to come to his help, financially, more than once. Jas was not lucky. Even his fishing-smack had dragged her anchor, one wild night, and had foundered on the rocks under the Tower, almost at his feet. That had happened when he was still young enough to enjoy putting forth at sunset to set the nets, and spending the night gossiping with his crew, smoking and drinking porter, and hauling the nets at dawn, and racing the other boats back to harbour with his catch. When the *Kathleen* was lost, the Captain had immediately requisitioned a successor. John Weldon said that God alone knew where he'd conjure the money from; but the feat of legerdemain was accomplished.

The celebration of the arrival of the *Eileen Oge* in Cloonabinnia Harbour, took place one stormy November afternoon in the *Eileen Oge*'s cabin. It was a ceremony that involved the consumption of a great deal of whisky, in drinking luck to the vessel, and companion compliments. Towards its conclusion, when, as Mr Weldon told himself, spirits were up as well as down, he had produced the draft of a lease of the demesne-lands of Ross Inver, of which he proposed to become the tenant. He explained to Captain Jas that his signature on this document would automatically cancel the debt on the *Eileen Oge* and, so generous was the 'fine' (or premium) that he was prepared to pay for the tenancy, there would even be something over to put into the Bank, that was getting (so John said) a bit nasty about the overdraft on the Demesne farm account.

The rent was low, to be sure, candid John Weldon admitted, but the Captain had only lost money with his farming demesne, and it was indeed a bit of a gamble himself taking it at all.

What Mr Weldon did not go into with any great minuteness was the duration of the lease. Possibly he thought that after the last cup drunk to the future of the *Eileen Oge*, her owner might not be able to master details. Possibly, on the other hand, he feared that he might; because the expiration of the lease was fixed at very many more years ahead than the Captain was likely to see.

'The only little difficulty might come from Mr Nicholas,' John Weldon had said, apologetically. 'He might make an objection—'

Mr Nicholas was Jas's first cousin, son of that Robert who had resented the purchase of Jas's commission, and had held fast to the pony-phaeton. He was Jas's heir presumptive, and, secure in that position, he had not concealed his disapproval of the Captain's career.

'Show me the pen here!' Jas shouted, with a hiccough.

Mr Nicholas had indeed made a protest, but this was all that had been needed to reconcile the Captain to the ratification of what Mrs Nicholas (who had been a D'Arcy) called 'The Half-Seas-Over-Lease.'

'A nice thing when a man can't do what he likes with his own!' Jas said to John Weldon, who warmly agreed with him.

This incident took place in 1887, when Jas was no more than sixty-three, and still owned a fair share of the good looks of his youth. His complexion had certainly deepened to a rather pulpy purple, his long moustache had gone from gold to grey, and his blue eyes were bloodshot, and would fill with water on slight provocation of either wind or emotion. But neither his age nor his potations had had serious effect upon his figure, and he was still what the Widow Hynes and her friends called him.

'A fine, big, *grauver* man, God bless him!'

It was typical of Jas that while he accepted with unconcern the steady decrease of his income, owing to the depredations of successive governments, combined with difficulties with tenants, (as well as with other factors for which he had only himself to blame), the thought that his cousin should have an interest in preserving what was left of the property rankled in his mind.

He was, not for the first time, discussing this fact with his confidant, John Weldon, when an idea, novel and stimulating, flashed into his mind. Having once more observed that it was a dam' funny thing if a man couldn't call what belonged to him his own, he was inspired to add.

'But Begad! I might give the dam' feller a bit of a take-in yet! It's never too late to mend they say!' He laughed with pride in his own brilliance. 'Listen to me now, John! Do you look about you—' (the Captain used the verb in the imperative)— 'and see if you can't find me a good sensible lump of a girl, that'd know which side of her bread was buttered supposing I asked her to marry me!'

The confidant received this suggestion with rallyings of his patron that, though crude, offered the requisite satisfaction and encouragement. He assured Jas that it was the best notion he had heard this long while, and he even went so far as to assure him that he would do himself the pleasure of getting blind drunk on the day that saw the christening of a son and heir to the Captain! He then set about the search for a lump of sufficient sense and goodness, and presently found it—a small lump indeed, but one of good material—in the person of a little Miss Esther McKnight, a young lady who had assisted her mother, a highly respectable widow, in the highly respectable office of house-keeper at the County Club in Monarde, and there, on one of the rare occasions that Jas had 'set foot' in the Club, favourably attracted his attention.

'Sure you know her yourself, Captain. She's living now with her brother and his wife outside the town, on the Ardmore Road, since the mother died,' thus the Messenger of Cupid reported, 'and she's trusting to them now for her keep, and she doesn't greatly fancy it. She's an independent cut of a girl—I beg your pardon, Captain, a young lady, I should say! Sure her father was a very high up Methodist Minister in Dublin! I b'lieve herself and the sister-in-law are liable to have a bit of a scratch now and then. She mightn't be sorry not to be beholden to them much longer! She's a nice, good, decent young lady. She remembers you well. She got a smack for the gentry, helping the mother that way in the bar of the Club.'

Miss Esther McKnight was all that John Weldon claimed for her. Her taste for gentry was undoubted, and it enabled her to ignore such disadvantages in the proposed alliance as may have been deduced from what has been told of Captain Jas. John Weldon presented her to the Captain as her namesake was offered to King Ahasuerus.

'And the thing pleased the King, so that he set the royal crown upon her head.'

Even though something tarnished by wear of a more or less illicit nature, the crown fitted Miss McKnight very successfully. She established herself at the Tower, and took command of her husband and his household with all the niceness, goodness, and decency that John Weldon had ascribed to her. Having undertaken to love, honour, and obey the Captain, she, being a gentle and conscientious little creature, made a very creditable attempt at keeping her word. Also she set herself to make friends with the real ruler of the Tower, who was not the Captain.

Jas's household had known no change since the day that that skilled and determined schemer, the Widow Hynes, had installed

27

herself and the superfluous little Pindy, in the Tower of Inver. The Widow had outlived her character. She was now not far from ninety, and the long and stupefying years of illiterate old age had wiped out her personality, and had left her, a mere presence, a creature no more effective or individual than an old cat, drowsing out its life in the embers. It was now the superfluous little grandchild who, singlehanded, administered the affairs of the Tower, and it was with her that both Esther and old Ahasuerus had to reckon.

In Ireland there is a good-natured convention that youth stays long and is determined only by marriage. The village people still spoke of Mrs Hynes' grandchild as 'that Pindy girl above at the Tower,' even though it was nearly thirty-five years since the little Isabella, holding fast by the corner of her grandmother's apron, had left the village of Cloon, and had taken up her residence in the ancient home of those forefathers of hers to whose name she had no claim. That she should have been christened by the name first brought by the Lady Isabella Devannes into the House of Prendeville, was an instance of what would sometimes seem to be the bitter playfulness of Fate. Lady Isabella's daughter had dragged the name through dirt; now, a hundred years or so later, for, perhaps, a further chastening of her pride, her name, that she had given to her eldest daughter, having endured tavern usage among that daughter's descendants, was bestowed upon a creature born in the worst inn's worst room, another living blot on the much blotted family escutcheon, yet, none the less, the Lady Isabella's lineal descendant.

'Shibby Pindy,' was what the Widow Hynes' compeers had called her grandchild, 'Shibby' being the easy-going diminutive that the century of tavern usage had given to the name Isabella. And as Shibby Pindy, Isabella Prendeville went through life, silently, without complaint, the servant of her father, making no claim on him, her single protest a proud refusal to take wages. When she was three and twenty Jas had offered to pay her for her work. She had faced him and said 'I want no wages from you!'

She was nearly as tall as he, and when her angry blue eyes looked straight into his, Jas had felt guilty and uncomfortable for a moment. Then the memory that, also for the moment only, had shamed him, appealed, paradoxically, to his conceit.

'She's a deuced handsome girl!' he thought. 'She's got my eyes in her head right enough!'

And after that Shibby became his purse-bearer, and had all things at the Tower in her control.

When her father brought in Esther McKnight to reign at Inver, Shibby, recognising that a Prime Minister exercises considerably more power than a constitutional monarch, made a resignation of the household keys that, though formal, was mainly symbolic, since the locks to which they appertained were for the most part broken. Young Mrs Prendeville, with tactful wisdom, handed back the symbols, and begged the Prime Minister to continue in office, and thus laid the foundation stone of friendship.

Later, when Esther produced the son and heir prophesied by John Weldon (who, it may be added, did not fail at the christening to fulfil his promise), there was discovered in Shibby a passion for babies that had not before found an outlet. She took her half-brother in her arms with rapture that for all her self-control she could not hide, and became thenceforward his slave, and his mother's most faithful ally and supporter. The alliance held and strengthened, but Esther's reign was a brief one. A daughter was born to her, and she made a slow recovery. A year later another son came into the world, and finding, perhaps, the Tower of Inver a blank and cheerless place in November, left it again with all speed, having done no more than open his eyes, and give one disapproving cry.

Young Mrs Prendeville went with him to the unknown when he came, with a weak arm round little Kit and his sister, as though she would bring them with her, and one hand in Shibby's strong clasp, and her eyes on poor old Jas (who had been, after all, a good husband to her, according to his lights), with his head down on the footrail of the bed, sobbing.

Chapter 5

'Truly the light is sweet, and a pleasant thing it is for the eyes to behold the sun.' Thus the Preacher, in a rare moment of admission that the world has anything to offer that is worth having.

But even he must have allowed that young Kit Prendeville, long, lithe, and golden-haired, riding a red-golden blood filly over the wet-golden sands of the Long Strand of Ingard Head, with an azure sea beyond him, and above him an azure sky, flecked with circling white seagulls, was a pleasant thing to behold. It is even possible that he might have so far forgotten his pessimism, and been enough moved by such a poem in movement and colour, as to have adjured the young man to rejoice in his youth, and spared him the threatening climax.

Kit needed no such adjuration. He sat down in his saddle, rejoicing consciously in the filly's youth, and unconsciously in his own while the creature that—on the whole—he loved best in the world—thought most of, certainly—also, in her own fashion, rejoiced with him. She danced fractiously beside the snowy serpent that edged the curving run of the sea, flitting sideways, light as a fly, when a stem of seaweed with a wrinkled brown knob of a head, and a tail of glossy streamers, lay in her path; stopping short, in absurd panic, at a piece of driftwood; plunging, rearing, and whirling away, when the foamy terror that ran beside her, so thin, and swift, and noiseless, stole nearer.

The faint wind of early summer blew her sparse mane in the air, so that it looked like a gold fringe on her shining neck. It caught Kit's cap from his head, and sent it spinning landwards along the smooth sand. One would say that the wind, this exquisite morning, was in league with the sun to find playthings for its beams to sparkle with, so bright and crisp was the boy's hair, so gay the young mare's floating mane.

Kit sat a horse thoughtlessly; it was easy to see that it was no more an effort to him than breathing. There are those who with a great sum obtain this freedom, but others are freeborn, and Kit was of the company. The dancing filly knew it, and at last, submitting herself to him, let him steer her out over the writhing white snake into the blue mystery beyond it, staring, snorting, and stepping high, so that the water struck up from her knees and fell in diamonds on her and her rider.

Kit thought: 'She'll not mind the water any more now—I'll give her a spin to the Mile Point before I pick up me cap—'

He was quite unaware of being a poem, and his method of expressing himself left a good deal to be desired, even though a high standard might not be exacted. The National School at Cloon, followed by Mr Kilbride's Commercial College at Monarde, had done their best, or worst, for the son of Captain Jas's old age. By the time that his schooling had to be taken in hand, the steady erosion to which Jas's income had been subjected, from more sources than need now be enumerated, had reduced it to a figure that did no more than suffice for the plain necessities of life, and certainly left no margin for embroidery, which was the aspect in which an education more liberal than that afforded by the united efforts of Cloon and Monarde, presented itself to Kit's guardians. At the first of these seats of culture Kit learned how to read and write (indifferently, both), how to chuck a stone, underhand, with unerring aim, how to climb a thin Connaught stone wall, and to jump a fence like a hound running a line, as well as some slight smatterings of arithmetic. He was on the best of terms with his fellow scholars, but was in chronic revolt against the master; there came, at length, a black day when he was caned, struggling, kicking, and shouting that he was a gentleman. After this effort of discipline its object ran home and refused to go to school again, and was supported in his refusal by his half-sister, Miss Shibby Pindy. After a year or two of idleness, and of riding any horse that he could cajole or steal from its owner, Shibby sent him to Mr Kilbride's, an establishment that for her ranked far higher than Eton (the more so that she had never heard of Eton), and there Kit acquired the rudiments of the 'sound commercial education,' guaranteed by its prospectus, and the knowledge that he was good-looking (a knowledge which was shared by the young ladies of Miss O'Reilly's neighbouring seminary) and a tone of voice that was considerably less attractive than the soft brogue of the National School with which he had entered Mr Kilbride's Academy, as well as an infiltration of what—for want of a more explicit term—must be called commonness of mind and manner that Jas, sunken and debased though he was, had somehow escaped.

Having passed through Mr Kilbride's hands, Kit discovered a wish to become a Veterinary Surgeon, and proceeded to one of the Queen's Colleges, financed by Miss Pindy, she alone knew how. He then, after a brief, but lively course of study, failed to pass even the preliminary examination for his chosen career, and with that, abandoning his ambition without a regret—Kit's was the fortunate temperament that forgets to regret—he succeeded in getting himself taken into a racing-stables near Dublin, where he learned much that was useful, as well as a number of things that were the reverse, among which was a taste for whisky. There, he presently distinguished himself by an abortive elopement with the trainer's daughter, a pretty and precocious young person of sixteen, which was frustrated by the unexpected and inconvenient return from Dublin of the trainer, who met the young couple at the railway station in the act of taking their tickets. Kit was sent home to Inver next day, and the young lady went back to school, and there the matter ended.

Whether Kit's half-sister would have been prepared to forgive her young brother his faults unto the full measure of seventy times seven, cannot confidently be asserted, but after this, his first serious misdoing, her forgiveness was ready, and her arms were open to him when he came home to them.

After this episode Kit stayed at home. Inver held him fast, as it had held his race for so many centuries. He took to training young horses, the single art for which his gifts and his fancy fitted him. He earned enough to keep himself, and occasionally to do a deal on his own account. Even had he earned nothing, it was all Shibby asked, to have him at home, to be her inspiration, to plan for him, even only to care for him in every day's most common need, and to see him happy.

The red-golden blood filly, who, as an undersized two-year-old, had been one of Kit's earliest efforts in horse-coping, had accepted the discipline of the sea with the resignation that experience was beginning to teach her might as well come soon as late; but having trampled to and fro, knee deep, at, as it chanced, as near as need be to the very place where Kit's grandfather had waded out to meet his death, she did not disguise her joy when she found her face turned landwards again. She came out of the water with a rush, and Kit headed her for the Mile Point, and was prepared to let her go, when he heard a gallop of hoofs on the hard sand behind him. A heavy brown horse was coming fast along the shore, ridden by a girl. The pair thundered past Kit at best pace, the rider pulling hard at the horse's head, without, quite evidently, influencing him at all.

The chestnut filly's highly-strung nerves wanted but this, and with the passing of the brown horse, she went off like a firework. When she touched ground again, tense as a tennis-ball, tearing at her bridle, mad to be off, Kit sympathised with her, and let her start in pursuit of the runaway.

'It's that brown horse of Johnny Weldon's—a piggish brute— only fit for a cart—'

It was characteristic of Kit that he considered the horse first.

'And that's Peggy, I suppose. They said she was coming home soon. She never was any good to ride, anyhow.'

The filly went as fast as his thoughts; he was beside the girl now.

'Don't try and stop him at all!' he shouted to her. 'Hit him and make him go! Give him enough of it—he'll not like that! You've plenty of room before you—'

The girl's face was very red. Her hat, hanging by its guard, bumped on her back in time with the horse's galloping stride. Through locks of loosened hair she looked, with knitted brows, at her instructor.

'He feels as if he'd never stop,' she said breathlessly.

'There's no fear he won't stop! He'll be jolly glad to stop soon enough! Come on, I'll race you to the Point!'

'My father—' began the girl; but Kit was ahead, and the brown horse's heavy shoulders still worked so hard under her that she could only sit as tight as she could, and keep his head straight, reserving explanations.

The Mile Point, where the grey-green bent-grass came down across the sand nearly to the sea, was still a good half-mile away when the brown horse began to show signs of having shot his bolt. Kit, floating effortlessly ahead, heard the faltering beat of the big feet and turned in his saddle.

'Hit him now! Now's your time!'

He checked the filly and let the horse come up on his near side.

The girl, who was Peggy Weldon, grand-daughter of that John Weldon of whom mention has already been made, had little of either breath or strength left in her, but pluck is an efficient substitute for most disabilities. She was, besides, very angry, and anger is an efficient prop to pluck. So she hit the brown horse twice, hard enough to revive his energy, and kept him as nearly abreast of his leader as the filly, chafing and furious at being held back, would permit.

At last, and none too soon for the brown horse's feelings, Kit drew rein at the crumbling spit of sandy cliff, held together by grey grass, and pock-marked with rabbit burrows, which was known as the Mile Point, and was itself a full mile from the far end of the headland, where the white light-house sat, like a great swan, holding erect a stiff white neck, shining in the sun. The brown horse, who, like John Gilpin, had little thought when he set out of running such a rig, was now blowing hard, his sides heaving, his short, thick tail quivering, his neck a lather of white foam. He had, very obviously, had something more than was good for him.

Peggy Weldon turned on Kit a face that blazed as much with indignation as with heat. Her dark hair had been shaken down, and hung like a cloak over her shoulders, and her big, round, grey eyes, that were like those of an angry cat, looked at him as though, as he said to himself, it had been he who had bolted with her, and God forbid that he'd bolt with a woman that was like a sack o' meal on a horse's back!

'You're Kit Prendeville, I suppose? Why did you make me gallop

34

this horse like this? I believe his wind's broken!'

'Yes, I'm Kit all right, and you're Peggy,' said Kit, grinning (if so unlovely a word can be applied to so charming a thing as young Kit Prendeville's smile), remembering Peggy's short temper of old, and how easy and amusing it had been to arouse it. 'What started him? If you were so anxious to stop him why did you turn the whip on him?'

'*Why?* Because you told me to, of course! And I was fool enough to mind you!' Peggy flashed out at him, while, with hands that shook from effort, she tried to twist her hair and stuff it into her hat. 'It was a man shooting at gulls that started him. I suppose his wind's broken, and that's thanks to you! Father will be very pleased! He's behind there somewhere!' She jerked the sentences at him, stabbing such hairpins as remained to her into the dark mass of her hair.

'You've time enough. There's your father now. He's a good mile away. The horse'll have got his wind again before he's here,' he reassured her, but without, as she told herself, the least sympathy, and laughing all the time too!

She swept the wild hair from her eyes and stared into the distance. Far behind, on the long curve of the shore, a horse and rider could be seen, dimly, against the misty blue and green of the woods of Inver. Kit surveyed the girl with interest. He and she and his sister had played together as children, but he had not seen her since she was fourteen. She had grown into a fine big lump of a girl, he thought, and, as far as he could see through all that hair, devilish good-looking too, by Jove—he'd never have thought she'd have made such a good fist of it in the way of looks!—but if that horse hadn't a sore back after her, you might call him, Kit, Blackbird (a permission which is of the nature of an affirmation). And she was all to bits, and girls had no business riding, if they went to bits with a half-mile of a gallop. And she was Johnny Weldon's daughter; but—here he relented a little—she seemed to have pluck anyway—she was always a little devil to fight when he and Nessie used to play together, and the least thing would set her mad. It seemed, he thought, like that was the way with her still!

'It's a long time since I saw you. When did you get home?'

'Last night,' said Peggy, shortly.

'I was always away when you were back,' said Kit. He looked her up and down with a gleam in his eye, taking stock of the ruin brought about by the brown horse. 'I daresay you didn't get much riding in France!'

Peggy did not fail to catch the implication. 'So likely I should get riding at a convent school in Paris! Or at St. Rule's either!'

Her cat's grey eyes looked at him so fiercely that Kit began to laugh.

'Easy for you to laugh! I don't suppose I shall get any more riding here, either, when father sees what I've done to this horse—'

The horse and his rider that both were watching had come perceptibly nearer. To have laughed at her made Kit feel more friendly and look like old times—and she certainly was good to look at! He took up the brown horse's rein that Peggy had let fall on his neck.

'Get off and I'll lead him about a bit—he'll be all right. You needn't be afraid at all.'

Peggy let herself drop from the saddle to the ground. It was as much as she could do to stand, so spent and strained were her muscles. She would have fallen had she not clutched at the hand that Kit reached down to her, grinning in what she felt to be a very offensive way. Then he slipped from the filly's back and began to lead both horses slowly to and fro. His arm was through the filly's bridle, but the precaution was unnecessary, as she followed him like a dog, touching his shoulder now and then with her soft muzzle, assuring him that she loved him. Kit began to search his pockets for a bit of sugar for her, standing still on the wet sand, just above the sliding white lip of the out-going tide. The filly's red-golden coat shone iridescently in the sun; the shimmering, silky, blue and silver of the sea made a background of delicious colour. Even the brown horse was glorified to a bronze, and had his share in the charm of the group.

Peggy's eyes were on Kit. She thought nothing of the picture, being very angry at his grin, as well as humiliated at having had to accept his help. In that grin she had been aware of the touch of the conqueror—for which Miss O'Reilly's seminary was, no doubt, responsible—and anger burned the hotter in her because of her reluctant admiration of his looks.

'Of course he knows he's a beauty!' she thought. 'Anyone could see he's full of conceit! . . . And why should he think I can't ride? And his voice is common, not like a gentleman's . . . Heavenly Powers! Father's awfully near!'

This was indeed the case, and Kit had realised it as soon as had Mr Weldon's daughter. He led the horses back to where Peggy stood.

'You'd better get up and ride back to meet him,' he said, still grinning. 'He might think it queer you to be waiting here—I'll mount you—'

Peggy put her foot into his hand, and was shoved up on to the saddle with an effort that said more for Kit's strength of arm than for her skill in the fine art of being mounted. Then she moved slowly away to meet her father. She thought, 'He's no fool—but I did think he'd have been more like a gentleman . . . His voice is as bad as father's! I can't say more than that!'

Kit thought, straightening out his arm, 'They must feed 'em mighty well in France! It wasn't cracking blind nuts made her that weight!'

Chapter 6

Miss Shibby Pindy (to give her the style and title by which she was generally known to her neighbours) sat alone in the drawing-room of Inver House. The time was the afternoon of a brilliant June day; the high windows of the great room were bare of blinds and curtains, and the hot afternoon sun beat in unchecked. It was a corner room, looking south towards the demesne, and its longer, western side was built out in a wide, shallow curve, with two massive pillars of green Galway marble marking at either end the spring of the curve, and supporting a heavy gilt cornice above the broad window. Standing there one could see away across the harbour to Ingard Head, and beyond it to the open sea; the high stand-point made a high horizon, and the great window was full of the sea.

Everything that had survived of the original conception of the room, the heavy, tall teak doors, with their carved architraves and brass furniture, the huge brass-mounted fireplace, the high mantelpiece of many coloured marbles, chipped and defaced, but still beautiful, the gorgeous deep-moulded ceiling that Lady Isabella's Italian workmen had made for her, from the centre of which the wreck of a cut-glass chandelier still hung, all told of the happy conjunction of art and wealth, and of a generous taste that could make the best of both. But a very cursory glance would show how long past were the glories of the great room. The few portraits that remained on the discoloured walls dated from a century and more ago. The later generations of Prendevilles who had roystered there, the Reverend Harry D'Arcy and his crew of topers, the hiving Pindys who had clung to their roosting-places under the family roof-tree, had left their own mark on all its splendours in that coarse and wanton destruction that is the sign manual of brutalised human creatures, a deliberate destruction that transcends all other forces, animate or inanimate, of ruin, and one that neither cattle nor swine can equal,—

they at least, are unable to confer that final touch of defilement, the scribble of an ignoble name.

Nevertheless it is not too much to say that for one faithful though unacknowledged daughter of the old house, this room, defaced and dishonoured though it was, was as a secret temple to which she could retreat, to renew her energies, and to enforce her inspiration. It was thirteen years now since, after long and fierce battle, she had wrested it from a Pindy matron and her brood, and had put padlocks on the tall teak doors, of which none but she kept the keys. That had been the first and greatest of the fights. Following on it she had patiently and unrelentingly undermined two groups of Pindy squatters who had continued to exercise in the basement a privilege that, since the death of the last Madam Prendeville, had again asserted itself as a hereditary right. Sometimes emigration had abetted Shibby, but more often death had stepped in, and Shibby had stepped in behind him, and had locked the door on the outgoing tenant as inexorably as Death himself.

Thus it was that on this sunny afternoon Shibby was alone in the Big House, and all its many rooms were as clean as her strong hands could make them, and as empty as her strong heart could wish. When her great idea had come to her, young Kit had been no more than eleven years old, a lovely lad, fair and slender, the traditional good looks of the Prendevilles having triumphed over all opposing strains of heredity. He had followed his half-sister one afternoon, into the Big House, and into the room from which she had but just ousted Mrs Bob Pindy. Pictures of the Lady Isabella and of her husband, hung on either side of the mirror above the mantelpiece. That of Beauty Kit was painted when he was a boy, of just Kit's age, fair, slender and young, as was Kit. He was dressed in blue velvet, one lace-ruffled hand on his hip, the other on the head of a fawn-coloured greyhound, who yearned elegantly to his master, as did all well-bred dogs of his period, if the testimony of the portrait-painters can be accepted. Young Kit stood in front of the fireplace, in a shabby blue serge jacket and knickerbockers; one long thin hand on his hip, the other on the head of a long-legged yellow mongrel terrier (who, however, was too common and ignorant to yearn, and was suspiciously watching a rat-hole).

It was then, looking at the boy and at the picture, so strangely alike in every way, save the one that was for her the important of all—the glory of wealth, that glowed in every detail of the portrait, from the jewel at the boy's lace collar to the loaded magnificence of the frame—that Shibby had been smitten with her idea, and with such force that she had staggered to one of the windows, and had been obliged to seat herself on a window-sill, since there was no furniture in the room.

'The King shall have his own again!' Inver should once more worthily house a reigning Prendeville! Her boy should live as a gentleman should, as his ancestors did. He was as good as any one of them! She felt as Flora MacDonald possibly felt when the chance came to her of saving the Prince whom she adored.

Kit was four and twenty now, and still the Big House was empty. 'But wait till the poor Captain's gone,' Miss Pindy was in the habit of encouraging herself. 'There's time enough—there's not so much to do now after all! Thanks be to God I have the roof well mended, and that was the biggest of the trouble!'

It is a great and useful thing to be narrow-minded, and to have a will that drives a sharp wedge into life, instead of making vague and indeterminate assaults upon the positions to be carried. Even though the assault may fail, the assailant knows no remorse for neglected alternatives; if concentration upon a single point could avail, Shibby had no need to fear failure.

Sitting in one of the wide windows though she was, with as fair a view of sea and sands on the one hand, and of sunny grasslands and woods, and distant mountains, on the other, as Ireland could show, Miss Pindy's face was turned inwards towards the room, and her eyes, fixed upon an atrophied Chesterfield sofa, had in them a lover's ardour. The sofa had been the latest of her achievements. She had bought it at an auction, at which, with swift and resonant bids, she had intimidated and quelled opposition. From the sofa her gaze travelled to two starveling arm-chairs, 'a pair' that she had plucked from a huddle of second-hand furniture on the pavement outside a dealer's shop in Monarde. A three-legged table, covered with green plush, studded with brass nails, stood on its three shabby, contorted legs, a contemptible little intruder in front of the splendid mantelpiece. For Shibby it represented but another point of satisfaction, another milestone on the long road that she had set herself to travel. Dotted about the bare spaces of the big room were other spoils, gained at auctions, or fought for and won in long private haggles. Chairs such as no person, save a visitor *in extremis* would every sit upon; a three-fold embroidered Japanese screen, with its storks and bamboos ravelling into ruin; fret-work brackets, a fender stool covered with faded woolwork, and a cupboard with a cracked marble top and looking-glass doors, that, in Shibby's eyes, was only less of a triumph than was the aged and abject sofa.

Yet for anyone who had known what efforts of self-denial, of painful economy, of strategy, and of resolution, had gone to these purchases, their very commonness would have invested them with a halo of pathos, even though the pathos—as pathos often will—wavered away into absurdity. Shibby sat and gazed upon them, ticketing each with its story, brooding over her resources, trying to decide if, now that the drawing-room was furnished— 'or near enough for a while, anyhow'—she should proceed to the restoration of the dining-room, or begin on another bed-room. She rose from the *prie-Dieu* chair on which she had been sitting, —a chair whose iron discomfort would have disconcerted the devotions of a saint—and tramped across the great room, counting aloud the number of each slow stride.

'There's no carpet in this country, no, nor no two carpets, that'll cover it,' she murmured. 'It's no good for me going to Father Walsh's oxtion unless, unless maybe . . .' Her mind began to grope through what she could remember of the effects of the departing Father Walsh, while her eyes travelled, as by an accustomed road, to those of the blue velveted boy in the picture, and for a few seconds were still, communing with them.

'Very well,' she said aloud, nodding her head, 'I'll hold on now till I have the pig sold. That should be eight pounds to me—' She laughed, sardonically; 'Eight pounds! That'll go far! And twenty bare bedrooms above me!'

Well, no matter. Kit was young yet; when she had the house finished and furnished, he should go to England, or maybe America.

41

With his looks and his name there was no fear but some grand rich lady would treat herself to him, and then he needn't be ashamed to bring her home to the Big House! As grand as she might be, she wouldn't get a grander house than what it was! . . . only for the want of the Demesne . . . that was the point at which her visions would ever check and pause . . . Could the Weldons,—the Grabbers,—be induced to let it go? . . . The grand lady, to be sure, would want to buy it, but would they give it up to her? . . . After all, what had the Weldons to come after them but the one daughter? What would the like of Peggy Weldon want with the Demesne? For certain sure she'd rather the money! . . .

Shibby's contempt for her own sex was characteristic of her time and her class. Daughters were only pawns in the game of life, cyphers that required a masculine figure in front of them to give them value. Now, into her racing mind, that other idea, which before now had sometimes found entrance, forced itself, masterfully, refusing to be kept out . . . The like of her . . . Peggy Weldon . . . The mother, after all, was a decent little woman, too good for Johnny Weldon . . . And there was no dount but the Old John was a warm man . . . Such a solution would have at least the merit of simplicity, and, as she said to herself, loftily, there was no fear that there'd be any trouble dealing with the Weldons if she came to them offering a marriage like that! (It was also characteristic of Shibby's time and class that the possible views of those most concerned were not even remotely taken into account in her design.)

Her eyes, fixed, and made sightless by thought, were still on the picture. She dragged herself back to the present, and it seemed to her that the blue-velveted boy smiled at her encouragingly.

One of the doors of the room was open, and a voice calling her name came echoing through the marble-paved hall, a soft contralto voice, calling on a low note.

'Shibby! Are you there? The Captain wants you——'

'That's no news to me!' said Miss Pindy, grimly, to the empty room. 'Thank God he didn't come mooching after me here!'

She strode forth from the drawing-room and locked the door. Then she turned to the messenger, who was her half-sister, Nesta.

42

'On earth what does he want with me? I declare he has me bothered with him! Is it to get into this house? He was above here in the forenoon. I seen him sitting on the steps, smoking his old pipe; waiting for me I suppose he was, to get in. The door was shut, and I was too busy scrubbing to open it for him.'

'It's only his tea he wants now. Kit's come in, and they're wanting their tea.'

'Let them want!' replied Shibby austerely. She banged the heavy hall-door as if she were banging it on the supplications of her family, and followed her young sister down the steps.

'I wouldn't have bothered you,' apologised Nesta, 'but I couldn't find the keys.'

'That'd be hard for you seeing they're in me pawket!' Shibby responded, with a touch of satisfaction in her voice, evoked by the thought of the impatient suppliants who had to await her pleasure. 'Tell me where was Kit, Nessie?'

'Kit was exercising—and, oh, Shibby! Peggy's home! He met her!'

Nessie's colour rose with the excitement of her news, and her voice, the gentle western voice, with the sing-song rise and fall, had an unwonted spring in it. She was twenty-three, yet she had never been away from the old Tower of Inver for as much as a night. To go to Monarde, or Clytagh, by the morning train, and to return by the evening one, was the extent of her experience of the world. Shibby had taught her her letters; a monitress of the National School had imparted some further rudiments of education, and then Mrs Johnny Weldon had compassionately intervened, and Nessie had shared with 'the Grabber's daughter' the teaching that Peggy received from her mother, preliminary to being sent to schools, English and French, of a class to which the daughter of 'the Grabber's' employer could not aspire.

Nessie was like her mother, gentle little Esther McKnight, with no token of the Prendevilles about her except her bright blue eyes. She was of those whose inveterate unselfishness can only be explained by the theory of a heredity of slave ancestresses. Creatures so submissive as to have no independent existence, so unselfish as to become the centre of a vortex of practically enforced selfishness;

born slaves, perpetual servers of the domestic altar, whose single redeeming vice is their self- indulgent virtue, who can only urge in self-defence that they do not often transmit their infirmity to their male offspring. Certainly Esther's son had no reason to reproach his little mother on this score. Nessie had absorbed it all.

The news of Peggy Weldon's return came to Miss Pindy with something of a shock. She stood still at the foot of the steps of the Big House, and looked down the long avenue into the demesne. At almost the farthest point that was visible from where she was standing, the roof and chimneys of a house showed above the trees.

The Grabber's daughter come back! The one that'll have it all! It was no new thought to Shibby, but now it held her rigid. Was Fate taking the game out of her hands into its own?

'What like is she now?' she demanded. 'What did he say about her?'

'He said she'd got very big, and she was no good to ride— that's all he thinks of!' said Kit's younger sister, who, his adoring slave though she was, shared with the rest of humanity a certain satisfaction in exposing the foolishness of one of the opposite sex. 'I asked what she was like, but all he would say was that she weighed the best part of a ton and she had his arm broke mounting her!'

Nessie laughed, and looked to her sister for response. Shibby uttered a sound expressive of assenting contempt for the uselessness of such as Kit, and marched on down the weedy cart-road that led from Inver House to its predecessor, now its supplanter, Inver Tower.

Chapter 7

A stranger who had seen Shibby as she stood in front of the Big House, her gaze seemingly fixed on the small house among the trees of the demesne, but the eyes of her soul on the man to whom it belonged, might, if he were a man of fancy, have thought of a Norn, one of those fatal and tremendous maiden-goddesses of the North, whose decrees were generally baleful, and always irrevocable; or, more obviously, of Lady Macbeth, watching and waiting. But one of the neighbours of Cloon (since the Irish peasant is a shrewd person and little influenced by looks) would probably have grinned and said:

'Look over at Shibby Pindy! Isn't it she that's the big proud gable of a woman! And as cross as briars she is too! Faith if she'd be vexed I'd rather meet a burning mountain!'

The neighbour would not have been far out in his estimate. Shibby was indeed a big woman, following in that her father's family. She stood a full six feet in height, her broad shoulders and massive limbs in noble and well-ordered proportion to her great stature. Her hair had been black, as had been that of her country-girl mother, now it was grey. It grew low on her low forehead, and flowed back over her ears with a silver ripple in it that made one think of a sunny river. Under her dark, thick eyebrows were the blue eyes that heredity dealt out alike to Pindys and Prendevilles, with a stubbornly stupid disregard for those who were or were not eligible for entry in Burke's Landed Gentry. Her nose and jaw and chin were firm as marble, strong and heavy. In her mouth only was there any hint of the gentleness that hid in her heart, and its gentleness was held in check by the look in her great eyes that made the neighbours shirk her glance, and whisper that it was best to stand out from the like of her . . . wasn't there some that said she had the *Droic h'uil*—the Bad Eye, the Lord save us!

Shibby owed very little to her father, but one gift she had had

45

from him. Since her childhood she had led the choir in the chapel of Cloon. The neighbours told it of her that there had been strange priests, and men from Dublin itself, and they to go down, as you might say, on their two knees, asking her would she go sing for them in their chapels and their music halls. But no she would not. Sure, said the neighbours, she wouldn't leave them children of the old Captain's if they were to put their eyes on sticks for her! (which is, of course, a recognised form of inducement, but is one that is never recorded as having been successful.)

Shrove after Shrove Shibby's grandmother had tried to make a match for her, heaping her savings into the scale to outweigh such disadvantages as her birth might involve. Shibby was a beautiful girl in those days. Those who had seen the portrait of the Lady Isabella would declare that no better likeness of Shibby Pindy could be imagined. Lady Isabella had left Shibby more than her looks, and perhaps it was thanks to her that the Widow Hynes' match-making had no success. Shibby held high her handsome head, and would listen to no persuasions. 'I'm neither fish nor flesh!' she would say with arrogant self-depreciation, 'I'm meat for no butcher!'

Once, and once only, the wind of the wings of romance had nearly swept away her resolve. A young doctor had come to Cloon, and had—as was said—been 'given the Dispensary.' In other words, his father, a prosperous merchant of Monarde, had, by a dashing employment of material arguments, procured the post for him at the hands of the Committee. That was thirty years, and more, ago. The little house in Cloon, in which the young doctor had then installed himself, held him still. Willy Magner was a good fellow and a good doctor, and, as his father said, 'If you can buy a practice from another doctor, why, in God's name, shouldn't you buy one from a Commy-tee?' which was sound sense.

Doctor Magner and Shibby were much of an age; they soon became friends, and the Widow Hynes' hopes had run high. But the Doctor had never married. Shibby alone knew the reason why.

'Willy, I wouldn't wrong you or your children,' was what she had said when the young doctor had interrupted their friendship by asking her to marry him.

'Shibby!' he had answered, putting his arm round her, 'What do I care for children, born or unborn? Why wouldn't you have me? I love you, and I believe you love me!'

'And if I do, Willy,' Shibby said, 'isn't that reason enough?'

She put her proud head down on his shoulder—he was a tall, thin fellow, taller than she—and wept.

But all he said, and he said much, could not shake her.

The ancient Tower of Inver had, like many of its contemporaries, but a single living-room, but, in the great days of Inver, a small dwelling house had been built on to it for the housing of Lady Isabella's grooms, and in the conglomeration of small rooms that had thus been evolved, Jas and his family lived in reasonable comfort. The chief sitting-room was in the Tower itself; one of its windows looked out into the immense stable-yard of Inver House, a vast square, with a row of horse-chestnut trees in its centre, shading a long shallow stone-paved tank, in which, in the old days, the carriages were washed, and, surrounding it, coach-houses, and barns, and stabling for the five and twenty horses that had been the minimum of Lady Isabella's requirements. Opposite the Tower window was a wide, arched gateway, in which was now but one half of the iron gates that had once guarded the high-walled garden. Its four acres had been held to be the pick of the lands of Inver. Now they were given over to thickets of briars, out of which, here and there, a grey lichen-covered fruit tree thrust its forlorn branches, as it might be an old and antlered stag, assailed by wolves. Dense stretches of docks and coltsfoot, thistles and nettles, rioted in the rich ground, and yielded place only to the ravaging snouts of a sow and her progeny, and to the devastating scratchings of the fowl, agents of destruction, that together represented Miss Pindy's sole independent source of income.

Since the day, now nearly forty years past, when Jas had constituted Shibby as his purse bearer, she had ruled all things of his, faithfully, with rigid economy, absolutely, as an eldest daughter should. For her the fact of her relationship was never forgotten, but for the old Captain it had passed into oblivion. For him Shibby had become, quite simply, one of the basic facts of life, whose origin is neither questioned nor considered; like his house, his bed, his meals, the stick that he leaned on, without which he would fall. As far back as his memory would go, she had always been there. But his memory now would hardly reach to yesterday. He lived in a cloud, through which he could peer at the near faces, and, as it seemed, realise their personalities; but between him and the past it hung, and lifted rarely and unpredictably. 'A very useful girl,' he would say of Shibby. 'I have a great confidence in her.' Once or twice he had wakened suddenly, and had stared at her, and asked if she were Margaret, but before a reply could be made, the cloud had closed in again.

Close to the turf fire, that was smouldering in the cave-like depth of the fireplace, the Captain awaited his daughters, sitting there, huge and old, a dramatic, even a stagey impersonation of the tragedy of old age. He was eighty-eight, and the burden of the years lay heavy on him. The cruelties of Time need not be catalogued, nor the scars it leaves detailed. Jas had drunk hard all his life, but not harder than many others. He had lived dissolutely, but not more than those that had gone before him. He had been one of the predestined failures, standard examples of a bad heredity, whom the stars in their courses would seem to have doomed that in weakness only they should be strong, and only in disaster pre-eminent. He had, in his life, ruined himself, and considerably disappointed his friends; now, even in the matter of his death, this single point of consistency he had maintained, and he continued to disappoint the long succession of prophets who had in turn predicted for him the speedy death proper to a constitution undermined by drink.

But Jas had outlived all his old friends, and made no new ones. Even the succession of the prophets, which is ever renewed, had ceased to find inspiration in his legend. No one now, not even Shibby, expected anything of him but that he would for ever sit, wrapped in an orange-brown frieze coat, with a sailor's blue woollen nightcap on his head, and an old horse-blanket over his knees, by the turf-fire in the little sitting-room of the Tower of Inver. To the two children, born to him out of his time, he was no more than a permanent and rather troublesome fact of nature, as it might be the stump of an old

48

tree in their path, impossible to root up, but—or so Kit found it—
not too difficult to evade or ignore.

In front of the fire, beside the Captain, sat three dogs of indeterminate breed, that, for no very obvious reason, were given the courtesy title of collies. Erect as cormorants on a rock, they sat with their noses set for the red pit of fire, like guns trained on a mark. A large turf-basket, piled with the brick-shaped pieces of hard black peat, that is the common fuel of the West of Ireland, stood on one side of the hearth; a kettle on the hob was putting out little puffs of steam.

Miss Pindy, with a single adroit and circuitous kick, obliterated the cormorants, who vanished instantaneously, establishing themselves in their trusted refuge under the Captain's big armchair.

'Them three thinks the world was made for them!' she said, 'and it's them knows how to enjoy it!'

Old Jas woke up, and rolled an eye, timorous as those of the dogs, at the ruler of his house. Was she going to sweep the room and send him to bed? He never could be sure of what might not happen. He was tired; but that might be because he had walked up to the Big House this morning. Certainly he had felt like teatime; but one never knew. It might be bedtime, and he might have had his tea and forgotten it. If that were so he ought to have his pipe. One of his swollen blue old hands began to paw at the pocket of his coat. He was still able to fill a pipe for himself, even though they wouldn't let him have the matches, damn them—what harm was it if he had burnt a hole in the old coat one day? It was time he went into Monarde and bought a new one. The fellows at the Club would be laughing at him. But they— 'they' were his family—never would let him have any money—damn them! He found his pipe. Now where had the pouch got to? He began researches in another pocket.

Nessie intervened.

'Your tea, Captain. It's not time for your pipe yet.'

The Captain's faint activities subsided. His tea was placed on the seat of a chair beside him. He enjoyed his tea, and translated his enjoyment of it into sounds that would have mitigated the enjoyment of theirs for people less accustomed to them than were his son and daughters. The white beard, that was the last barrier old age

49

had raised between him and his youth, was apt to be an unpleasing sight by the time one of his meals was ended. The gods could have had small love for Jas in that they had delayed so long his summons.

The little sitting-room was crammed with furniture, old and precious, yet, by its present owners, unvalued and regarded as superfluous. When Madam Prendeville had gone to live at the Tower, she had conveyed there from the Big House all of its furniture that could possibly be bestowed in so small a place, and ancient mahogany tables, tallboys, bureaux and cupboards of the great period of Irish furniture, fought for floor space with the shabby necessary additions of later years.

At a black mahogany cabuchon-legged table in the middle of the room Miss Pindy sat, and dealt with food and drink to her family, with the same swift decision with which she would fling scraps to her hens.

'Kit,' she said, looking him up and down, 'I hear you're after meeting Johnny Weldon's daughter. She's a great lady now, I suppose! And you a disgrace to the world in them old clothes! I wonder she'd speak to you! Why wouldn't you make yourself decent when you go out?' Her voice was reproving, but her eyes, as they moved from Kit's square spare shoulders down his long legs to his small feet, contradicted the reproof.

'She was glad enough to see me, I can tell you, in spite of my old clothes!' Kit hit back at Shibby. 'She thought that brown cart-horse of her father's was running away with her. It'd have been no light job for him if he had! I made her ride him out, and it wasn't long before he'd had his 'nough!'

'Well, the pair of you, Nessie and yourself, must go see her now she's home,' announced Miss Pindy, 'she might be glad as to see Nessie as you, for all as grand as you think yourself!'

It was her way to mask her feeling for her young brother in a species of grim chaff. It was an effort of self-preservation, a floodgate behind which she penned that master-passion of her life, which had seized and subjugated her on the day that Esther had confided her first-born to her care.

'I didn't see Mrs Johnny myself this long time,' she went on, 'I might go over with you myself—'

She was interrupted by an outcry, confused and protesting, from her father. One of the dogs, protruding her head from beneath the valance of the chair, had very gently taken the Captain's piece of cake out of his hand, and in his effort to save his property, he had upset his tea. It stood, a brown steaming pool, in the valley made by the horse-blanket between his knees, and he gazed down at it, bewildered, afraid to move, dreading, like a child, the scolding that he supposed he deserved.

The door was open, and Fly darted through it with her loot. The sod of turf, snatched from the basket by Kit, and hurled after her, did not expedite her departure, since it would have been impossible to do so. Kit began to laugh. Shibby said:

'I wish to God the whole pack of them dirty dogs was dead!'

Nessie went to her father's aid.

'It wasn't my fault, Nessie—I couldn't help it— The dam' brute gave me a start——' He was almost crying.

'Never mind, Captain, there's no harm done. I'll get you some more——' Nessie's voice was like the oil that the Good Samaritan poured into the wounds of the man that fell among thieves.

The old Captain took heart, and brought out his stock response for the moments, and they were many, that Nessie comforted him in adversity.

'I'll do as much for you when you're my age and I'm yours! I can't speak you fairer than that, can I now?'

'You cannot indeed!' said Nessie, making the rubrical reply. 'And I promise you I'll be greatly obliged to you!'

Kit looked at his father; a look of which it would be easier to say what it did not express than what, precisely, it betokened. A vigorous young dog will sometimes thus survey an elder, lying somnolent and sick in the sun; with a sort of curiosity; not exactly with contempt. One could only say, positively, that there was no pity in it.

Chapter 8

The four generations of the Weldon family, from old Mick, the first of the dynasty to emerge from the paternal boghole, to Peggy, its latest representative, were like nothing so much as a set of cement steps (rather shabby as to the lower ones) of which no two correspond in height. Mick was but a little above the ground level. From Mick to John the First the rise was noticeable in affluence and position, but was unimportant in cultural elevation, and it was reserved for John Weldon the Second to make an upward move on the social ladder which was nearly double that of his sire.

The younger John was one of the successful people who make their success rather by what they are not than by what they are. He was not adventurous, nor imprudent. He did not drink, not was he extravagant. He was not brilliant in any way, but he was cautious and careful, and if his faculty for taking care, sometimes (with regard to his own affairs) was expanded (by force of circumstance) into cunning, he could defy his conscience and the catechism to charge him with having failed to be honest and just in all his dealings.

There had been a time when young John Weldon and Shibby Pindy had been spoken of in hopeful whispers by the Widow Hynes to her gossips. The talk had grown in fervour and volume, when, very suddenly, all that had inspired it ceased. Not the most acute and persevering of the gossips, not even Shibby's grandmother, ever discovered the reason of the abrupt departure of young John Weldon to Dublin. These things had happened when he and Shibby, who had been born in the same year, were but little over twenty. It was reported that someone had met Johnny Weldon going home one evening, with a severely swollen face, and that he had said he was forced to go at once to Dublin to see a dentist, and would be away in the morning. He did not return , and his father said, pleasantly enough, that he was no loss, and that it would be no harm for him to learn to do something useful; the boy was thinking for the Law, John the elder said, and he was smart enough at his books, and it'd be a handy trade these times, with all the litigation that was going in the country.

That Shibby Pindy, young and handsome, strong, and very proud, had known how to give a knave an answer, was a fact that neither she nor young Johnny Weldon had thought it necessary to divulge, but it is possible that old John had made a guess that was not far off the truth. It is at least certain that he had always, throughout his long life, showed Shibby something far more like affection than he had ever exhibited to his son.

It happened to Johnny, sore in head, and wounded in spirit, to arrive in Dublin at a moment when an Evangelist Revival, as sincere as it was vehement, was in high progress. Young Johnny, who, in spite of occasional lapses, was a serious youth, attended the meetings, and learned to sing hymns, and to groan religiously, as well as other matters, more important in theory, but less simple in practice. At one of these assemblies he fell in with a solicitor of a like way of thinking; they sang together out of the same hymn-book, and groaned in friendly emulation. Thence forward the path was clear before young Johnny Weldon. When, some years later, he returned, a solicitor, learned in the Law, to his native village, he was already higher up the social ladder than his father had ever even wished to be.

It was regrettable that when he thus returned, a converted and thoroughly respectable character, old John liked his son less than ever. But this Old John kept to himself, and it did not interfere with his satisfaction at the rise in the family fortunes.

It has been told how, with the assistance of that jovial celebration aboard the *Eileen Oge*, John Weldon had achieved the tenancy of the Inver Demesne lands. He had been in possession for some fifteen years when the Land Purchase Act of 1903— that measure which instilled into Irish landlords the painful truth as to the economic value of half a loaf—revolutionised the land tenure of Ireland. Old John had been eighty-three then, and had declared that he was well pleased enough with things as they were. His son, however, took a different view of the position, and it was he who had induced Captain Jas (to whom ready money never came amiss) to sanction the purchase of the Demesne 'under the Act.' Shibby's opposition had been violent, but unavailing. She had faced the younger John Weldon, closeted with the Captain, and had told him that the Captain didn't rightly know what he was doing—('and I tell ye so up to his nose!' she had shouted)—and that until Kit was of age nothing should be settled. Shibby had been tremendous and awe-inspiring in her rage, and the old Captain had trembled, but the enemy had held the winning cards. Finally he had compelled Jas to order his daughter to leave the room, and Shibby had left, breaking like a thunder-cloud into terrible tears that watered her hatred of her adversary, renewing and strengthening it, making it strike its root deeper still into her deep heart.

The sale of the Demesne, although the work of Old John's son, was of necessity carried out in Old John's own name, and even though he had been content to remain a tenant only, now that he found himself its absolute owner, he knew how much possession meant to him.

Old John's lot in life was happy beyond the lot of most men. He had had his dream, and it had come true. He found it almost incredible that those broad and beautiful acres, that from his boyhood he had known and revered almost too worshipfully to dream of possessing them, were inalienably his. Yet the incredible had happened, and all that was now required—not to enable him to sing the *Nunc Dimittis*, since the last thing he wished for was to depart, in peace or otherwise—to round off a life-history of success, was a suitable house.

The Big House, that had hitherto been to the Demesne its very heart and culminating point, had no share in John's dream. It was, he said, too big entirely. What was this the Captain had called it long ago? 'a d——d barracks!' And he was right— 'which he wasn't often the poor man!' John would add kindly. The old Prendeville house, that had intervened between the Tower and the Big House, had gone with the Demesne. It was a ruin; but there were the stones, handy enough, on the spot. Old John, with a spirit of enterprise that at the age of eighty-three is unusual, summoned to himself a contractor, who was also 'a bit of an architect,' and laid down his requirements. Two good, honest, square, little rooms with the hall door between them, that'd be handy for an office for Johnny, and the kitchen behind that again. And four bedrooms above them—sure that'd be enough for any family—and a garret in the roof that'd do for a servant gerr'l.

These had been John's instructions to the contractor who was also a bit of an architect, and this particular bit, no doubt, it was that had inspired the two small bow-windows that had broken out, like pimples, on either side of the hall door, and had cost so little more than the stipulated price, that John had acceded to them, and had felt in so doing as much a patron of Art for Art's sake as Pope Julius might have felt when he authorised the plan of St. Peter's.

John Weldon had contradicted his character, and had run contrary to all his own theories of conduct in his marriage. His wife had been the daughter of a poor farmer. She had no 'fortune.' She was not of John's religion (which was that of the Protestant Church of Ireland), and he had married little Molly Casey for the sake of love and her looks, and had snapped his fingers at old Mick's indignation, and the disapproval alike of priest and parson. John's worldly wisdom, of which he was extremely proud, had not often failed him, and this, its most noteworthy lapse, was justified by the care his wife took of him, and her skill in fattening a pig, allied arts of equal merit in John's eyes. (Also, it may be said, by her transmission of her good looks to her granddaughter, Peggy—and for this, also John gave credit to his own perspicacity.) Mrs Weldon had died a couple of years before the accomplishment of John's other sentimental venture, the purchase of the Demesne, since when his son had come to live with him, and his daughter-in-law had managed his house and seen to his comfort.

In the year 1912, John was ninety-two, four years older than this feudal lord, Captain Jas, but time and little Molly Casey had served him well. He had, as he was accustomed to say, 'minded himself better than the poor Captain'; by which he implied that his self-restraint in getting drunk only on state occasions, such as young Kit's christening, and his fidelity to Molly Casey (who, it may be said, had seen to it that this was not only a virtue, but was also a necessity) had had their reward in his hearty and prosperous old age. His mind was no less alert and shrewd than it had been in the great days of the 'Half-Seas-Over-Lease'; he still kept a firm hand on all his affairs.

'I make that old son o' mine work for me!' he would say, 'and I pay him well. But what's mine's me own, and it'll stay mine till I'm rowed out to Deer Island with me two feet foremost! Ho, ho, ho!'

This was a picturesque reference on John's part to his funeral, which, as is not unusual in his class, he was accustomed to treat as a joke of a subtle character, and the jest did not lose in flavour from the fact that he was entirely aware that his son found his firm hold on life and property was the reverse of amusing.

In spite, however, of the lagging of a veteran who was not only aware of his superfluity, but gloried in it, young Mr Weldon's career moved upward from strength to strength. He established a fish market in Clytagh; he married an Englishwoman, both acts of considerable local distinction. He was one of the main pillars of the little Protestant church of Cloon, and although he was a small man, his voice, when the hymns were to his mind, left no one in the parish in doubt as to the strength of his lungs and the fervour of his piety. It was a source of deep irritation to him that in order to distinguish him from his father, who, for ninety odd years had been known as John Weldon, he was generally spoken of as Johnny Weldon, often as Young Johnny, which was, as he legitimately felt, an unsuitable designation for a godly solicitor of sixty-two years of age. He felt that his father's preposterous longevity caused him annoyance enough without his sharp incessant pin-prick.

Young Johnny's marriage was, as has been suggested, something of a rise in the world for the grandson of Old Mick, and the son of Old John. Miss Louisa Owen had been governess at the Rectory for several years, until, in fact, her pupils had outgrown her and gone forth into the world. She was English, and well-educated according to the standard of an earlier and less exacting time; and she had 'the name' of a little patrimony of her own. The Rector's wife, who was something of a strategist and administrator (as be-

56

comes a Rector's wife) and was anxious to keep Miss Owen in the parish (to play the harmonium, and to teach at Sunday School) being well aware that patrimony and matrimony are often allied terms, had let fall a hint as to Miss Owen's 'fortune' into the younger Mr Weldon's receptive ear. The younger Mr Weldon ('a church-warden and a *very* superior man to his father,' as the Rector's wife pointed out to Miss Owen) took the hint without delay, and never, as he had often, very handsomely, remarked to Mrs Weldon, had reason to regret it.

Whether Mrs Weldon regretted it or no was a matter known only to herself. If it had been enquired of her, on her honour, as a truth-telling Englishwoman, what were her reasons for having married Young Johnny, she might have found them a little difficult to re-member. Such reasons, if after twenty-three years of matrimony they are to preserve their cogency, must be kept well dusted, and carefully polished and handled, even massaged—especially if one has espoused Mr John Weldon the Second. The chances are that she would have replied, rather uncertainly, that he used to walk back to the Rectory with her after evening church, and that poor Mrs Brownrigg— (who was the Rector's wife, and was dead, and therefore, in Mrs Weldon's phraseology, poor)—had advised it; and that her mother had died at just about the time, and that 'John' —(he had desired her to call him John)—was a very considerate husband, and she had been quite happy; and then she would probably have said, brightly, brightness being a part of her duties in the past that she still consci-entiously cultivated:

'Oh, I don't know! I'm sure I ought to be very thankful—I sup-pose everything is ordered for the best! John and I have always got on very well indeed—— And now there's Peggy—— !'

There, in the sense of being at Demesne Lodge (for Old John there was but one demesne in the world), Peggy certainly was, and she, who was the fourth step in the ascent of the Weldon family, marked a rise even more considerable than either of those that had preceded it. It was, to be sure, unfortunate that a son had not been vouchsafed to Young Johnny to carry on the growing greatness of the House of Weldon, but both he and Old John agreed that, in spite of the disaster of her sex, Peggy was an undoubted credit to the family. One never knew. Even, in virtue of that very disaster, the family position might be consolidated by an alliance with one of the class still known as the Landed Gentry of Ireland, even though the qualifying adjective was, in 1912, not often based on more than such lands as were comprised in their flower-gardens.

'There isn't any reason, with her prospects and her looks, and all we're doing for her, why she wouldn't go so far as to marry a title!' Young Johnny had said to Mrs Johnny, magnanimously condoning her failure in the matter of a son. 'And thus, my dear, we may be able to say, as the hymn says:

> *'Joy hath budded from each thorn,*
> *That round our foot-steps lay!'*

When Peggy, her education rounded off by a course of music at the Conservatoire, returned from Paris, a finished product in Mrs Weldon's eyes, her father's acceptance of the fact of her sex no longer required the prop of religion, not was it damped by resignation. The thorn had budded most creditably.

'I spared no money to give her the best of edjication,' he would say. 'She's brought home a boxful of prizes! Literachoor and Music, and all sorts; and she's remarkable at figures, so her school-teachers tell us. The Mother says she gets that from me. But indeed *I* find it's subtraction, and that out of *my* pawket, that she's best at! Addition isn't in *her* line of business at all!'

Young Johnny (who was in some ways an ingenuous little man) was much pleased with this ingenuous little jest, and for several successive weeks it brightened the unofficial conversation of the Clytagh Bench of Tuppennies—which was the profane term then current for the magistrates of Mr Morley's creation—in whose court Mr Weldon plied his calling.

Old John was no less well satisfied with his granddaughter. She was wonderful to him, wonderful, even mysterious in the splendour of her attainments. That one small head should carry all she knew was his perpetual glory and amazement. Old John, though he had stood on the shoulders of his father, Old Mick, was still a primitive.

'Well now!' he would say to a friend. 'There's no bounds to that little gerr'l, the learning she has, and the smartness of her! I declare to ye she's that cultured ye'd say she was born in a droign-room! Upon me soul ye would. And to hear her play the p'yanna—oh, t'would delight a Turk! And as for French—Honest to God! She talks it as nice and as easy as meself talks the English!'

Then, if Old John considered his companion safe as a confidant, he would probably continue, though in a lowered voice.

'And a downright handsome gerr'l she is too! The very dead spit of my poor wife, God be good to her! . . . I d'no what way in the world was me son Johnny her father! I d'no at all how did I breed an ugly thief like him! Though, faith, for the matter o' that, I hadn't but me poor wife's word for it that he's me son at all!' with which old John, who might have posed very successfully as Falstaff in extreme old age, would fall into bronchial chucklings that put a stop to discussion of this delicate point.

Chapter 9

Mrs Johnny Weldon, seated in the bow-window of the dining-room of Demesne Lodge, which was just large enough to contain her and her work-basket, darning Young Johnny's socks, gave precisely the pleasing domestic finish that the contractor's artistic effort required. It is said that two years in Ireland suffice to turn an Englishman into an Irishman, but a quarter of a century had only intensified Mrs Johnny's adherence to her native type, and had done no more than teach her to endure the outrages on her sense of fitness that had confronted her on her entrance into the household of her mother-in-law, Mrs Johnny Weldon, née Casey. The old Mrs Weldon and the young Mrs Johnny Weldon had begun their life under one roof on a basis of mutual dread, if not dislike, and had slowly progressed from fear, through respect, to affection. Mrs Johnny found a faithful, even an admiring ally in old Molly, and a staunchness that responded to the tune of her own steady soul. The old Irish countrywoman, wearing the brown habit of her Church, with the blessed oil on her brow, died in the arms of the English Protestant daughter-in-law, and it was her savings, left by will to 'her dear daughter-in-law, Louisa,' that stiffened Mrs Johnny's resolve to give her daughter those opportunities of education that her own youth had known of, but had not attained to.

Mrs Johnny, like many of her class and nation, was both sensible and sentimental. To combine these divergent qualities is an essentially English endowment, and by straining both to their ultimate ounce, Mrs Johnny had, as she said, 'got on very well indeed' in her married life. But, since no woman of sense, however sentimental, could idealise Young Johnny into anything more romantic than 'a very considerate husband,' Mrs Weldon had, as is not unusual with mothers, fallen in love with her offspring. If her statement that 'now there was Peggy' was merely meant to express the fact that the prefect triad, *Monsieur, Madame, et Bébé,* was now achieved, it was indisputably the case; but if the implication was that her daughter was of the nature of a link between herself and that daughter's father, her sincerity might have been doubted. By the end of Peggy's first month in the family circle, the dispassionate observer would by no means have regarded her as a bond of union between her parents. It had, on the contrary, become Mrs Weldon's difficult part to function as a buffer-state between her husband and her daughter, and even she, faithful little upholder of the domestic sanctities though she was, could hardly have denied that life for her was less strenuous when this duty was not required of her.

This was the case on this steamy July afternoon, when Mr Weldon's socks were occupying his wife's attention. He was away, on business, and his only child, seated on the table in the little dining-room, was encouraging her mother's industry, in a manner not uncommon among daughters, by looking on, and contradicting most of her mother's observations, with a freedom that Mrs Weldon would have checked severely in the little Brownriggs.

'But Mother,' Peggy was saying, 'if he's sleeping in Clytagh to-night, why can't I have Nelson to-morrow? Father won't want him, I settled with Kit that I'd ride with him in the morning.'

'I don't know what Father may have told George Pindy——' began Mrs Weldon.

'George has had no orders,' broke in Peggy, 'and he said Nelson wants exercise. Did Father tell you I wasn't to have him?'

The note of rebellion was perceptible to Mrs Weldon. 'My darling child, I do beg of you not to swing your legs like that! It distresses me to see you——'

Mrs Weldon was what is known as sparring for wind, while she summoned her forces. Peggy jumped off the table and stood in front of her mother.

'Now Mother, I want to know why Nessie and Kit are to be boycotted! I always played with them when I was small. Why on earth shouldn't I play with them now? There's no one else here to play with!'

'The Prendeville family,' began Mrs Johnny sententiously, her early profession coming to her aid and bringing her courage, 'may be of very high and ancient lineage, and no one respects Birth more than I do, and there's nothing to be said against poor little Nessie—'

'Father allows that, does he?' How kind!'

'—But,' went on Mrs Weldon, ignoring the interruption, 'I fear that there is a good deal to be said against her brother——'

'Who says it?'

'I say it,' said Mrs Weldon, faithful to Young Johnny, 'and your Father says it. He doesn't care for you to be so much with them—with Kit at least;' she corrected herself; 'All this riding and lawn tennis—I'm afraid he doesn't think Kit very steady. He knows a great deal more about him than you or I do.'

Mrs Weldon's voice expressed, perhaps, a rather more sincere sympathy for the views of Peggy's father than she felt—(Kit had been in her Sunday School class, he was such a pretty little boy then—he was pretty still! She banished the thought, and said to herself that Peggy ought to remember the Fifth Commandment.)

'Father knows best, dear!' She nodded her tidy head, compressing her lips, while her long needle wriggled like a worm over the ball that was temporarily filling the place of Young Johnny's heel.

'Oh, Father!' said Peggy, in a voice that was far from conforming with the precepts of the Fifth Commandment, 'Father approves of no one except himself! I don't know why there should be all this fuss about the Prendevilles. I don't care very much about Kit myself—Nessie is the one I like—but of course Father thinks the worst of everyone! Especially me! I believe he thinks I'm a daughter of Satan, and he had nothing at all to say to me!'

Mrs Weldon was shocked. No little Brownrigg, or even big Brownrigg, would have spoken thus of its parent. Was it for this that she had economised to send her child to expensive schools, and had foregone her dear companionship for so many years? Was it for this that she economised to send her child to expensive schools, and had foregone her dear companionship for so many years? Was it for this that she had overcome John's distrust of Paris, his horror, hardly overborne, of a convent school? And those troublesome and expensive holidays in France and London, those visits to her own English relations, so full of social anxieties, and demanding so much laborious gratitude—were all these efforts that she had made in order to keep the child free from undesirable village relatives and companions, and an Irish accent, made in vain?

First Paris, and then St. Rule's, that very modern school, at which Mrs Weldon had been so proud to think of her girl officiating as assistant teacher of French and music. But oh! these modern schools! poor Mrs Weldon thought, what had they not taught Peggy! Here she had come home, at the age of two and twenty, full of accomplishments, and without a brogue, but full also of what some people might call independence, but what she could only think of as naughtiness. Yes, naughtiness was the only word for it. Whatever excuse there might be for this friendship with the young Prendevilles— ('and after all, they *had* always played together, and there *is* no one else for the child—I ought to have thought of that,' she reproached herself). But to speak in such a way of her own father! Mrs Weldon felt herself getting hot at the thought of what the naughty girl had said——

Before however she could find words to express something of what she felt, Peggy had overwhelmed her in the bow window and had implanted a swift kiss on her forehead.

'Don't look so shocked, darling! You really are the dearest pet of a little old maid! I'll go out now and tell George you said I could have the horse to-morrow——'

Another kiss silenced Mrs Weldon's protest, and Peggy was gone. Her mother heard her snatch a stick and hat from the stand in the little hall. ('Just like a man!' she grieved, addressing her plaint aloud to Young Johnny's sock, sure of its sympathy.) Presently she saw her daughter pass the window and take the path that led into the main avenue through the demesne.

'She's gone to the Tower again! How put out John would be!' she thought, distressfully. 'Well, as long as it's only Nessie——'

She watched Peggy's active figure swing along the path till it was lost to sight. Her anxious thoughts followed it. Only Nessie? But that was just what it was not—it was also Nessie's brother, quite another matter. How unfortunate it was! John and she should have thought of all this before they brought the child home. And those two poor half-educated Prendeville children—she could not be sorry for them—suspended like Mahomet's coffin between two worlds! Naturally they welcome a girl like my Peggy! . . . But that old Shibby— the stream of thought checked, and broke over a snag, a large snag.

John always said she was a schemer. Was she scheming now? It was certain that lately the Tower had extended tentacles towards Demesne Lodge. What did they mean? . . .

Mrs Weldon had never felt quite at ease with Miss Pindy. She was so vast, so incalculable. And she had found it so difficult to know what to call her. 'Miss Prendeville' was impossible. 'Miss Pindy' would amount to acceptance of a position so equivocal that Mrs Weldon could hardly bear to think of it, much less acknowledge it. And then she had found 'Miss Shibby' so difficult to pronounce. It gave her a horrid feeling that she was trying, in a state of intoxication, to say 'Mississippi.' Finally, on the not very frequent occasions when they met, Mrs Johnny had compromised on 'Miss Isabella.' (And it would be hard to express the gratification that this title afforded to Shibby, she who was Mahomet's coffin indeed, without so much as a name on the coffin-plate to which she could lay a claim!)

The grey fog, stabbed through with rain, that is so often the Atlantic's contribution to July, in the West of Ireland, enveloped Peggy as she walked to the Tower. She had to pass the Big House, looming large and mysterious in the dense air. She stood still at the beautiful old wrought-iron gates, that had been meant to keep inviolate the great circle of gravel in front of the hall-door, but that now hung crooked on their hinges, always open. The gravel was greened over with weeds; a goat, standing on its hind-legs, was eating the ivy that grew on the area wall. Peggy looked at the house meditatively, considering it and its history. It was so dominating, and yet so appealing; so splendid, and so neglected. It could remember a past so lordly and so brilliant, and now had to endure this miserable present, forsaken, given over to desolation. It seemed to Peggy to eye her through its many windows appraisingly and censoriously, and to find her, with her rough frieze coat and skirt and her walking stick, an outrage, standing on the very spot over which the silken Lady Isabella, in her coach-and-four horses had so often passed.

'It thinks that I and my people are *canaille* who have robbed it of its demesne!' Peggy thought, returning the scrutiny of the house boldly. 'And so we have, and I'm not a bit ashamed of it!' —

(Peggy knew none of the circumstances of the 'Half-Seas-Over-Lease')— 'And I only wish we had robbed the old house too, instead of having to live in that little poky hole we're in now! *We've* got the right of competence! The Prendeville's couldn't hold what they had, in spite of their bragging——' She was looking at the stone over the hall-door, that was carved with the clenched, mailed hand, and the arrogant moot, *Je Prends,'* had caught her eye.

'You can take!' she tossed the taunt to the old house, laughing. 'But you can't hold, and I and my sort can!'

The two strains of blood that were in her, the tough acquisitiveness of the Irish peasant, and the hardy practicality of the English middle classes, were speaking, little as she knew it. They had not yet had opportunity to assert themselves. They awaited their hour.

The heavy hall-door stood wide open, Peggy yielded to impulse and went in. The air in the great hall was chill, and the green marble flags were clammy with the cold sweat that the weather drew out of them. Every door was open, and in the drawing room Peggy could see Shibby, a stupendous figure, with her head tied up, turban-wise, in a towel, operating vigorously with a broom.

'May I come in, Miss Isabella?' she asked, when the onslaught neared the doorway at which she stood.

'Indeed you may, and welcome!' responded Miss Isabella, with the graciousness always evoked by this mode of address. 'Come in my dear! You were never in this room I think since it was furnished?'

'I've never been in here at all,' said Peggy, 'it was always shut up—what a splendid room.'

She advanced into the centre of the room. The spoils of auctions had been massed in one corner, their attractions shielded from dust by coverings of newspapers and old linen. Shibby felt a pang that they should thus be taken at a disadvantage.

'Ah, wait awhile till you see it nicely settled out!' she said quickly, 'I can tell you it's something like then!'

Peggy stood still, looking at the rich decorations of the ceiling, at the carved architraves of the massive doors, at the marvellous man-

65

telpiece, with its inlaid bouquets of flowers of rare and precious marbles. She had never seen anything like it. The house fascinated her. She stared at the old portraits in the stucco panels on the damp-stained walls. The portraits, sentient and conscious, as old portraits can be, stared back at her. Suddenly she met the bright eyes of the boy in blue velvet.

'But that's Kit!' she exclaimed, 'when was he painted like that?'

'Ah-ha! That's a mistake you couldn't be blemt for making!' said Shibby, beaming at her, the white turban nodding approval. 'Wouldn't anyone say it was Kit himself? But it isn't him for all that! It's his ancestor, Beauty Kit, the man that built all the stables. And there's the lady he built them for.'

'Why she's exactly like you, Miss Isabella!' said Peggy, gazing respectfully at the dark and haughty beauty that had so strangely reproduced itself in Shibby Pindy, and comparing the small white hand that held the rose, inevitable in portraits of the time, with Shibby's hand that held the broom. 'It's a lovely picture! But—if you don't mind my saying so, Miss Isabella—I don't think she's quite as lovely as Kit——'

As she spoke the name she turned to Shibby, and found her eyes fixed on her face. Shibby's gaze could sometimes have a singularly unhinging effect. The intensity in it startled Peggy, and then the thought that it might seem that she had compared the beauty of the Lady Isabella (and therefore that of Shibby herself) disparagingly with that of the living Kit Prendeville, instead of with the looks of the bygone lad of the name, caused a blush, one of those uncontrollable blushes that are the bane of the young, to sweep over her face, deepening and growing of its own consciousness, till its victim, standing in the full light of the curtainless windows, felt as if she were being simultaneously pilloried as a laughing-stock, and burnt alive. Her normal self-confidence failed her. She knew herself to be no better than any blushing girl of the despised Victorian period. 'And all for nothing—nothing at all! What do I care about Kit's looks, good or bad!' she said to herself, furiously, while Shibby's pitless eyes dwelt on her. The floor seemed to melt under her feet. She felt as if all sensation were concentrated in her burning face.

66

The moment had hardly passed when Nessie ran into the room, calling her name.

'I was upstairs. I thought I heard you! I want to show her the house, Shibby, and now all the rooms are open. Kit's upstairs opening the shutters——'

'Do so, my dear,' Shibby commanded, her eyes still fixed on Peggy.

Peggy turned quickly and followed Nessie, passing Shibby without looking at her. She had courage, but not enough to meet the steady gaze of Miss Isabella's blue eyes.

Nessie flitted before her to the end of the hall and opened a door.

'This is the dining-room. Do you see the light patch in the table? That's where it was broke when Lord Ballyfaill tried to jump his horse over it. I believe Kit would do better with the chestnut filly! If Kit asks a horse to do a thing at all, it does it!'

'No one that wasn't a fool would want to do such a thing!' said Peggy, hotly. 'But young men are fools enough for anything!' She was still angry and discomposed, and ready to visit what she felt to have been her humiliation on the first object that offered itself. 'I don't suppose Kit has more sense than the rest of them!'

'What's that about Kit?' said Kit's light voice. 'What are you saying about me behind my back?'

'Nothing that I wouldn't say to you to your face! Do you think I'm afraid of you?' Peggy flung the challenge at him, ripe for battle. Her grey cat's eyes were very clear and bright, her black brows and lashes gave them emphasis. The blush that had stormed her unawares, still glowed with a moderated fervour in her cheeks; her ruffled temper gave vividness to her expression.

Kit looked at her with an open approval and amusement that she found exasperating.

'Why my goodness, Peggy! How could a poor chap like me think such a thing? Sure I know as well as you do that the boot's on the other leg! I'm trembling all over this minute, you're looking so cross at me! Though the Lord knows what I've done to vex you!'

Shibby's slow stride, like that of an excessively heavy dragoon, was heard in the hall. Her white-turbaned head presented itself at the door.

'I heard you come down, Kit. Mind you shut them shutters after you before you leave the house!'

'I will to be sure—For as little sense as some thinks I have!' He looked at Peggy, laughing at her. His face was brilliant with enjoyment, knowing that she was angry, and that he was teasing her.

Shibby also looked at her; a side-glance, swift as a savage's, on which, swift as it was, nothing was lost.

'Nessie-girl, I want you a minute. Come and give me a hand to get the room over tidy again——'

'Can I help, Miss Isabella?' Peggy made a step towards the door.

'No, my dear, you cannot. And I must go find the Captain. He's about the house some place for ever! If you were to be looking at him, you'd say he wasn't stirring at all, but he's going on always!'

The turban was withdrawn. Then it reappeared.

'But why wouldn't Kit show Peggy the house when she never seen it? There's the long gallery above she didn't see, Kit, and the middle-room too—sure don't they say the ceiling in the middle-room is worth I d'no what!—and there's the Italian chimbley-piece in Lady Isabella's—and there's all the pictures in this room too—what good are you that you couldn't show them to a young lady when she comes to see them! Come on, Nessie-child—' She extended a long arm and caught Nessie's hand, and pulling her through the doorway, closed the door.

Kit thought, 'Don't I know well why she did that, the old divil!' He went a little closer to Peggy.

'Tell me, what did I do that you won't so much as look at me?'

She felt his nearness and it disquieted her. She had lost her self-confidence. She wished Nessie had not left her. It was Nessie whom she had come to see, not Kit. Kit was troublesome and disturbing. She had seen too much of him lately—why was it she could never see Nessie alone? If she had known he had been in the house she wouldn't have come into it——

68

'I don't *want* to look at you!' she broke out, turning and glaring at him, her grey eyes alight.

Kit gave a shout of laughter.

'Then why do you do it?'

He put out a hand, thin and strong, and scarcely larger than Peggy's own. 'Ah, come on, Peggy! Don't be cross to me! Whatever I did, I'm sorry!'

His charming eyes smiled at her. Suddenly he found her very attractive, and he was resolved to use the power that he knew was his to compel her to make friends.

Peggy's eyes fell before his; she half turned away her head, with the simple action of a child that turns from a fire that scorches it; again the courage that she was so proud of, failed her. Kit came a step nearer still, and took her hand that was hanging by her side. It was brown, from playing lawn-tennis, and hard from rowing, but there was something that was like Peggy's self, at once feminine and generous, about it.

Kit held it tightly, and thought: 'Shibby's right! She's a damned nice girl!'

Then he yielded—as he had often yielded before—to impulse, and catching Peggy close to him he kissed her lips.

For a bewildered instant Peggy was still. Then, with the hand that was free, she tried to push him away from her. She felt that only half her will was in the effort; the other half was hypnotised, stunned by the unexpectedness of the assault. She knew that nothing but instant action could save her from being delivered over to the enemy. The enemy was certainly very near, smiling into her eyes, holding her fast, his lips on hers—an experienced enemy, for whose masterful attack she had been unprepared—a nearly victorious enemy, into whose power she felt suddenly that some inward traitor threatened to deliver her.

She dragged herself from his grasp, and began to utter stammering, angry reproaches.

'Ah, Peggy, what harm was there in that? Me and you that are old friends!' wheedled Kit, in his soft brogue, 'Sure that was only a little kiss of peace, like St Paul talks about! Wasn't it very forgiving of me to kiss you, after you being so cross to me all for nothing! It's you that ought to kiss me!'

And, unfortunately, the sheer impudence of the apology made Peggy laugh.

Chapter 10

Once in what is picturesquely if obscurely called a blue moon, old John Weldon would summon his physical forces from the torpor of old age, and obesity, and the armchair by the kitchen-fire in which, regardless of the expostulations of his daughter-in-law, he spent most of his time, and would inform his family that he was going to pay a visit to the poor old Captain. Thus, ignoring his own seniority, he was accustomed to speak of his late employer and patron. Old John's mental forces required no special effort of assembling. In spite of his ninety-two years, they were still vigorous and standing to arms, ready for action at a moment's notice. Indeed, as his elderly son occasionally, in thwarted moments, remarked to his wife, there was something hardly decent in an old man of his age keeping so tight a grip on worldly matters.

'It is full time he should be thinking of his soul, and his eternal salvation,' Young Johnny would say, with what was, in a son of sixty-two, legitimate irritation; 'He won't so much as let me sign a rent-receipt for one of them little village houses! He must do all himself!'

'*Those* little houses,' Mrs Johnny would murmur under her breath, quite without her own volition, just from old habit; she had long since learned that John's grammar, though on the whole passable, was not, in those minor matters, susceptible of correction. 'It isn't youshl, John, dear,' she had sometimes said (her pronunciation of her native tongue, governess though she had been, being, in some respects, no more impeccable than John's grammar), 'to employ the pronoun *them* where the definitive adjective *those* is indicated.'

But this was a colloquialism rooted in the very depths of John's being, and Mrs Johnny had practically lost hope about it.

The up-hilly half-mile of avenue that intervened between Demesne Lodge and Inver House, might have proved for Old John a barrier instead of a connecting-link, were it not that recognising the impossibility of undertaking any expedition on his own feet, he had defied gentility, and the remonstrances of his family, and had taken unto himself as a means of transit the conveyance familiar to his early youth. This was a small donkey-cart, one of those low, spring-less vehicles that are familiarly known as 'ass-butts,' and do the greater part of the work of the poorer parts of Ireland, and Old John, enormous though he was, had never lost his boyhood's knack of hitching himself backwards on to the front part of the cart, and sitting immovably there, with his legs hanging down beside the right shaft.

In this humble but adequate manner he took the road at the full of a July blue moon, an astronomical event that occurred a few days later than Peggy's visit to the Big House.

'G'wan Jack!' said Old John at rhythmic intervals to the donkey, beating it without animosity, and as matter of routine, just as he had done when he was a bare-foot boy.

The little donkey toiled on; it seemed a miracle that so small a creature could move so monstrous a load. Yet ever when a blue moon rose, the little donkey rose also to the occasion. On this hot afternoon the miracle was again accomplished. The Tower of Inver was gained, and Old John, with the aid of his thick stick, and a firm grip of the long hair on the donkey's back, began to lower himself from the front-board of the cart on to his feet. Out through the open doorway rushed the three dogs, with zealous barkings, which continued in a crescendo of indignation during the disembarcation of the visitor, while he, ignoring the reception in a very wounding manner, proceeded, according to his habit, to tie the donkey to the stem of the single white rose-tree, whose straggling branches, snow-flaked with blossoms, draped the doorway.

He had but just accomplished this, puffing and blowing over the effort, when Shibby's tall figure filled the narrow entrance to the Tower. A low, stone mounting-block was near the door, and Old John, disregarding invitations to come in, waddled to it and seated himself upon it.

'Wait, my dear, till I draw me wind,' he said. 'To be sure, I'm getting younger every day, but for all that——' the end of the sentence was blocked by a laugh at his own wit, that developed into a long fit of coughing.

'Don't stir now, Mr Weldon,' Shibby said, 'till I bring you a small sup o' whisky. You're dead with the heat!'

It was one of the contrarieties which govern likes and dislikes, that Shibby had always held Old John Weldon as one of her few friends, in spite of the part he played in the pillaging of Captain Jas, and in spite also of his being the father of Young Johnny, for whom she cherished one of the unalterable hatreds of a country in which though memory for benefits is often brief, for injuries it is ever eternal.

'Well, Shibby, my dear, and how is the Captain?' asked Old John, smacking his lips over the sup o' whisky, and looking as Falstaff might have looked had he continued to hear the chimes at midnight until he had seen some ninety jolly years.

'Ah, he's the same way always—just trying to live,' said Shibby. 'Isn't it a pity now, Mr Weldon, to see him that way, and yourself to be so hearty and strong!'

'And he that has four years the advantage of me!' replied Old John, well pleased. 'But look,' he went on, 'at the fine, dashing young son he has to come after him! That's where he has me beat! What have I but that old psalm-singing show of a fella! I declare to ye that little girl he has is a better man this minyute than ever he was!'

'It's after yourself and the old lady she's taken, Mr Weldon,' replied Shibby politely. 'Indeed, she's a great credit! She's after leaving that school where she was, for good, I believe?'

'Ah, she was in it long enough. There was no occasion for her to be working for her living that way,' said Old John, with pride, 'though faith! She was able for the best o' them, with French and music and all sorts!'

'There's no doubt but she had a fine edjication, and was worthy of it,' said Shibby, pensively. 'Well, well, money's a fine thing! You'll be looking out for a grand husband for her now, I suppose!'

'Time enough, time enough, there's no fear she won't get a husband when she wants one! She'll be well worth any man's while I can

73

tell you that, Shibby, my dear!'

'Why—then that'll be according to what the father will give her, I suppose,' said Shibby, carelessly.

Old John looked hard at her over the rim of the tumbler from which he was draining the last drop of whisky.

'And that'll be according to what the father has to give, Shibby, my dear!'

He handed back the empty tumbler to her, with a quivering wink of one wrinkled eyelid, of a rollicking cunning that Falstaff could not have bettered.

'Well, and that's the case indeed,' assented Shibby, ignoring the wink, even though it was immediately stored in her quick mind for future consideration. 'It's hard to give what you haven't got, says you!'

She gave a short laugh, and taking the tumbler from his hand, put it down on a table inside the door. Old John evinced no desire to move, and Shibby, rejoining him, leaned against the rounded wall of the tower and resumed the conversation.

'I was above at the Big House four days ago. I'd like you should see it now, Mr Weldon. I believe you weren't in it at all since them dirty Pindies, Mrs Bob and her family, left it.'

'I was not then,' said Old John, wagging his big head.

'I have a deal of things bought for it——' said Shibby.

'——The two children was showing it to Peggy,' went on Shibby, in a voice airy as thistledown. 'I was sweeping out the dining-room the same time. Peggy wasn't in it ever before, she was saying. She was admiring it greatly.'

'Ah, it's a fine house, no finer,' said Old John, nodding like a China Mandarin, 'and a fine young man to own it! Not a finer in the country! There's no blood can touch the Prendevilles', when all's said and done!' He paused, and sighed. 'Ah, well, it's all that's wanting to him is the money to live in it! He'll not earn that with training young horses!'

'That's no more than a pastime for him!' said Shibby, proudly. 'He's young yet, and it pleases him. If he went to England it wouldn't be long before he'd meet a lady of blood and birth—' Shibby made the faintest pause before she continued—'and fortune, too, that'd

74

ask no better than to marry him!'

'Very like, very like, indeed, Shibby, my dear,' responded Old John, very amiably; 'but what'd he do if the young lady was to say to him: "I see your house, but where's your demesne?" she'd say! What'd he say to her then? Ho, ho, ho!'

Old Falstaff rolled his big head on to one shoulder and looked up archly at Shibby.

'If that was to be the way,' said Shibby, firmly, and looking, apparently, at one of the dogs, who was thoughtfully eating grass near the door, 'I'd say let him leave her standing, and marry one that could join the two together again!'

'Why—then I'd be of your opinion!' said Old John Weldon, quickly. 'Well, I'll go see the Captain——'

He descended from the mounting-block, and waddled into the house.

Shibby did not follow him. She remained where she was, thinking deeply. 'That's what he's after, is it?' she thought. 'He's not the only one that got the notion! Don't they say great wits jump! I'd like well to know what he's worth, the old rogue! I'll want more than the demesne for a fortune with the one that gets my lovely boy! Old John shall show me the whole story, fair and square, in his will, before I put hand or foot to it! I'll take no risks with Young Johnny!'

She seated herself on the mounting-block, and sat there motionless, all activity concentrated in her working brain. She was still there, twenty minutes later, when Old John came forth from his interview.

'Ah, the poor Captain! He's failing greatly. I'd see a great change in him since last I was here! Well, well, Shibby, I declare to you when I thinks of old times, I'd nearly have to cry!'

He was untying the donkey from the rose-tree-stem as he spoke; 'Come here, my dear, and let me ketch your arm the way I'll get up easy on the cart——'

Shibby came near, and with her help he hoisted his great bulk on to its accustomed place in front of the wheel. He took the driving ropes, and in doing so let his stout walking-stick fall from his hand.

'Give me up me stick now, like a good gerr'l—— Ah, time was when I could ha' tumbled like a cat for it! Well, well, we can't be young always!'

Shibby put the stick in his hand, and the old man worked himself back on to his bundle of straw. Then he leaned toward Shibby, and said in a lower voice:

'Tell me, Shibby, is it to the Captain, or to me son Johnny, that Connor pays his rent?'

'To neither!' said Shibby, with a short laugh; 'He brought me a couple o' pounds three years ago, and I seen none since! Nor no one else did neither!'

Old John reached out a fat hand and held Shibby's arm, drawing her nearer to him.

'Shibby, whisper! Don't let the boy folly the father!' His voice was very low and wheezy. Shibby bent down.

'What's that you say?'

'I'm saying,' Old John's voice got lower still, 'Keep the boy at home. He'll get no good out of Connor's pub.—G'wan Jack!'

The little donkey's spindle-legs broke into a tottering trot. The way was down hill, and the rattle of the cart would have drowned Shibby's reply had she attempted one.

Chapter 11

Hot days come rarely in the West of Ireland, sultry days, fierce and implacable, such as other countries know, when a pitiless sun burns the world to dust, and not a cloud intercedes with him for his victims. On the shores of the western ocean some mitigation does not fail, some gentle wind, some veiling mist, will be given, as indemnity perhaps for those other things that the west knows too well, the fogs, the storms, the week-long rains, all the miseries with which the Atlantic, like an ungracious giver, embitters gratitude for its gifts of beauty, and purity, and freshness.

There came to Inver, near the end of July, a day that as nearly succeeded in being overpoweringly hot as was possible, in view of Inver's position on the map; and, by a happy chance, it came on the date selected by the Committee of the Clytagh Races on which to hold their annual fixture—a fixture, let it be at once admitted, entirely 'illegal' according to accredited Rules of Racing, and one that was governed by no authority save that of its own 'Commy-tee'. This independent attitude, however, in no way lessened its popularity, a fact to which the little engine of the Cloon and Clytagh Light Railway could testify, as it laboured along, with several extra coaches rumbling in the rear of its ordinary contingent, and every coach of them crammed to bursting with race-goers.

The line, which was a benefit of civilisation that Mr John Weldon, Junior, had been instrumental in bringing to his native village, was laid on the high-road to Clytagh that followed the course of the river Fiddaun, and on this gorgeous day, half-stifled though the occupants of the train were, they had at least the consolation of looking upon the cool and lovely river, with the suave meadows reclining along its banks, and the cattle to whom they appertained, standing, at peace, out in the shallows of the slow stream, among the water-lilies and the rushes, having left their pastures derelict, for the flies to do as they pleased with them. A low line of blue mountains, thinly veiled by a shimmering haze of heat, lay on the horizon. Here and there thatched and whitewashed cottages made points of varying size, on differing planes of distance, that helped the eye to estimate the breadth of the level lands that stretched from the river to the Iveragh hills.

In the hot heart of the crush in one of the aftermost carriages Peggy and Nessie were enduring the half-hour of transit with the philosophy of which the young, in such adversities, have a greater store than their elders. Kit had preceded them early, riding Nora, the chestnut filly, whom he had entered for a race.

That Miss Pindy was also in the train was consequent on the double attraction of a furniture auction and an excursion ticket. From the last payment of the old Captain's scanty income that had been made by his agent, Young Johnny, Shibby had withdrawn as much, joined with her own hoardings, as justified her in the extravagance of this expedition, and no big-game hunter could know a keener thrill than she, when another acquisition for the glorifying of the Big House fell to her conquering bow and spear. She had, as was her cautious custom, taken her seat in the train a full half-hour before its appointed time for starting, and the period of waiting had not seemed long to her because such leisure was rare for her, and she had much to think of.

Her mind moved in pictures, and these, apart from the bright visions based on the auctioneer's catalogue, were more disturbing than agreeable. She looked back, and saw herself seated beside Old John on a bench in the little garden of Demesne Lodge. They had then come to closer quarters in connection with the match that, for differing reasons, seemed to both of them desirable.

'He might do better, but he *should* have the Demesne!' had been Shibby's thought.

'He hasn't but the Big House and no money to live in it, but I have enough for both, and I'd like well to see my grandchild married to the Head of the Family!' was how Old John had put it to himself, being still in the bond of the feudal idea. And to Shibby his thought was as obvious as was hers to him. To each the other's schemes appealed, each of them held trumps, and knew it, and they were sympathetically prepared to play into each other's hands.

The single possible source of disaster might be the intractability of the cards. The hint that Old John had dropped, as casually as he might have tossed away a burnt match, had fallen on the inflammable stuff of Shibby's hot heart and had wakened it to flame. He had not repeated it, but the terror of it was constant for her, hanging over her head, black as a thundercloud, menacing as a guillotine.

He had recalled to her mind an anxiety that she had almost dismissed—the time, during the preceding winter and spring, when, evening after evening, Kit would slip out, as it were casually, after the last meal of the day, and Shibby, lying awake in her room over the entrance door of the Tower, would hear him come in in the small hours of the morning, and would listen, with a disturbed soul, to his unsteady footstep passing her door. 'Playing billiards with Tom Pindy at the Hotel,' he would tell her next morning, and with this she had been forced to content herself. The billiards had ceased since Peggy Weldon's arrival—(and, since Old John's hint, Shibby had feared a peril more acute than billiards)—and the lynx-eyed watch that she had kept over Kit's movements had revealed to her no more than the gratifying progress of the friendship between the Tower and the Lodge. 'For all that,' she had said to herself, 'I'll see what Judy Davin can tell me.'

Judy Davin was a distant cousin of Shibby's grandmother, the late Widow Hynes, and in virtue of that relationship, she was the channel by which was conveyed to Miss Pindy the gossip of the village, which, profoundly as it interested her, she was too haughtily withdrawn from 'the neighbours' to collect for herself. The result of old Judy's investigations had been the endorsing of Old John's hints, together with the definite emergence of the name of Judy's near neighbour, Maggie Connor, Foxy Mag, product of the most degraded of Cloon's many public houses, whose mother had died in the County Lunatic Asylum, whose father had drunk himself into premature old age, whose brother, on one of his many appearances before the Bench of Magistrates, had been described by the Sergeant of Police as being what he might call 'a heredithery blackguard'.

Judy's report having thus given terrible life to Old John's suggestion, round Maggie Connor, Shibby's thoughts had clustered, like wasps round a bait, an object on which she might concentrate the strength of hatred which was the shadow-side of her power of devotion.

And, as fate would have it, it was into the carriage in which Shibby was seated that Foxy Mag, with a crowd of other girls of her own standing, had, at the last minute, pressed her way.

If a chance observer had seen Miss Pindy seated in dignified aloofness in the corner of the carriage, and had noted, as he could hardly fail to do, her impressive personality; her serious, wide-brimmed black felt hat, with the wing of silver hair on either side of her face, covering her ears and uniting in a polished knob at the back; the beaded cashmere dolman, the sweeping black skirt, the respectable portly umbrella, the brown kid gloves; and if the observer, noting all these things, had noted also the noble carriage of her head, the severe splendour of her look, he would scarcely have accepted her own words, had she told him of the nightmare phantasms, extravagant to absurdity, that were hurrying, one after the other, through her restless brain.

She would picture herself asking Maggie Connor to tea at the Tower, and putting something, she knew not what, strychnine perhaps,—it was a word that she knew—into her cup, something that should darkly and instantly work her will on her enemy. She went through the scene, inventing for herself the required details of the action of the poison.

'But I mightn't be able to get the right stuff— There's rat-poison to be sure——' She pondered for some time the administration of rat poison to Maggie Connor, not as a practical possibility, more as a bright ideal that could never be realised. The thought then of inducing Maggie to follow her to the top of the old Tower presented itself; it would be easy enough to give her as much of a push as would send her over the low parapet . . . Or could she get her into one of the cavernous cellars in the Big House, and lock her in, and leave her there, crying for help, and no one to hear her? . . . It can hardly be said that these projects took definite shape in Shibby's mind, or that they possessed any of the substance of serious intention. They were rather malign fancies possessing a mind as ungoverned as it was ardent, visions akin to the phantasmagoria of evil faces, ever changing from one hateful grimace to another, that will sometimes poison a sleepless pillow.

Maggie Connor, the inspirer of these scenes of melodrama, sat quietly enough among her gabbling fellows, the black shawl, that covered her red head, held discreetly across her mouth, in the fashion that obtains in the south and west of Ireland and suggests something of the reticence and mystery of the East. Maggie was not wont to sit in silence, least of all on such a day of festival as this, and in the depths of the black shawl she muttered curses on the mischance that had brought her into the carriage with Miss Pindy. She was not afraid of her, it would be hard to say of whom or of what Maggie was afraid, but the Big Woman with the Bad Eye—which was how Maggie and her friends in the village were accustomed to speak of Shibby—was a disquieting companion in the close quarters of a railway-carriage, and there was besides for Maggie an uncomfortable uncertainty as to what Miss Pindy knew, or might have suspected, of matters that Foxy Mag, even though not, as a rule, a respecter of persons, would prefer, for the present at all events, to keep quiet.

Kit met his sister and Peggy Weldon at the Light Railway Station at Clytagh, fighting his way along the narrow crowded platform to the carriage from which they signalled to him, being temporarily held fast in it by the crush below. To a stranger, accustomed to regard a railway station as a point of departure, rather than as the focal centre of a conversazione, the scene would have been amusing or annoying according to his temperament and engagements. Country girls, dressed in all colours, save those that a study of their own appearance might have suggested; country boys in their Sunday best, dark blue cloth suits, pale green frieze caps, and ties whose hues competed in brilliance with those of their sisters' hats. Massive, slow-moving mothers, many of them, despite the heat of the day, wearing the heavy blue cloth cloaks, with satin hoods, than which no female garment is more dignified and imposing. Black-jowled, black hatted fathers, shoving their way through the boys and girls, with the patient relentless obstinacy of a glacier; car-drivers, brandishing their whips, shouting invitations to the racecourse; while, leaning against the wall of the station-house, two tall Royal Irish Constables surveyed the scene with a benevolent remoteness suggestive of friendly visitants from Olympus.

Shibby stood by her carriage door without attempting a move, confident in the power of height and weight to make a way when she required one. That moment had not yet come for her. She saw Kit arrive, and she watched with the quiet intensity of a hunting cat, the passage through the crowd of Maggie Connor. Would she look at Kit? Would he look at her? Not even Shibby's concentrated observation could detect an exchange of recognition. Kit devoted his whole attention to Peggy and Nessie, and Maggie swung away with her gang of fisher boys and girls, apparently oblivious of any attraction outside her own group.

'The damned slut knows well I've me eye on her!' thought Shibby. 'That poor child isn't thinking of her at all—surely it was lies John Weldon and Judy Davin told me, as far as it was him was in the story!'

Outside the station the streets, from house to house, were crammed with people, traps, and donkey-carts. Here and there above the heads of the crowd, the upper part of a youth's figure, with a gay-coloured band over one shoulder, and the tossing head of a horse, would indicate the presence of one of the competitors at the coming races. The sunny, dusty air vibrated with noises of all kinds. Up through the steady din of talk flickered the shrill cries of little boys selling the local paper and cards of the races; horses whinnied to each other; donkeys, immured with their carts in entries to back yards, uttered their souls in those strange and hideous sounds from which familiarity cannot, for the civilised ear, eliminate the element of shock. The town bell-ringer forced his way backwards and forwards, ringing his bell, and howling an announcement of the auction at the Town Hall, that had been the lure which had brought Shibby to Clytagh. The sixty public houses, that had been licensed for the refreshment of the little town of some two thousand bodies (which in this connection seems a more suitable term than souls) were already doing a trade, which, in the literal sense of the word, roared.

Miss Pindy made her stately way through the narrow crowded streets. It had been said of her by a neighbour, resentful of what was considered her arrogance, that she 'walked Cloon like a ship in full sail.' A battleship at a regatta would have been a better simile for her on this summer day, as purposeful, heavy, and black, she strode

82

through the chattering crowds, intent on her business, thrusting on either side those light craft that interfered with her advance.

It was not unusual for those that interfered with her to get the worst of it.

Chapter 12

The racing was not to begin until three o'clock. Kit and the two girls were swept slowly along with the tide of pleasure-seekers, without any special object beyond an ultimate arrival at the solitary tea-shop of the town. The terminus of the railway line that linked Clytagh with Monarde and the outer world, was at the end of the main street, and the three found themselves held up in a backwater of the crowd near its entrance.

'Why wouldn't we go in here? We might get something better than tea and buns in the refreshment-room,' Kit suggested, 'and we might get it quicker too; there'll be the deuce of a squash at Mrs O'Brien's. I haven't much time. I met a man that told me they were making Nora carry I d'no what weight! I've got to go and see the Commy-tee about it—I'll not ride at all if she doesn't get fair play! They're all mad jealous of her winning at Monarde.'

'Oh, Kit, that'll spoil everything!' lamented Nessie.

'Coward!' said Peggy.

'Say that again and you'll be sorry for it!' said Kit, flinging his defiance to her with a light of his eyes.

'How are you going to make me sorry?' Peggy flung back, her grey eyes defying his blue ones.

'You'll know that some day!' replied Kit, the assurance of victory in his voice.

Under the pretext of protecting the two girls from the crush round them, he encircled them both with a long arm. Peggy was nearest to him, and it seemed to her that the protection was unnecessarily prolonged. She moved away from him, and looked up at the station clock.

'Father's coming by the 1.15,' she said, anxiously. 'It's due now! He'll be mad if he sees me here. He doesn't approve of races—I could hardly get mother to let me come to-day——'

'No fear! He'll not see you,' Kit began easily. 'We'll be safe to ground in the refreshment room—by Jove! There's the whistle!

84

Hurry!'

The small town of Clytagh was possessed of a certain consequence as being the portal of a chain of lakes of which the fishing
was sufficiently attractive to bring anglers from afar to its hotels, and
the stations had responded to their presumed needs by installing a
bar and a restaurant. Into the latter the girls and Kit betook themselves, and they had but just seated themselves at a table when they
heard the commotion betokening the arrival of the train.

'He's come!' said Mr Weldon's daughter in a fateful voice, sitting
rigid, gazing at her companions.

Kit began to laugh.

'I'll go out and ask him to come in and have a drink!' He looked
at Peggy. Her lips were parted, her eyes were very bright, she was
enjoying the tense moment.

'By Jove! She's a ripper!' thought Kit.

'Oh, Kit, you mustn't!' said Nessie, apprehensively. Kit had had
a whisky and soda, and, as Nessie said to herself, 'In *any* case, one
never knows what Kit wouldn't do——'

He did nothing, however, but look into Peggy's eyes, as if waiting
for her to reply. He had discovered that he could make her blush
when he could succeed in gathering and holding, as it were a physical grasp, the gaze of her eyes. He found it a delightful and stirring
game. It was trial of strength in which he always won, and Kit, like
most people, liked power. Peggy also liked power, but in these silent
contests it seemed as though she had met more than her match.
None the less, she took up his challenge.

'Ask him if you like——' she began, when the look of consternation on Nessie's face froze the words on her lips. Her back was to the
entrance. She turned quickly, and saw her father advancing towards
her. She was dimly aware that he was not alone, but for the moment
she thought only of him and his probable attitude. 'He'll make me
come home with him—I shan't see Kit ride the race——' The
thoughts flashed simultaneously, as thoughts will, several thoughts
together, like a chord of music. The tense moment had ended badly,
and was no longer enjoyable.

They all three stood up, and Young Johnny advanced, smiling,
almost beaming upon them, and especially upon his daughter. How

wonderful, she thought, how almost awful! What could it mean? Didn't he know about the races?

'Why, Peggy, me child! Who'd have thought of finding you here?' Paternal affection irradiated Mr Weldon's countenance. The glow subsided a little as he greeted Kit and Nessie, but it regained control as he turned to the companion who had followed him. 'This is me daughter, Sir Har'ld. Peggy, this is Sir Har'ld Burgrave—you've often heard me speak of him—that owns Moyroe. I had no notion I was to have the pleasure of meeting him, till I had the good fortune to find he was on the train, and I made bold to introjuce myself—I had the pleasure of knowing his poor fawther—he's coming to have a little fishing on the lakes here——'

'Well, not exactly,' interrupted the companion, stolidly. 'My father's dead.'

Mr Weldon was for a moment struck dumb by this correction, but rapidly recovering himself, burst into apologies and explanations, during which Peggy, trying not to laugh, shook hands with the subject of her father's address, and realising that the latter had omitted to introduce Nessie and Kit, did so herself.

Sir Harold Burgrave shook hands with his new acquaintances solemnly, with three stiff inclinations of a shiny black head. He was a tall young man of solid build, and with an expression that seemed to denote an equally solid brain. His father had been one of Young Johnny's absentee landlord clients, and it is possible that when, in conjugal seclusion, Mr Weldon had hinted at the possibility of the joys that might bud from thorns, the thought of old Sir George Burgrave's son and heir had stolen into his mind, a ray of alleviating sunshine.

'And now,' went on Mr Weldon, benignly, 'what are all you young people going to do with yourselves? I suppose we should begin with a bite o' lunch, at all events! And then my friend, Sir Har'ld here, talked of having a look at the Races——'

Mr Weldon's friend, Sir Harold, regarded him with a stony eye and said nothing, but Young Johnny continued with a gaiety that suggested nothing so much as a little dog frisking round an unresponsive master; 'I'll warrant he never saw races like these! But indeed I'm not one to speak—races are not my line, I'm afraid! I'm not even acquainted with where they may be taking place! But I daresay Kit——' Mr Weldon's tone chilled a little— 'can supply us with such information?'

'They're a mile out of the town, where they always are,' said Kit, curtly. He looked at his watch. 'I'm riding. I must go and see about different things. I'm sorry I can't wait for lunch.'

He looked at Peggy, and she was aware of a sudden darkening of her sky. The day wasn't going to be such fun after all. Why had they come into this hateful situation? She had known from the first that it was a mistake—and, being a young woman who had no hesitation in showing her feelings, she drew down her black brows, and lowered her dark eyelashes, and refused to return Kit's glance.

'I can run the ladies to the course in my car,' said Sir Harold Burgrave, civilly, but without enthusiasm.

'Now, isn't that the very thing!' exclaimed Mr Weldon, delightedly. 'That makes it all easy and nice! I can do my business quietly and I'll know my young ladies are in good hands! Now, sit down please, all of you, and we'll have something to eat——What, Kit, you won't stay——?' He indicated to Burgrave the chair beside Peggy that Kit had vacated. It was evident that he, unlike his daughter, found his sky distinctly the brighter for Kit's absence.

An impartial observer could not but have respected the gallantry with which Young Johnny accepted the situation. An obviously hostile daughter; the daughter's friend who (as he said himself) was bound to back up Peggy in her impudence, and in any case was no better than a dummy; and a young man with whom his acquaintance had progressed only far enough to show that he was one of those who have command of a silence that can strike like death to the heart of a host. But Mr Weldon did not falter. Having requested the young lady behind the counter at the end of the room to transmit his order for lunch, he resumed his place at the head of the oil-cloth covered table, and did his best, as he subsequently complained to Mrs Weldon, to keep a little cheerful chat alive until lunch came. The minutes wore on; and the chariot wheels of conversation drave ever more heavily. Nessie, oppressed by shyness, but obedient as ever to the voice of duty, assented faintly to all Mr Weldon's utterances, but initiated nothing. The chief guest sat in stolid silence, and, when directly appealed to by his host, responded with a brevity that stamped out all continuity of subject. His heavy brown eyes had no more expression than have those of a bull; they rested, for the most part, on Peggy, but whether in admiration, or because it was evident that she had no intention of trying to compel him to talk to her, Mr Weldon could not determine. Peggy, leaning back in her chair, made no attempt to look less out of humour than she felt.

'It would have done me good if I could have taken the stick to Peggy!' Mr Weldon told his wife, later. 'There she was, lolloping back in her chair, looking as cross as the cats, and not a word out of her, good or bad!'

Lunch began at last to come, very gradually, by the hand of an old waiter, who, having placed a plate, on which were four slices of stale bread, on the table, retired, apparently for ever. Intermittent use of the table-bell receiving no response, Mr Weldon applied to it an unmoving finger.

'Who rang that bell?' said the old waiter, emerging suddenly from a distant lair behind a screen.

'I did!' replied Mr Weldon, with violence. 'Why——'

'Well, don't do it again!' interrupted the old waiter, angrily.

'What's that you say?' shouted Mr Weldon, in responsive fury. 'Why don't you bring what I ordered?'

'Sampson was a sthrong man,' said the old waiter, more calmly, 'and Solomon was a wise one. But nayther o' them could bring ye a mutton-chop when they hadn't got one!'

He withdrew, chuckling acidly.

Sir Harold Burgrave uttered a sudden and loud guffaw, that was a consolation to the heart of the sorely-tried Mr Weldon, nerving him to further exertions. He started from his chair in pursuit of the waiter, and was lost to sight behind the screen. Sounds of battle from the waiter's hiding-place arose, and the young lady behind the counter of the bar, who had hitherto regarded the company with remote and elegant nonchalance, suddenly sprang into action, and flying from her place, could be heard engaging Mr Weldon 'off' (according to the formula of the stage).

When, at length, Young Johnny returned, in restored amity with the management, having achieved a plate of ham-sandwiches, and a piece of cold roast beef, hoar with age, and attended by a retinue of blue-bottle flies, he found that a slight improvement had taken place in the situation.

Peggy was talking to the guest. The inveterate Irish need to make herself agreeable, combined with her father's absence, and what she felt to be the interest, if not the admiration, implied in Burgrave's steady gaze, had mastered her ill-humour, and the guest himself had at least awakened, and was listening permissively, responding suitably, even, at intervals, showing very white teeth under a small black moustache in a not unfriendly smile.

'He was something livelier after he had a tooth driven into a bit of beef,' said Mr Weldon to his wife that night, as he recounted, with what may be defined as legitimate Christian peevishness, the trials of the day, 'but, indeed, Loo, my dear, if it hadn't been for me knowing all about him, as I might say, his father owning Moyroe, and those big ironworks in Scotland, and the Lord Mayor of — the year he died, let alone him being a Bar'net himself now, and rich enough to do nothing——'

'Oh, John,' interrupted Mrs Weldon, listening with interest, 'is that really the case? Isn't that a terrible temptation for any young man?'

'I think it's one most young men would be very ready to face, my dear!' said Mr Weldon, unable, in spite of his peevishness, to repress a snigger, 'but indeed, as I was saying, if I hadn't known what his position was, I may say I'd har'ly have thought it! I don't know if that's the way in your high English circles—only opening the mouth to put food in it—— ! You'd say he was despising us all!'

'Perhaps the young man was shy,' Mrs Weldon suggested, 'or he wanted to listen to what you were telling him, John.'

The suggestion was soothing.

'Well, I'll say this for him,' said Mr Weldon, pleased to be able to mitigate his severity, 'he seemed greatly struck with Peggy. His eyes were stuck into her! It might be that he was listening to me, but there's no mistake that he was looking at her!'

Chapter 13

The fields in which the races were to take place were far enough from the town to promote the trade of the car drivers, since a mile of dusty and stony road, under the sun of this July day, was a feature of the case that inclined any race-goer with a shilling in his pocket to expend it in a seat on a car. It is little to say that the car drivers were alive to their opportunity. Miss Pindy, walking to the auction at the Town Hall, was challenged at almost every step of her progress by a raised whip, or an insinuating proffer of 'a lift' to the races. She pursued her course unheeding, when a hope was kindled simultaneously in the bosom of three jarveys, by seeing the possible fare stop abruptly, and look across the street, as it might be she were looking for a car.

'Here y'are, ma'am!' yelled the quickest of the three, 'a bob, and I'll land ye into the judge's box itself!'

He whirled up to the pavement beside her, but not soon enough to prevent Shibby from seeing what she had stood still to see—a tall young man, with a small head of close-cut yellow curls, emerging from a public-house in company with a thin little man with a long nose, who wore a loose overcoat and white riding-breeches and top-boots.

'One o' them dirty jockeys!' she thought.

Then she caught her breath, as a girl followed, evidently of their company, a small and picturesque figure, with a mass of gleaming red hair, over which she was readjusting a black shawl, a girl whom Shibby identified as easily as she did Kit.

She felt a shock as distinctly physical as might have been the thrust of a knife under her breast-bone.

'My God!' she thought. 'Is it that way he's going?'

Then John Weldon had been right, better advised than she, when he had warned her not to let the son follow the father. To follow the father—what did it mean? What would be the end of it?

'The life o' meself!' she thought bitterly. 'That's all that will come of it! A miserable poor creature that no one wants—that's a disgrace to herself and all belonging to her! Wasn't it the funny set-out for Old John to be warning me against meself!' She gave a derisive snort of laughter that made a passer-by turn and look at her. The thoughts hurried through her mind while, almost without her own volition, she was keeping pace with Kit and the jockey and Maggie Connor, on the opposite pavement.

They were talking earnestly. It seemed to Shibby that Kit was arguing a point with the jockey and Maggie. They stood still to talk; Shibby saw Kit push back his cap and rub his head, looking irresolutely from one disputant to the other. Then Maggie caught the lapel of his coat, as if to insist on his attention. Her back was turned to Shibby, but the movements of her head and shoulders told of emphasis and the enforcing of a point. Then the jockey moved close to Kit, and, standing on tip-toe, said something close to his ear. Kit looked from one to the other, and then it was plain to the watcher across the road that he had yielded whatever had been the point at issue. The jockey, evidently well pleased, looked at his watch, and after another word or two, touched his cap and went away. They had stopped to talk outside a milliner's shop. Maggie turned to the window and pointed at something she saw there. Kit's face was flushed, he threw back his head and laughed, then he pushed Maggie before him into the shop, and followed her, a little unsteadily.

'He's had a drop!' thought Shibby; 'what do they want of him?'

The bellman clanged past her, shouting between the clamours of his bell that the auction was now beginning.

'What is that to me?' she thought. 'Let him bring her to an empty house! It's little I'll go buying beds for Maggie Connor! Let her lie in straw, the way she was born!'

She was standing at the gates of the yard of a chapel, and had moved just inside them to escape observation. A rosary hung on the handle of one of the gates. The sight of it turned her thoughts to her need. Her own rosary was round her neck under her dress. She groped for it with trembling fingers beneath the beaded folds of the black dolman, and almost unconsciously began to mutter prayers, whilst her great eyes, like those of some fierce, caged animal, stared

91

through the bars of the gate at the milliner's shop across the road.

The chapel clock beat out two heavy strokes. The air was still vibrating, when those for whom Shibby was waiting came out of the shop. On Maggie Connor's red head there was now a large straw hat, trimmed with brown ribbon and yellow and orange roses. She was a pretty girl, with vivid, quick-glancing hazel eyes, and with the brilliant pink and white complexion that sometimes is seen with red hair. The hat, with its flamboyant adornments, suited her, but her charm had passed with the black shawl. Kit looked at her, laughing, and said something to her; and the wild skirl of laughter with which she greeted it, rose, like the cry of a seagull, above the noises of the street.

Shibby's prayers ceased. All thought was fused in the heat of her hatred. She watched the couple out of sight before she moved. The she tramped deliberately to the Town Hall and paid her entrance to the auction. Her purpose, that had wavered, had hardened again. She had said to herself that she would not be turned from her intention by 'the like o' Maggie Connor!'

It was some minutes past three o'clock when Peggy and Nessie, driven by Sir Harold Burgrave at a high rate of speed, arrived on the race-course. Not one of the three had ever before been to an Irish race-meeting, and their fears that their unpunctuality might have lost for them some of the sport, were a proof of their ignorance of the usual procedure on such occasions as the Clytagh Races. Several hundreds of lookers-on had indeed assembled, and a few samples of the apparently essential accessories of the sport of racing—bookmakers, roulette-tables, and barrows of oranges, biscuits, and ginger-beer, were establishing themselves round and about the rough timber erection from which the judge was to issue his verdicts. The judge, and his attendant officials and committee-man, had still to come, but the gay and garrulous groups of pleasure-seekers, who were momently gathering in great numbers, were in no hurry to shorten the enjoyments of the day by a too rigid adherence to the timetable, and it may be said with confidence that Burgrave's was the only voice that expressed either surprise or condemnation.

A few moody young men, badged with coloured scarves, shirts, or sashes, moody with the stage-fright of prospective competitors, were riding slowly about the fields, moving from one to the other through the openings that had been broken in the banks for the flat races, or contemplating in deep silence the red-flagged jumps. In the central field a large tent, whose mission it was to supply restoratives to those for whose needs a special 'One-Day-Licence' was granted by the sympathising authorities, was already bulging with clients.

The fierce afternoon sun blazed down on the wide slopes, doubling their area twenty times at least, or so it seemed to the two on whom the care and entertainment of Mr Weldon's young friend had been laid. 'Mind now you make it pleasant for him!' he had whispered threateningly to his daughter, and his daughter was now, in dutiful compliance with the order, conducting the young friend over the race-course and examining with him the jumps.

The unwonted heat that had robbed Nessie's small face of all colour, had given a glow to Peggy's cheeks, and had intensified by contrast the light in her eyes. It was quite evident that these facts were not unperceived by Sir Harold Burgrave, and although his eyes, now wakened from the bovine slumber in which they had at first been plunged, dwelt upon Peggy with more eloquence then his lips commanded, he was very evidently taking trouble to make such conversation as would hold her attention and ensure her turning her face towards him.

The lie of the country lent itself agreeably to the planning of a course. From the first three fields the mark-flags could be seen for nearly a mile. At the farthest point at which they were visible, a large plantation intervened. The course ran through its centre, along a road, and then diverging again to the fields, traversed some broad meadows by the bank of the river, and turning right-handed, finished, slightly uphill, below the judge's stand. Groups of people dotted the first couple of fields; knots of experts were gathering at the jumps; a solitary enthusiast, a girl, could be descried, following the line of the course until she was lost to sight in the plantation.

'She's determined to know all about it!' Peggy said. '*I* don't care if I never saw another race-course in my life! Oh, for pity's sake, Nessie, don't let's walk another step! I'm dead!'

She threw herself down at full length on the dry yellow grass, and pulled her wide-brimmed hat over her eyes.

'Tell me when a race starts—if one ever *does* start—I'm going to sleep. Sit down and put up your parasol and keep the sun off me—'

Burgrave looked down at her.

'Oh, I say! You're not really going to sleep, are you? That's not playing the game! Your father told you to take care of me——' He became almost voluble in remonstrance.

Peggy moved her hat sufficiently to see his face. The constraint, whether of arrogance, stupidity, or shyness, that had afflicted him at lunch, had left him. He was staring down at her with, as she said to herself, a wakened-up look in his eyes. 'He can talk all right when he likes!' she thought. 'Lazy pig! But he's better than I thought—and now that he's come down off his high horse, he looks as if he might be good-natured—perhaps he was only shy——'

From far off some faint shouts came to them. Some boys standing on a bank near them began to run. Peggy sat up quickly. 'That's a race starting! Kit's not on in this, Nessie, is he?'

Nessie looked at the card. 'Not till the next one.'

'Then I shall go to sleep again——'

Nessie, obedient as ever to command, had seated herself on the ground and opened the parasol; Peggy threw her hat on one side and laid her dark head on her friend's lap.

'Mayn't I hold the parasol?' said Burgrave. 'I should like to feel I was being useful——' He knelt beside Peggy, close to her, leaning over, and smiling down into her eyes, as he stretched a hand across her and took the parasol from Nessie.

'Please don't trouble, Sir Harold,' Peggy said, frowning. 'I think I'll stand up—I suppose it's our duty to see the races now that we're here——' She thought: 'The shyness is wearing off—he's getting a little too good-natured!'

The first race had been started in one of the riverside meadows, on the farther and lower side of the hillside on which they were standing. It was a flat race, the distance being twice and a half times round the course. Only seven horses were running; they came cantering along in an amicable bunch, apparently devoid of emulation, and passed a little below the spot where the two girls and Burgrave were standing.

'There's only one man among the lot of them know what he's at—that long-nosed fellow in the pink cap—' said Burgrave. 'And that weedy brute he's on looks as if it could gallop a bit—but as for the rest of them!' He laughed. 'Come now, Miss Weldon, what are you going to back? I'm for the pink cap!'

'None of them!' said Peggy, watching the progress of the ambling group till it was lost to sight in the wood, 'I don't believe any of them will win!'

'Oh, but one o' them must win,' protested Burgrave, 'That is to say, unless——'

'Well, I don't care which it is,' broke in Peggy, petulantly. 'If this is what racing is like, I call it deadly!'

'We'll go back to the bookies and you shall have something on the next race—you'll think it's better fun then!' said Burgrave, looking at her with approval as well as amusement. He preferred young women who were ignorant of matters in which he could instruct them.

'Back Nora,' murmured Nessie. 'Shibby tossed Kit's cup for him last night and she said she saw luck for a horse!'

'How can you believe such rubbish?' said Peggy, laughing at her. 'You'd believe anything that glorified Kit! Didn't he tell us himself when we met him after lunch that he couldn't win? And you saw that awful belt that he said they wanted him to wear? He said it would break Nora's heart! Perhaps he's scratched! I hope he has! Poor Nora! I'm sure it weighed a ton!'

'Come, come,' said Burgrave. 'Not all that, surely!'

'Every bit of it!' declared Peggy. 'I suppose you call that fair play!'

Burgrave had begun sententiously to explain that this sort of show wasn't racing—not what *he* would call racing—when the horses reappeared beyond the wood and entered on the second round. The pace had improved, and the pink cap was pushing in front. Burgrave checked in his disquisition, and pointed with satisfaction to his selection.

'Let's go back and see my man win!'

Peggy agreed. 'He's becoming a bore!' she thought. 'But anything's better than standing here in the sun to be preached at!'

Nessie hung back. She said she wanted to see where the horses

had to jump out on to the road—Kit had said it was a nasty place—
if Peggy didn't mind?——

'As long as you don't ask me to go another inch further away from
Sir Harold's car,' said Peggy, airily, 'you can do as you like!'

Chapter 14

Nessie walked slowly along the slanting fields just above the line of the course, surveying it attentively, her thoughts all on Kit and Nora. The jumps were not formidable, for the sufficient reason that they had been supervised by one of the Committee, a prudent man, who was running a horse that 'fled' his banks (which means that he did not change feet on them, and in consequence ran a very good chance of falling on his head over one of them).

Nessie said to herself that Nora would jump them all backwards, if Kit asked her to do so—they wouldn't stop a donkey! If only she could stay the course, three miles, and part of them uphill—Kit had said she had the legs of them all, if they didn't handicap her out of it— 'and they will if they can!' he had said, and had added: 'But I'll not see the mare wronged! I'll see she gets fair play in spite of her teeth!'

But Shibby had said he'd win. Nessie's thoughts went from Kit and the mare to Shibby, and dwelt upon her, while she toiled on under the merciless sun over the dry, slippery grass. Nessie was an innocent creature, who believed, with a touching confidence, in her own people. She said to herself that Shibby was sure to be right. She always knew, somehow—tea leaves, or cards, or just setting herself to 'consider' a thing—that was what she called it. It came to Nessie's mind how, one day before the fair in Clytagh, she had come upon Shibby up in the Lady Isabella's room in the Big House, sitting down before an old mirror, and brushing her long white hair over her face, and peering at herself through its veiling strands. Shibby had told her it was the way she had learnt from a Wise Woman, back in the country, long ago, when she was a girl, if she wanted to find a thing out. 'And it was to find out what would she get for her pig!' thought Nessie, laughing, in spite of her fatigue, and her anxiety about Kit, and remembering how Shibby had seen the number Seven, and how, sure enough, it was seven pounds she got! Her thoughts moved on along the line of Shibby's activities. The Big House—would she ever get it furnished and fit for Kit to bring a bride to? And even if she did, were she and Kit going to agree about who should be the bride . . . 'Both of them like to have their own way!' thought Nessie, respectfully; Nessie, who never permitted herself a way of her own to like, brimmed over with love and admiration for her masterful relatives.

But this was too abstruse and complicated a point to be dealt with at such a moment as this of heat and fatigue. She put it from her, and pushed on, downhill now, to the next pair of flags.

She was near the turn of the course. The tents and the people looked very far away; she could see nothing of the race that was probably just finishing. A haze of heat hung over the flat country ahead of her, she was walking into the blaze of the afternoon sun and she felt blinded by the glare. Everything was strangely still and remote. But for the flags, and the hoof-marks on the grass, she could have believed that she had strayed from the course. She saw the wood below her, not far ahead now, and soon she came to a wide, low place in a bank, with white mark-flags indicating that it was the last jump on the outwards journey. Beyond the bank was the high-road, a very narrow road with but scant room in which to stop and turn a horse. ('But,' as the Committee said, 'sure they must turn somewhere——') The trees met the road here and red flags told that the course continued down the road through the wood, but a sharp turn round a projecting spur of rock made it impossible to see for more than a hundred yards ahead. Nessie said to herself that if there were going to be an accident, this was the place for it, and there was no use in going any farther.

It was restful to turn her back on the sun, and get into the scented shade of the fir-trees. She looked at her watch, and saw that the next race—Kit's race—was not due to start for fifteen minutes, a blessed time of respite, she thought, in the day's exhausting pleasurings; she could rest now for awhile. The road had been cut down several feet below the level of the wood. Nessie climbed up the steep, fern-grown bank, and went on through the undergrowth for a little way. Then she came to a great spruce fir, and pushing in under its low branches, she sat down on the mat made by its shed needles, and rolled her knitted coat into a cushion to put between her face and the tree's rough trunk, and was still.

Through a gap in the branches she could see the road from where she lay, herself unseen. The projecting rock faced her, a little lower down on the opposite side. It was a perfect place. Here she would stay, and it would be time enough to go back when she had seen Kit safe past the dangerous turn on the last of his three rounds.

Warmth; and stillness, and the green gloom of the wood, and the sleepy hum of winged things, high overhead in the sunshine above the trees, soon soothed Nessie's tired senses. She slept, deliciously, irresistibly, the unpremeditated sleep that is worth hours of sought-after-repose.

The sound of hoofs on the road below awakened her. She sat up and saw three horses go by at a fair rate of speed, that was, nevertheless, not too fast to interfere with an incessant and abusive interchange of opinion between their riders. They slackened speed at the corner by the rock; Nessie could hear them yelling at each other to give room. Kit was not among them.

'He's saving Nora—I won't show myself, it might only distract him,' Nessie thought.

The next instant the long-nosed jockey came into view. He checked the horse, while he looked from one side of the road to the other, and shouting, 'Come down! He's just after me!' he went on out of Nessie's sight.

From the bushes on the high ground, above the spur of rock at the turn of the road, a girl in a large hat looked out, and then came scrambling down the bank. At the same moment Kit and Nora came on. The young mare was going at her ease and steadily; Kit stopped her beside the girl, and let something fall that dropped in the grass at the roadside, close to her, something that looked like a broad strap, and fell heavily.

'Here you are?' he said hurriedly, setting the mare going again. 'I believe she'd win anyhow!' he called back over his shoulder, as he disappeared round the corner.

The girl in the hat picked up the strap, and climbed up the bank, and returned to her hiding-place. The profound stillness settled down again upon the wood as though it had never been broken.

Nessie leaned back against the great trunk of the spruce-fir. Her heart was beating so hard that it felt as if it had filled her whole body, and had left no space for breathing. The remembrance had assailed her of a story that Kit had told her, of how a race had been won by dropping the handicapping weight, and getting it back before the finish—it had happened more than once, he said. And then he had said it would depend on the course, but that anyhow it'd take a smart fellow, with good help, to work it. . . .

Nessie had absorbed, unconsciously, something of the country-woman's view of young men. They were privileged—a law unto themselves—'there was no good expecting too much from them, for you wouldn't get it but as little!' Thus Shibby; and her philosophy had dovetailed with Nessie's power of hero-worship. The King could do no wrong! . . . But that Kit should swindle in a race, even to save Nora——! She endured the thought for a moment of horror, and then she flung it from her as one might fling away a snake. No! she said it aloud, facing her own soul, clenching her small fists, defying her conscience. It was no swindle to outwit injustice—— Kit was all right . . . Kit——

Nessie dropped her head upon her knees and wept. Sheer exhaustion, mental and bodily, overcame her. She neither could nor would try to think it out. All she could do now was to lie close in her lair under the tree, and stifle thought, and see the thing out, whatever way it went. It seemed a long time to her before she again heard the beat of the hoofs on the grass as the horses came on in the second round. Soon the sound changed. They had jumped into the road. Another moment, and the leaders came on into sight, and had passed her. Nora was first now, with the pink cap not far behind her. There was an appreciable pause before Nessie could hear the angry shouts of the three remaining riders as they jumped into the road, and came hustling along in a bunch, trying hard to make up the ground they had lost. They passed in a cloud of dust out of which their harsh and hideous voices rose, as it were a running fight between big dogs. Nessie lay quiet in her hiding-place. There was nothing she could do. This was a matter beyond her scope.

She could not have made even a guess as to what time had elapsed between the passing of the horses on the second round, and the moment when, for the third time, she heard the sound of hoofs on the road at the entrance of the wood. This time Kit came on alone, galloping very fast. He passed from Nessie's view round the projection of rock, and then the listener heard him shout at the mare, stopping her. The hoof-beats ceased. She heard his voice, low and quick.

'Ketch her head! . . . Give it to me now! . . . Look sharp!'

In less than a minute the clattering hoof-beats told that he was off.

From round the rock the girl in the big hat came quickly, and stood, just below Nessie, looking up the road. This time her hat had been pushed back, and Nessie could see her face. It was scarlet, her eyes blazed, her red hair held the sun, it was like a fire round her excited face. Nessie recognised Maggie Connor. In the same moment the pink-capped jockey galloped into view. He looked behind him, checking his horse, a little and shouted to the girl.

'Is it all right, Mag?'

'It is! It is! He has it—he's just before ye!'

'Well done, Mag!' and then: 'Jim got a good price for us!'

He passed from view.

Maggie Connor scrambled hastily up the bank again, and was securely hidden for what seemed to Nessie a long time before the remaining horses, now only two in number, passed, dripping with sweat, and evidently much distressed, their riders silent, and already using their whips. Close after them followed a riderless horse, his head plastered with earth, and with a long gash from a spur on one shoulder, while a broken rein and swinging stirrups did their part in inciting him to persevere in the race. It was plain to see that the precautions of the prudent Committee-man, his owner, had been insufficient.

Then, all, once more, was still, in an incredible silence, a silence that felt to Nessie as though it shut her in, like a wall built round her in an instant, so that there was neither past nor future, nothing had ever existed, or would exist, but the numbed present. She lay dead still; as one lies in a moment of intermission from some nerve pain, knowing that a movement will stir it into fierce life. She saw Maggie Connor descend to the road, and set off quickly in the wake of the

101

horses. Nessie waited till the sound of her hurrying feet had ceased. Then she too climbed down into the road, leaving that quiet place beneath the fir-branches where the first great disillusionment of her life had come to her, and walked heavily back towards the distant crowd on the hill by the way by which she had come.

Chapter 15

It may already have been gathered that the Committee of the Clytagh Races were men of independent judgment, who recog-nised no laws save their own, and were superior to that fetish of consistency, which, as George Meredith has well said, is the hobgoblin of small minds. That a time should be decreed for the start of each race was a detail that looked well on the green card (which had arrived, damp from the printing-press, not unreasonably long past the hour at which it announced the start of the first race). But the Committee, holding, very properly, that time was made for slaves and not holi-day-makers, permitted such delays as suited the convenience of all, save perhaps, that of such pedants and precisians as make a business of pleasure. At Clytagh, on this day of sport and merry-making, these were in a minority of one, and Sir Harold Burgrave was, it must be conceded, adapting himself with remarkable complacence to the local conditions. Ireland, with its customs, was, to be sure, absurd, a country *pour rire*, but it certainly had some pleasing features, and among these he had quite decided to include those of his agent's daughter, Miss Peggy Weldon.

Clytagh was the central point of a remote and primitive district; Burgrave, strolling back with Peggy towards the Judge's stand, bor-ing a way through the congested throng of jovial friendly people, found himself remembering a recent visit to the West Indies, and the fashions that had prevailed at a Plantation Party. The costumes here, as there, recognised no laws of fashion except those dictated by the taste of their wearers; the hats of the younger ladies had, equally, the charm of individual fancy, and glowed with a variety of colours that suggested a rainbow in high fever. Burgrave looked at Peggy, with approval. 'She's dressed like a white woman, anyway!' he thought,— 'jolly well-turned out, good-looking girl!'

A big countryman shoved his way past them, and Burgrave put out his arm, as a measure of protection, and encircled Peggy. She was pressed against his side, and he held her there for a few seconds, his opinion of her rising in proportion to her nearness.

'A bit rough, these fellows,' he said in her ear, 'but I won't let them hurt you!'

As he spoke, he felt himself caught by his other arm and whirled round, while a female voice said ecstatically, 'Oh, Johnny! Look down at Mary Ellen for God's sake! Look at the black velvet dress she have on her, and the holt she have of it at the back!—Oh, beg paurdon!'—his assailant, who was a solid, red-cheeked country girl, checked herself in much of confusion—'I thought you were a friend o' mine!—Oh, Johnny! Is it there you are? I'm just after making a grab at this gentleman be the way he was you!' She laughed hilariously.

'Please don't mention it,' said Burgrave stiffly. Peggy had withdrawn herself from his protecting arm and was laughing at him, and he disliked being laughed at.

'Isn't Mary Ellen splendid!' she said, as the lady who had been indicated moved by, slow and majestic as a widowed Queen—a widowed queen with a handful of gown clutched in a red fist, and raised high enough to reveal laced boots and white knitted stockings. Peggy's eyes dwelt, fascinated, upon her until she was lost to view in the neighbouring whisky-tent. 'She's wonderful!' she said with a sigh. 'How I wish I had borrowed Mother's Sunday black satin!'

What did she mean? She seemed quite keen about it—Burgrave was bewildered—these Irish people—women, anyhow . . . But the fact that he didn't know what she was driving at did not lessen her attractions. He stared at her a little harder, and noted afresh the charm of the line of brow and cheek which was all that her study of Mary Ellen's costume permitted him to see.

Borne outwards on the stifling breath of the whisky tent came the voice of a reveller.

'I never had anny taste for singin', but if I'd be cot in a corner of a shebeen I'd sing! I'd sing all round me! That's my way, an' I don't give a dam' if it's good or bad! Me heart, d'ye see, is as big as wings! If y'insult Ireland y'insult me! That's my way,an' I don't give a—,

'Ah, shut yer mouth, Jim!' said another voice, 'Y're dhrunk!' The

104

first voice broke into song.

> *'Oh, mother, dear mother, when Ireland is free,*
> *Your Barney'll return to your arrums!'*

'Here, we've had enough of this!' A tall and serious R.I.C. constable advanced upon the tent. 'Come out o' that!'

The song ceased abruptly. The singer staggered forth from the tent.

'Why, it's Jimmy Connor!' said Peggy.

The singer heard his name, and recognising Peggy, swung off his hat and pushed his way to her. 'Take my adwice, Miss Peggy! Put yer money on the one you knows! Be faithful to yer frinds and yer frinds'll be faithful to you! That's my way, an' I don't give——'

A shout from the crowd. 'They're off!' interrupted Mr Connor's watchword. Farther down the course the race had been started; Peggy could hear the horses pass, but the crowd was too dense to permit her seeing then.

'Oh, I can see nothing!' she lamented. 'And this is Kit's race!'

'Here! Stand back there!' Burgrave's broad shoulders gave weight to his words. 'Let the lady see something!' He forced a passage ahead, and a lad standing on a large packing-case by the tent was pushed off it. In a moment Burgrave had lifted Peggy on to it.

'That's better, eh? Now, will you stand here while I go and put something on Pink Cap? . . . What? You want a bit on the filly, do you? Number two, isn't she?——'

He elbowed his way to one of the bookmakers. When he returned, he mounted on the packing-case beside Peggy, steadying her against the pressure of the crowd.

'Now, if the filly wins, you'll get seven sovereigns, and if she don't I lose one!'

'But why should you lose anything? Isn't it my bet!'

'It's your bet, but it's my sovereign, and I shall lose it because you insist on backing an outsider!'

Her ignorance enchanted him. His manner became increasingly protective.

'Your father put you in my charge, and I can't let you lose your money because you want to back your brother!'

'He's Nessie's brother—he's not mine,' said Peggy quickly.

'I thought he must be your brother you were so keen to back him!' He watched her face.

'I don't see what that has got to do with it!' Her colour rose; she looked at him angrily.

Burgrave said to himself that he liked a girl who would rise to a fly like that.

'Then perhaps it's because he's *not* your brother—?' he suggested, stooping a little to meet her eyes under the shading brim of her hat. 'If I were running a horse would you back me? I'm not your brother, y'know!'

'No! Thank goodness you're not!' retorted Peggy hotly.

Burgrave laughed out, beaming at her. 'Quite so! I entirely agree!'

Peggy turned from him as far as the encompassing crowd would permit. To leave his side, and with it the security of the packing-case, was impossible. Why had she so idiotically consented to Nessie's wandering away, like a stray donkey, and leaving her to compete alone with this forward and aggressive young man?

'I ought to try and find Miss Prendeville,' she began, with all the formality she could command; but at the same instant a surging movement of the crowd told of the return of the horses and the end of the first round. The crowd and the bookmakers uplifted their voices with redoubled energy, and the five horses went by at an easy gallop, entering on their second round with but little gained or lost since the start. Nora was sailing along at her ease in the lead, the pink cap, on a long-legged, competent-looking brown horse,—the shouts of whose name, 'Lively Lad,' indicated him as the people's nomination—following close after him. The remaining three horses coming up the rising ground, strung out a little, but not far behind.

'Go on, Con!' shouted the crowd to the long-nosed jockey, 'Up, Lively Lad!'

'Up, Nora!' came from a solitary voice. Peggy followed the sound, and saw it had proceeded from Jimmy Connor.

'Up, Nora!' she echoed stoutly.

'Bravo!' said Burgrave, 'stand to your guns! But I'm afraid she can't win for you. She might have beaten the brown horse if they hadn't penalised her as they have—they've put eleven stone on to her, and—let's see—' he looked at the card—'Yes,—here you are Lively Lad, Con Brendan, ten-three!'

'It's abominably unfair!' Peggy broke out. 'Why shouldn't the best horse win?'

She could hardly have given Burgrave an opening that would have pleased him more. He was a young man with a very special passion for informing the ignorant (an amiable trait, though one that is not always appreciated).

Peggy, it may at once be admitted, heard not a syllable of the dissertation upon the rules of racing, that was offered for her instruction. Burgrave's heavy explanatory voice boomed on over her head, while she stood with a leaping heart and straining nerves, waiting for the second return of the horses. It seemed to her an hour before a sudden outburst of wild voices told her that the moment had come.

Burgrave's harangue stopped with a jerk. 'By Jove, there's one o' them out of the wood! Can you see?' He put up his field-glasses. 'Yes. By Jove, it's the chestnut mare! Here! You have a look!' He thrust the glasses into Peggy's hand. 'Can you see! It's your brother—beg pardon, *not* your brother!—leading—going strong too! That's a better mare than I thought her——'

Peggy's hands were shaking so much she could not hold the glasses steady.

'I can't see, I can't see! You take them! Tell me——'

'Here's the Pink Cap coming along! He's sticking to him well! Don't be too sure of your seven sovereigns, he's not beaten yet!'

In a storm of noise the horses went past, encouragements, execrations, personalities, and the shrill yells that are the Southern Irish form of cheering, speeding them on their journey.

'It's going to be a thundering good race!' said Burgrave, shaken a little from his attitude of facetious superiority to all things, specially all things Irish. 'D'you mind moving a little and I can get the glasses on to 'em! There now, they're at the first fence—good! Well over!... Go on, Pink Cap! By George, there's one down——!'

'Not Nora?' panted Peggy.

'No, no, she was first over it—took it in her stride—made nothing of it—By Jove, she's going ahead now!—Have the glasses—— ?'

'No—please—I couldn't see with the beastly things—tell me!'

'Now they're at the big double! . . . Oh, well jumped, by God! That's a topping good mare! . . . Pink Cap's down! No, he's not! Well saved! Did you see? The loose horse nearly put him down! . . . The other two are done . . . not an earthly . . . There's Nora into the wood! She's a long head, Pink Cap'll hardly catch her . . .'

There was a breathless pause. One minute, two, three.

'Oh, are they never coming! Oh, where on earth is Nessie? Why isn't she here! . . . *Will* Nora win?—Oh, do you think there's been an accident? . . . *Why* don't they come!' Peggy shook with excitement, and Burgrave, more pleased with her than ever, held her more tightly still. She was quite unaware of it. It was the first race she had ever seen, and she twisted herself in Burgrave's arms and gazed into his face, with tears shining in her eyes.

'Steady on!' said Burgrave, laughing at her. 'You'll bring us both down off the box if you're not careful! Here's Nora out of the wood now! By Jove, it's her race after all! . . . Here's the other fellow now . . . he'll not catch her!'

'Come on, Con! Come on, Lively Lad!' yelled the crowd, whose money was on the favourite.

'Nora! Nora! Come on, Kit!'

Peggy saw Jimmy Connor in front of her, and lifted up a half-choked voice in unison with his, 'Nora, Nora!'

Nora was still nearly half a mile away, and was leading the brown horse by a hundred yards or more. Soon she came to the last jump. It had once been a bank, but the stress of the races had worn it down to a mere ridge of mud, and, on the landing side, what had been a shallow drain was now almost filled with earth and sods, kicked into it by the successive horses all jumping it at the same place. Nora came at it at full speed, prepared to gallop over it, as she had done on the second round, but this time she miscalculated the distance. She took off too soon, and landing with her fore-feet in the hidden drain, she turned a somersault that left her prone, with her head almost facing the remains of the bank. Kit was shot from the saddle clear of the mare, rolling over and over, head over heels.

A hoarse gasp rose from the crowd, pierced with the squeals of country girls.

'He's dead! He's dead! The mare's dead! She's killed! Be dam' they're both killed! . . .'

'The divil a kill in it!' rose the voice of Jimmy Connor. 'Look at him now!'

Kit was already on his feet. They saw him stagger to the mare and catch her head. He dragged at the bridle, and the young mare, with a violent struggle, raised herself from the mud in which she lay and scrambled on to her legs. A couple of moments later Brendan, on Lively Lad, went past.

'Get up, Kit! Come on, Kit! Ye'll win yet!' roared Jimmy Connor, and with that broke into a storm of curses.

'The girth's broke! Look at the girth hanging down!'

Then rose an indescribable din, every throat on the course uttering its ultimate howl of exultation, rage, sympathy. Kit had flung the saddle on to Nora's neck, had vaulted on to her bare back, and with the saddle hung over one arm, had started in pursuit of Lively Lad.

The young mare, shaken by the fall though she was, recovered herself by sheer force of the good blood that was in her. In less than a dozen lengths she had settled down again to gallop, and at each stride she gained a little on her adversary.

Brendan, cantering home, to win, as he believed, as he liked, heard the new note of excitement in the yells of the crowd. He looked back, and saw that the walk-over, that had seemed inevitable, was not to be quite uncontested.

It will be understood with whom, at this crucial moment, were his sympathies. But the eyes of the crowd were upon him, he was riding the favourite, and he had no alternative but to go on and win. As he rounded the last flag before addressing himself to the straight run home, he again looked over his shoulder and saw with astonishment that the mare had not only succeeded in pulling herself together sufficiently to follow him in, but was now galloping strongly and was fast drawing up to him.

'She'll have him cot! She'll bate ye yet! Come on, Con! Belt him! Turn the whip on him!' howled his supporters.

Then the passion of emulation, spurred by the pressure of circumstance, awoke in Con Brendan. He 'turned the whip' on Lively

109

Lad and set to work in earnest to win.

Kit sat still. Peggy, half blinded though she was by tears, could see that he was speaking to the mare, leaning forward, calling on her to do her best for him, to spend herself to the utmost, to the last throb of her gallant heart.

And Nora did not fail the rider she loved. At each instant the distance between the two horses was lessened. Now the mare was up to the horse's quarter, now she was level with his girth. Half a dozen more strides and her nose was ahead . . . And there she kept it, despite Brendan's best efforts, until she was past the judge's stand and the race was won.

Chapter 16

The River Fiddaun, of which some brief mention has already been made, was a slow, wide stream of no great length, that forsook its parent lakes, up the country, beyond the town of Clytagh, and, in the words of geographies, debouched into the harbour of Cloonabinnia. At the point where it widened to meet the sea, Cloon village had established itself; its thatched, whitewashed cottages were clustered together on the river's western bank right down to the water's edge, in indifference to the fact that there were but few winters that did not see the bog-brown water standing, half-door high, at the lower end of the chief street of the three that composed the village.

The Fiddaun's further bank was, for a mile or more upstream, the bounds of the Inver Demesne. Were it not for the Crooked Bridge the people of the village would have had to walk nearly two miles, to the Moyroe Bridge, if they wanted to sell fish at the Big House, or to steal firing in the demesne. It was owing to the enterprise of Jas's grandfather that these industries were fostered by means of the Crooked Bridge. Mr Nicholas Prendeville had improved the occasion of his year of High Shrievalty, as well as the means of communication between his house and his subject village, by inducing the Grand Jury to bring in a bill to build a foot-bridge across the Fiddaun at a point a little above the village and convenient to one of his avenues. Mr Prendeville's enterprise had not stopped short at the mere exercise of influence. He himself undertook to build the bridge, with the county grant, and thus it came about that although its two slender arches were barely high enough to be clear of the winter floods, they supported a road-way wide enough for his coach-and-four. The bridge was, to be sure, crooked, thanks to the rock that sat immovable in mid-stream at the place most convenient to the avenue, but this only imparted a tough of picturesqueness and originality, and troubled no one save Madam Nicholas's coachman when the horses were fresh.

A stone seat was built in the thickness of the wall at the middle of the bridge, with a complimentary reference to the builder, and the benefit he had conferred on 'The Poor of this Parish,' carved on a fine limestone slab that formed the back of the seat. On the seat, leaning against the worn letters of the inscription, Maggie Connor was sitting, knitting. The needles flickered in her nimble fingers with, as it were, a self-contained intelligence. Her bright eyes flickered like the needles, glancing from the avenue that joined the bridge, to a point of rock that projected beyond the trees some little distance higher up the river.

It was a misty evening, very still and warm. The river glided past, dead smooth, the reflections of the Inver trees so deep in it that one would say they had stained the water with their heavy green and were pictured there for ever. Occasionally a fish broke the glassy surface into rings that shook the quiet of the painted trees for a moment; a heron stood in a reedy patch above the bridge, sunk in moody meditation. Lower down, by the village, at the mouth of the river, some seagulls swooped in dreamy, lovely curves above the anchored fishing boats.

Foxy Mag knitted on vigorously, caring for none of these things, until a sudden storm of rooks, rushing to rest in the tall trees of the demesne, darkened the sky. The creaking whirr of their wings made her look up. She was reminded by them that the hour was late.

'He's not coming at all,' she thought. 'The Pup! And me waiting this way . . .'

She put her knitting in her pocket and stood up, her eyes on the Inver avenue.

'. . . For all, he might come yet . . . He might be waiting below on Carrig-a-Breac . . . Maybe it's mesel' is keeping him waiting——' she swung her black shawl over her head and went down the steep, twisting curve of the bridge and into the Inver woods.

The avenue turned soon to the right, plunging into the deep of the trees. The undergrowth of hazel and birch closed it in on both sides. At wide intervals there were openings that showed where trees had been cut, to make 'rides' for hounds and woodcock shooters, but the blocks of blue-grey limestone, draped in briers, that some ancient vagary of cosmic force had strewn on this side of the river, took the meaning from the term, as far, at any rate, as horsemen are concerned.

Maggie turned aside down one of these paths. The hazel bushes grew close on either hand. Their branches, thick with leaves, made the path a tunnel, dark and dank. The track wound on for a little distance between the trees; as it neared the river the bushes thinned, and the tunnel opened on a narrow space of grass that ended abruptly at the top of a low limestone cliff, at whose foot was the river. An immense rock, that rested part on the grass, part on a projection of the cliff, hung out over the water. Its flat top was eight or ten feet above the surface of the stream. Close beside it a contorted oak-tree had started out from the bank, and made a dense screen between the rock and the bridge. The river eddied oilily around its foot; it was called Carrig-a-Breac, the Rock of the Trout, even though no angler had ever been known to have succeeded in rising one of the giant trout fabled to dwell in its shadow.

Maggie went out of the shade of the trees and seated herself, as in an accustomed place, on a branch of the oak, that curved inwards over the great rock. There was no restfulness in her attitude. She leaned forward, listening, her small brilliant face tense, her eyes gleaming. She had not been there many seconds when a distant whistle made her start to her feet.

'That's like it'd be his whistle,' she said. 'It might be he's calling me——'

She hurried back to the main avenue. Again she heard the whistle, and then Kit's voice, evidently cheering on a dog.

'That's the way! Me to be waiting like a fool, and him sporting with his dogs!'

She pressed on, and soon, following the voice, came on him whom she sought.

Kit was lying at full length on the ground in front of a big boulder, shouting encouragements to a dog of whom only a twitching hind-foot was visible, the rest of it being buried beneath the boulder.

'Oh, and is it there you are?' said Maggie, less in inquiry, since the answer was obvious, than in angry statement. 'Didn't ye tell me ye'd be waiting below by the bridge for me at seven o'clock, and it's gone

113

eight by the church clock now!'

'I didn't know then I'd meet a weasel,' Kit replied without moving. 'I'm hunting him from one stone to another for a half-hour.'

'And isn't it a shame for ye to hunt a weasel!' Maggie demanded of Kit's prostrate form. 'You know well it is! Wasn't John Daly drowned last year, and the people said it was for him stoning a weasel that was swimming across the river the week previous——'

The hind foot kicked convulsively and a smothered yelp came from under the boulder. There was a tiny rustle in the bracken behind it.

'Tally Ho! There he goes!' yelled Kit. 'Hulla, Tinker, good dog!' He dragged the dog from under the stone and flung him into the brier patch in which the quarry had vanished.

That it had not stayed there was soon evident. Tinker burst his way through the briers, and could be heard hunting on through the wood. Kit followed him, and in less than two minutes Maggie realised that the scene she had come in upon was being repeated a little farther ahead. She stood still, and a rush of rage, so sudden and fierce that it made her giddy, boiled up in her brain. Should she instantly go home and leave him, or should she wait and tell him what she thought of him? Which would hurt him most? She stood, undecided, digging a hole in the ground with the high and crooked heel of her shoe. A beetle scrabbled by her, and she stamped on it; there was satisfaction for her in hurting something, if, as she feared, she couldn't hurt Kit.

'How well he can keep me here, waiting all night for him! I'm sorry to me heart I came at all! I'll go home——' She turned.

'Hold on, Mag! I'm coming! We lost him!' Kit was swinging down the avenue towards her. He had his cap in his hand. His face was flushed, his yellow hair lay in damp rings on his forehead, his eyes were shining, alive with the fun of the hunt.

For all her anger Maggie's peasant heart bowed down before his princeliness. 'How could I resist him at all?' she thought, her eyes drinking his beauty.

'That was a great hunt!' Kit said laughing, oblivious of the anger in Maggie's face. 'Tinker and me've been at him this last half hour. But he's beaten us. I wish I'd had Fly with me—Tinker's not much

114

good—he's too big for one thing——'

Tinker, who was one of the collies by courtesy, grinned apologetically at the mention of his name, and sidling up to Maggie, jumped up against her, pawing at her hand.

'Get down, ye dirty brute!' Maggie said, slashing the dog's face with the fringed corner of her shawl. She turned on Kit. 'I suppose it was to tell me about the dog ye brought me here, or maybe the weasel!' she broke out. 'If that's all ye have to say to me I'll go home out o' this!'

'Oh, all right,' said Kit, good-humouredly. 'Go if you like!'

'Then what for did ye bring me here?'

Maggie hurled the words at him, her voice running up the scale to the high-pitched note assigned by the women of her class and country to denunciation, and the expounding of injuries, experienced, or expected. 'It's a week this day since the races, and you not to come next or nigh me from that same day, nor to say as much as a common thank-ye to me after all I done for ye! That's a nice way to treat one that done for ye what there's not another girl in the Globe of Ireland would do—No, nor could do! Con Brendan could come out of his way to find me after the race, and to pay me the compliment that neither man nor woman could surpass me for what I done, and for the nate, clever way I done it. But what did you do only to hyst your sails, and away with ye to Miss Peggy Weldon! *Miss Weldon* indeed! A fine Miss she is!'

'Come, now,' said Kit, roughly. 'That's enough about that! We're not talking about Miss Weldon. You'll kindly let her alone——'

'I'll kindly do no such thing!' Maggie's voice became a scream. 'I'm not your negro slave! I'll say what I like!'

Her shawl had fallen off, her ruffled red hair made a dark setting for her small wild face. She threatened him with a clenched fist. Kit snatched at her wrist and dragged her towards him.

'What's all this rot about? Blackguarding me for nothing before you know why I wanted to see you! Here! Have sense and listen to reason!'

He caught her chin with his other hand and turned her face to him and kissed her, an angry kiss, that yet delayed, as though to prove his power. In an instant she had flung her arms round his neck

115

and returned his kiss many times. Then she pulled herself free from him, and sitting down on a boulder in the grass beside the road, she began to cry, quietly at first, then with loud sobbing.

'What on earth's wrong with you now?' Kit said, impatiently, looking down on her bent head. 'See here. Ten pounds is all I got out of that rotten race, all told. I'm sorry to my heart I minded you and Con. The mare would have won easy, weights or no, without all that botheration, and I knew it too—I was drunk when I minded either of you!'

Maggie sobbed wildly, but did not speak.

'Anyhow,' resumed Kit, exasperation in his voice. 'Here's the bloody money, and do what you like with it! You were in such a devil of a hurry to ballyrag me, I didn't get time to tell you it was to give you this I wanted you. There's nothing to cry about.'

His voice, half angry, half conciliatory, checked Maggie's tears.

'I don't want your money,' she said, wiping her eyes furiously with the end of her black shawl.

Kit sat down beside her. He hated scenes, being too young, as well as too lacking in imagination, to understand or sympathise with another's emotions. He said to himself that this was a damned bad beginning, but he had to go through with it.

'Look here, now, Mag,' he began again. 'For God's sake don't cry. I tell you there's nothing to cry about—I want to talk to you, and you must have sense and listen to me——'

'What is it?' said Maggie, without looking at him.

'Well, first of all, here's the ten quid——' ('That ought to please her, anyhow,' was his thought.) He rooted in his breeches pocket and extracted a roll of notes.

'I tell ye I don't want your money!'

'Ah, nonsense!' Kit said, and pushed the notes inside the breast of her dress. His hand was small, and it rested there an instant.

Suddenly Maggie snatched at it, and pressed it to her bosom.

'Kit—Kit——' she began, and stopped, with a harsh and hard-drawn breath.

Kit put his other arm round her. He said to himself he wished to God she would take things quietly, and not go raging mad this way about nothing.

116

'Listen now, Maggie, my dear girl——' She pressed his hand more tightly to her breast.

'—What I've got to say is this. Shibby's found out something about you and me. I don't know how, or who from, or how much she knows, but I've got to be careful. You know jolly well she's top-dog. I haven't a penny, you may say, but what comes through her hands. If I don't come down to the village——' he stammered a little— 'I mean if you don't see me—for a while——'

Maggie tore his hand from her bosom and flung it from her and sprang to her feet.

'Say no more! Ye've said enough! Ye've had enough o' me! God knows ye've had all you want! Throw me out now, like dirty water—that's all I expect from ye!'

Kit, spoilt and self-willed boy though he was, stood silent before her, afraid to risk a reply.

'And how frightful ye are of old Shibby!' Maggie shrieked on. 'Little ye'd mind her if it wasn't pleasing to yourself! I'm no fool to swallow lies the like o' that! Ye'll have to make out a better story than that for me!'

'I'm telling you no lies! As long as the Captain's alive I haven't a damned ha'penny I can call my own, and well you know it! The little I earn you've had it!' His voice told that his temper was rising, and with it his courage.

'That's a nice thing for a gentleman to say! Throwing it in me teeth that you paid me!—Paid me!' she gave a wild cry that was half a laugh, half a sob. 'God above knows I asked no payment from you! Too big a fool I was——'

'Shut up!' broke in Kit, in a swift and fierce whisper. 'There's a trap coming down the road! Get back into the bushes! Look sharp!'

The instinct of secrecy that is so deeply implanted in Maggie's race, the instinct that makes men turn their backs on a stranger, that sends the women in the villages to hide within their doors, like wild animals in their holes, should those of another class come by, came to Kit's aid. In a moment Maggie had slipped behind the screen of hazel bushes that filled the spaces between the trees. She was, in fact, quicker in concealing herself than was Kit, who, realising that he was too late in taking cover, began to walk away from the small pony-cart that had just come into view. It was coming, as a glance told him, from Demesne Lodge, and in it, alone, was Peggy Weldon.

She slackened speed, and then, as she came level with him, stopped the pony.

'Where are you off to now!' she called out, surprise in her voice. 'I'm going to the station to meet father. He's coming by the last train.'

'I have business in the village, and I *was* walking there,' replied Kit, 'but now I'm going to drive!' He made a jump for the handle of the door of the trap, but Peggy was too quick for him and had her right hand on it before his hand reached it.

'What cheek!' exclaimed Peggy, full of pride at having foiled him. 'No you don't! Not until you say "Please"!'

'To be sure I will! And more than that!' He put his hand on hers, and began gently to turn the handle with her. 'Please, Peggy, dear!' The pressure on her hand increased.

Peggy slapped the pony's back with the reins.

'Go on, pony!'

The pony started instantly, but not before Kit, releasing the hand and the handle, had lightly stepped into the trap over the unopened door. 'Now then!' he said, triumphantly. 'What'll you do now?'

Peggy whipped up the pony.

Chapter 17

On this same misty afternoon Miss Pindy stood at the top of the steps of the Big House, and watched with satisfaction the arrival of two carts piled high with furniture. That auction, that had lured her to Clytagh on the day of the races, had proved not only unusually seductive, but, owing to the rival attraction of the races, buyers had been so few that bidding was feeble, and the consequent bargains more seductive than Shibby was able to resist.

'I did well to go!' she said to herself. 'There mightn't be a chance like it again forever!'

Her eyes gloated over her bargains as they were unloaded and borne past her into the hall. This was the third load that had come up from the station at Cloon, 'and nothing but what's good in the whole of them!' she gloried: 'Maybe I spent too much, but I have good value whatever!'

She had been at the Big House all day, and it was evening now, and she was tired, but it is little to say that she would have fallen where she stood from fatigue, rather than forego a moment of this her greatest pleasure. The mood of despair that had seized her in Clytagh had not been able to hold her strong spirit in bondage. She had wrestled with it and conquered, when, as it seemed to her, all her plans were going astray. Now, a week later, she felt that though she still sat in darkness, dawn was not far off. It is convenient to describe the processes of Shibby's mind in some such metaphor as this, but she was too primitive, too essentially elemental, to analyse or define her moods. She lived them wordlessly. She was not conscious of uplift in spirit when things moved in accord with her manœuvring, or of gloom when they went as she would have said, 'agin her'. She was happy or distressed; she was being successful, or being baffled; her plots were prospering, or failing—that was all there was about it. She did not discuss with herself her emotions, being entirely occupied with the facts that produced them.

'Leave the big brass bed in the front room on the first landing,' she directed the carriers.

She looked at it with innocent pride. Wasn't it the grand bed! Worthy of the house, worthy of the lovely lad that should bring his bride to it! The thoughts of Kit, and of the glorious future that she was preparing for him, sprang up and danced like sun-sparkles on a morning sea. It was long since she had been so happy. Had she not seen only half an hour ago, Kit and Peggy riding past the house. It was only then, she thought, Peggy was going home, and it was a good three hours that the two o' them had been out together! She wouldn't be too sure of him yet, but she had said to herself, with a laugh of satisfaction:

'There go the House and the Demesne together again!'

She tramped down the long corridor in the rear of the grand bedstead and its bearers, and watched the assembling of its exuberantly ornate sections with the air of a victorious general reviewing his forces.

'There isn't a stick in the room now but what's good!' she said aloud, listening absently to the sound of the departing footsteps of the carriers. 'Lady Isabella herself wouldn't want better!'

The hall door shut with a resounding bang. She was alone in the house, and it was past her supper hour, but she could not tear herself away from the delightful survey of her new acquisitions.

Things were going right at last. She sat down in one of the new arm-chairs, and let the tune that had been singing itself in her, in that mysterious, indefinite region of the being in which tunes carry on their independent life, find its external vehicle in her voice, her voice, that even now, for all her sixty odd years, was as honey-sweet as it had ever been, while in those long, strenuous years it had gained the shaken reed tone that is the very heart of pathos.

> 'Ah, there's nothing half so sweet in life
> As Love's young dream!'

sang Shibby, and began to wander up and down the room, moving in measure with her music. The old tune filled the room, and slipped out through the half-open door into the long corridors. Who can say what listeners unseen were gathered there! Viewless creatures, drawn there by the viewless strength of Music? . . . Shibby sang her song out. Then she uttered a long sigh. It was as if the regrets, the contritions, the longings of the unseen generations who had gone before her, had been stirred by her voice, and were finding in her a channel of expression. 'What do I know of Love's Young Dream?' Then she said to herself: 'Too much, and too little, and a quick awakening! It was for Love's sake I was born, but sure Love has no pity for bastards!'

On the wall that faced her was a tall mirror that had somehow survived the reigns of the Pindys. A wide-winged gold eagle was poised over it, amid carved open-work tracery of branches and scrolls. It was late now, and the light was dim, but Shibby's glance fell on a piece of the gilded scroll-work of the mirror, broken off, and lying on the floor.

'Look at that now!' she exclaimed with annoyance. 'It was them careless chaps done that, bringing in the wardrobe . . .' She picked up the piece and fitted it to its parent scroll.

'Ah, that'll mend easy,' she comforted herself. The reflection of the sole window of which the shutters were open was bright in the glass. It caught her attention, and then, beyond her own image, she thought she saw, in the depths of the great shadowy room, some definite shape of greyer shadow move. Almost it seemed to her that she had seen a figure cross the room from the door and pause by the bed. She swung round. There was nothing . . .

There are people who live on a plane a little nearer to that shifting border, which is between what may be called sense, and sensibility, than the rest of the world. Things happen to them that cannot be explained in comfortable accord with that self-respecting quality that throws a protecting mantle over prejudice or ignorance, and calls itself common-sense. Shibby's enormous practicality, the stern practicality of the Irish peasant woman, enabled her to accept with composure occurrences that defied recognised standards of proof. There was, she felt, no use in trying to explain them away. They happened, unexplainably, incontestably; and they had, from her youth up, happened, and that was all there was about it. Certain dreams were inevitably followed by certain events; premonitions assailed her, senseless in their impotence to avert the trouble they threatened—so that a disaster for her would sometimes stretch both ways, before and after—and sometimes, more mystifying still, the threat would be made, and the stage set for disaster, and nothing would follow. The Tragic Muse had missed her cue.

'Certain things were foreshown to me,' she would admit, 'but sure, what could I do? I have no certainty. Only to leave it to the Will o' God!'

Therefore it was that now, as she stood, staring hard into the shadows, the thought in her mind was a question as to what this showing might portend. She stood thus for perhaps a minute, without fear, only in deep questioning. And then through the deep silence of the house a faint sound began to assert itself, an uneven shuffling sound, difficult to ascribe to any known agency. But Shibby had no moment of hesitation or uncertainty. She strode across the room and flung open the door.

'Is it there you are, Captain? Sure I didn't know you were in the house at all! It was the Mercy o' God I didn't go home and lock you in!'

Old Jas, standing, wavering, as if a wind shook him, at the top of the wide stair-case, looked at her bewilderedly.

'Why, Shibby?' he said, 'Shibby? Is that you?' He fumbled at the pocket of his long orange-brown coat, and extracted a red cotton pocket handkerchief with which he wiped his eyes, and gazed at Shibby again.

'To be sure it's me!' she said loudly. She thought he had not seen or heard her distinctly. 'Who else would it be?'

'I give you my honour and my word,' said Old Jas, helplessly, 'you passed me here on the landing not two minutes since!'

It was then that Shibby, as she said afterwards to Nessie, felt 'quare'. The twilight corridor stretching away into silence, might still hold that which the Captain had taken for herself. Versed though she was in things that were 'quare', that the Captain should 'have seen meself at all, was something out o' the way altogether! I wouldn't wish that at all,' she had said, gravely, to her young sister, shaking her head in disapproval, 'I wouldn't like it.'

Nessie had come to the Big House in search of her father, and the three walked back through the dusk to the Tower. From the high place where the house stood one could look down across the tops of the trees to the narrow harbour. On the father shore, in the village, the few lights were coming out, here and there, like stars on a cloudy night. The thin turf-smoke lay like a film over the houses. The open sea beyond the harbour was pale with the last reflected light from the west. A fishing-smack lay at anchor off the whitewashed coast-guard station. The young moon hung over her mast like the crescent on a Turkish flagstaff. A fishing sloop was putting forth for her night's work. Her brown sails were idle, only the throb of her little engine faintly shook the air.

'I wonder will we get a bit o' fish to-morrow, and it Friday and all?' said Shibby, 'or will they have it all sold away out o' the place to Johnny Weldon's dirty fish-store! It's a disgrace the way we couldn't get a bit o' fish here, if it was only for the fast-day itself! I wish to God Kit would take out the *Eileen Oge*, the way he'd get us something now and again——'

'He came in just when I was coming over here. He said he had to go to the village. He was riding with Peggy all afternoon,' said Nessie, apologising for the absent, and saying, as was her custom, the thing that she hoped would please. 'He says he'll teach her to ride before he's done with her. I'm so glad they've taken to each other, like this,' Nessie went on. 'I was afraid at first Kit wouldn't——'

'Sure I thought that meself,' Shibby replied, rather absently, because her thoughts had fastened, swift and thronging flies, on the project, never far from her mind, that Nessie's words had suggested.

They had nearly reached the Tower before either spoke again. Old Jas had fallen behind, and was wandering after them, standing still sometimes, to strike with his stick at a weed, seldom hitting it, never doing it an injury.

'Shibby,' Nessie began suddenly, 'do you remember the day we went to Clytagh?'

'Why, child alive, of course I do! It isn't hardly a week since we were in it!' Shibby answered quickly, with surprise. 'I couldn't but remember it, if it was only for the heat! Indeed, I'd say that yourself wasn't the better of it yet. It was only a while ago I was thinking you were looking poorly enough, and I was blaming it in me mind on the heat and the races.'

'It's about the races I want to speak to you—' Nessie went on, hesitantly, 'about that race that Kit won—I was in the village this afternoon, and Jimmy Connor—you know, the Connors that have the public-house——'

'You may be very sure I know them!' said Shibby, ominously.

'He followed me. He was asking me where he could see Kit—he said he wanted to talk to him—and he began to shout something about the races—— He had taken drink——'

'I'll go bail he had!' Shibby cut in.

'I didn't answer him. I went into the Post Office away from him. Shibby'—Nessie put her hand on her sister's arm to arrest the long, swinging strides, one of which was equal to two of her own steps, 'Shibby, I didn't tell you—I didn't tell anyone—but listen, something happened in that race—I saw it!' Her voice had sunk to a whisper.

The mention of the Connors had caught Shibby's attention. 'What are ye saying at all? Speak up, child!'

'It was that belt of lead Kit had to wear. Nora—they said because she had won at Monarde she must carry more weight. It wasn't fair—— Kit was mad about it——'

'What's all this about?' said Shibby impatiently. 'What business is it of Jim Connor's?'

'Oh, but Shibby, only listen one minute—— There was a place on the racecourse that the people couldn't see; trees hid it; but I was there. No one saw me. Oh, Shibby, I saw Kit throw off the belt, and Maggie Connor picked it up——'

Shibby caught Nessie by the shoulder.

'Who d'ye say? Maggie Connor?'

'Yes, that little girl with red hair—she was hidden there,' Nessie went on, miserably. 'She gave it back to him for the finish—there was one jockey who knew—only one—and he didn't care, he was laughing—— But, oh, Shibby! Could Kit be punished?'

'Maggie Connor that was in it!' repeated Shibby, with a brow of thunder. 'The brazen tinker! . . .'

'But, Shibby, Kit—if it were known—what would people say?'

Shibby flung up her head and laughed, the laughing as it might be of the war-horse, when, among the trumpets, he smelleth the battle afar off.

'Faith, I know well what I'd say! I'd say what'd the other fellas be doing? Let them look out for theirsel's! That's what I'd say! Maybe theirsel's were doing the same and worse!'

She stood still, with set face, seeing again the sordid Clytagh public-house, and Maggie Connor and Kit coming out of it with the jockey.

'It was then they made up their blagyarding!' she thought, 'giving him drink and deceiving him!' Unconscious that she spoke aloud, she said, in a voice that ground out the words as the wheels of a traction-engine grind down stones:

'That the Almighty God may strike Maggie Connor dead!'

Old Jas had shuffled up close behind his two daughters   unnoticed by either of them.

'What's that? What's that?' he mumbled. 'Is poor Maggie dead? I thought she died long ago!—— She was a very pretty girl. I'm dam' sorry to hear it——'

Chapter 18

The evening meal at Inver Tower was of a composite and thoroughly practical character, varying according to the requirements of the moment, and regulating itself, mainly, as to time and constitution, to suit the needs of the son of the house. But when the time had come to a quarter past eight o'clock, Miss Pindy refused to wait any longer for Kit.

'What a time he chose to be going down to the village! Seven o'clock! and he knowing well I had a chicken designed for his tea! Run, Nessie, and tell Delia to bring in what there's left of it before it's boiled away entirely!'

At nine o'clock the Captain was sent to bed. At ten Tinker slid in unobtrusively, and having made a hurried and fruitless examination of a dish from which his fellows had been fed, retired to his sanctuary under the Captain's chair with the crust Nessie gave him, glad to evade being sent out to the stable.

'Kit must have gone out fishing,' said Nessie. 'Here's Tinker come in.'

'Well, so long as he brings in a bit o' fish——' Shibby said, relenting a little. 'But if that's the way he'll hardly be back before morning. You'd better go to bed, child—I'll wait up a bit longer.'

There are not many days in Western Ireland that a fire in the evening can be dispensed with. Shibby sat in the Captain's chair in front of the quiet glow of turf in the wide old fireplace, and applied herself to the task, unfamiliar to her active, violent soul, of systematically reviewing the general position.

'I have enough to think of!' she said to herself, drawing together the blocks of turf, and flinging, with a skilled hand, a log into their low, steady redness. This story, now, that Nessie had about the races. She must find out the rights of it all from Kit. There might be more trouble out of it than she had let on to Nessie. There was no good frightening the child. Anyhow, there was one thing certain, if it was to be Jimmy Connor that was to make the trouble, she had the way

126

to put him down. He had better mind himself, and not forget who it was owned his father's public-house, and how many years' rent there was owing!

The main thing was to keep a quiet tongue . . . She sat and stared at the fire. Its tongues were quiet enough; they were having their own way of the log, devouring it, unresistingly, surely. Shibby put her foot down, in its thick, country-made shoe, on the wood, and crushed it down into the glowing turf. It was as though she were aware of an analogy and was metaphorically crushing out the Connors, root and branch . . . . But on earth why wasn't Kit home, and it near twelve o'clock! Young men were a fright! No sense at all in them! . . . But if he were indeed taking a notion of Peggy Weldon, the way Nessie said he was . . . Could Old John be trusted? What good would the girl be without the demesne? Young Johnny, that had stolen from the Captain in spite of her, might want to keep it himself . . . And the money too, that should bind the Big House and the demesne together with a golden wedding-ring; would Old John make that sure, or would they have to wait for it till Young Johnny was done with it, and God knew he might live as long as the father! . . .

Disturbing thoughts, and behind them all was one that she had not permitted herself to dwell on, driving it out with those which she told herself were more important—the thought which had power to cut at the root of all her hopes, to ruin all her building . . .

The lamp on the table beside her was burning low, and the fire was going grey. Tinker came out from under her chair, looking behind her towards the door. He growled faintly. Shibby stood up. She knew not why. It was, perhaps, the subconscious expectation of Kit, wakened in her by Tinker's movement, which brought again before her eyes the vision of Maggie Connor, laughing and insolent, in the big hat with the yellow roses, as she had seen her that day in Clytagh. The dog growled again, a nervous, half-uttered growl, like a series of little bubbles breaking in his throat; with his head still turned towards the door, he crept away as close to the wall as possible, and hid himself under an old couch at the opposite side of the room. Shibby was unaware of him. On her in that moment, there had fallen a possession of hatred that shook her, as only such a wind

127

of deep emotion, love or hate, has power to shake. She felt as if it came from without, meeting and joining hands with what was in her soul. Something stronger than she, strong as she felt herself. Her fists were clenched, her head was bent forward. To one who had seen her then she would have looked like a snake ready to strike. Thus she stood, held by the power that had mastered her. She had gone outside Time. Her mind could register the intensity of her hatred of Maggie Connor, but for how long she stood there, numbed in her body, living only in the blackest deeps of her soul, she knew not. Only that when the possession passed, she found the lamp-flame rising and falling to a finish, and the fire gone grey.

She heard a step outside the window and the tension broke. Shuddering, she wrapped her shawl more closely round her, and strode to the outer door.

'Is that you, Kit!'

Tinker, who had run in front of her, began to bark rejoicingly. She opened the door, and Kit came in. He pushed past her into the sitting-room and sat down heavily in his father's chair.

'What kept you? Where were you? What a time o' night this is for you to be coming home!' said Shibby, following him, her voice angry and low. She lighted a candle. 'What are ye sitting there for? Aren't ye going to bed to-night at all?'

'I've had the hell of a row with Jim Connor!' Kit growled, without looking at her. He smelt of whisky. He kept his face averted from her, and his voice was unsteady and excited.

Shibby snatched up the candle and held it to his face. He was very pale, there was a cut on his forehead, a smear of blood and mud went from it down his cheek, and one of his eyes was half-closed and already a deep purple stain surrounded it. The other was bloodshot, and had evidently fared little better.

'My God!' exclaimed Shibby, regarding him with horror. 'He made a show of you altogether!'

'I did as good for him!' said Kit, fiercely. 'I'd have damn' well killed him only for Maggie, and Con Brendan—they pulled me off him when I had him down!'

''Twas little they had to do when they went saving Jimmy Connor!' commented Shibby, scornfully, 'and what foolishness was

128

on you to be dirtying your hands with the like o' that blackguard?'

Her voice was harsh, but her eyes were soft, and the smile that came and went as she spoke, told that though she might condemn a fight, she loved a fighter.

'But on earth,' she went on, 'what call had you to go fighting with Jimmy Connor? I thought it wasn't but too great with him you were always——'

Kit remained silent.

'Can't ye answer me?' said Shibby, impatiently. 'Was it out o' the races that the trouble was?'

Kit looked at her as sharply as his damaged eye would permit.

'Who says there was trouble out of the races?' he demanded.

'Never mind who says it. It'd be as good for you to tell me the whole story first as last.'

'I'll tell you nothing till you tell me who said anything to you.'

'Why then it was your own sister—and a good job for you it was herself and no other!'

'It's a dam' funny thing she never said a word to me——'

'Never mind whether it's funny or no—she has more sense than you! *She'll* keep her mouth shut and not go down the village taking drink and fighting like a mad dog!'

Kit, battered as he was, began to laugh at this negative tribute to Nessie.

'Stop your laughing now, and go on and tell me the whole story. I'll not go out o' this, nor you neither, till you have it told.'

'Well, it was this way——'

He plunged into a rambling account of the race meeting. He said the whole show was illegal. That what he did wasn't a bit worse than many a thing that was done. It was Con Brendan's notion from start to finish—his and Jim Connor's between them. What money was in it they got it—except only the prize, and a few shillings he put on the mare— and anyhow, the mare'd have won easy enough, carrying the weight and all, and he told them so, damn them, but they wouldn't mind him—all the three of them tearing at him, giving him no peace.

Shibby cut short the transference of the blame to other shoulders that was so usual a feature of Kit's explanations of a scrape. 'I suppose Maggie Connor wanted a new hat!' she said, bitingly.

'She got it too! Blast her!' said Kit, with a sudden burst of rage that did much to soften Shibby's displeasure.

'And the money yourself got,' pursued the inquisitor, 'was it to her you gave that too?'

'To be sure it was,' said Kit, angrily. 'D'ye suppose a hat would satisfy that one?'

('He's tired of her, thank God!' thought the inquisitor).

'It was she took the belt from you, wasn't it? She earned it well!' Shibby commented, with a concentrated bitterness that stung Kit to rejoinder.

'She earned it a dam' sight better than Jimmy did, anyhow! It was she did the work, I'll say that for her. All he did was to go to the bookies and put money on the mare, and now trying to collar it all!'

He stood up, and swayed as he did so, and caught at the back of the high chair to steady himself. Then he hurried on, excitedly, with his story, falling into intricate technicalities, shouting down Shibby's interrupting questions, continuing to distribute the responsibility, impartially, on all concerned, with the single exception of himself.

'Con Brendan's the one who had better look out for himself! He made a pot out of it! He's a professional—*he* doesn't want to lose his licence, you may take your oath of that! It's him will get the worst of it if Jimmy lets his tongue loose! But I tell you Con knows that as well as I do! He's no fool! He'll have an eye to Jimmy Connor all right! It's nothing to me——'

Suddenly he paused. The excitement sank. His tenor voice that had been loud and fractious, like that of a naughty child, had trailed away into weakness. Then he said: 'Oh Shibby, for God's sake let me go to bed! There's no more to say——'

'I think ye have enough said!' Shibby said, gloomily. 'And I'll say no more meself. Come on now until I wash the dirt off you. The sight you are! Did anyone ever see the like! And worse you'll be to-morrow! Well, well! I'll see you clean and decent in your bed before I'm done with you——'

Her voice had lost some of its severity, and Kit knew that her unfailing forgiveness was at hand. He dragged himself away from his father's chair to which he was clinging, and followed her, submissively, with Tinker at his heel.

Chapter 19

The arrival of a large and important-looking yacht in the harbour of Cloonabinnia was an event sufficiently unusual to stir the village of Cloon to its depths. Every little shop—which, in such a village, is nearly equivalent to saying every little house—roused itself from the torpor that is habitual to such little shops, and confident in the spending powers of Jacks-ashore, set forth its choicest wares. Mr Tom Prendeville, (né Pindy) of the Prendeville Arms, put on his Sunday clothes, and laid himself open for conversation in the doorway of his hotel; the lesser public-houses seemed to exhale a special and welcoming perfume of porter, and when Sir Harold Burgrave's four-oared gig came accurately alongside that pier on which, so many years back, the American ship had deposited her famine cargo, there was scarcely a fisherman, boy, or child in the village who was not there to take stock of it. Not a detail was lost on those all-observing eyes, from the white tiller-ropes, the shining brasses, the dark blue cushions, the ordered and conscious splendour of the crew, to the still greater splendour of the owner of all these wonders. Burgrave proceeded up the village street in company with a fisherman, and closely attended by a pattering, whispering throng of infant admirers. He had asked to be shown the way to Mr John Weldon's, and the fisherman had offered to show him the way to the hotel, and had advised him to get a car, for the reason, (here he looked at Burgrave's snowy canvas shoes,) that the day might throw a shower, and it was a good mile back to Weldon's. (The fisherman's grandmother had been a Pindy, and had taught him to resent the rise of the Weldons.)

'A bad mile, you mean! I know your Irish roads!' Burgrave had replied, with the genial and condescending facetiousness that he thought suitable in dealing with the people whom he was accustomed to call 'The Paddies'; and the fisherman had laughed politely, and said that it was true for him, and that indeed the road wasn't so good that it mightn't be better.

Mr Tom Pindy's livery-stables responded to Burgrave's requisi-

131

tion with an outside-car of primitive type, with a raw young mare in the shafts, and a raw young driver on the box, and it was therefore scarcely surprising that Sir Harold Burgrave's first experience of an Irish jaunting-car, was not devoid of incident of a minor kind. The young mare had been in harness just often enough to have learnt that convention insisted on a heavy swerve on encountering any of those objects among which her previous life had been passed. Heaps of stones were greeted with swinging shies that shook to his foundations the English passenger, unversed in the adhesive seat peculiar to the native. The sight of a pair of coupled goats, poised, after their manner, on the knife-edged top of a bank, flung her into panic in which she remained rigid, unable to move, until restored to animation by flail-like blows from the boy who was driving, when she fell again into the untidy trot that the goats had interrupted. At the summit of the crooked bridge a sow, strolling pensively in the middle of the road, nearly brought the drive to an untimely end. The young mare, in an attempt to turn and fly, wedged one wing of the car against the wall, and Burgrave only saved his legs from injury by a rapid and precarious scramble on to the seat.

'Can't you pull the brute straight, you young fool!' he roared, only maintaining his position by clutching with both hands the rail of the car. 'Can't you see she's jamming this side against the wall? Hit her, can't you!'

'I can not. Me whip's broke,' replied the boy, simply, and without emotion.

'Then get down and go to her head——' Burgrave had begun, when the mare, for her own dark reasons, suddenly wrenched the car clear of the wall, and breaking into a shambling gallop, left the bridge and its dangers behind, and set off up the road through the wood.

By the time the approach to Demesne Lodge from the main avenue was reached, her ardour had flagged, and the boy dragged her to a standstill at the gate of Mr Weldon's little drive. Old John himself was standing there, and Burgrave hailed him.

'Hi! You there! Open the gate, will you?'

Old John received this command in silence. He looked slowly at the visitor, and then at the lad who was driving. In his mind was a contest between the inveterate politeness of his generation and class; and displeasure at its absence in the stranger. Displeasure carried the position, even though he had quickly guessed who it was that had so crudely demanded his services.

'I'm getting on in years, Sir, you must excuse me,' he said, ceremoniously, and then, like the bark of a cross old dog. 'Blast ye, Timmy Lyons, get down and open the gate for yourself!'

Timmy Lyons, whose mother was one of Old John's many tenants, hurled the reins at his passenger, saying hurriedly, 'Ketch the reins, Sir!' as he leaped to the ground and sped to the gate.

Burgrave had not expected Old John's refusal, and was feeling in his pocket for sixpence with one hand, while he gripped the rail of the car with the other. The reins fell on the ground, and before the boy had time to pick them up, the mare made a sideways rush through the gateway, the wing of the car struck the old man, and he fell heavily on the grass beside the drive. The mare broke into an uncertain trot, the reins trailing on the ground beside her, and what might have been the fate of the enraged and now alarmed Burgrave it is hard to say, had not Peggy at this moment emerged from the house, and, seeing the approaching car, had quickly seen, also, something of what had happened. She was dressed for riding and had a cane in her hand, and she ran to meet the car, demonstrating with outstretched arms. The mare checked and swerved, Burgrave jumped off the car, and snatching up the reins, pulled her to a stand, with her nose in the laurustinus bushes that encircled the small gravel sweep in front of the Demesne Lodge hall-door.

'The car's just knocked down an old man at your gate!' he said to Peggy, breathlessly, and with the crossness of a man who has been both shaken and discomfited. 'I hope he isn't hurt—a fat old fool who stood in the way——'

'Good heavens! Grand-dad!'

Peggy set off down the drive at the best speed that a habit-skirt would permit, while Burgrave, still further shattered by his unfortunate reference to Peggy's grand-father, could think of nothing better to do than stand at the young mare's head, and straighten his smart, white-covered yachting-cap, and pull down his brass-buttoned blue coat, and curse Ireland and all things Irish.

Burgrave was a young man not without parts. He was a capable person in a boat and on a horse; he had a fairly equable temper; it is not enough to say that he was not a bad fellow, because, in some ways, he was quite a good fellow. But he was unaccustomed to frustration and the disintegration of his plans. He had looked forward to meeting his agent's handsome daughter again with more interest than he chose to admit to himself. There was just a pleasing hint of King Cophetua about the situation, and with a sideways thought to the subjugation of the Beggarmaid, he had given rather special attention to his attire as the ideal yachtsman. Now he felt that all had been disorganised by this damned Irish car. He reflected, with growing wrath, how perfectly ignominious had been King Cophetua's entry, clinging to the side of a shabby hack-car, being trotted away with—(not even run-away with)—by a common, hairy-heeled brute of a cart-mare, and being rescued by the Beggarmaid herself! He said to himself that he wasn't used to looking like a fool, and he didn't like it . . . Then he reflected painfully on his reference to Peggy's grandfather, and tried to console himself by disparagement of Old John. How the deuce was he to know who he was? The old boy looked like a pauper inmate out for the day—not worth all this excitement . . .

Here the young mare tried to tear herself free, and, snatching at a mouthful of laurustinus she smudged the rusty foam on her lip on Burgrave's beautiful coat sleeve. He dragged her back roughly, and, while he sacrificed a clean silk handkerchief to his coat sleeve, his anger strengthened in him.

Where was Weldon? Dash it all, he had told the fellow to expect him. He was his agent, confound him, and he paid him jolly well too. Why the devil wasn't he here when he was wanted? He'd be damned if he'd stand here holding this dirty-mouthed brute all day——

His soliloquy was interrupted by the sight of a group advancing slowly towards the house. In the centre was Old John, as broad as he was long, Peggy and the driver on either side of him. They suggested an armorial bearing—Old John's vast waistcoat the shield, with male and female supporters. The group, taking no notice of the visitor, moved, intact, but sideways, the door being narrow, into the house.

There followed sounds of commotion; doors opening and shutting, running feet, and loud, agitated voices. Then the sounds gradually faded away, as when a band marches down a street, and silence fell.

Anger deprives most people of their sense of proportion. Burgrave's face, as he sought and found a piece of rope in the 'well' of the car, wore an expression of hatred that might have beseemed the avenger of a family blood-feud.

'Now!' he said, between his set teeth, to the mare, while he tied her with the rope to a branch. 'Pull away, you devil, and be damned to you! I shall walk back to the boat!' He flung the decision at her. If looks could have killed, Mr Tom Pindy's young mare would have fallen dead where she stood.

A little calmed by this assertion of independence, Burgrave had turned to depart, when he found himself face to face with another horse, a chestnut, on whose back was seated that young Prendeville whom he had met at the races at Clytagh. Burgrave was not one of those who form prepossessions at first sight, but an aversion was a simpler matter. At Clytagh he had merely decided that he had no use for young Prendeville; now, at this ruffled moment, he felt that he disliked him excessively.

'H'ar-ya'? he said, in condensed response to Kit's greeting—(confound the fellow, sitting up there on that good-looking mare, when he, Burgrave, had to walk in the mud, or hang on to the side of a filthy car!)

'Did you want to see anyone?' said Kit, civilly, slipping off Nora's back and going to the hall-door. 'Will I ring?'

'No 'ank-ya!' replied Burgrave, with still greater condensation,— 'can't wait——'

('He looked at me,' said Kit, recounting the interview to Nessie, 'as black as any dog! *I'd* done nothing to the fellow!')

'Ah, that's a pity!' said Kit. 'Let me tell someone you're here——'

'They know it!' said Burgrave, with a sudden and uncontrollable burst of fury.

('I declare, I was near laughing in his face!' Kit told Nessie.)

At this point, Timmy Lyons, deposed from the office of supporter (which he had, as a matter of fact, exchanged for that of valet and sick-room attendant), emerged in haste from the house.

'I'm to go for the doctor, Sir!' he called out to Burgrave. Then he saw Kit. 'Oh, Master Kit, for God's sake would ye go fetch Doctor Magner! Ye'd be quicker to ketch him in before his round than me——'

'What's the matter? Who's ill?' said Kit, quickly.

'It's the old gentleman—— He got a knock like with the car. He's not too bad at all—only giddy-like in the head——'

'Oh, I'll go, I suppose——' Kit hesitated for a moment, then he said sharply: 'Run in, Timmy, tell Miss Peggy I want her in a hurry.'

Burgrave wondered to himself what it was about this fellow Prendeville that he couldn't open his mouth without annoying him. Even now, for instance—what right had he to order his, Burgrave's, hireling about? And the girl, too–as if she belonged to him! He, Burgrave, would damn well show him that they didn't!

'Look here!' he called, dictatorially to Timmy Lyons, who was starting to do Kit's bidding. 'You can give that message, but look sharp about it. I'm going back at once!'

Kit looked curiously at the English stranger. Was he intentionally asking for trouble? If so, Kit would be very happy to oblige him. A cross thief—that was what he was! And he had told Peggy the same the first day he had laid eyes on him . . . Ah, here was Peggy at last, and in her riding-kit too—good!

'Kit!' said Peggy. 'Have you heard? Poor old granddad's had an awful shake! I wish you'd go and ask Doctor Magner to come and see him. And he's asking for Miss Isabella too. He says he's dying! He's not, you know, but he says he is, and that he wants to see his "old friend!" I think his head's bothered by the fall—— He's really all right——'

'All right,' said Kit, gloomily. 'I'll go. I'll tell them.' He paused. 'I thought you were coming for a ride with me this morning? Wouldn't you come with me now?'

Peggy looked at him dubiously. 'I'd love to——' she began. Then she saw Burgrave. 'Oh, Sir Harold—I'm so sorry—Father's just coming. I told him you were here—but you see—the accident——'

'Perfectly, I quite understand,' said Burgrave stiffly. 'Please don't trouble your father. I shall hope to be able to see him another day——'

Timmy Lyons, at this juncture, came out of the house like a

136

bolted rabbit, and close on his heels came Young Johnny.

'Oh dear, dear, dear!' Mr Weldon began, rushing upon Burgrave with outstretched hands. 'How unfortunate this has all bin! Sir Har'ld, I cann't say how shocked I am you to be kep' waiting this way! The fawther gave us all such a fright—— !'

He caught sight of Kit, who had remounted, and turned quickly to Peggy. 'I heard you had sent Kit for Dr Magner?' he said, indignantly. 'What's delaying him this way?'

Peggy paid no attention to her father's inquiry. She walked across the gravel to where Nora stood, and putting her hand on the mare's shining shoulder, said in a low voice, 'It's no use waiting for me, Kit. I can't come—quite impossible!'

Kit leaned down.

'Well, then, to-morrow morning—say seven-thirty, at the Big House gates,' he whispered.

'No, father wants Nelson to-morrow,' she whispered back, hurriedly. 'It must be Saturday—he'll be away——'

Kit's quick eye had seen Mr Weldon's hostile and suspicious gaze fastened on his daughter. 'All right,' he said aloud. 'I can go for him now,' then, without looking again at Peggy, he said in a voice that she, only, could hear: 'Damn! I don't want to wait till Saturday!'

He touched Nora with his heel, and she walked away down the drive, with the springy, rhythmic, sedate elegance of a well-bred, well-mannered young horse. Peggy, unconscious, or rather, regardless of her father's disapproving eyes, stood still, and watched horse and rider out of sight, Nora's long, fine, pale-gold tail swinging a little from side to side as she moved, Kit's head very erect, his shoulders very square.

Burgrave's eyes were on Peggy. Why should she watch the fellow off like that? Was she never going to turn round? He wanted to see if his remembrance of her as he had seen her last, at the races, was correct. He had only seen her for a moment, properly, without her hat, that time when she was lying on the ground, and he had leaned over her to hold the parasol between her and the sun. He thought to himself that—if she only knew it—he had come precious near kissing her then—if only the other girl hadn't been there—not because he thought so much of her—rather the other way on—just for a

137

lark, to see how she'd take it! He laughed a little at his thought, and Young Johnny, who had not ceased from apology and welcome, immediately laughed too. What at, he did not know, just out of pure relief because Sir Harold's obviously lost temper seemed to have been regained.

Chapter 20

The lunch that in its own good time ensued, with Sir Harold Burgrave as its brilliant focal point, was, for Mrs Weldon, immensely simplified, and relieved of anxiety, by the absence of the venerable master of the house. She had done all the occasion demanded of a kind and attentive daughter-in-law, and had performed her ministrations not only from a sense of duty, but because she was fond of Old John, and had always tried hard not to disapprove of him. Old Falstaff had been put to bed, and had been given hot whisky and water, and his pipe, and his spectacles, and the Clytagh weekly *Vindicator*, and, after a last hurried yet careful inspection of him, as he lay, looking like a recumbent balloon, in the wide bed that nearly filled his little room, and having received his assurance that he was grand, and wanted no more at all—at all, Mrs Weldon had slipped noiselessly down to the kitchen (so that John and the guest should not be disturbed) and had there achieved what John—when the *status quo ante* had been restored and the guest had departed—had praised as 'a nice, ladylike little luncheon'.

The man's part in such a crisis is necessarily, mainly, a humble and negative one, but Young Johnny had also done his best, and had played efficiently into the hands of the more active partner, by, at the first moment possible, immuring the guest and himself in his office, thus leaving the field of her operations undisturbed. The rendering unto Cæsar an account of the things that were his, filled what remained of the morning very thoroughly, and when Cæsar, all having been found in satisfactory order (and Cæsar was a clearheaded and businesslike young man), had proposed to summon Timmy Lyons and return to the yacht, Mr Weldon had been so pained, that the point had been yielded, and Mrs Weldon's effort was not made in vain.

It was certainly (as Mr Weldon said, later, to Mrs Weldon) the Hand of Providence that had put Old John out of action for the moment. His table manners were embarrassing, and his conversation, especially when stimulated by the presence of a stranger, was often of the kind that is said to leave nothing to the imagination—a criticism that would seem to reflect unfavourably on the imagination referred to.

Peggy's behaviour, which her parents were beginning to fear could not always be relied on, was, on this great occasion, wholly to their satisfaction. She had changed her riding-things, and had put on the pale green linen gown that her mother liked best; and when the rendering of accounts was ended, she had swept the acquiescent guest into the flower-garden, and had there held him in play, what time her father got out some whisky and decanted a bottle of port, and her mother, having herself laid the table, and given Bridget, the sole retainer, final and, as it were, death-bed instructions as to the ritual to be observed, had gone to prepare herself for the ordeal.

Poor Mrs Weldon, hurrying into her tight black satin 'Sunday dress,' had an eye on Peggy and the visitor, strolling about the flower-garden.

'How well she looks!' thought the mother. 'I'm so thankful she put on her green linen! . . . She's talking to him easily as if he were a nobody, and not a gentleman of wealth and position! . . . John says he's taken with her . . .' Here the difficulty of arranging a lace *jabot* interrupted her thoughts, but they pursued a subconscious course, and the last definite words that rose in her mind, as she gave a final glance of resigned self-depreciation at herself in her glass, were '—A Baronet's lady! . . . My daughter, Lady Burgrave!'

Then she ran down the little passage to Old John's room.

'Had your broth, Father? . . . That's right! The doctor will be here soon, but you're looking quite well again, thank God!'

Old John only grunted in response, but it was a friendly grunt, and to himself he said: 'That's a decent little woman. It's a wonder to me why did she marry Johnny at all!'

The nice and ladylike lunch went well. Burgrave had the hearty and not over-fastidious appetite that is reassuring to a hostess as nervous and unversed in entertaining as was Mrs Weldon. He 'went Nap,' as he said, tranquilly devouring all that was offered, without even using the formula hallowed by custom, and saying that he yielded to Mr Weldon's entreaties out of 'pure greed'. 'Ate all before him!' was how Bridget reported his efforts to Timmy Lyons, feasting secretly in the tiny back-scullery. Young Johnny, who had a delicate digestion, found himself compelled to eat far more than was good for him, in order, as he said, to keep the guest in countenance. And Peggy continued the good work she had begun in the garden, and looked so handsome, and talked so successfully, that Mrs Weldon felt she could almost cry from sheer love and pride in her. Burgrave found the port quite tolerable, far better than he had expected, and Mrs Weldon's coffee was irreproachable. He liked Mrs Weldon; the expression in his brown eyes changed and softened when he spoke to her. She reminded him, he thought, of his mother, the late Lady Mayoress, and he was deferential to her, and praised the coffee, and complimented her on her cook.

'I'm sure he has a kind heart,' Mrs Weldon thought, wondering if it were deceitful to suppress the fact that it was she who had made the *meringues*.

When Mrs Weldon, in obedience to a marital wink, rose to go, Burgrave made a protest.

'What, leaving us?' he said, as in a couple of strides he reached the door. 'Why go, Mrs Weldon? I'm sure Miss Weldon would like a cigarette!'

'Yes, but Mother wouldn't!' said Peggy, laughing, and looking at him over her shoulder as she passed him.

'She *is* a good-looker!' thought the guest, returning to his second glass of port. 'Funny how she managed to be this old outsider's daughter!'

The tide of conversation ebbed after the ladies had left. Burgrave drank his wine reflectively, and again exhibited to Mr Weldon his gift of keeping silence when he had no desire to speak. Mr Weldon, whose attitude towards his employer might be compared to that of a cautious fisherman who is playing a salmon with a trout rod, toyed with a wineglassful of hot water and a biscuit, and did nothing to disturb the quiescence of this large fish. Presently the fish stirred. Burgrave abstractedly lit a cigarette, and turned to his host.

'How many acres have I in that Moyroe property, Weldon?'

'About seven hundred, Sir Har'ld,' replied Mr Weldon eagerly, 'and you have the best half of the best reach of the river running through it. I've known your last tenant to take forty pounds of white trout out of it in a day!'

'By Jove!' Burgrave woke up. 'I won't let it again! There *is* a house there that I could put up at, isn't there? The governor used to go and stay there sometimes, didn't he?'

'Ah, 'tis a roon, Sir Har'ld, your poor fawther would never let me spend as much as a half-crown on it——'

'Isn't that like the governor!' said Burgrave with a laugh. 'I say, Weldon, d'you think you could fix it up? I rather like messing about in bricks and mortar—I might stay there now and then. This harbour is handy for the ship—and I'd have a bit of wild   shooting—'

'Ah, t'would be like building a new house. 'Tis very out of the way, too. I'd say you'd find the hotel at Clytagh——'

'I can't stand your Irish hotels,' Burgrave broke in, in his bullying voice. 'They're not fit for white men!'

Mr Weldon accepted this comment on the civilisation of his native land without a protest. He would probably have endorsed it, were it not that a thrilling idea had occurred to him, and he was swiftly determining how it should be developed.

'If you were not in too great a hurry, Sir Har'ld,' he began, 'I should like greatly to show you a little of the place here. There's some fine timber in the demesne—It's mine now, y'know,' he went on lightly. 'Or at least, strictly speaking, it's me old fawther's. We bought it from old Captain Prendeville, the fawther of the young man you saw here awhile ago.'

'Oh,' said Burgrave, shortly. 'That cub. Yes, I met him at the races.'

('Why doesn't he like him?' thought Young Johnny. 'I must look into that.')

'Then there's the old house, Inver House. The Big House, the people call it. It's worth your while to see it, Sir Har'ld! 'Tis said to be a perfect example of its period. Queen Anne, they say——'

Burgrave found himself getting bored; he leaned back in his chair and looked at his watch, and stretched his long, thick legs, and yawned. Three glasses of port and a solid meal, in the middle of the day, dispose to sleep. He did not think it necessary to stand on ceremony with his agent.

'You've given me such a devilish good lunch——' he said lazily.

'Oh, Sir Har'ld! If it wouldn't interest you, please don't think of it! It was only I thought——' Mr Weldon was almost incoherent at the idea of inflicting an unwelcome plan upon his guest.

' ——However,' continued the guest, regardless of the apologies, 'it just happens that architecture is rather a hobby of mine. I'll have a look at the house if you like. I daresay it's better for me than going to sleep, anyhow!'

There came a faint tap at the door, and Mrs Weldon's voice said, very apologetically:

'John, dear—just a moment——'

John dear joined his wife in the little hall.

'Well, what is it? Be quick!' he said, with impatience permissible in an angler whose fish is lightly hooked.

'The doctor's been,' said Mrs Weldon, in the chosen idiom of her class, 'and he says your Father's had quite a shake—he thought it might be a slight stroke—and he's to be kept quiet and in bed—'

'Well, keep him!' said Mr Weldon in a pettish whisper. 'I can't go see him now——'

Mrs Weldon glanced apprehensively at the dining-room door. 'Is he going soon?' she breathed.

'No, he's not!' said Young Johnny, still more pettishly. 'I'm taking him up to see the Big House.'

'It's only that your Father is asking to see Miss Isabella, and I was just wondering how to send word to her——'

'What nonsense! What does he want with her? He'll have to wait——'

Burgrave's large figure appeared, filling the little doorway.

'Tell him I'll leave a message,' said Mr Weldon, hurriedly, to his wife. 'Have tea ready when we come back—Now, Sir Har'ld, if you're quite ready?'

Half-past three o'clock on a hot July day, after a very ample lunch, is not the most propitious moment for a walk. The half-mile that lay between the Lodge and the Big House had never seemed longer to Young Johnny, even though he shortened it by taking a path across the grass and under the trees. The sea breeze of the morning had fainted in the blaze of noon, and though the over-arching trees baffled the direct assault of the sun, they could not keep out the dull persistence of the heat. Overhead, in the leaves, was the continuous hot roar of a furnace, seven times heated. Out of the bracken and briers and hazel-bushes that muffled the trunks of the great trees, heavy, purposeful horseflies came, dogging passers-by like detectives, planning their silent attacks.

'I thought you told me it was less than half a mile!' said Burgrave, stopping to wipe his forehead. He brought his big hand down on a horsefly that had settled on his leg. 'Got you! you brute! Ugh! Look at the mess his beastly blood's made on my clean breeches! I say, Weldon, have we much farther to go? These flies are the very devil!'

'We're just there now, Sir Har'ld,' apologised Young Johnny. He thought, 'I was a fool not to wait till after tea! Maybe he'll hate the whole thing now——'

'There now are the big gates!' he went on brightly. 'They're greatly admired by the cognosenties—as they call 'em, I believe! I'm afraid I'm only an ignorahmus in such matters——'

The Big House received the two hot gentlemen with forbidding, shuttered aloofness. The drip-courses over the windows had the expression of angry eyebrows, drawn over implacably closed eyes. Burgrave seated himself on one of the big stone blocks that were the stops for the gates, and regarded the house with interest.

'Jove, it *is* a fine house!' he said, with surprise. 'That's a fine portico!—well proportioned—and that stone balustrade along the top—jolly good I call it! How many rooms are there, Weldon?'

'Twenty, I believe, on each floor, Sir Har'ld, more or less—I declare it's so long since I was in it, I'm not rightly——'

'Can't we get in?' Burgrave cut short Mr Weldon's disclaimers. 'I'd rather like to see what it's like inside.'

Mr Weldon hesitated. This was a development that, though favourable, might be embarrassing. He was only too well aware that the guardian of the Big House was unlikely to comply with a request from him, save for very good reason shown.

'I'll try can I get the key,' he said, concealing his uncertainties, as is, in such case, the part of wisdom, and setting forth stoutly on his doubtful quest.

Burgrave sat and smoked, and contemplated the house with grow-ing admiration.

'It's just the stamp I like,' he thought. 'Who'd have expected to find a house like this in this God-forsaken place? . . . Pity it isn't at Moyroe!' . . . Then his mind, moving along those subconscious step-ping-stones that link such unlikely lands, arrived at the tract that was beginning to be occupied by Peggy Weldon. She, also, was an unexpected find . . . like the house . . . Why hadn't she come along too with him and her father? . . . Or the old boy might have stayed at home without particularly disappointing anyone . . . Then Peggy could have shown the house to him. How jolly it would have been to get in out of this blazing sun, and to have had her to show him round instead of her rotten old father! He cursed himself for not having asked her to go with them. He thought of the look she had given him as she left the dining-room. 'She'd have come fast enough if I'd asked her!' He saw in thought her dark-lashed grey eyes and her smile, and cursèd himself again. 'She's just the looks I like,' he said to himself. 'Up to a bit of weight, but plenty of quality—though God knows where she gets it, seeing how she's bred!'

He laughed, and getting up, strolled across the wide enclosure to the hall-door steps, and began to examine the carved marriage-stones. 'Prendevil-Martine,' 'Prendevill-O'Rorke', 'Prendeville-Devannes'. The names with their archaic spelling, and the roughly-carved coats, blurred and lichened by age, deepened in Burgrave the sentiment of respect for the old house, and of jealousy for its owners. He thought of his father, and of how he had paid a whacking price to the College of Heralds for the coat-of-arms, and the crest that now adorned the back of his watch. These people, these Prendevilles here, had 'em for nothing. Well, they couldn't have paid for them if they had wanted them—and that was that!

Then he heard his name called, and saw Mr Weldon and a young girl crossing the enclosure.

'The door's open all the time, Sir Har'ld! Miss Nessie kindly says we might have walked straight in, no harm done, and no offence taken! You've met Miss Prendeville, I know. You went to the races together, to be sure!'

145

Burgrave wondered a little at the faint colour that rose in Nessie's face. He took it as the innocent tribute of girlish rusticity to his personality. He seldom forgot that he was a fine young man of over six feet high, and never that he had fifteen thousand a year and a title. For Nessie, he was a rather alarming, strange Englishman, who was connected in her mind with the altogether hateful episode of the races, and the remembrance of which never failed to frighten and shame her.

'You'll find all the rooms open, Mr Weldon,' she said.

'Miss Shibby isn't in it, is she, my dear?' asked Young Johnny, anxiously. Nessie was his point of friendly contact with the household at the Tower.

'Didn't you meet her? She's gone to see old Mr Weldon,' said Nessie, surprised. 'Dr Magner came for her and drove her to see him. Would you like me to show you the house?'

'Ah, we came the short cut—that's how we missed them. No thank you, my dear child,' he continued. 'I'll not trouble you. I know the house—I've known it longer than you have, I'm afraid I must say!' Young Johnny showed his glittering false teeth in the middle of his thin grey beard, in a friendly smile, offering to youth the pathetic, truckling homage of the elderly. Then he pushed in the heavy door, and stood aside, deferentially, to let Burgrave precede him into the house.

Chapter 21

Sir Harold Burgrave was a young man who possessed in a marked degree the great quality of thoroughness. It is one that is more often met with in England than in Ireland, the axiom 'If it'll do, it'll do,' with its seducing obviousness, its ultimate demoralising power, being less generally accepted on the sterner side of the Channel. The position with regard to Inver House postulated itself, almost unconsciously, for Burgrave, much as follows. He was interested in architecture. Inver House was pronounced to be a perfect specimen for its period. (As to that he would judge for himself, whatever old Weldon's authorities might say.) He had a large, idle balance at his bank; and, finally, the fishing in the river was of the best and there was nothing but a ruin at Moyroe.

These various considerations worked together to the common end of impelling Burgrave to an examination of the Big House that should leave nothing in connection with it undiscovered; and they had the secondary result of reducing young Johnny—(who, it will be remembered, was not as young as he was, and had decidedly over-eaten himself at lunch, out of sheer politeness)—to a state of really pitiable exhaustion. Burgrave paced the great pillared hall to and fro, estimating its every measurement, with the ardent pedantry of the amateur. A staircase of white stone, splendidly wide, classic in its simplicity, faced the entrance, rising from the end of the hall to a broad landing. Burgrave mounted it with enthusiasm that grew at each step, as the noble proportions of the great house unfolded themselves. From the landing, two broad flights of stairs sailed upward to the first floor, thence a single flight led to the topmost story, and, having arrived there, Burgrave set about the business of 'viewing the premises' with ordered and steady zeal. He strode up and down the corridors that ran, east and west, the full length of the house, going into every room, noting where the walls were stained by damp, (what time the roof had still awaited Miss Pindy's restoring hand) appreciating the solid finish of the woodwork, the stucco decoration of the ceilings, the brass-mounted fireplaces, the old hinged brass handles of the door locks.

'We'll leave the rooms on the ground-floor to the last,' he said to Young Johnny, trailing along at his heels like a faithful tired old dog. 'We'll take the first floor now.'

Young Johnny agreed humbly, and with awe. He had believed himself to be a practical person, and a man of business, but here was a rich young Bar'net, this proprietor of Heaven knew what palaces in his native land, excelling in methodical competence any professional house-agent whom he had ever met. Did he, thought Young Johnny, with aching legs and a sinking heart, intend to leave none of these many dim and dusty bedrooms unvisited? It appeared not. Door after door was opened and the rooms appertaining to them examined. Young Johnny, with the disabilities already mentioned, and a more than incipient touch of indigestion, crawled after his leader, feeling that nothing earth could offer would equal the simple yet debarred happiness of sitting down upon a chair.

Burgrave opened a door at the end of one of the corridors, and disclosed a very large room.

'I think they call this "Lady Isabella's room", Sir Har'ld,' Mr Weldon announced, faint yet pursuing.

The shutters were shut. Burgrave crossed the room with long steps and let in the hot afternoon sunlight.

'By George, it's furnished!' He stood for a moment taking stock of the room, and of the furniture that Shibby had recently installed. 'Not half bad those Victorian wardrobes. But oh, good Lord! What a bed! What a brute of a thing! How could anyone put a beast of a modern vulgarity like that, under that gorgeous ceiling!' Burgrave shouted his contempt, proud of his excellent taste. 'There's Nehushtan for you if you like!'

Mr Weldon had been quite prepared to admire the brass bedstead, which, indeed, as he subsequently confessed to Mrs Weldon, he reckoned very handsome. But he knew that if Sir Harold, who was evidently an authority called it 'Nehushtan,' it would be worse than tactless to contradict him. He felt very uncertain about Nehushtan, who, or what it was. 'But Louisa will know!' he thought, restfully.

Burgrave was pleased with himself and his Scriptural allusion.

'Not bad that, eh, Weldon? The brazen serpent, don't you know? I thought I had forgotten the whole thing! It's a goodish time since my mother used to push Bible lessons into me!'

'Very apt, Sir Har'ld! Very apt indeed!' replied Mr Weldon, leaning, in a condition bordering on collapse, against the brazen snakes that had had so stimulating an effect on Sir Harold's brain cells. This assimilation of the Big House had gone far beyond his expectations, beyond what had been, even, his hopes; it was, in fact, becoming a nightmare. Who could have imagined that so devastating a success would have attended his suggestion?

'—and by Jove!' went on Burgrave, 'that's a topping old mirror—Hullo! Who the devil's that?' He swung round quickly. 'I'll swear I saw someone in the mirror!'

Had Apollyon himself appeared in the mirror, Young Johnny was now incapable of what might have been considered suitable enthusiasm.   .

'Maybe it was me you saw in the glass, Sir Har'ld,' he suggested feebly. 'I'm just in the line of it for you——'

What Burgrave might have said to this prosaic suggestion cannot be told. It is probable that he would have been as indignant as are most people when they are offered a normal explanation for what appears to them to be supernatural. But as Mr Weldon spoke, the door of the room was slowly pushed in, and the figure of Captain Jas stood in the doorway.

'Ah! It was the Captain you saw!' said Mr Weldon, quickly. He went over to old Jas and took him by the hand. 'I'd no notion you were in the house at all, Captain. And how are you? I didn't see you this long time! Why you're looking grand! May I introjuce Sir Har'ld Burgrave to you? He's bin admiring the house—Sir Har'ld, this is Captain Prendeville—the owner of this fine house!' he added, with a flourish.

Burgrave came to the door and took the huge, purple old hand that Mr Weldon relinquished to him, murmuring a salutation.

Jas was wearing the blue knitted nightcap and the long orange frieze coat. A thick brown muffer came up so high round his neck that the grey locks of his hair and the strands of his thin white beard were displayed on it. In spite of the heat of the afternoon, his hand was so cold that Burgrave let it go quickly.

'I am glad to meet Sir Harold Burgrave,' the old Captain said, with the touch of old-fashioned formality and deference, and the accent of good-breeding, that still were evident in his manner and voice. 'It is kind of you, Sir, to have a good word for this poor old place. We've—we've——' he groped for a word, 'neglected it, eh, Johnny? That's it, neglected it; that's what it is, I'm afraid!'

The smell of the coarse tobacco that fishermen smoke, was heavy about him. In his left hand was the pipe, still alight, that he had taken from his mouth at sight of the stranger, and was now keeping in retirement. 'My poor mother would never live here,' he continued, 'she used to say it was too big——' He looked at Burgrave alertly. The rare excitement of meeting a stranger had aroused him. 'I always said it was a d——d barracks! Didn't I, Johnny? I'd had enough of barracks in my soldiering days! Hadn't I, Johnny?'

'You had, Captain, you had indeed!' agreed Young Johnny.

'It's a very fine house, Sir,' said Burgrave, respectfully. He thought: 'The old chap's a Sahib! How on earth did he come to be the father of that cub?'

'Ah, it was a fine house in my grandfather's time——' said the old Captain, 'or was it my great-grandfather's time, Johnny? I forget——?' The old voice wavered, the slender jet of vitality began to fail. 'My son will have to—to——' the old voice tottered and failed.

'Do it up again, Captain, isn't that it!' consoled Young Johnny, who was a kindly man up to a certain point; 'or you might make a fortune for Kit, and sell it to someone that'd give you a nice price for it! That'd be better than spending money on it, don't you think?'

Burgrave looked hard at Mr Weldon, and then at Jas. Was this a put-up thing between them? *He* wasn't going to be rushed——

But Mr Weldon was only regarding the old Captain with a friendly smile; and the Captain had raised his left hand, and was gazing at the pipe in it, with a yearning eye; he was obviously oblivious to all other earthly concerns.

No, there was no conspiracy, Burgrave was satisfied as to that. For himself, he told himself, he would keep an open mind in the matter; he would do nothing in a hurry. Burgrave was young, and not without his enthusiasm, but heredity and training had made him wise beyond his years.

'Well, Mr Weldon,' he said, 'with Captain Prendeville's permission, we might have a look at the rest of the house——'

As has already been said, Miss Pindy and Doctor Magner had once been very good friends, and the friendship, having survived one serious check, had weathered well, even though it had changed in character, as, inevitably, such friendships must. Each still held the other, instinctively, a little higher than the rest of the world. They met seldom, but the mutual confidence held.

The drive from the Tower to the Lodge was a short one, and the more so that the Doctor always drove a good pony, and made it go. There was but little time for conversation, and Shibby, who had been startled by the sudden summons, lost no time in inquiring into Old John's condition, and soon gathered that in the Doctor's opinion he was shaky enough, though he wouldn't say he mightn't puck on for a while yet. 'But isn't he ninety-two years old!' said the Doctor. 'And isn't that a terrible age for any man to be! Ah, the old man is worn out! It's only the force of habit keeps him going. He's been at it now so long it's chronic with him. There's nothing else at all keeping him alive. Some little thing it'll be, and the old boy'll go out like a candle!' Then he temporised, as doctors must. 'But after all, there's no saying——' He gave the pony an unnecessary touch of the whip. What was the good of prophesying? A patient would always make a fool of you if he could, one way or the other——

'Well, I'll be sorry for old Mr Weldon, whenever he goes,' Shibby said. 'There was something about him I always liked. Keep him alive, now, Willy, as long as you can.'

'Well, to be sure I will!' said Doctor Magner, impatiently. 'Isn't that what I'm here for?'

Women were like that, he thought, telling you to do the obvious thing—even Shibby! And why should Shibby, of all people, be asking him to keep old John Weldon alive? What on earth affair of hers was it? The day was very hot, and the doctor had been at the Dispensary all the morning, and was tired, and his temper was, perhaps, not quite what it might have been had Shibby thought more of him than of those unborn children.

They had come near the gate that had been the means of Old John's overthrow, before Shibby spoke again. For the Doctor there was no continuity in her thought, yet its sequence had been as closely related as are the definitions of a problem of Euclid.

'Willy, d'ye know anything of a fellow in the village by the name of Jimmy Connor?'

'I do. Plenty.'

'What sort is he?'

'He's a dog-idle blackguard, and he comes out of the worst-conducted pub in the place!'

Shibby nodded her head. 'I knew well that was the way, but I wanted to hear what you'd say. And the girl——?'

Dr Magner looked sideways at Shibby, and paused for an instant. 'Well, the girl—yes—the girl—well, if you want the truth, Shibby, I'd say she was 'no any good' as they say.'

'I'd say the same,' said Shibby.

'The mother is in the County Asylum,' the Doctor went on, 'and the father's destroyed himself with drink—there's none of them fit company for any decent people!'

'He knows!' thought Shibby, with a pang through her heart.

'The people in this village have been marrying and intermarrying in a vicious circle since the days of Adam!' continued the Doctor, in a large generalisation, 'and those that aren't mad are bad, and mostly they're both! Here, catch hold of the reins till I get down and open the gate,' he ended, getting out of the trap as he spoke, glad of a reason for discontinuing the conversation.

Old John was sitting up in his bed, propped high with pillows, when Mrs Weldon brought his two visitors to his room.

'Here's the Doctor back again, Father,' she said, 'and he's very kindly brought Miss Isabella with him. You said you wanted to see her.'

'And so I did, and so I did!' said Old John, cheerfully. He had a red cotton pocket-handkerchief tied round his head. His white shirt, whose services were demanded as much by night as by day, was unbuttoned at the neck, and permitted a view of a puffy chest, overgrown with grey hair as an old tree trunk is overgrown with grey lichen. The bed clothes were strained over the great globe of his stomach. On its summit rested his right hand, in which he held a long blue envelope. His broad face was yellow, instead of its wonted crimson, and was netted with purple veins; but his manner was no less alert than its wont; his little pale-blue eyes, with their yellowish irises, twinkled with cordiality, and his voice as he spoke his salutations was but little more husky than usual.

'I'm greatly obliged to the two o' ye, coming this way to me, on the minyute! When the Doctor was here, awhile ago, I thought I was for dying, and says I "B" Jingo! I'll see me old friend Shibby again before I go!" But now, sure, I'm grand!'

'As grand as you are,' said the Doctor, repressively, 'you can keep quiet in your bed till I see you again.'

'And so I will too, and welcome,' replied the patient. 'I'll do that much for ye, if you'll oblige me now. It's just a little matter o' business I had——' The little eyes rolled towards his daughter-in-law. 'I wonder, my dear, did the grand gentleman you had below leave e'er a drop of port wine after him? I wouldn't wish it that me old friends here would go away and have it to say we didn't as much as ask them had they a mouth on their face!'

Mrs Weldon took the hint in good part.

'Indeed yes, Father,' she said, quickly. 'That would never do, would it! John's out with Sir Harold, but I'll go down and see about it. Of course they must have some refreshment.'

She left the room.

Old John twisted himself on his pillows to see if the door were safely shut. Then he took a long paper out of the blue envelope and handed it to Shibby. 'Read that now, my dear,' he said, watching her.

Shibby went red all over her face, a sudden fierce flush. She walked to the window, and unfolding the paper, began to read it.

'See that now, Doctor, how she can read it without the glasses!' Old John said, admiringly, looking down from the height of his ninety-two years on what he regarded as Shibby's youth. 'Isn't it well to be young!'

'It's more than *I* could do!' said the Doctor, 'and I believe there isn't more than a year between her and me!'

'For shame for ye to talk about a lady's age!' said Old Falstaff, faithful to his rôle as gallant. 'We'll change the conversation, and I'll tell ye what I sent for ye for. That's my will she's reading, that Turnbull in Monarde is after drawing up for me——'

'What a hurry you're in to make your will!' said the Doctor, playfully, 'why, you're not turned the hundred yet. Time enough then to think of such things!'

While he spoke he was asking himself what affair Old John Weldon's will was of Shibby's. 'She's not mentioned in it, anyhow! Nor I neither! Worse luck!' he thought. 'But why has she got to read it!'

Old Falstaff shook his red handkerchief head and leaned back among his pillows, coughing a little. 'No, no, there's no time like the present——' He was watching Shibby narrowly, trying to see her face.

The Doctor had his finger on his pulse. 'You're tired now,' he said, 'wouldn't you leave the will alone till to-morrow?'

As he spoke, Shibby turned from the window and came to the bedside. She placed the paper in the old man's hand.

'Well?' he said, eagerly.

Shibby's face was flushed, and her large blue eyes were as bright as if she were indeed the girl that Old John felt her to be.

'I think you've done what's no more than fair and right,' she said, deliberately. 'I think it's a good will, Mr Weldon.'

Old John looked hard at her. 'Are we justified, Shibby, my dear? Will it go right?'

'I'd say it will,' replied Shibby. Then she met Dr Magner's interested eyes. She held up her head and met his gaze, defiantly. It was no affair of Willy Magner's. He might think what he liked. 'It surely will, Mr Weldon,' she repeated with decision.

'Well now, you'll keep your mouth shut, my dear?' said Old John, his eyes ever on her face.

'No fear but I will!' said Shibby.

Her voice satisfied him. He raised himself again. 'There should be pen and ink on the table behind there,' he said, trying to turn, 'and a big book——'

'Here, I have a pen,' said the Doctor. He took a fountain-pen

155

from his pocket.

'Wait awhile now,' said Old John, 'give me first me book off the table——' He opened it, and from between its end page and the cover he took a sealed envelope. He handed it to Shibby. 'Put that in a safe place, my dear, and don't open it at all till I'm put away in Deer Island!'

Shibby saw that on it were written the words, 'For Miss Isabella Prendeville (or Pindy). Not to be opened until after my death. J. W.' Silently she took it from him and put it in her bosom, fastening her gown over it. The old man, also silent, watched her with approval.

'This is me old ledger, that has all me accounts in it,' he said, patting the big brown book, and cocking a humorous eye at Shibby. 'Isn't that a shuitable thing to sign me will on! Now Doctor, the pen, if you please——'

He took the pen in his big, pudgy, pale old hand; he pointed it first at the Doctor and then at Shibby.

'Take notice the pair of ye, Doctor Willy Magner, and Miss Shibby Pindy, that this is my last will and testament, me being in me right mind, Glory be to God! and you being the same—as far as I can see! He! he! he!' He wrote his name clearly and carefully. Slowly he took a piece of blotting-paper out of the ledger, and blotted the signature. Then he handed the pen, ceremoniously, to the Doctor. 'Sign you here! . . . Very good! That's easier read than your prescriptions! . . . And now you, Shibby, my dear——'

Miss Pindy's small iron hand shook a little as she wrote her name in the tidy script that she had learned at the National School—'Isabella Hynes (or Pindy)'—her mother's name, the only name that was legally hers, and the detestable nick-name by which she was known, that she shared with those she despised. It was seldom that she had occasion to sign her name, never before, thus formally and importantly, and it is hard to say which of those two designations she found more hateful to write, she, who knew herself to be a Prendeville by every token of race, hands, feet, eyes, and stature.

'Never mind,' she said to herself, 'a good work is done this day, and what do I matter, one way or th'other!'

Old Falstaff looked critically at the two signatures. 'Time was,' he said with a wink at Dr Magner, 'when I thought ye'd have had but the one name between ye!'

'Come, come!' said the Doctor, 'you're getting light-headed! Shibby, would you please ask Mrs Johnny for some hot milk, and a half-glass of whisky in it? I'd like to see the patient drink it before we go.'

Chapter 23

It appeared to Peggy that Saturday morning took a long time in coming. Each of the three intermediate days had held so many arduous moments that they had undoubtedly doubled their natural length. Through all the three days Sir Harold Burgrave had held the stage. 'He was like Juggernaut!' she told Nessie, who had stolen over on Friday evening after Juggernaut had been put away for the night in his yacht. 'We all went down before him! Father was the high-priest, of course, and saw to it that the burnt-offerings were not over-cooked, and I'm the human sacrifice!'

'Ah, Peggy,' said Nessie, in her soft, singing voice. 'Don't be sacrificed! He's not good enough for you—I wouldn't like him. And Kit hates the sight of him. He was talking to Kit about the Big House—saying what a pity it was to see it the way it was, and wondering why the gates weren't painted, and things like that. Kit was mad!'

'You'd better talk to Father about him then, and tell him you'll forbid the banns!'

'Oh, *Peggy*!' says Nessie, shocked, just as Peggy intended her to be.

It was her rôle with Nessie to be daring, a woman of the great world that little Nessie had never seen; she tried to mock and swagger, and none the less hid a frightened heart. This big, devouring young man, with his loud, confident voice, and his large appetite, who looked at her as if he wanted to eat her up too, and took her father's homage, and everything else, as his right—did he mean to take her too? It was all very well for Mother to like him, and to say he had a kind heart, and that there was something reliable about him—that was only because he was English, and he was polite to her. Mother wouldn't have to marry him . . . (And she had married Father! She couldn't be very——) Peggy began to laugh, and told herself she had better try and think of something else. But it wasn't easy, and Sir Harold was very incessant . . .

He and she and her father had driven on the outside car to

Moyroe, and had picnicked in the ruined house. The roof was like a rotting skeleton leaf, with network of sagging rafters, and a few patches of slates clinging to them. The windows and the doors were gone.

'Ah, the people stole them,' her father had said apologetically. 'You couldn't expect but they would. But that was before *my* time, Sir Har'ld. It was like a wreck for them—they just came and got what they wanted, when they wanted it!'

'What a country!' Burgrave had responded, 'you Irish are all thieves! The men rob decent Englishmen's houses, and the girls steal their hearts! What have you got to say about that Miss Peggy!'

'I'm half-English!' Peggy had defied him. 'My mother's English!'

'That doesn't count!' Burgrave had replied, exulting over her. 'Women have no nationality, only what they get from men! If you want to be English you'll have to marry an Englishman!'

And then her father had sniggered sycophantically, as she told Nessie, and had sneaked away and left her alone with him. 'But I said I had a headache—which was a lie, of course—and I went off and sat on the car in the shade. He thinks he's only got to want a thing to get it! And he does too, if Father can get it for him!'

Another of those heavy days was devoted to the yacht, a day that gave Peggy a headache in earnest, and that tested the endurance of Young Johnny to the core. He had accepted the invitation with the respectful enthusiasm with which he enveloped his liege-lord as with a garment.

'It'll be like new life to Peggy and me to get outside the harbour! But I'm afraid we'll har'ly coax Mrs Weldon to come beyond the moorings——'

Mrs Weldon did indeed show the strength of character proper to her country and to her early profession, and had held to her resolve of being put ashore after luncheon. But for her daughter and husband no such escape was possible. Peggy watched the gig that conveyed her mother to the pier, with such feelings as Andromeda may have known when she was deposited upon her rock: (and the rock was at least stationary, and was not shared with her by the sea-monster). Then she resigned herself to what might be in store and a deck-chair.

It was a windless day of burning sun, when the sea was as molten glass, and the air trembled over it as if in the blast of a furnace. The *Clio* slid out of the harbour under her auxiliary steam, with snowy awnings keeping the sun from her scarcely less snowy decks, and with her owner, clad in tropic white, standing astride the tiller, steering with his legs, splendidly ignoring the fact that he had any occupation or duty save that of talking to his guests. The *Clio* was soon outside the harbour and beyond the lighthouse on Ingard Head. Soon she had left the wide bay of Monarde behind her, and holding a left-handed course, she headed west for the open sea. The horizon, miraged in the white glare, was high in the sky, with pale bands of blue and silver joining it with the lower planes of ocean. A school of dolphins were wheeling over and over in front of the yacht, their circular black bodies and sharp fins made them look like parts of some huge piece of machinery, broken loose and run mad. A flight of oyster-catchers whirred across the *Clio*'s bows, glittering, as their swinging, twisting course showed them now black and now white, like sparks lit, and extinguished, and relit, quicker than thought. Snake-necked cormorants rose and fell, passive, on the blue oil of the long, gentle, Atlantic swell, until the sound of the yacht's engines roused them from trance to bend their long necks and to dive, with that utter perfection of curve which seems the inevitable sequence of their serene poise, is almost part of it, so imperceptible is the absolute moment of disappearance. On the long, long slopes of the swell a couple of open fishing-boats were climbing and descending, with the unconcern of the gulls that were floating beside them. It seemed as if their red lug-sails were set for no purpose but to blot with their reflections the pale hollows of the sea. They were as intimately in the picture as the dolphins, or the cormorants, or the gulls—which was more than anyone, even her skipper, who adored her, could say for the *Clio*, bustling along with a throbbing heart, like a fine lady late for an appointment.

Burgrave left the tiller to his skipper, and came and sat beside Peggy and her father.

'Feeling all right, eh? I've got a nice day for you, what! You can't say I've not squared the Clerk of the Weather, can you?'

'*Quite* all right, Sir Har'ld!' replied Young Johnny in eager italics.

'It's all *most* enjoyable!'

Which was heroic of Young Johnny, because, as a matter of fact, he was feeling both dizzy from the heat and sleepy from a large lunch, but seeing—as he subsequently complained to Mrs Weldon—that Peggy 'wasn't even trying to be so much as civil, *he* did his best to show a little decency of behaviour!'

The effort was ignored by the host. Burgrave was determined to extort the approval of his other guest. He rather enjoyed her mutinous attitude.

'I'll bring her to a small helm before I'm done with her!' he told himself, looking with the pleasure of anticipated possession at Peggy's shaded face, and watching for her curly eyelashes to lift and release the grey flash that he had begun to find as enchanting as it was amusing.

'Well, Miss Peggy? Had enough of it? You've only to say the word "'Bout Ship!" and about she comes! I'm not running away with you!' He leaned towards her and murmured, with studied audacity: 'Though I'm not saying I shouldn't like to!'

The flash that he had played for, came.

'If it came to running away, I might run faster than you! I should *want* to run away!'

'That's all right!' said Burgrave, laughing delightedly. 'So should I!'

Peggy stood up, looking pale; she felt that controversy of any sort was, at this moment, beyond her power.

'I wonder if I might go downstairs and lie down? The sun's given me rather a headache——'

'We don't call it "downstairs" aboard ship,' said Burgrave, enjoying the ignorance that he could instruct. 'Let me help you——' He took her hand, and, Peggy's unwilling spirit had to submit herself to the weakness of the flesh, and accept his support. He saw her safely on to a sofa in the saloon, and stood over her, grinning with the heartless grin of the inured yachtsman at the victim of misplaced self-confidence.

'You'll soon be all right. I'll put her about now, and we'll get out of the swell— We'll run away! Eh?'

'I wish to goodness *you'd* go away!' said Peggy furiously, made

161

reckless by misery.

Thus it was that Young Johnny's endurance was tested, not so much by the action of the deep (though it did certainly predispose him to silence) as by the necessity of keeping his host entertained.

'All I could do was to discuss the Big House with him,' Mr Weldon told his wife. 'And I can assure you, Louisa, he's thinking seriously about it! I'm to go over it again with him to-morrow, and he'll see the gardens and the stables and all that. It's my belief he'll buy it. He says he'd like a house here. I just said, quietly, you know, that it was a pity the demesne wasn't going with the house, but that it was mine—or the same as mine. And o' course that's the same as saying that it'll be Peggy's one of these days.'

Mr Weldon paused, and his eyes and Mrs Weldon's met, in question, as to the mother's, in confident satisfaction as to the father's. Joy was indisputably beginning to bud from the thorn.

'I tell you,' went on Mr Weldon, emphatically, 'that if I ever saw a man reely gone on a girl I saw it to-day! *He* has his mind made up about that right enough! . . . And the work he made about her because she had a bit of a headache! Up and down stairs a dozen times, and asking how she was feeling——'

'Yes, I do think he has a good heart,' said Mrs Weldon, thoughtfully. 'There *is* something nice about him——'

'"Something"!' said Mr Weldon, indignantly. 'It was only too nice to her he was! Having the steward to open a bottle of champagne for her—and only a mouthful she would take! *I* was glad enough of a drop—I considered that it wouldn't be held to invalidate my pledge, being that I wasn't feeling too well myself——'

'You were quite right to take it, John dear,' said Mrs Weldon, authoritatively. 'It would be regarded in the light of a necessary restorative.'

'I felt sure you'd think so, my dear,' said Young Johnny, (whose conscience had its sensitive spots) with gratitude.

Sir Harold and Mr Weldon were hardly seen at Demesne Lodge on Friday. The further inspection of the Big House and its surroundings occupied the morning, and, after lunching again on the yacht, Mr Weldon returned alone, bearing with him Sir Harold's farewells to the ladies.

162

'He's going off to a regatta on the Clyde,' Mr Weldon reported. 'But he'll be back again shortly. He says he won't be satisfied till he pulls a big fish out of his own stretch of the Fiddaun! He asked me would I like to go with him to the regatta!' Young Johnny added, trying not to look too elated, 'but I told him I was too busy. I had to be in Clytagh collecting rents for himself for the next three days, and the Quarter Sessions coming on at Monarde after that——'

'Well now, John, wasn't that a pity? Wouldn't it have been a pleasant change for you?' said Mrs Weldon, moved by that impulse, common to most people, and specially active in wives where their husbands are concerned, to urge upon another the acceptance of an invitation to leave home, which the advocate herself would not consider for so much as an instant, were the positions reversed.

Peggy said quickly: 'What time are you starting, Father?'

'Oh, I must ketch the early train,' said Mr Weldon. 'I've got a lot to do—and that reminds me—run out like a good child, and tell George I'll want the mare in the trap, at 6.30 sharp.'

'Nothing could be better!' thought Peggy, going on her errand. 'Mother won't matter!'

Everything, after these days of stress, was now going to be pleasant. The yacht gone, father away, and good old Nelson, the brown horse, available for rides. Peggy was down in the narrow stableyard next morning, a full quarter of an hour before George Pindy had saddled Nelson, and it was still five minutes to the half hour when she rode up to the gates of the Big House.

Kit was not there. She rode in through the half-open gates, and across the weedy gravel sweep to the foot of the steps. The hall-door faced south, and the sun had come round the corner and was touching with gold the more salient devices of the marriage-stones, like a skilful illuminator. What a wonderful house it was, Peggy thought, how perfectly wonderful to feel that one owned it, that to live in it was your right, your birthright! That was what Kit could feel! And Sir Harold, never! It was Kit's house, with Kit's crest over the door, and all those coats-of-arms belonged to Kit's ancestors. Happy Kit, to be able to look back through the centuries and to know that— then she checked herself as she thought of Kit's half-recognised kin— 'Never mind! *He* isn't a Pindy! *He* comes straight from that lovely Kit in the picture! Not that the boy in the picture is really any more lovely than——' She checked herself again. 'What nonsense I'm talking——' and just then Kit came cantering round the end of the house on a long-legged young bay horse that he was training for a farmer. He swung in at the gates and cantered up to Peggy. He looked extraordinarily handsome, like some bright creature from another sky—St Michael or St George, she thought. As he laughed a greeting, mocking her for her too-early rising, she felt something stir in her bosom, something that rose and fell and trembled . . .

'Where shall we go?' he said, airily. 'You've the top o' the morning and all the world before you! This beggar wants a gallop. What about the lighthouse? It'd be jolly on the Long Strand—and there'd be no flies!'

Chapter 24

Shibby had for two days considered in silence the contents of old John Weldon's will. They had satisfied her. Nevertheless, it was only after deep reflection that, on Friday night, she had decided to disclose to Kit the substance of what she had learned. It had been plain to her for some time that Kit was going in the way she had planned for him. Since the night that he had fought with Jimmy Connor, he had kept clear of Cloon and its public-houses, and also of that other danger that she feared most of all.

'It wasn't but a notion he had of her, and she couldn't hold him! She did for herself entirely with that blackguarding that they had at the races——' Then she considered Peggy. To be sure her beautiful boy might easy do better than the like of her . . . But to join once more the Big House and the Demesne, and a good penny to the back o' that, that would hold them together . . . And indeed she was a fine girl enough, a good big handsome healthy girl, and sensible; that was the English drop she got from her mother . . . and there was no doubt but that he was thinking of her. Not a day but they were riding together, or playing—what's that game they have?—back in the big yard . . . But for all, it might be no harm to say a word. There was, she told herself, no good in saying too much. Shibby had ever an inherent reluctance to letting a cat out of a bag. It would be sufficient, she felt, with Kit, to show but the tip of the cat's tail—and safer too, for all reasons.

So it was that on Friday evening the tip of the tail was exhibited to Kit, and Kit had regarded it with a disappointing lack of enthusiasm.

'Peggy's to have the Demesne, is she? She'll not make a fat lot o' money out o' that!'

'She won't be trusting to the Demesne alone, I can tell ye!' Shibby had retorted indignantly. Whereon Kit had shut his mouth and would say nothing, and Shibby had to content herself with thinking that when Kit kept his mouth shut he meant business.

Shibby was an early riser; on Saturday morning she had heard Kit going early to the stables and mounting his horse, and she had then followed him down the lane from the Tower, and had watched him down the lane from the Tower, and had watched him and Peggy ride out together through the old gateway. She stood there until they were out of sight, looking at them as they rode down the long straight avenue, Kit's young horse dancing along sideways beside the stolid Nelson, the riders turning to each other, talking and laughing.

'Well, I can do no more!' said Shibby, and went back to the Tower to get the Captain his morning cup of tea.

Kit and Peggy meanwhile, rode on under the trees, and turned off the main avenue into the way that led to the Crooked Bridge, and so on into the village of Cloon. They trotted through the village, bringing sleepy, rosy children and yapping cur-dogs out on to the doorsteps. People go to bed late, and sleep late, in the listless western villages; only one house showed other signs of life, a small public-house from which a red-handed young man, came forth, and stood and watched them coming, and continued to watch them until they had turned the next corner.

As they passed him, trotting fast, the young bay horse plunging and pulling, and scarcely taking two steps of equal length, Peggy called out a good morning to him. The young man made no rejoinder.

'He's not very polite!' said Peggy, laughing.

'He wouldn't be!' Kit replied cryptically, but Peggy was too much engaged in keeping Nelson going to hear what he said.

The village was soon left behind, and leaving the road that led to the lighthouse, they turned down the side road, through the sand hills, that went to the Long Strand.

There is a fascination in a long stretch of sandy shore which is hard to explain, but is none the less irresistible. Perhaps it is the simple perfection of the substance, its uniformity, its colour, its smoothness, its greatness, its smallness, the endlessness of the supply, and yet its elusiveness; the magic way that a handful, gripped however tightly, will run and pour away through the fingers that try to hold it. Ingard Head was all compact of the finest, purest sand, banked up during the ages against the long reef of rocks that was its western rampart against the Atlantic. Its humped back had somehow consolidated itself into pale green pasture, from which little sheep, like white mice, gnawed a scanty living. Lower came the grey bent-grass, sparse as an old man's hair, and lower still, in the loose sand above high-water-mark, the sea holly grew in spiny clumps of exquisite colour, turquoise, and pale grey, and seagreen. The tide was going out; Kit led the way across the dunes, between the road and the shore, and on, across the sand, to the edge of the thin receding wave, where the going was sound and hard. The harbour was all of gleaming silver, just ruffled by a light morning wind that had no strength in it, and would draw its last breath soon, when the sun had gained fuller power; but the day was young still, and the little wind came lightly ashore with the freshness of the night and the sea in it, and the tiny wavelets hissed and seethed, and fizzed like champagne, as they ran back over the yellow sand.

The way from the road to the shore that Kit, by chance, had taken, led them through the dunes to the very spot where that earlier Kit Prendeville, his grandfather, had waded out to meet D'Arcy of Milltown. The cross that his widow had put there to his memory, stood just above, among the sand-hills, stained with patches of orange lichen, roughened with the storms of nearly ninety years. Peggy gave it a glance, and thought how distinguished it would be to say that one's grandfather had been killed in a duel. Kit, oblivious to the privilege that was his, as soon as he felt the firmness of the wet sand, set the prancing bay horse going in earnest, and went away at speed, shouting to Peggy to follow him. She followed, at Nelson's sodden bone-shaking gallop, for a half mile, while Kit and the bay, thundering on, passed the Mile point, and rapidly dwindled to a speck, hopeless to overtake. Then Peggy pulled her horse to a walk, and turning his willing head homewards, let him pace on, in sunshine that grew more fierce at each moment, giving warning that on a blazing August morning it was well to be at home by nine of the clock.

And then, in this moment of peace, and beauty, and solitude, thoughts that for these last few weeks she had been evading and refusing to entertain, at last forced themselves uppermost and insisted on being considered.

Is it worth while, is it even possible, to try and crystallise into set words the swift, capricious, shy emotions of a young girl? In Peggy's mind, round a single centre, fancies like soap-bubbles, formed, and glowed with many colours, and broke . . . or like butterflies that flutter about a flower, falling and rising, dwelling, and whirling away, her thoughts quivered and played round the thought of Kit. She mocked at herself, and mocked at her thought of him. She summed up all that seemed to her against him, and while she told herself that he was nothing but an illiterate country-boy, she saw him, in the mirror of her mind, coming galloping to her through the big gates, with the sun in his hair and the blue of the morning in his eyes. Again came that stir and tumult in her bosom, that was a physical thing, and could not be gainsaid, and left her shaken and afraid of herself.

'I'll not wait for him! I'll go home by myself!'

She pushed the reluctant Nelson into a slow trot, and tried to set her mind to hope that she could get away before Kit discovered her flight. But she had gone only a very little way before she heard, as she had known she would hear it, his voice shouting her name; and the rhythmic sound of his horse's galloping feet came nearer and nearer, a sound and a rhythm which can have in them a quality as thrilling as the beat of a drum calling to action.

'What a dirty trick!' laughed Kit, ranging along side of her, leaning from his tall horse towards her, looking into her eyes with the delightful smile that was so confident, so possessive, so beguiling. 'Getting away with a start, when my back's turned! Come on! Make the old beggar gallop this last half mile!'

They were still some distance from the place where they must return to the road, when Kit pulled in his horse abruptly.

'Better not bring 'em in too hot,' he said quickly, looking hard at a small figure, that was a couple of hundred yards or so from them, the figure of a small girl, barefoot, with a black shawl over her head; she was alone and was walking very fast, and had just passed the old cross among the dunes. Kit's brow had clouded and his voice had changed. 'We'd better walk these horses for a bit, it's getting infernally hot——'

The girl hurried on, sometimes running, sometimes walking, steering an irregular course, but making for the sea. She crossed the dark strip left by the falling tide, and ran to the very margin of the water. Almost, to the two watching her, it seemed that she stood in the sea. The Big House of Inver, grey amid its surrounding trees, faced her, high on the opposite shore across the blue water. The girl, her back to the riders, stood still for a moment; then, as they watched her, she flung out her arms from beneath the shawl. Her fists were clenched; it was as though she was denouncing the Big House. The black shawl slipped from her head, and the sunshine lit up coils of red hair, heaped untidily on her head.

Kit's fears became definite, he recognised Maggie Connor.

'I know who that girl is,' he said hastily. 'She's mad. Her mother's shut up, and she should be the same. Come back, we'll keep clear of her—we can get up to the road back here—come on!'

While he was speaking Maggie walked straight in front of her into the sea, and stood, with the water above her knees, still gesticulating with waving arms. They could hear her voice, gabbling, shrilly and incessantly.

'Is she going to drown herself?' whispered Peggy, in horror. 'We must stop her——'

At the same instant Maggie turned and saw them. She came out of the water, and leaned forward, staring at the riders, shading her eyes with her hands, the sun full in her face.

'Come on, I tell you!' said Kit, roughly. 'She'll come to no harm—there's no good waiting here——'

He gave the bay horse an angry dig with the spurs. The horse, with a tremendous plunge, sprang into a gallop. Peggy, taken by surprise, was slower in starting, and before Nelson had begun to go, she heard loud calling from the little figure by the sea's edge. Inarticulate cries, and then, Peggy asked herself, had she heard a shriek of Kit's name?

She caught up to Kit, where he had checked on the road beyond the sand-dunes.

'She was calling to you! She was saying "Kit, Kit!"'

'Very likely she was,' said Kit coolly, 'there's plenty here knows me and my name well enough, loonies and all! There's the full o' th' Asylum in this village always, if you only knew it!'

He laughed a little as he spoke, but it seemed to Peggy that his voice was strained, and he looked pale.

'He thinks I was frightened!' she thought, with a melting heart.

Chapter 25

The inward serenity imparted to Miss Pindy by the knowledge of old John Weldon's dispositions had enabled her to endure with a fairly easy mind the visits of 'the Englishman' to the Big House.

'Let him look at it till he's tired looking!' she said, in discussion of the matter with an old cousin of her mother's, whom she occasionally imported to assist in her cleaning operations, and in whom she placed a certain share of confidence. '*He'll* never have part nor lot in it!'

The cousin, whose name was Judy Davin, gave an assenting snort indicative of her contempt for Sir Harold Burgrave. Then she said, cautiously, 'Did ye hear, Shibby, that that Connor gerr'l— Foxy Mag they calls her—isn't well this while back?'

'What ails her?' said Shibby, her face hardening.

'Going quare-like in the head, they say she is. Faith, I can hear her all times meself—screeching singing she'd be; or maybe roaring crying. I'd hear be night through the wall o' me house.'

'Kind mother for her!' commented Shibby, shortly.

'There's some that's saying too,' resumed Judy Davin, in a lowered voice, 'that she's carrying a child!'

The two women were working in the drawing-room of the Big House; Shibby was dusting the furniture, her cousin was sweeping. The pause in Shibby's dusting was only momentary.

'I believe it,' she said grimly.

'And wasn't that too the same way with the mother! Wasn't it old Father Scanlan that made James Connor marry her before all came to all!' said old Judy Davin, with the usual laugh allotted to such a theme, the laugh that is not so much depraved as stupidly traditional.

Shibby's eyes had met those in the portrait of her ancestress, the Lady Isabella Devannes, and upon her spirit a shadow fell. A hopelessness. Who could struggle against this force, this inevitable drag of the tide of blood on to the rocks! The word Heredity she did not

171

know; what, in the case of Maggie Connor, it implied, had long since been burned into her. She knew herself as one of its victims, and knew too that its force had not spared the boy she loved.

'There's no doubt but they have chat enough in that dirty village!' she said scornfully. 'If ye were to put as much as one foot in it, ye'd come out of it with the mud all over ye!'

'Faith there's plenty mud, and black mud, going in it,' assented Judy Davin, cheerfully, 'and surely to goodness it's a fact that Jimmy Connor have a bad tongue!'

That this was a challenge to her curiosity was obvious to Shibby, but, in order to keep old Judy in her proper place, she continued her polishing of the cupboard door for some moments, before she said, disdainfully, 'I suppose it's on his own sister he's wiping his tongue!'

'No, but telling meself of some blagyarding they had at Clytagh, at the races, a whileen back. It was the way I should tell you. I told him when I'd seen yourself I'd tell ye what he said. But look, I wouldn't mind what that boy'd say! I know his carackther. He couldn't face you to look at you: there's something bad standing always between his eyes! God forgive me for saying it, and the father me own husband's cousin b' the mother! But sure I wouldn't like them Connors!'

Judy Davin resumed her sweeping with a preoccupied zeal that implied lapse of interest in the subject.

Shibby finished her work in the cupboard. Then she strode across the great room to where little old Judy Davin, now on her knees with a dust-pan and brush, was collecting the harvest of her broom.

'Judy Davin!' said Shibby, fiercely, 'what was the message Jimmy Connor had for me?'

Judy Davin, still kneeling, looked up at her cousin. 'I'll tell ye the truth the same as if it was before the Lord Almighty's altar I was kneeling!' she responded solemnly. 'It was what he said: "Let you tell Miss Pindy above at the Captain's I have my own way and my own means," says he, "and let her see my sisther righted", says he, "before I disgrace the one that disgraced her!" says he.'

Shibby drew herself up to her full height, all the pride of that ancestress, whose children had begun the downfall of the Big House of Inver, in her face. She stood, strong as a tower, looking past Lady

Isabella's portrait to that smiling boy in blue velvet, her inspiration, the *ikon* before which she renewed her vows, from which, through all these toilful years, she had drawn courage——

'I'll lie down dead in my grave first,' she said deliberately, 'and you may tell him so.'

Judy Davin was an old woman, nearly twenty years older than her cousin, and not very brave. She said to herself that she had said what she could say, and that Shibby was a fright, and it was better to stand out from her—'Let her pull out for herself now!' thought old Judy Davin, rising from her knees and waddling slowly out of the big drawing-room to the hall door steps, thence to empty her tray of dust into the area.

It was five o'clock when Miss Pindy dismissed her coadjutor and set about her usual preparations before leaving. The first duty was the search for the Captain, whose practice it was to stray after her as she moved about on her various occasions, and, specially, to follow her when she visited the Big House.

'If it wasn't for the old pipe he had I might give the day looking for him!' Shibby would complain; 'But sure the like of it for stink there isn't in Ireland!'

On this afternoon her task was light, and the potent aroma of 'shag' tobacco led her no further than the dining-room.

'Yes, yes, I'm coming,' said the old Captain, 'I was just examining the place a little. I'm afraid this feller who's after it will have something to say about "Barrack damages", eh?' He looked pleased with himself, as was his way when a word from his old days of soldiering came back to him.

'Who's after it?' Shibby was startled, and the speed of her question scattered old Jas's ideas for a moment.

'Oh, some dam' feller—some dam' feller—Kit knows—the letter came just now—what was it the feller said?' He looked at Shibby, bewilderedly, accustomed to be put right by her.

'How can I tell ye! Isn't that that I'm asking ye!'

'Wait a minute—yes—I have it—it was that English gentleman I met here. I have it all now!' Jas looked delighted with himself.

'Three thousand pound he's offered for the house! "A d——d barracks" I called it long ago! But we'll ask a good stiff price all the same! I talked to Kit about it. Kit said four thousand. It was Johnny Weldon's man—that Pindy feller—brought it, and he waited for an answer——'

'Surely ye didn't give him an answer like that, on the minute?' broke in Shibby furiously.

'Oh I don't know, I don't know what Kit did,' said old Jas, querulously. 'The letter was to me, but he took it and said he'd answer it—a great liberty I call it! A boy like that, my own son, taking my letters!—in very bad taste I call it—' Mumbling and grumbling, old Jas shuffled down the steps. Shibby waited to see him safely on level ground. Then she demanded:

'Where is Kit?'

'He was there just now—in the stable-yard—you must speak to him, Shibby. Tell him I won't have it! Tell him——'

Shibby did not wait for the Captain's further instructions. She had heard the noise of a horse's hoofs in the yard. Kit was there surely, and she hurried to find him, full of bewilderment and misgiving.

Kit was in the stable, with his coat and waistcoat off, strapping the chestnut mare with a pad of straw.

'Kit,' said Shibby, advancing upon him with a brow of storm, 'what's this story the Captain has about a letter?'

Kit straightened himself, with a hand on the mare's well-polished quarter. 'Oh, I was waiting to see you about it,' he said nervously, 'it came this afternoon—you were out——'

'I wasn't so far off!'

Kit ignored the interruption. 'It was from Johnny Weldon—it's—it's a sort of an offer from that chap that was here in the yacht—Burgrave. Johnny Weldon's his agent, y'know—' he hesitated.

'What do he want?'

Still Kit hung fire. Shibby waited, every nerve tense and strained, ready to respond, like the strings of an instrument tuned to concert-pitch.

'Well—it's what he wants——' He looked apprehensively at Shibby. Then he said, with an effort, 'He's made an offer of three thousand pounds for the Big House and the gardens.'

'And what do yourself think o' that?'

174

The storm he feared had not burst, but the clouds were black.

'Well, it isn't hardly two hours since the letter came. I d'no what I think of it yet. There's no hurry. Weldon says Burgrave'll be back in a fortnight and he'll get the answer then. I just wrote a line——'

'What did ye say?'

'I said—I said we'd consider it——'

Shibby was too angry to see how wild were his eyes, and how troubled his face.

'You know as well as I do that there'll never be money enough for anyone of us to live in it,' he went on, speaking very fast, his voice running up the scale. 'He's offering a damned good price, and——'

'And do ye tell me ye'd take it?'

'I don't know why I wouldn't! What good am I doing here in this rotten place? The sooner I'm out of it the better for me! But here I'm stuck, tied hand and foot for want of money!'

'What a hurry ye're in all of a sudden to get away! Is the want of money all that's tying ye?'

Kit looked hard into Shibby's ominous face. Her great eyes were fixed on his. The terror that had lain on his spirit since the morning, had been lifted by the excitement of Burgrave's offer, and what he looked on as the prospect of release that it brought. To Kit, who had never known what it was to have money, money meant power, omnipotence. It had seemed to him that money would open a way of escape as nothing else could. Now, with Shibby's opposition, fear fell on him again, with a rush. The prison gates, that had begun to open, were closing again. He went red up to his forehead. Tears came into the blue eyes that had the beauty of Shibby's own, but none of their force. He felt suddenly that he had better rely on Shibby. She would stand by him; he would trust her now.

'Shibby, I'm in the damndest hole any fellow ever was in! Won't you help me!'

In an instant the cloud that had threatened him was swept away. Kit knew that he had not trusted in vain.

'My child! My child!' said Shibby. Her arms were round him. She pressed him to her bosom, as she had done many times before, from his babyhood, when he had run to her for shelter, for pity, for her infinite forgiveness.

Thus she held him for a moment, murmuring over him the little peasant words of love that she used to comfort him with when he was a child; smoothing, with her small, hardened hand, the curling fair hair that she adored.

A wooden corn-bin stood near the door of the stable.

'Let me sit down, my child,' she said. 'I'm tired.'

She sat down heavily; she had worked hard all day, but it was not work that had tired her.

'Tell me now the whole story,' she said, looking up at his troubled face, with the childish yellow curls astray on his forehead, and a childish tear still wet on his cheek. 'Don't be afraid now; tell it all to me.'

Kit's spirit, quick to rise as to fall, rose with the familiar task of self-justification before a judge from whom he knew well he need not fear justice. He stood in front of her, lithe and graceful, feeling the relief of confession, telling her everything, hinting, knowing it would please her, at what he was feeling about Peggy, explaining how Maggie Connor was now standing in his path, making unlooked for trouble. 'She chucked herself at me!' said Kit, and Shibby nodded her head. Her countrywoman's heart went with him, assenting to a young man's right to act as it pleased him, reserving all her condemnation for the woman. That Kit should thus allot the blame, and, in doing so, confirm her low opinion of Maggie Connor, seemed to her no more than was natural. She heard him to the end, almost in silence. He ceased, and she sat, still silent, her eyes fixed, unseeingly, on his perturbed face, thinking hard and fast. Then she said, as if thinking aloud, 'If we could get her to th'Asylum—where her mother is this minute——'

Kit turned away from Shibby's intense gaze. It made him uneasy, he could not have told why. He had the grace to feel ashamed, and he put his hand on the young mare's quarter and fell to strapping her again.

'—Willy Magner would certify her—if we could get her put away before—before anything'd happen——?' She turned suddenly upon Kit. 'For God's sake, Kit, can't you be easy a minute, and leave the horse till I'm done with you? Didn't ye tell me just now ye seen Maggie Connor walk out into the sea, like she wanted to drown

176

herself?'

'I suppose I did,' said Kit sulkily. Into his mind the vision sprang. The bright water, and the little figure dark against it, with arms outstretched towards the Big House. 'Cursing the house, and me too!' he thought.

'Well then!' said Shibby, with a grim satisfaction, 'isn't that evidence enough? Couldn't you swear to that? Wouldn't it be the Mercy of God if we could get her put away?'

'How could I swear to such a thing as that?' Kit broke out, angrily. 'What d'ye think would be said of me if I did, no matter how mad she is?'

He said to himself that women had no decency. The very notion of him, of all people in the world, to be the one to swear he saw Maggie going to drown herself!—on his account! As if that wouldn't come out fast enough if he shoved himself in!—And how could he know if it was thinking to drown herself she was, or only just wanting to bathe her feet in the salt water! He'd have everyone laughing at him! It'd make a cat laugh at him! . . .

Shibby rose, wearily, from her seat on the corn-bin.

'I'm thinking there'll be more said of ye before all's said and done. Finish your horse now—that's all you think of!'

She went out of the stable walking slowly and heavily.

Chapter 26

The evening meal at the Tower was over. Miss Pindy was sitting by the window of the sitting-room, working, by the last light of the summer day, at something white and useful. Kit was standing by her, leaning against the curved wall, smoking a cigarette, looking down at her bent grey head with the unconscious patronage that youth bestows on age, yet admiring her, respecting her, feeling that he loved her—not as much, naturally, as she loved him—but quite a lot, yes, an awful lot. He felt shriven after that confession. His load of anxiety was as though it had been transferred to Shibby's strong shoulders. He thought, with satisfaction, that although he had generously refused to back her up in that plan about Maggie, that was no reason why she wouldn't put it through somehow, she and old Magner. 'If those two give their minds to a thing they'll mostly do it,' he said to himself, and felt comforted. It was wonderful, after all that had been on his mind all day, since he had seen Maggie on the Long Strand, to have this feeling of absolution and relief, this sense of a shifted burden.

It was past eight o'clock. Nessie was helping the Captain to his room, as usual; putting his pipe and his tobacco-pouch where he could reach them, and his candle-stick where he couldn't—'But he'll have a good try to knock it down just the same!' Kit thought, picking up his cap, and whistling to the dogs. Then he came near to Shibby, and said, 'I'm going out. I—I might meet Peggy——' His heart felt blissfully soft and happy. He stooped over his sister and kissed her forehead and whispered, 'Wish me luck, Shibby!'

Shibby's work fell to the floor. She caught Kit's hand that was on her shoulder, and kissed it.

'God bless the work!' she said, in the Irish that she had learned as a little child from her grandmother. '*Bail ó Dhia ort!* A blessing from God on thee, my fair-haired boy!'

It was the end of the last week of August. Even in that far western place, where the sun lingers on the shores of Erin as if he loved her best, the red warmth of his setting was yielding to the green pallor of dusk as Kit left the Tower and passed from the lane into the wide avenue of the Big House. He stood for a moment by the gates, facing the west, and looked down across the tree-tops to the quiet harbour. The sea, asleep, still faintly tinged with the dying colours of the sky, was like an opal. The air was languid with the lingering heat of the day. As he stood there, the colours died, and the sea went dull and grey. The long promontory of Ingard Head was like the back of some sea-monster, the nebulous rays from the lighthouse making a glow-worm light on its snout. Kit's eyes and thoughts were on the paler strip of shadow that was the Long Strand, where that morning he had seen Maggie Connor standing in the tide. He shook his head angrily and kicked a stone out of his path; then he tossed the thoughts from him.

He walked on in the growing gloom under the trees. The wood was so quiet that even the dogs, Tinker and Fly, followed tamely at his heels, mistrusting the dark silence of the undergrowth. Kit stood still when he came to the turn that led to Demesne Lodge, and waited there for a few minutes. He hated waiting; soon he struck a match and looked at his watch. It was near nine o'clock. He hadn't thought it was so late. Maybe she was ahead of him after all. It was to see the red harvest moon rise over the sea she had said she was going, on the far side of the place, and he had told her how to get to the little lake in the demesne, that was called Polranny, the Hole of the Ferns, for that there she'd get a good view to the east; up the Bay of Monarde. Of course she was ahead of him, he was making a fool of himself hanging about here. He pressed on, taking a short way through the trees to the Hole of the Ferns.

The ground, beyond trees, sloped downwards steeply; it was strewed with grey boulders whose rounded backs rose here and there above the dense growth of the ferns from which the lake took its name. The lake lay at the foot of the slope, half encircled by Scotch firs. A couple of them stood, like outposts from the wood, at the top of the slope. There had been a third of their company, but it had fallen, and now lay at their feet. Beyond the lake was a narrow, rushy strip of bog, and beyond it was a mole of great round pebbles that the sea had cast up, making a barrier for its own hindering. The wide Bay of Monarde, dim and mysterious, stretched away eastward as far as one could see.

Peggy was sitting on the fallen tree, watching for the moon to rise above the pale outline of the hills on the distant shore of the bay. She had been waiting there for some ten minutes, in the perfect solitude and silence, thinking, and her thoughts had been all of Kit. Her father and mother had discussed him and his family that evening. Her father had spoken of the letter that he had had from Sir Harold Burgrave, authorising him to make an offer for the Big House. Then he had expanded eloquently on the chance—a chance that might never come again—that this offered to 'the old Captain and the rest o' them.' What good was the Big House to them? Now, a man like Sir Harold . . . Panegyrics of Sir Harold followed . . . Then had come Kit's turn. 'Idle and good-for-nothing as he was,' this money would give him and Nessie a chance—start them in the Colonies—much more to the same effect. Then her mother had joined in, without bitterness, but in agreement. Only old Granddad had grunted disapproval, and coughed and spat, and muttered something about a damned Englishman, and as fine an old family as there was in Ireland. Peggy had met his eye. She knew that there had been sympathy in her face, perhaps gratitude. Was it her imagination, or had Granddad winked one of his crinkled old eyelids at her? Peggy was fond of her old grandfather. She thought of how he had tipped her a fiver the other day, and of how he always had a good word for her friends at the Tower—even for poor Kit . . . .

A glow came up behind the hills, darkening them, and making their outline definite, and then the red rim of the August moon stole, like a creeping fire, over the horizon. It moved up the green sky, incredibly huge and red, and a long beam of warm gold came trembling down the sea, and was echoed in touches of light in the dark little lake at Peggy's feet. She heard footsteps behind her, and stood up, pretending to herself that she did not know whose they were. Then Fly ran up to her, barking a greeting, and Tinker followed. Both knew her well. They danced round her, barking, and jumping at her hand.

'Down, dogs!' Kit called to them. He came nearer, and stood a little way from her. 'I—I knew I'd find you here,' he said, awkwardly.

He suddenly felt that he was nervous and not sure of his ground. He tried to hearten himself with the remembrance that she was 'only Johnny Weldon's daughter', but all the unnerving thoughts that he believed he had long since set aside, of how she had been 'at swell schools', and could speak French, and play the piano, and had seen the world—or more of it than he had—and was—(oh! specially now, with that gorgeous moonlight on her face)—stunning to look at. All these her advantages, crowded inopportunely into his mind, inducing a very unusual self-distrust. So he stood, and looked at her, and wondered what his next move should be.

Peggy's heart was shaking her, making her breath come too fast. She steadied herself with one hand on the rough red scales of the Scotch fir. She had ridden alone with Kit many times, but the horses and the daylight were company. Here, in this utter loneliness, on the edge of the world as it seemed, she felt stripped of protection. That other daylight world, that Kit credited her with knowing, was only a world of schoolgirls and schoolmistresses. She felt very young, and, for all her courage, frightened.

'I nearly lost the way,' she said, for the sheer sake of breaking the silence, trying to keep her voice normal, 'but I remembered that you told me to steer for the Scotch firs——'

Kit made no reply. He was silhouetted for her against the green-blue moonlit sky. She knew only that his face was turned towards her. Still he stood silent, looking at her, and then in a moment, all plans and methods of approach were swept from his mind by the rushing tide of a feeling such as he had never before known. His self-consciousness was, for the first time, lost, drowned in that flood. There was for him but one thing in the world that mattered. In three quick steps he was beside her. He put his hands on her shoulders, looking down into her eyes, leaning ever closer to her. He tried to say her name, but her nearness made the word faint on his lips.

'Oh, Kit, no!' Peggy murmured, but knew that the protest was of no avail.

Chapter 27

Miss Isabella Pindy sat in the best armchair in the drawing-room of the Big House, holding a thanksgiving service in which she was at once priest and congregation. She had left Kit and Nessie seated in the sun on the hall-door steps.

'Telling her his story he is, the poor boy!' Shibby thought. 'Well, well, little I'd ha' thought long ago that I'd be jollying myself with having a match made between Johnny Weldon's daughter and the Heir of Inver! Thrown away I'd ha' said he was—and I'd say it now, too, if it wasn't that I seen Old John's will!'

She rose from the best chair, too absorbed in thought to notice that one of its castors was off, and strode across the room to the window from which she could see a smooth green stretch of the demesne. A bunch of Young Johnny's bullocks were grazing there. 'Wait awhile, my lad!' she exulted. 'It isn't your beasts will be feeding in it by and by, when all's said and done and you're put under the feet of my boy!' There was no doubt in her mind but that much would have to be said and done before Young Johnny was subdued, and put in his proper place under Kit's feet, but as she sorted the cards in her hand, she knew she held the best of the trumps. The only question now was how best to play them.

It was with a new and delightful feeling of security that she roamed round the house, opening shutters and windows, and debating with herself as to what her next spendings should be devoted to. Let the Englishman offer what he liked. There was no fear now that Kit would have cut, shuffle, or deal with him. Then she thought of old John Weldon. The morning was still young, and she decided that a visit to him, to tell him the news, was no more than his due, and bareheaded as she was, she set forth across the grass, by 'the near way' to Demesne Lodge.

Old Falstaff, somewhat shrunken in body, and less lively than his wont in soul, after three weeks of rest and seclusion, was sitting in the sunshine of a garden bench in front of the Lodge.

'Why, Shibby, girl! I didn't see you this long time! Not since that little business matter——' he rolled a filmy eye, that had not lost its cunning, at her, and laid a fat finger to his nose.

'Tell me, Mr Weldon, when is this Sir what-shall-I-call him, coming back?' asked Shibby, swinging a swift glance along the open windows behind them.

'Next week,' said Old John, in a creaky whisper. 'Johnny has his mind made up to ketch him! You know what for!'

'He's late,' said Shibby, sitting very erect, a light in her eyes. She sat quiet for a moment, tasting again her triumph. Then she turned to the old man, nodding her head.

'They're in bonds!' she said, deeply.

Old John was speechless. His toothless mouth fell open, and it was a full thirty seconds before he gasped: 'Begad, but that's the best news I heard yet!' He drew a long breath. 'My God! When I thinks of the Old Madam, that was Miss Moore of Gurtha, and no better in Ireland! And me father, Mick, that was her servant! By gosh, it's like a merracle to me that I should live to hear the like!'

'Please God you'll live to see them married!' said Shibby. 'He's mad for her!'

'The sooner the better, if that's the way, the sooner the better!' said old Falstaff, to whom the news had brought an access of vitality, wheezing, and leering at Shibby; 'But whisper, Shibby. D'ye remember of what I said to ye this good while back—? ye do! Well, ye'll want to mind yourself, there might be work out of it yet!' He spoke so low that she had to lean towards him and listen intently to hear what he said. 'Jimmy Connor was here twice to see Johnny; but Johnny won't be back in it till after to-morrow. There's talk going that Kit beat him, and he wants to have the law of him.'

Shibby's great eyes blazed. She stood up. 'I thank you, Mr Weldon, for what you've said. I'll take this business into my own hands. If that dirty hound comes here again I'd be obliged if ye'd send him to me! *I'll* deal with him!'

She stood for a moment, towering over the old man, looking straight before her, wrapped in her rage. Then, with the effortless dignity that comes of perfect poise, she swept away across the grass, her head up, the grey mass of her hair shining in the sun like a silver

183

crown.

Old Falstaff watched her out of sight. 'By the powers!' he muttered. 'There goes the finest Prendeville o' the lot o' them, whatever way she was got!'

Nessie was waiting for her elder sister at the gates of the Big House.

'I came here looking for you, but you were out.' Nessie was pale, and her voice had a shaken sound in it.

Shibby looked closely at her, and said sharply: 'What's the matter?'

'Jimmy Connor was here just now. He wanted to see Kit. Kit was out; I was thankful. He was half drunk, and I shut the door and told him it was no good for him to wait. He went away, raging! I saw him fall down twice. He was like a madman!'

'I wouldn't doubt him!' said Shibby, grimly. 'Where is Kit?'

'He and Peggy are in the drawing-room. She wanted to see the pictures again———'

Shibby stood in thought. Then she said: 'Don't say a word to Kit at all. I'll go see Jim Connor meself to-morrow.'

In the drawing-room of the Big House Kit and Peggy were sitting, hand in hand, on that central jewel of Miss Pindy's achievements, the atrophied Chesterfield sofa. They were looking at the portraits of Beauty Kit, and of his wife, the Lady Isabella.

'He's supposed to be like me,' said Kit, looking approvingly at his namesake, 'what do you think?'

He put a possessive arm round her, and took her chin in his hand, turning her face so that she must look at him. Kit was as much in love as it was in his power to be, and he looked deep into her eyes and laughed, out of sheer delight in her.

Peggy's clear grey eyes, that had lost something of their peculiar and cat-like directness and independence, dwelt for an instant on his face, in which the beauty of the portrait was so strangely repeated, but deepened and matured. A week ago she would have laughed at his vanity, despising it a little. Now, in this overwhelming phase of subjection to his physical attraction, she had lost her power of criticism, and had forgotten her first distaste.

'You're only trying to make me pay you a compliment!' she said, flushing, and laughing a little, back at him. 'But I won't! The compliment shall be to Beauty Kit up there——' She looked up at the picture. 'Yes! he really is like you, but not——' Her eyes turned foolishly, tenderly, to Kit's again, '—not so pretty!'

Kit was justified—or thought he was, which is nearly the same thing, though not quite—when he said to Shibby that night:

'Of all the girls I ever met there isn't one to touch her!—Is it she loves me? She's mine to do what I like with!'

Chapter 28

Old John Weldon had been mistaken as to the time of his son's return. Young Johnny came home that same evening, his various operations having been accomplished in record time, and that same evening it was that Jimmy Connor achieved the interview with him which had that day twice been denied to him.

He came late, at nearly nine o'clock, and the consultation took place on the gravel outside the hall door, and Mrs Johnny, accustomed though she was to the prolixity of her husband and his clients, marvelled at the length of time that the statement of this case demanded. Old John was seated by the fire, that even in the height of summer he could not do without. Peggy had found the room 'stifling,' and had, as Mrs Weldon had explained to Mr Weldon, 'just run up to the Tower to see Nessie about something.' Mr Weldon had frowned.

Old John, who was accustomed to sleep in his chair until nine o'clock, when he went to bed, was roused to unusual interest by the lateness of the visit, and by the fact that Mrs Weldon was unable to tell him the name of the visitor. He showed his interest, after the manner alike of the very old and the very young, by incessant questions of a futile character.

'Who is it at all, coming at this time o' night?' 'What is he come about at all, my dear?' he said at frequent intervals. 'Are they near done talking, d'ye think?' to all of which his daughter-in-law responded with appropriate patience and inanity. But when, at last, Young Johnny rejoined his family, though his brow was dark and fateful, he showed no inclination to explain what it was that had darkened it. He said, briefly, that it had been James Connor who had wished to speak to him, and he then sat down opposite to his wife, and with a glance from her to his father, in explanation to her of his silence, he took up the newspaper and began to read. Old John bore this reticence for a few moments, then he said, fretfully:

'Well, Johnny? Well? What did the fella' want? In God's name can't ye open your mouth, man, and not be sitting there as dumb as an image?'

Young Johnny gave Mrs Weldon another look, the look interchanged by the mature in connection with the futile questionings of age and youth. Then he said, solemnly:

'I am sorry to say, Sir, that what James Connor came to speak about was a very distressing matter. I don't know that I should mention it, seeing it was not my affair, and that it concerns someone who is no relation of mine—and never will be—or at least—' he added in a lower voice, looking at his wife—'I trust not!'

'What are ye mutthering there?' said Old John, turning in his chair, and striking the ground with his stick to secure attention. 'What difference is it to me whose affair it is? I'm asking ye what brought Jimmy Connor here? No good, I'll be bound! I know himself and his father well, and his grandfather too, and I never knew any good o' one o' them, root or branch?'

Mrs Weldon said in a low voice: 'The Doctor said not to annoy him——'

''Tis a most unpleasant story,' Young Johnny began, slowly, and with more apparent reluctance than he secretly felt, 'and I'm sorry to say it concerns a young man whom we have known all our lives——'

'Do you mean Kit?' whispered Mrs Weldon, quickly; she glanced, as if involuntarily, out of the window, towards the way that Peggy had taken, the way that led to Inver House.

'I do!' replied Young Johnny, portentously.

Old John, as is usual with slightly deaf people, had heard both question and answer, though neither had been intended for his ears. Again he struck the ground with his stick.

'What had that blackguard to say about Kit?' he bawled. 'Plenty o' dam' lies, I'll engage! Can't ye speak up, ye bosthoon? Holy and merciful God! What a son is given to me to incense me!'

'Better tell him, John,' whispered Mrs Weldon, whose own curiosity was now awakened. 'There'll be no peace till you do—you'd better not vex him—one doesn't know what might happen——'

Young Johnny walked round the little dinner-table and stood over the old man.

'You can believe it or not as you choose, Sir,' he began formally, observing, with a praiseworthy effort, the admonition of that hampering Fifth Commandment. 'What Connor told me, in the first place, was that Kit Prendeville was a party to a shameful piece of swindling at the Clytagh Races. In the second place, he asserts that Kit has seduced his sister, Maggie, who will have a child, and he refuses to marry her.'

Mrs Weldon gasped. She said to herself that John must be very angry indeed to permit himself to use such language. Aloud she breathed:

'John! Can it be true?'

'I see no reason to doubt either of these statements,' replied Young Johnny, coldly.

Old John banged his stick on the floor, and laughed, until his laughter merged into a violent fit of coughing.

'Is that all ye have to say?' he shouted, when power of speech was granted. 'Kind father for him! What's bred in the bone will come out in the meat! And why shouldn't he plaze himself when he's young! He's the finest young man in this country and you may be the proud man the day he marries your daughter!'

'Who says he'll marry my daughter?' responded Young Johnny, shouting in his turn, quite forgetting his filial duty as he looked at his father's face, large and purple and twinkling with satisfaction. 'If these stories are true—and I'll make it my business to find that out—there's no fear I'll let a dissolute young ruffian like him marry my daughter!'

'What?' roared Old John. 'What's that you say? You cur! You——' his old voice thinned and broke like a boy's—'I tell you she's promised to him! Break the match if ye can!'

'There's no match! There's no promise!' Young Johnny was too angry to hear Mrs Weldon's reiterated entreaties. 'John! John! Be careful! John, come away! The doctor said——'

'Ah-h-h! Ye'll be sorry yet!' Old John screamed, struggling to his feet. 'Get out o' me sight before I strike ye! Ye whipper-snapper, ye!' He choked and coughed, and, raising his stick, made a step towards his son. But the blow failed. The stick fell with a crash into the fireplace. The huge, unwieldy old man staggered, his outstretched hands groping aimlessly in front of him, the purple colour deepening in his face.

'John! He's falling! Catch him, quick!' shrieked Mrs Weldon.

Young Johnny, taken, awfully, by surprise, lost his head, and stood, paralysed; but Mrs Weldon, small and quick, sprang to her father-in-law as he stood, tottering, and catching one of his arms, so steered his great body that it toppled sideways, and, as a stranded ship, left by the tide, rolls on her side, so he sank in a huddled mass upon his chair.

His son and daughter-in-law stood in consternation, gazing at the wreck. Old John lay quite still. They would have thought him dead but for his loud breathing.

'It's a stroke!' whispered Mrs Weldon, at last. 'John, what shall we do? We can't move him——'

'I'll go at once for Magner—watch him, you—Don't stir him at all——'

Mrs Weldon was left to her lonely vigil.

The house was very quiet. Peggy out, and Bridget gone down to the village on an errand. If any change came to the old man, if he recovered consciousness, and wanted to be moved, what could she do? John and the doctor couldn't possibly be back in less than an hour——

But Old Falstaff lay very still. His head was sideways, sunk in his shoulders, his grey-bearded chin in his chest. Mrs Weldon had the courage in illness that is more often found in women than in men. Very cautiously she put her finger on the fat, old wrist. At first she could feel no pulse; then some movement came through to her. His left hand hung over the arm of the chair. She picked it up. It was very heavy and cold, and it slipped from her hand and fell on his knee as if it were dead. She looked at the black marble clock on the mantelpiece. It was nearly ten o'clock, 'and Peggy not home—what could be keeping her?' Mrs Johnny wondered if she had been wise during this past summer—was it really Nessie who was the attraction? Should she have discouraged all intercourse with the Tower? . . . But it would have been so dull for the child here, with no one of her own age . . . and oh, to think if these terrible stories about Kit were true! . . .

She looked at Old Falstaff. His breathing was quieter, almost

189

imperceptible. What had he meant by saying 'Break the match?' What an idea to come into his head! The poor old man! But he was always mad about the Prendevilles. It was the wish that was father to the thought! The aphorism, familiar and well-worn, brought its accustomed bromidic consolation, and soothed her. Yes! That was it. John was silly to fight him about such fancies! . . . How dreadful it would be if he were to die that night! . . . And to think that the very last thing he said to his only son would be to call him a whipper-snapper! Mrs Johnny considered it gravely and regretfully. What painful things life was full of! . . . Why didn't Peggy come in? She was fond of her old granddad. This would upset her . . . Whatever was keeping her? Her father was sure to ask where she had been—he would be so annoyed . . .

She heard steps outside, and Peggy's voice (thank God!). The voice said, lingeringly, 'Well, good night . . .' and then again, 'Good night!' and then silence. Then Mrs Weldon, afraid to leave her post, straining her ears, heard Peggy's voice once more.

'No, not again—you *must* go—Dear, good night!'

But when had the mother heard in her child's voice that tender intonation? Was it with Nessie that this reluctant good-night was exchanged?

She heard Peggy's step in the hall. In another instant she would come bursting into this stricken place—Mrs Weldon sat up, her hand uplifted, ready to hush the expected voice to silence. But the step went on, past the door, and upstairs. The listener heard the door of Peggy's room open and shut, and was conscious of a sudden, irrational, intuitive certainty that Old John had been right.

'It was Kit to whom she was bidding good night,' thought poor Mrs Johnny, consternation overwhelming her brave spirit. 'What, oh, what would John say?'

It did indeed prove that the opprobrious epithet 'whipper-snapper', and that addressed to his only son, a respectable professional man of sixty-two, or thereabouts, was old Falstaff's last utterance on this lower earth.

'He'll not come round,' Dr Magner had said, and he had been right.

At the turn of the night, those that watched by him, in the little dining-room that had been one of the complacencies and satisfactions of his long life, were aware of some deepening in the silence, some sense of a departure.

'Before it was making day,' Shibby said, afterwards, 'I knew he was gone. I was awake, and the thought of him came to me, and my window shook though the night was still. I wouldn't say but that it was himself that was in it—coming to say good-bye to me, like. God rest his soul!'

John Weldon had a great funeral, such as he would have desired. All the village, and half the country round, had assembled; and solid, solemn business men from Clytagh, even from Monarde, walked in the dragging procession from Demesne Lodge down to the pier in Cloon, whence Old John was to take ship, and to go, as he had often said, with his two feet foremost, out to the ancient grave-yard on Deer Island. A long line of boats went with him, and as the oars struck the water, the women, crowded on the pier, raised the Irish Cry for the old, old man, who had been one of the best-known figures in Iveragh since before ever they or their fathers or mothers were born. So Old Falstaff departed from Inver, and from the life that had interested him so much, and was deposited in the Weldon burying-place, a barbaric pyramid-shaped stone hut, a resting-place but a shade less repellent than the ground by which it was surrounded, a soil in which generation after generation had been buried, old coffins exhumed to make place for new ones, their rotting timbers hardly containing the piteous remains of long-forgotten ones; sometimes too crumbling to be replaced and laid on the coffin of a new-comer, fit only to be shovelled, indiscriminately, upon its lid; a ghastly travesty, one would say, of Christian burial, yet persisted in from one century to another.

Mr Turnbull, the solicitor from Monarde, was one of the followers of the hearse that conveyed Old John's enormous coffin to the pier; but he had gone no farther.

'Thank you, Mr Weldon,' he had said, when Young Johnny had offered him a seat in one of the boats. 'I'll walk back to your house and wait for you there.' He tapped the breast-pocket of his coat. 'I have your late father's will here—the most recent,' he had added.

That night, when all was over, and on Mr and Mrs Weldon the solitude of the conjugal apartment was at last bestowed, Young Johnny told his wife at some length how, when Turnbull had added them words ('Those words,' murmured Mrs Johnny to the pillow), a certainty had come over him that there was something wrong. 'But who ever could have thought the old man would have played such a trick on me!'

'But John dear, surely it's all the same——' Mrs Weldon tried to comfort her lord. 'You would have left it to Peggy in any case——'

'*After my death!*' replied her lord, in a tragic voice, and turned over on his side and went to sleep.

Old John was what is known as a warm man; warmer, in fact, than had been generally believed. His testamentary instructions were quite clear and decisive. To his beloved granddaughter, Margaret Owen Weldon, he left £12,000 and the Demesne Lands of Inver; the rest of his property he left to his son, with the exception of three legacies of £50 each, one to his 'dear daughter-in-law, Louisa Mary Weldon, as a mark of gratitude and affection,' and the two remaining fifties went, free of death-duties, to the amazed and delighted Kit and Nessie, 'the children,' said the will, 'of my best and oldest friend, with the hope that they may be as happy and prosperous as I wish them, and that the ties between the Prendeville family and mine may become even stronger in the future than in the past,' and it was added that to his respected friend, Miss Isabella Hynes, or Pindy, he had already given a token of his life-long esteem and regard, which explained the omission of her name from this, his last will and testament.

The aspiration as to the Prendeville family had been Mr Turnbull's modification of Old John's instructions.

'Say now that it is my desire that my granddaughter shall marry the Captain's son!' dictated Old John.

'But is there an engagement, Mr Weldon?' Mr Turnbull had inquired, in rather scandalised tones.

'There is not,' said Old John. 'But what I'm sayin' is the way that'll make an engagement, and a marriage to the back o' that!'

Then Mr Turnbull had urged the modification, 'as being, if I may say so, more discreet, Mr Weldon, and less likely to arouse opposition.'

'Ah-ha! I see you know what my son Johnny's after!' Old Falstaff had replied, chuckling, and consenting. 'But young Kit's a match for any bloody Englishman!'

Old John's will was read in the presence of his immediate family in the dining-room of Demesne Lodge, whence, with grunts of effort from his bearers, he had that same morning, being toilfully removed. Young Johnny had invited Dr Magner to be present at the ceremony, partly as an old friend of the family, and partly, also, from a feeling that in such a rite, the testator's physician should, properly, take part.

Thus it was that although Mr Turnbull's letter, announcing the legacies of the Tower, made no mention of the aspiration as to the union of the families of Prendeville and Weldon, Miss Pindy was not long kept in ignorance of it. Late that same afternoon she met Dr Magner in the village.

'It would have done you good to see Young Johnny's face when Turnbull was reading the will,' the Doctor said to her. 'The poor fellow didn't fancy those legacies at all! And what he fancied still less was Peggy getting the demesne and that fine lump of money! When Turnbull read out the bit about the ties between the families, I thought Miss Peggy got rather red. But indeed the room was warm.' The Doctor paused, and looked hard at his old friend, Miss Pindy. 'I was wondering had Old John anything to go on beyond his pious hopes?'

'Well, I wouldn't say that he hadn't,' Shibby replied noncommittally. She, too, paused; then she said, in a low voice, glancing right and left down the narrow village street, in the centre of which they were standing, 'Tell me, Willy, what way is that girl, Maggie Connor? It was told to me she was going wrong in the head.'

'She comes of a tuberculous family,' said the Doctor, evasively.

'Well, but is it in the head she's wrong?'

'She's wrong every way,' said the Doctor, with the manner of one who closes a conversation.

Shibby stood still for a moment.

'Could you certify her that she was going mad?'

He shook his head.

'Willy,' she persisted: 'tell me one thing only, is she fit to go to America?'

The Doctor again looked hard at Shibby. He thought: 'Well, she's a great schemer!' but thought it with respect, even with admiration. Then he said, deliberately: 'As far as her head goes, I should say she'd pass muster. As for the rest of her, she has about five months in hand, but mind, this isn't a professional opinion, I've not been consulted.'

'I didn't think it likely you were,' returned Shibby, 'or I wouldn't have asked you!'

'I'm not so sure of that!' said the Doctor, laughing at her.

'Well, I'm obliged to you, Willy,' said Shibby, beginning to move away.

'Don't mention it!,' said the Doctor, politely. 'But whisper, mind yourself now! Don't let yourself in for a libel action!'

'Never fear but I'll mind myself!'

She turned from him, and walked on down the street, deep in thought. Yes! she said to herself, with her stern, confident smile, she'd mind herself, no fear but she would! Hadn't she a hundred good weapons in her armoury! Fifty, that that good, decent old man—might the great God give rest to his soul!—had given her, and fifty more that she had forged for herself in long and patient years of self-denial,—put aside, not to be touched, save in some great emergency. And wasn't America over there; a land where all things were forgotten; a place, if one so wished it, of oblivion? What more had anyone heard of that girl from back in Moyroe, that had been dairymaid with a farmer, and when her father and mother wondered what was on her that they had no word from her, it was found out that her master had paid her way to America? And didn't the same fellow, a man of the Flahertys he was, do the same to another girl after? The low hound! . . .

Michael Connor's public-house had the distinction, not easily earned, of being the worst kept and worst conducted of its four rivals in the village of Cloon. Shibby stood for a moment outside a portal that could not be accused of trying to make vice attractive, and peered into the dark interior. The shop was empty. Behind the counter Jimmy Connor sat, in his shirt-sleeves, reading a newspaper. At the farther end of the counter a low doorway permitted a view of a kitchen, and of the hooped back of an old man, on a stool in front of the fireplace.

'Good evening, Jimmy,' said Miss Pindy, graciously, entering, and standing at the stained and battered counter, from which a reek of stale porter rose disgustingly.

'Evenin',' said Jimmy Connor.

He was a heavy young man, with a fat red face, a bristling red moustache, and a nasal tenor voice. He put down the newspaper as he spoke, but his manner would not have beguiled the average customer, and he remained seated.

'I've been wanting to see you this while back,' said Miss Pindy, in a voice whose silver smoothness could not have been bettered by the most conciliatory diplomat.

'I'm here always,' said Jimmy Connor, gruffly.

'I know that,' replied Miss Pindy, 'and that's why I'm come late, this way——'

Her hearer looked at her with concentrated suspicion.

'Well, here I am,' he said.

'Is there no place I could talk to you for five minutes? I can't speak to you in the shop this way, with people maybe coming in.'

The voice was velvet, but there was a touch of steel in it.

Whether it was that hint of steel that found out the cur in Jimmy Connor, or the blue light in Shibby's eyes that had before now quelled better men than he, is of no concern. The singular fact remains that he rose from his chair, and saying, sulkily, 'Ye can come

195

into the snug, if ye like, Miss,' he opened a door beside that leading to the kitchen. Then he stood in the kitchen doorway and called roughly to the hooped old figure by the fire, 'Come in and mind the shop!'

The 'snug'—which is the pet name in Irish public-houses for an inner den of confidential drinking—in Mr Connor's establishment, made no attempt to justify its name with allurements of comfort or decoration, and relied solely on its primary attraction. There was a central table, covered with a ragged skin of black American cloth, marked with the rings of many slopping tumblers. Some chairs stood in front of a small fireplace, in which were the white ashes of an extinct turf fire. A few framed advertisements of purveyors of drink, flaunted on the walls. A glass-fronted press, with bottles on its shelves, and a small sideboard with tumblers on it, completed its equipment.

When Jimmy Connor joined her, Shibby had already seated herself in an arm-chair behind the central table.

'Shut the door!' she said sharply. The velvet had gone, and the silver; the voice was all steel.

'Now, listen to me Jimmy Connor. You came up to the Tower last week, drunk, threatening Miss Nessie. I'll not have it! You went the same day trying to see Mr Johnny Weldon with stories about Master Kit. I heard that from old Mr Weldon the day he died, I'll not have that either!'

'I never seen him,' lied Jimmy Connor. Then, plucking up a little courage, he added, 'The stories were true, anyway!'

'The truth's something new from you!' said Shibby, mastering him with her terrible eyes. 'I don't care are they true or false. I'll not have it! Listen to me! I have you, and your father, and your sister, in my hand. I can put you out on the roadside to-morrow! This is the Captain's house, and you know as well as I do how many years' rent is in arrears!' Shibby paused, but her eyes never left Jimmy Connor's face, whose usual crimson hue was now mottled with a variety of unpleasing colours, induced by conflicting emotions of rage and fear. 'I can do this,' Shibby continued, 'and if I see fit, I will do it. It'll depend on yourself, Jimmy Connor!'

Jimmy Connor, wriggling in what he believed to be the death-ray of Miss Pindy's eyes, tried, with futility that was almost pathetic, to respond with bluster. What about the races, he asked, and all the blagyarding that was in it? What about that, he'd like to know? He repeated the question, with emendations and slight variants, several times. Branching then into irrelevant matters in connection with the rent and its non-payment, and the reasons for its non-payment, he spend some time in describing, with gathering courage, the defects and dilapidations of the house, and said that if it wasn't for that misfortunate old man of a father he had, he'd go to America to-morrow, and the house might be throwing after him, for all he cared.

Then he returned to the matter of the races, and was, according to the customs of such as he, proceeding to repeat all that he had already said on the subject, when Shibby's hard and authoritative contralto broke in on his whining tenor.

'I've heard all that. Enough's enough. Yourself and Con Brendan can settle it between ye as suits ye best. The two o' ye can have a nice story to tell in Clytagh! You can tell how yourself and your sister tormented Master Kit till ye got him to oblige ye; and how all the money that was got by roguery went between Brendan and Maggie and yourself! You may tell that story, Jimmy Connor, and I wish ye joy of what good it'll do ye!—and it'll be a nice help to Con Brendan when he's looking for a mount!' she added, her eyes always on his face.

Jimmy Connor had been standing near the door of the small room, having backed away from Shibby as far as possible. But now he came close to the table at which she was sitting, and leaned across it, resting his thick hands on its torn cover, his red head held low between his shoulders.

'There's another story I can tell——' he began, menacingly, but with a shake in his voice that told of trepidation, like a dog that growls and shows its teeth but is afraid to bite,— 'and if I don't get satisfaction——'

Shibby struck her fist on the table.

'Be silent!' she said, imperiously. 'Don't dare to speak to me like that! I'll have none o' your stories!'

The Lady Isabella Prendeville herself could not have spoken more autocratically, or looked more awe-inspiring, than did Shibby Pindy, the descendant whom she would have repudiated.

'Listen to me!' Shibby continued, 'I've come here to make you an offer. You can take it or leave it. Please yourself. But I'll not make it twice!'

Jimmy Connor, surprised into silence, waited, wondering, staring at Miss Pindy, his mouth hanging open.

'You were saying just now ye'd like to go to America. Did ye mean that?'

'O' course I meant it!' he began again to bluster. 'But first I'll have justice——'

'Stop that!' Shibby silenced him with a flash of her great eyes. 'Now, attend to me.' She spoke very slowly, each word hard and sharp-cut as a block of dressed stone. 'The day you show me a letter from the steamer agent in Monarde, saying you have Maggie's and your own berths taken to New York, you'll get a clear receipt for the rent, and twenty-five pounds for yourself, with it. And when you get to New York, there'll be seventy-five sovereigns,' she dwelt on the golden words, 'waiting for ye there! I'll give ye till to-morrow to think it over, but it'd be as good for ye to give me your answer now. I can tell ye one thing. As long as you live, you'll never have the like o' such an offer again! It's now or never for ye!'

She ceased and waited for his answer.

Jimmy Connor reared himself up from the table, his shifty eyes wavering from the flaring advertisements to the bottles in the cupboard, and on, round the walls, to a stained print of Mr Parnell, over the fireplace, anywhere rather than meet that fixed gaze of Miss Pindy's. He passed his hand over his bristling mouth, and fidgeted, while he tried to hustle his whisky-sodden mind to a decision, or rather—since the offer had been infinitely better than his wildest hopes—to a response that should express reluctance, without running any risk of scaring out of reach so wonderful a bird of Paradise as a hundred pounds! The only question was, could he knock anything more out of Miss Pindy.

Miss Pindy herself answered the question, with what seemed to the wavering Mr Connor an appalling knowledge of his thoughts.

'Ye needn't think ye'll knock more out o' me, for ye'll not. And mind this! If you dare to draw down the name of Master Kit between your lips—and I'll know if ye do—not one damned ha'penny will ye get from me, and shortlong it'll be before y're out in the street without a roof over your heads!'

'She doesn't know I've been to Weldon!' thought Jimmy Connor. 'God! I'm done if she finds that out on me!'

He drew a quick breath. 'I'll do it!' he said, breathing short, 'I'll go!'

'You'll do well to go!' said Shibby, grimly. 'It'll be the best day's work ever you done for yourself. But don't forget what I'm saying. You'll get nothing if you don't keep your mouth shut, nor nothing if you don't clear out o' this as quick as you can, and Maggie with you—mind that! Not a ha'penny, if the two o' ye don't go. I'll see to your father. He'll be all right.'

She stood up. She seemed to fill the low room with her presence. Great and terrible she was to Jimmy Connor, and his soul trembled before her. Out of a deep pocket she drew a purse, an old-fashioned, brass-bound leather bag.

'Here's a ten shilling bit,' she said, throwing the gold coin down on the ragged table cover. 'That's earnest for you. Go to Monarde to-morrow.' She paused, her eyes searched his face and found submission there. 'I have no more to say,' she said, moving past the cowed Jimmy Connor like a queen.

Chapter 30

Old John Weldon had been buried for a week. Old John was thoroughly dead and out of the way. That was one good thing, Young Johnny thought, could not help thinking, as he ploughed his way through all the papers that Old John had accumulated during his long life; papers of all sorts, crammed into old desks and chests of drawers in his bedroom, access to which he had rigorously denied to his son. All Young Johnny's labours were embittered by the thought of that outrageous bequest to Peggy.

'Me that was his son, and did everything for him! Only for me he'd never ha' had it to leave at all! And then to put me down under me own daughter!'

Not even the discoveries of many investments, sound and profitable, of which he had had no knowledge, all accruing to him as residuary legatee, consoled him for losing the demesne. 'It is plain enough to me what he was driving at,' thought Young Johnny. 'Didn't he say "Break the match if ye can!" I'll break it and no thanks to him, the old—' here Young Johnny (who had never quite recovered from his early conversion in Dublin) remembered that his father should be honoured, and, with some difficulty refrained, from the unfilial epithet of rogue.

The door opened, and Mrs Weldon came in. 'The post, dear— there seems to be one from Sir Harold——'

Mr Weldon took the one from Sir Harold, and opened it carefully, even reverently, with a pocket-knife. Such thick and creamy paper, and so gorgeous a seal required special treatment. Mrs Weldon stood waiting, while he read it; once through, and then again, beginning this time near the end. Mrs Weldon was patient, but there are legitimate limits to a wife's patience.

'What's it all about, dear?'

'Read it!' said Mr Weldon, in a pregnant voice.

Mrs Weldon took the letter and read, summarising aloud, as people do on the stage.

'"offer you my condolences on the death of your father—coming this week, leaving yacht here,"—where? Oh, I see, Kingstown, "since you and Mrs Weldon are good enough to offer to put me up—anxious for a reply about Inver House"—Oh, John, I thought they had refused to sell?'

'So they did, in a way, my dear, but not very definitely; and refusals aren't always final!'

There was a subdued triumph about him that Mrs Weldon could not understand. She went on with the letter. '"I have quite decided not to repair the house at Moyroe— " Oh!' Mrs Weldon gave a gasp, and read on, quickly, to herself. Mr Weldon watched her face. '*John!* What does he mean?'

'It's very plain what he means! And, what's more, I believe he had his mind made up before he left here at all!'

Triumph, even glory, shone in Young Johnny's face. Mrs Weldon read again the end of the letter. This time she read aloud the sentence that had given her pause.

'"I hope Miss Peggy will be with you when I come. I am particularly anxious to see her."' Mrs Weldon opened her mouth to speak, but words failed her.

'Now!' said Mr Weldon, proudly, 'what did I say!'

Mrs Weldon sat down on the side of Old Falstaff's dismantled bed, and gazed at her husband. At length she said slowly: 'Yes. It's quite plain what he means. I only trust Peggy will have sense.'

Mrs Weldon, it may be suggested, had not forgotten that lingering leave-taking at the door that she had been aware of on the night that Old John had died, but she had not thought it advisable to mention it to John.

'What d'ye mean by that?' Mr Weldon inquired sharply.

'One never knows what girls may do,' said Mrs Weldon, putting up a species of smoke-screen of generalities, 'and you see, John, he's said nothing definite. I would advocate——' (experience had taught Mrs Weldon that a word that might recall to her husband her superior education, was often very compelling)—'I would distinctly advocate that we say nothing to the child——'

'She must be told of Kit's behaviour,' said Mr Weldon, obstinately. 'I consider she's too great altogether with him and Nessie.

She's for ever with them it seems to me. I only put off telling her before out of decency—the funeral and all—and it's not a thing to talk about without proper caution. We mustn't forget the law of libel, my dear!'

'You need have no anxiety that I would wish to discuss such a painful subject with anyone, least of all with a young girl, John dear,' said Mrs Weldon, decisively, and with a touch of severity.

'She'll have to hear it sooner or later,' said Young Johnny, sticking to his point. 'It wouldn't surprise me at all if me fawther didn't have some understanding with Shibby Pindy about a match,' he went on, thoughtfully, 'she's clever enough for anything. Don't you remember how he declared she was promised to him, and——'

'Your father was very much excited,' Mrs Weldon interrupted, 'and so were you too, John dear. Believe me it is wiser to wait a little.'

The schoolroom still peeped out in all she uttered, and Mr Weldon, though he grumbled, crumbled.

It had been impossible during this past week for Mrs Weldon to keep any special watch on Peggy's incomings or outgoings. There had been the funeral, a heavy effort; and she had had to go to Monarde to see about mourning, and a hundred other things, as she said to herself, besides being summoned by John, every five minutes, to find some paper that he had mislaid, or to help him in his explorations of Old John's magpie-like hoards. It had certainly seemed to her that Peggy—like the classic example of the 'thronging woman'—had gone out of the house ten times for once she'd come in. But she was too busy every morning, and too tired every night, to go into the question. All she knew was that the weather was fine, and that she was thankful the child should escape the trail of trouble that death leaves after it, and that she should have Nessie to play with—'She would have helped me if she could—I sent her out myself,' thought the mother, exculpating the child, '—and she can't see too much of Kit, as he's always riding, and she couldn't have the horse.'

But now that this epoch-making letter from Sir Harold had come, the suspicions that she had stifled for a time, raised their heads like a nest of vipers, and hissed at her. While she hurried about her various tasks she was trying to assure herself that Peggy, with her expensive upbringing, and her fastidiousness, would never think twice of Kit. '—a young man with no education, and no knowledge of *les convenances* of society, and a brogue!' She thought, piling his disadvantages, trying to ignore the fatal point —'If only he were not so good-looking!'

After a worried day, she spent a no less worried night, considering the situation, and finding no solution of its difficulties.

'No other young people . . . such a handsome boy . . . No, I shouldn't have brought her here . . .'

Towards morning the sleep that had been kept at bay by thought, crept imperceptibly upon Mrs Weldon, and, without her knowing that relief was near, it came. Thus it was that, much to her annoyance, she had slept on far past her usual hour, Mr Weldon, in the softened mood caused by the glow of joy at his heart, having decreed that she was not to be disturbed. When she came downstairs she found that her husband and Peggy had both gone out.

'The master went down to the Post Office,' said Bridget. 'I think it is in the garden Miss Peggy is. There was one came to see her—'

'Who?' said Mrs Weldon quickly.

'A girl, I think, ma'am. She didn't come to the house at all. I seen her from me, meeting Miss Peggy down th'avenya.'

'Oh, Mary the Machine, I suppose, bringing up her black skirt,' thought Mrs Weldon, who had accepted with simplicity the title bestowed by the village on that local dressmaker who alone possessed a sewing-machine. She continued her usual avocations, overtaking as best she could the runaway minutes, and she was completing her morning task of dusting the drawing-room, when she saw Peggy coming towards the house. Peggy felt to her mother, after that momentous letter of yesterday, like a new Peggy, a Peggy of wondrous latent possibilities, a Peggy who might, some day, incredibly, be a Baronet's Lady! That was to say if—Mrs Weldon was caught up by the if. It preluded so many possible disasters, all the dangers and disadvantages that were summed up for her in one little word of three letters—Kit! She tried to keep herself from such thoughts. She stood a little back from the window and regarded her girl as if she were a stranger.

Perhaps it was that the window wanted cleaning. It seemed to her that Peggy's colour looked all wrong, patchy, not a bit like herself. Her dark eyebrows were drawn down, as if in concentration of thought; she was looking straight in front of her, but she was not, certainly, looking where she was going, as while her mother watched her, she missed the turn of the garden path, and stumbled over the edge of the grass, and nearly fell.

'The child isn't well!' thought the watcher, anxiously, and went out into the little hall to meet her. The two met, face to face, at the door. Instantly Mrs Weldon was aware of trouble.

'My darling, what is it?' she exclaimed, catching Peggy's hands in her own.

'Let me go, mother,' said Peggy, turning away her face. Her voice was rough and full of effort. She tried to draw away her hands. She was nearly a head and shoulders taller than her mother, and was a strong girl. But Mrs Weldon held her fast.

'No,' she said, firmly pulling her to the open door of the drawing-room, 'you're coming in here, and you must tell me what it is—perhaps I know already!' she added in a low voice that was almost a groan.

The habit of authority lives long; and the habit of obedience will cling, though it may be despised and resented. Peggy, despite herself, submitted to being brought by her mother into the drawing-room. Mrs Weldon released her hands, turning back to shut the door, and the girl walked over to the little cottage piano, that stood with its back to the room, and put her head down on a pile of music that lay on it.

Mrs Weldon's heart was thumping at her side and her knees were shaking. Half she feared that she knew what it was that had thus shattered her child, and half she feared that it was still left for her to tell her. She sat down on the sofa, feeling that she could not stand, and waited. Peggy did not speak. At length Mrs Weldon drew a bow at a venture.

'Is it something about Kit?'

The arrow went home.

'Then you know?' Peggy whirled round and faced her mother; 'it's true, is it?'

Had it then been of any avail, Mrs Weldon, stricken to the heart, would have lied unflinchingly. But, 'Oh,' she thought, 'no lie can save her!' With tears running down her face, she nodded her head. Peggy's wild eyes met her mother's. The tears were enough.

'Then it *is* true!' she said, breathlessly.

She tore at the front of her blouse and pulled out a ribbon that went round her neck. A ring was strung on it, a beautiful old ring that was a Prendeville heirloom, and had somehow survived all vicissitudes of fortune, and had been passed on, from one Madam Prendeville to another, since the time when it had sparkled on the white hand of the Lady Isabella; a lovely thing, composed of a single big ruby, like a rose, with a cluster of diamonds, like dew-drops, round it.

Peggy threw the ribbon with the ring on it across the room into her mother's lap. The colour had rushed into her face.

'Don't ask me to talk to you, mother! I can't!——Not now. Send that back to him. You needn't write. He'll understand!'

She crossed the room with swift steps. At the door she turned.

'Mother—— Don't let Father speak to me. I couldn't stand it—— Don't tell him about—about the ring!'

Little Mrs Weldon held out her arms to her tall daughter. She couldn't speak. Peggy shook her head, and in silence opened the door and went out.

Mrs Weldon sat quiet, listening, whilst the baffled tenderness, the vicarious pain that mothers have to bear alone, that sometimes, it maybe, is deeper than the child's pain which caused it, because of its impotence, because of the knowledge it brings of the child's separate existence, flooded her soul. She heard Peggy go upstairs and into her own room overhead, just as she had, that night, little more than a week ago, heard her go upstairs after that lingering farewell. This was a longer farewell for her.

'My child, my child!' thought little Mrs Johnny, looking at the lovely old ring through a dazzle of tears.

Mrs Weldon had sat there a long time, and had thought many thoughts, while one half of her mind, watchful as a dog's, listened for a footstep or a sound from Peggy's room, before she stood up, and picked up the cloth with which she had been dusting the room, and mechanically shook it out of the window before putting it away.

With the familiar task, the dreary, inescapable common-sense of the middle-aged awoke in her. She heaved a great sigh; much such a sigh as escapes from a patient when, recovering from an anæsthetic, the hard and mundane glare of the window fills his eyes.

The thought in her mind was:

'Thank God, *we* hadn't to tell her! She's young—she'll get over it——' And then, inevitably—'She can do better than Kit!'

Chapter 31

Miss Pindy's activities in the matter of the Big House had been much stimulated since that happy morning when she had sat in what it is not an exaggeration to call a trance of triumph in the great room which she felt to be the crown of her achievement, and knew that her heart's desire had been granted. Old John's sudden loosing of all the possessions to which he had held tight for so long, had brought the realisation of her plans into grasping distance.

'Peggy's two-and-twenty,' she thought, 'there's nothing can stop it now!' Hadn't Jimmy Connor been up to see her last night, and shown her the steamer-agent's letter? He and Maggie would be out of the country next week, please God, and then let Young Johnny pull out! He knew nothing, and if any gossip got to him later on, she'd know how to quench his stories, lies or truth, no matter what they were!

She had carried her sewing-machine up to the Big House, and was now, as had become her daily custom, sitting in the drawing-room working at the curtains that had been the latest of her purchases. The swift needle stabbed on; with each inch that it put behind it she felt that Kit's enthronement in his ancestral home came nearer. The purr and rattle of the machine so filled her ears, and her well-satisfied thoughts so occupied her mind, that she did not hear the door open, nor knew that Kit had come in until he stood in front of her. She stopped her work, and looked up at him with the look in her eyes that only woke there for him. Then she saw his face.

'Good God! What's happened?'

He threw into her lap the ring with the ribbon still strung through it.

'That's happened!' he said, 'and that!' He crushed into her hand a half-sheet of note-paper. 'By post it came, just now. She wouldn't as much as send a messenger up to me!'

On the paper Peggy had written but three scant sentences.

'Kit, I've seen Maggie Connor. Here's your ring. I don't want it.

207

Peggy.'

Kit watched Shibby's face turn to stone, ashen grey; nothing alive in it but her eyes. He gave a loud laugh, and sang out in his pretty tenor:

> *'The coloured man he went to France,*
> *And that's the end of this romance!'*

'That's about the end for me, too, Shibby, old girl! I've got the order of the boot all right! I might as well go to France, too—or to Hell, for the matter o' that!'

Shibby smelt the whisky on his breath, and knew its flush on his face, his beloved face—whisky or no, let him do what he liked, he was hers, her own, her dearest, bad or good. Hardly knowing what she did, she started up. As she did so her eyes met the painted eyes of Lady Isabella. In that whirling minute it seemed to her as though she read in them the satisfaction of one whose prediction has come true. The ring on its ribbon that Kit had thrown into her lap, swung from her hand.

'Ah!' she cried to the picture, flinging out the hand that held the ribbon, 'it was you begun it! You that drove your own children to ruin and destruction! God curse you that brought this on my innocent child! Look at your ring that I gave him! God in Heaven! Wasn't I the fool to think that anything belonging to ye wouldn't bring him bad luck!'

She staggered back and sank on to one of the light chairs. It creaked and swayed under her weight. 'Break! Damn you!' she cried, rising to her feet again. 'Who wants ye now?'

The chair fell over with a crash. She kicked it behind her, as if unable to endure the sight of it.

Kit watched her, bewildered. The effect of the whisky that he had drunk was dying down. He wanted practical help and counsel, and he felt himself overpowered by the tempest that his news had aroused. Only once before, as a boy, he had seen Shibby lose her self-control, and that was when his father had sold the demesne to John Weldon. Wasn't it, he said to himself, a lot worse for him than for her? If he had said that he was going to France, or to Hell either, that didn't mean that he meant it—not straight off, anyhow. A fellow couldn't be expected to mean all he said when he'd just had a knock-out like this. He had always come to her, for help; what good was she if she couldn't help him now? He took her hand.

'Hold on, Shibby, let's think! Isn't there something we could do?'

Shibby, standing silent, her mind like a tossing sea, her eyes still fixed on the portrait of her namesake and ancestress, came back with a jerk to the present.

'It's late now to be asking me what can ye do. Ye done enough in the past!' She turned away from the picture and looked at him, anger, pity, and love contending in her passionate face, 'No more, my poor child, God help ye, no more than your father done before ye!— And no more than them that came before him—but too much——O God! Too much!'

Kit began to curse. 'What good is it to go back on things?' he said fiercely, 'is there nothing to be done now?'

Even in this moment of despair Shibby was glad of the weight of his reliance on her. He was weak—like his father before him, she thought—but the very weakness that tossed him to her breast was dear to her strength. She began to think hard. 'What was that she said?' She snatched up Peggy's note and read it again. 'She "*Seen* Maggie Connor." Why then it was from Maggie to be sure she got the story so——' She stopped. 'Tell me, wasn't it with her you were when you seen Maggie going out into the sea?—Very well, then—'

Slowly, step by step, like a mountaineer fallen in a crevasse, faced with a wall of ice, Shibby hewed a way of escape—or, at least, a plan of action. Maggie Connor, (please God) would be on her way to America in less than a week. Jimmy was wild to be out of the coun-try—('He'll tell the people in America she's a widow!' Shibby said, with a bitter smile) —Let Kit write a letter and say Maggie is mad, and telling lies. Why would Peggy take a mad woman's word before his? And let Kit go away, down to that fair he was talking about, back in the Co. Clare. Wasn't it tomorrow or next day that the fair was?—Sure couldn't he stay there a few days with his mother's cous-ins, Janie and William—that were ever and always asking to see him and Nessie?—Sure Nessie would meet him there—She'd be better out o' this till the Connors were gone—that dirty blackguard fright-ened her!—Let Kit wire to Janie McKnight and say he'd be with her

209

this evening, and let him write to Peggy from there. There was time enough for Nessie, but let Kit get away for fear there would be any more trouble with Jimmy, and not come back at all till the Connors were out o' the place entirely. Peggy would be glad enough to see him come back to her, Shibby would go bail! It mightn't be well that he should go see her. She might cross-question him, or her father might cross-question him (and it was well known that Johnny Weldon could make a person swear a cow into a jackass). No; let Kit go away . . . and say nothing to Nessie at all. She wouldn't believe it if another spoke to her, but if she knew the truth she might tell it. You couldn't trust poor little Nessie!

The scheme flowed from her lips, gaining in volume, and in detail and explanation as it flowed. And Kit listened attentively, and with growing hope, and the portraits looked as if they also listened. The blue-velveted boy seemed to smile more gaily, and his greyhound seemed more alert; but no one, however sympathetic and imaginative, not even Nessie, could have persuaded themselves to fancy that there was any softening of the proud downward curve of Lady Isabella's perfect lips.

Chapter 32

The letter that Kit wrote to Peggy was sent to her by post, even as hers had come to him. It cannot be said of it that it was a success from a literary, or indeed from any other point of view. It was badly written, and badly spelt, and its explanations, refusals, and denials were verbose, confused, and carried no conviction. Poor Kit would have done better to have risked the cross-examination even of Young Johnny. Shibby, for all her astuteness, did not take into consideration the persuasive arguments of eyes and voice, of beauty and sex. These had been the conquerors that had broken down Peggy's initial reluctance, and her power of resistance; the bonds that held her were born of the magic nearness, of youth speaking to youth. Shibby would have been better advised had she permitted Kit to make his defence in person.

But the effect of Kit's letter, Peggy's first letter from a lover, was, for the lover, little less than a tragedy. She read it once, twice, three times, and with each reading the cold light of disillusionment beat on it more implacably. Then she lit a candle and held the sheet in the flame, and watched the words curl and turn brown, and the paper shiver and break off, and float in black scraps into the fender.

'I couldn't bear that Mother should see it!' was her thought. The disaster of his spelling almost softened her towards him. It made her laugh in spite of herself. It almost restored her belief in him. A creature surely must be as innocent as a baby, who spelled believe with three e's, and agony with two g's! Could it be, as he said, that that girl was telling lies about him, that her accusations were the hallucinations of a mad woman?

Peggy went over that horrible interview again. At the moment it had felt that these were not lies that were being poured in a hot torrent into her shrinking ears. Yet why should a mad woman's word be taken in preference to poor Kit's? Then Maggie's distraught face came back to her, it stared into her very eyes, her frantic voice sounded again in her ears, and Peggy's mind registered again the vow it had made in the moment of shock, never to speak to Kit again, never, as far as was possible, to see him, or even think of him again. Let him be clean forgotten—she tried to remember the verse—and become as it were a dead man out of mind? was that the way it went? . . . Oh, poor Kit! her heart said, mastering her mind . . . Dear Kit! . . .

Someone had turned the handle of her bedroom door, and found it locked, and was knocking——

'Are you there, Peggy, dear?'

Peggy unlocked the door and let her mother in. She was glad that there was no vestige of the letter remaining.

'Father's just had a wire from Sir Harold. He's coming by the afternoon train. We've got to tidy poor granddad's room for him. Will you help me, my child?'

Mrs Weldon had been aware of the arrival of the letter. Had, in fact, herself handed it to Peggy, not without a guess at its writer and at the probable nature of its contents. That Peggy should have immured herself in her room, made the guess a certainty, and had also the effect of making Mrs Weldon's voice almost aggressively tender, and of attuning it to the tone that she usually reserved for condoling with mourners. Peggy found it jarring. She walked to the window, turning her back on her mother, and said brusquely:

'Mother, I want to tell you. I've had a letter from Kit. He says that—that story is all a lie, and that——' She hesitated, then forced herself to speak the name, 'Maggie Connor is out of her mind, mad.'

Mrs Weldon listened silently. She had still a stone in her sling. Should she throw it?

She followed Peggy to the window and put her hand on her arm. 'I'm afraid Father is quite certain about it, and he knows more than we do. Don't let us think about it, darling. I only regret that you should even have heard such a story!' The tenderness of Mrs Weldon's voice was overlaid by the ineradicable primness that had been part of the professional equipment of her time. Peggy found the combination almost unendurable. It would have disposed her to rebellion, even if her father's pontifical utterance had not instantly done so.

'Why should Father know more than we do? I see no reason why Kit's word shouldn't be taken as soon as Maggie Connor's—or as Father's either!' she added, in a voice that threatened storm. 'Why

212

should Kit be condemned——' Her voice shook and failed.

Mrs Weldon struck in, an added primness and authority in her manner, assumed because she believed such to be the proper way to deal with the child for whom her heart was aching.

'I do not wish to argue the matter again. You have sent back his ring. I am thankful to think it is all at an end. There is nothing to be gained now by discussion of a very unpleasant subject.' Her voice was severe. This was how Mrs Brownrigg would have expected her to treat an erring pupil, but her eyes, as she looked up at her tall daughter, were full of the sympathy that her principles would not let her express.

'Come, my child,' she said briskly, 'we haven't too much time to get the room ready.'

Peggy said to herself, 'Mother doesn't understand,' and followed her without a word.

Very differently, and far more agreeably, was Kit spending his morning. He had composed his letter in the train, and had posted it at Cahirbwee station on his way to the hospitable house of the old cousins, Janie and William McKnight. These, a comfortable and well-to-do old brother and sister, had received him with effusion, assuring him of the pleasure that would be bestowed on them by a visit from him and Nessie, and promising a stable for his possible purchase.

Now, while Peggy's brain was engaged, endlessly, with the thought of him, turning over and over, like a mill-wheel, at one moment rolling downward, overpowered by her faith in him, to accept his word against that of his accusers, Kit, on the other hand, with restored confidence in the future, was strolling through the wide fields, outside the town, where the fair was held, full of optimism, and of the delightful feeling that he had fifty pounds in his pocket to spend as he liked. That rain should be falling in a patient drizzle distressed him no more than it troubled the throngs of draggle-tailed horses, standing in the mud of the fair field. He was clad in the frieze cap, the drab waterproof coat, and the brown gaiters that are consecrated to such occasions, and in addition to being indifferent to weather, he had the happiness of knowing that his costume differed not, by so much as a button, from that of every other man he

213

met: (a satisfaction, it may be added, peculiar to his sex, and in no degree shared by the feminine half of humanity).

Kit was as much in love with Peggy as was usual with him in such case, perhaps a little more than usual; but this was merely a temporary set-back. 'After all,' he thought, 'she has only Maggie's word against mine. Surely she ought to believe me sooner than Maggie!' He felt quite injured at the thought of Peggy's possible want of confidence in him. In the meantime weren't there always horses? It was a question in Kit's mind which interested him more, girls or horses. Both were able to disappoint you. On the whole, horses were safest. His thoughts were given a turn in a more congenial direction by the sight of a useful-looking grey four-year-old clearing a space round him in an effort, as a bystander observed, to kick the stars out of the sky.

'He's not half a bad cut of a horse,' Kit was thinking, 'I might see what the fellow is wanting for him——' when he felt his elbow caught in the grip of a hand.

Con Brendan, the long-nosed jockey, was beside him. 'Well now, Mr Prendeville, I'm as glad to see ye, by damn, as if ye give me the fair an' all that's there! I was thinking I'd be forced to go back, looking for ye, to Cloon.'

Kit did not reciprocate this cordial greeting. 'What d'ye want with me?'

Under the brim of his cap Con Brendan's small eyes slanted round him cautiously, his long nose pointing downwards. ('Like a jackdaw stealing out of a pig's trough!' thought Kit.)

'Come this way, Mr Prendeville, if you please, a small piece,' murmured the jackdaw.

Kit followed him to the side of a high furze-grown bank, a little beyond the scope of the moving crowds of men and horses.

Con Brendan wasted no time in preludes.

He scrambled up the side of the bank and peered over its summit to make sure that there were no listeners on its farther side. Then he descended, and standing as close to Kit as was possible, he began, in a low voice:

'Ye see Mr Prendeville, it's this way. Ronayne—that's the man that owns the horse I was riding at Clytagh, "Lively Lad" his name

214

is——'

'I know all that o' course——' said Kit, impatiently. 'What about him?'

'Well, Sir, ye see he got a word telling him the way you won that race, and he sent me a message to come and see him, and he talked to me very ugly——'

'What could he say?' broke in Kit. 'What can he know about it? Who is there could give him a word?'

'There is no one, only the Connors, could have anything to say, but——' Con Brendan looked still more jackdawlike as he glanced up at Kit, 'I wouldn't say that Jim Connor wasn't vexed some way. I was talking to George Pindy that's with Mr Johnny Weldon, and he was saying Jimmy was above at the Lodge one day—and I know meself that Mr Weldon collects rents from Ronayne——' He paused.

Kit said abruptly, 'What did Ronayne say to you?'

'There wasn't a name in Europe that he didn't call me. He had the full o' the house o' curses for me!' replied Con Brendan solemnly, 'I never heard his equal! It was what he said I pulled the horse! The lying——' Mr Brendan's own language as he recounted this calumny could scarcely have been excelled even by that of the cosmopolitan Mr Ronayne.

'What's he going to do about it?' asked Kit, coolly, lighting a cigarette with a hand that shook a little in spite of him.

'I was coming to that,' said Brendan, on whom the shaking of Kit's hand did not fail of effect. 'I b'lieve if he got the value of the prize-money it'd quieten him. Ye see——' The jackdaw's little dark eyes glinted up at Kit. 'If Ronayne blew the gaff on me, there's a thing or two I could say about him and his horses that might do him no good—and he knows that well enough, the——' again the repertory of Europe was ransacked for an appropriate epithet.

Kit thought for a moment, then he said:

'See here. Con, you meet me at Heffernan's pub in Cahirbwee this evening, and we'll fix the thing up. If it's only the prize-money Ronayne wants, it'll be all right. But we'll want to get a paper from him, saying he was satisfied it was all square——'

'Ye'll get that,' said Brendan, confidently.

'Then in God's name, don't let us waste time here any more,' said

215

Kit, with restored spirits. 'There's a grey colt I saw just now—come on and have a look at him.'

The grey colt did not satisfy Mr Brendan's critical taste.

'Ah, he intherferes in front, and he's not much better behind. He has the emblems of old marks on his knees, and he's growing a side bone. Don't look at him at all, Mr Prendeville!'

Kit was led away, not without reluctance.

'The chap said he knocked his knees schooling over stones—'

'Ah, them country-fellows have all the thricks as good as any old dealer in Dublin,' the mentor responded. 'If ye picked forty holes in a horse, they'd have fifty pegs to put in them!'

The morning, wet though it was, afforded Kit a variety of exquisite emotions. He 'tried' horse after horse; taking them out to 'the galloping field,' compelling them, over its broken and muddy banks, to justify their owners' asseverations that they would change feet on the blade of a knife; entering upon long and entrancing haggles, from which, at the last moment, abetted by his now constant adherent, Con Brendan, he would retire, only to select another 'likely one,' and to initiate a fresh contest. His affair of the heart, imperilled, and hanging in the balance, the dangers and difficulties that threatened him, were swept from his mind.

Miss Pindy's primary motive in sending her young brother to Cahirbwee Fair has already been recorded, but had she also wished to select a soothing medicine for his presumably wounded spirit, she could not have prescribed a more efficient restorative. At intervals Kit and his satellite would gravitate, as if unconsciously, to one of the tents in which refreshments (mainly in liquid form) might be obtained. The warmth of the fifty pounds that were burning in Kit's pocket, had rapidly communicated itself to the sensitive perceptions of Mr Brendan, and he did not fail to make the most of the happy chance that had thrown Kit in his way.

The afternoon had come, and with it the drizzle of the morning had become rain. Kit had returned to one of his earlier selections, and the bargain was pursuing a deeper and more earnest course. A recent visit to a tent of refreshment had softened the asperity of Mr Brendan's comments, and had intensified Kit's anxiety to bring off a deal.

216

'Thry her now!' bawled the owner of the animal under consideration, a young farmer who posed as a humourist, and addressed his remarks as much to the crowd of bystanders as to the possible purchaser. 'It's all I ask that ye'd thry her! Ride her at the bank below—any dam' place ye like! She's bred to lep! Didn't her mother jump a labourer's cottage one day, with me on her back, and the only mistake she made was to leave a hindleg in the chimney!'

This *jeu d'esprit* gained the approval of the audience.

'Very good, faith!' said a stout, slightly drunk, elderly farmer. 'Begor, I'll ride her over the wall below meself, if this gentleman that owns her will make no objection?'

The gentleman in question said that as far as he was concerned a young baby could ride her; which seemed irrelevant. The bystanders, on the other hand, were shocked, and protested in chorus.

'No, John! Do not, John!' they shouted. 'You're too weighty entirely, John! Oh, you're a very weighty man, John! Very weighty entirely! You'd be like to be killed, John, if ye fell off her!'

'Faith, if he didn't fall off her dam' quick her back'd break under him!' said Brendan, very ably bringing down, as it were, two birds with one stone. 'I wouldn't touch her at all, Mr Prendeville, she's too light——'

He turned away, brushing against Kit, and in doing so murmured under her breath: 'She's a nice quality mare—she might be worth buying—— We might get her cheap now. He'll have no business taking her home. All she wants is a bit o' food in her!'

The mare in question was a well-bred, four-year-old, iron grey, in very poor condition. She was shivering in the cold rain, with ears laid back, and a watchful eye. Her tail was tucked in, miserably, but there was a certain look about her hindquarters that suggested the potential activity of a live wire. Kit's last visit to the refreshment tent had exhilarated him rather more than was advisable.

'Here,' he said to the mare's owner, 'let down those stirrups for me, like a decent man, I'll have a trial of her——'

'Thry her any way ye like,' said the young farmer, 'belt her out round the big field! She's a sweeping fast mare, and there's no man in the fair that's better able to test her than yourself!'

Kit mounted, and rose out of the group towards the galloping

217

field. The mare was chilled and out of temper. She sidled along in a mincing jog, eyeing with hatred every horse she passed, and every now and then snatching petulantly at the snaffle, which was, as is almost invariable in Munster, the bit in which she was being ridden. Kit was in high good humour. All thoughts of his misfortunes in love were, for the moment, kept under, partly by the last 'shot' of whisky, and partly by the joy of a deal. He patted the mare's wet neck, 'Now, my lady, we'll see what you're good for!' he said, touching her gently with his heels. The mare swung sideways, half rearing, resentful of suggestion. Kit had a light cane in his hand. 'Very well then, what'll you say to this?' he said to her, and gave her two smart slaps with it.

The grey mare's response was instant. She sprang right off her hind legs up into the air, in a kangaroo-bound that would have carried her over a five-foot wall. Kit gave her another light slap, laughing at her, sitting down, and enjoying her silky, slippery activity. Then she began to gallop. The big forty-acre field had emptied; the fair's vigour was spent, and the mare, now exulting in comparative freedom, let herself out, forgetting her ill temper in the ecstasy of speed. Round and round the wide field Kit took her, twice, three times, till she had settled down into a beautiful, rhythmic gallop. Then he steadied her, and headed her for the muddy bank at the place in it that was least battered by the trials—in both senses of the word—of others. Possibly the mare realised its unreliability. She pricked her delicate ears as she approached it, and Kit thought, 'She'll have it all right!' Then she rose, like a lark, soaring up and up. Kit saw the trampled grass far below; not an iron touched it. 'No changing feet in a pudding for me!' gloried the grey mare, high in air, and landed, far out beyond the bank and its attendant ditch, as lightly as only a young and well-bred horse can.

It was a great jump, and though quite contrary to all the canons of Irish bank-jumping, Kit shouted praise to her as she came sailing down out of the sky.

'Come on, now! We'll have the wall!' he said, steering her down the hill for the lower part of the fair field, which was bounded by the wall over which, had it not been for the dissuasion of his friends, the weighty John had intended to prove the mare's mettle and his

218

own. She was galloping charmingly now; at each stride Kit felt more resolved that she should be his.

'She'd put Nora to her trumps!' he thought. 'I wouldn't say she mightn't be too good for her, if she were in condition——'

The wall was a typical western one, built without mortar, 'a dry wall,' of large round stones, single at the top, small ones, two or three deep, at the base. It was a full four foot, six inches high.

'Ah, it's nothing to the champion wall at the Horse Show, and she'd jump that all right, I bet!' thought Kit, gathering the mare together, letting her know what was expected of her. Her head went up, he could feel intention in her shortening stride. A storm of shouts and yells burst from the group of watchers on the hill above.

'They be damned!' thought Kit, 'the wall's all right! He told me I could try her out——'

Then the iron-grey mare rose like a stag at the wall. Not until they were mid-air did Kit realise why the watchers had yelled at him. A donkey-cart had been left in the lee of the wall, at the place he had elected to have it, resting on its shafts, sideways. Too late he and the mare saw it. In the mysterious way that a horse will sometimes lengthen his jump in the air, the mare tried to clear it, but her forefeet landed between the shafts, she pitched on her knees, and rolled over upon Kit, who had been flung out to the off side.

The mare was soon up and on her feet. She stood quiet, her head and off shoulder plastered with mud, and before she had time to collect herself, some men had rushed up. One of them caught the mare, the others went to Kit. He was half-stunned and lay still. The men turned him over cautiously.

'Is he dead?' said one.

'He's not dead at all,' said another, 'clean the gutther out of his eyes! sure the soft ground saved him!'

A minute or two passed, and already the crowd was ten deep. Brendan broke his way in, and Kit opened his eyes on his jackdaw face.

'Are ye hurted, Sir?'

'I don't know,' said Kit, slowly. 'Give a man time to think——'

'Go fetch Dr Handcock, he was here a while ago——'

'No, but give him a suppeen of whisky—— Run away to the tint

219

one o' ye, and get a drop in a glass——' Thus the bystanders.

'What about the mare?' murmured Kit. He tried to raise himself, and fell back with a grunt of pain, against Brendan's knee. 'I think my leg's broke,' he said, and fainted.

When he came to himself a doctor had been discovered, (as is not unusually the case in Ireland, where sport and horses are to be found) who had already taken off his gaiter, and was improvising a splint out of a piece of a packing-case that he had snatched out of the delinquent donkey-cart, emptying its freight of apples, with the splendid unconcern of a doctor to all interests save those of the patient.

'Where's he staying?' said the Doctor to Brendan.

'I b'lieve it's at Mr McKnight's he is, Doctor, back in the town,' volunteered a sympathiser.

That, the Doctor remarked, busily and skilfully bandaging and strapping, using the wrong things in the right way, as Irishmen and Doctors do on emergency, was as well, as his ankle was broken, and it was no harm for him not to have a long journey before him, as he couldn't do it, if he had.

'Go get a door, boys, somewhere,' he commanded. 'Pull it off the next shed! We must get him back to Mr McKnight's on a cart.'

Kit opened his eyes again.

'Con,' he said, feebly, 'here, whisper——'

Brendan bent down.

'Buy that mare for me!'

'I will so,' said Brendan. 'She's a sweet mare.'

Chapter 33

Old Judy Davin, albeit, as she would herself have said, pushing eighty years, made good speed up the last pinch of the hill to the Tower of Inver. Was she not charged with news of high consequence? No king's messenger could have been more convinced of the importance of his mission than she; she would have fallen in her path sooner than slacken speed. Inland, at Cahirbwee, the day had been wet enough, but here on the western coast the storm was driving rain before it in grey gusts of water, and though the wind gave old Judy a friendly shove up the hill, she was exhausted, and very wet, when at length she arrived at the threshold of the Tower.

The outer door was shut against the wind. The long thorny branches of the white rose whipped the grey oaken boards, as though the few blossoms that had weathered the storm were asking for shelter. An iron loop, contemporary with the rough bolts that studded the old door, was at once handle and knocker. Judy Davin rattled it until the barking of the dogs assured her that she had been heard. The door opened, and the three dogs rushed out, and, ignoring the familiar visitor, proceeded, vociferously, to scour the bushes that surrounded the Tower, in search of foes, confident in their non-existence.

'Holy Joseph! Aren't them dogs frights?' said old Judy to Nessie, who had opened the door. 'Ye'd think they'd ate ye, and for all, they're quite! Where's the sisther, asthoreen? I want her.'

'I'll fetch her,' said Nessie. 'I think she's in the yard, feeding the fowl.'

'Well, go fetch her in to me, and God bless ye! I'm bet out with the wind, and wet enough, too, faith! Tell her it's in the kitchen I'll be, striving to dry meself.'

Shibby found her ancient cousin seated on a low chair in front of the kitchen fire, with her boots in the fender, and her bare, skinny old feet on it, roasting in the glow of the wall of burning turf that lined the long bars of the open fireplace.

'Well, sich a day!' Judy began, after the usual salutations. 'I'd ha' come out but as little, if it wasn't for a message I have——' She paused and looked round the kitchen. Shibby stalked to the door of the scullery.

'Delia!' she called to an unseen handmaiden, 'the pig's food is ready. Take it up to her if you please.'

A kettle swung on a hook over the fire, and a blackened earthenware teapot was on the hob, ready, as all Irish teapots have to be, for action at any moment.

'Shibby, jewel,' said old Judy, 'for the love o' God give me a cup o' tay—I'm near dead!'

By the time the back door had slammed on Delia and the pig's food, old Judy and her hostess were seated sideways at the kitchen table, facing each other, each with a cup of tea in front of her.

'Now!' said Shibby, authoritatively, 'what is it brought ye?'

Old Judy leaned forward and clutched Shibby's knee with a twisted claw-like hand.

''Tis what Jimmy Connor says,' she began in a whisper, 'that I should tell ye the world wouldn't stir Maggie! He have the tickets—what day is this it is? Frida' is it? Well, it's Monday he's for starting, and the dickens a foot will she go with him!'

Shibby heard her old cousin out in silence.

'Why's that?' she said in a cool voice, looking past Molly into the red heart of the fire.

''Tis her head, the crathur,' said Judy, 'bothered in it entirely she is. Jimmy said to me there'd be times when she'd stand for an hour or more, saying nothing, only looking at the ground like, and then maybe to commince to screech and roar. Sure he said there was a couple o' nights last week she went out late, and she never come in at all, only running the woods back in Inver all night, like the fox! God forgive me! Not like a Christhian at all, the crathureen! God help her!'

'And who have she to blame only herself?' demanded Shibby, with the unconscious cynicism as to masculine responsibility in such a case that is innate in the women of her class, angry that compassion should be given where it was undeserved. The question was purely rhetorical.

222

Old Judy did not reply directly. She lowered her voice to the darkest of whispers, and said:

'D'ye mind what I said t'ye one time? Herself was in my house a' yestherday, crying and lamenting, and saying the young one that's to be, is Kit's!'

'Isn't it easy for her to draw down Master Kit?' said Shibby, scornfully, with a very slight emphasis on the prefix to recall Judy to her position. 'He's not the one man in Cloon!'

'Why-then the brother have the one story with herself,' said Judy, with a slight acerbity, 'but sure I says to him to put a ring on her finger, and to take her out o' this, and there'll be no disgrace on her in Ameriky, whatever man it is—Master Kit or another!'

'And what did he say?'

'Faith, he said he'd be thankful to take her, but she'll not go for him pleasant, and he said she'd rise the country on him if he was to pull her out of the house to put her on the thrain! She's walking the Crooked Bridge, and out to Carrig-a-breac, back and forth, day and night. "It's there I meets him," she'll say. She'll often come in my little house—she has a nature for me, the crathur— "He's gone away!" I says to her, "likely it's to Ameriky he's gone!" I says, coaxing her——'

Shibby had risen to her feet, and was paying no heed to her old cousin's discourse. Her face was dark, as it were a thundercloud when the lightning is near. That her plannings, the plannings of all these patient years, should be shattered by this mad old woman, this embodied scandal, this disgrace to herself and her sex! Not for an instant was Kit blamed. Could the lightning strike at her command, one victim only should know its power.

A sound made itself heard above the babbling of Judy Davin, more definite than the clattering of the door in the wind. It reached Shibby through her broodings.

'What's that knocking?' she said suddenly.

'It's nothing only the wind,' said Judy, anxious to continue her narration.

'That's no wind!' said Shibby opening the kitchen door and going into the scullery. The wind from the outer door rushed in and the fire belched forth a cloud of smoke.

223

Shibby returned, with a telegraph envelope in her hand. Telegrams were rare birds in Cloon.

'The Lord save us!' whispered Old Judy, crossing herself, 'what is it at all, asthore?'

Shibby read the message. Then she said aloud, more to herself than for the benefit of her cousin, 'Kit's broke his leg.'

She read it again.

'Is that bad or good?' she thought. 'It might be the best thing after all——'

She found a pencil and a piece of paper.

'Here, Paddy,' she called to the messenger, and thought again, and wrote, 'We will be with you to-morrow.'

Perturbed though the atmosphere of Inver Tower was by Kit's disaster, its perturbations were scarcely more profound than were those of Demesne Lodge, palpitating with the impending arrival of Sir Harold Burgrave. A levy had been made by Mrs Weldon, pale and purposeful, on the rest of the household, in order that the room dedicated to the guest should do honour to the Weldon family no less than to him. Peggy, mutinous and moody, yielded her dressing table candlesticks; Mr Weldon, with considerable effort and equal enthusiasm, conveyed the armchair pertaining to his office, up the narrow staircase to the guest's room. What Mrs Weldon thought, contrived, and accomplished, can only be understood by housewives in such a case as hers, on whom, as it were, the ends of the world are come.

Peggy's mind, like a weathercock in a storm, had swung incessantly from one extreme to another, since Kit's letter had that morning reached her. He had said, *'How would you beleeve her before me?'* and then, *'She's wrong in the head. Don't you remember me telling you so when we saw her thinking to drown herself that day on the Long Strand?'*——And yet when she thought of Maggie Connor's outcry:

'He promised me! He promised me! The blackguard! The bloody rogue that he is!'——

Which should she believe?

'She's going to the States with her brother,' Kit had written. *'Why would she do that if she was thinking I would marry her? Surely it is me*

you would beleeve before her, my darling?'

She could hear his voice in all he said. Could see the reproach in his eyes as plainly as she saw the face of his accuser. Oh, was he a rogue and a blackguard, or was he only a scapegoat, vilely slandered for her own ends by a mad, wicked girl? Peggy's mind raced, lashed from one extreme to the other by conflicting assertions. She was very young, and her way had hitherto been in clean and happy places. Was it Kit, whom she had likened to St Michael or St George, who was to teach her that the world was full, also, of darkness and cruel habitations? She wouldn't believe it . . .

'Peggy, where are you, my child?' her Mother's voice called, 'just run to the linen-press and get me out——'

Peggy ran.

Chapter 34

It has already been said that Sir Harold Burgrave was not a bad fellow, and although it has been said before, in the case of so unattractive a young man it is advisable to reiterate it. But it is a mistake, if it is desired to popularise an unattractive young man, to over-do the reiteration, and into this mistake Mr Weldon, and, in lesser degree, Mrs Weldon, fell. Sir Harold had brought gifts to his friends at Demesne Lodge. 'So aptly selected!' as Mrs Weldon said. To Mr Weldon, two dozen of port, of a vintage whose quality Sir Harold himself had proved (even though in the case of Young Johnny, whose besetting virtue was abstemiousness, the gift might have been apter.) On Mrs Weldon was bestowed a down cushion, of a size and splendour that ensured for it a cloudless future of respected idleness, and on Peggy, a huge blue-ribboned box of chocolates, so large and luscious, that to consume any one of them with decorum and satisfaction, would involve either a knife and fork, or, at the least, a quarter of an hour of silence and seclusion.

Sir Harold had been afflicted with an unaccustomed spasm of shyness, and had sent the box—which was round, and in size as well as shape, compared favourably with a cart-wheel—to Peggy's room by the hand of Bridget into whose amazed yet ready palm he had pressed a half-sovereign.

'Faith, I thought it was a sixpence he had for me! and a sixpence'd be handy enough, too, now and agin!' said Bridget. 'It would so,' said George Pindy, to whom the confidence had been made, 'but sure didn't he give meself the same! Me that never done a hand's turn for him!'

Thus, like Esau, had the ingenuous Burgrave smoothed his path with propitiatory offerings, and even though Miss Peggy's gratitude might have been more warmly expressed—(taking into consideration the blue ribbon and the diameter of the cartwheel)—and she was indisputably silent during dinner, still, he thought, one never knew—— Perhaps she had guessed what the chocolates betokened, and felt overcome by the greatness that was in store for her. No doubt the beggar-maid was shaken when King Cophetua proposed to her (and very suitably, too). Burgrave had talked to an elderly brother-in-law of his intentions with regard to Peggy, and had hinted that he was uncertain as to how she would receive them.

'My dear fellow,' the brother-in-law had said, after some ineffectual attempts to dissuade the lover from so unworldly an alliance, 'you may make your mind easy on that score! If you say "Snip!" she'll yell out "Snap!"'

Burgrave had, so far, said nothing even approaching to 'Snip,' but, he told himself, there was no hurry, he would feel his way, quietly; and there was this business of buying the Big House to be arranged. He would go into that at once, and would trust to the future in the other affair.

In accordance with this resolve, the young man, accompanied by his faithful adherent, Young Johnny, went forth early on the day following on his arrival, to view again the Big House and its surroundings. The gardens and the stable-yard were once more inspected, and then Mr Weldon diverged alone to the Tower, to get the key of the house. He did not return for some little time, and when he reappeared his step was unusually brisk, even hurried, his eye was bright; excitement, controlled, but deep, was manifest in his respectable countenance.

'I'm sorry to have kept you waiting, Sir Har'ld,' he said, breathlessly, 'but I was talking to the old Captain. He's the only one there. He was telling me that Kit—that's his son, you remember—is after breaking his leg at a fair down in County Clare, yesterday, and the ladies have both gone there to him——' He paused a moment, still breathing quickly. 'There's a notion I just got, Sir Har'ld. It may not commend itself to you, but I'll just mention it, and you will, of course, form your own opingen——' Mr Weldon cleared his throat, and shifted his position, as though the 'notion' that possessed him would not let him stand at ease.

'What's the old fool dancin' about for?' Burgrave thought. Aloud he said, 'Well, I can't form anything till I know what it's all about.'

'There is no doubt but that Captain Prendeville is in full possession of his senses,' began Mr Weldon, as if stating a case for a jury,

227

'and the Big House is his own absolute property. There's no entail—'

'What's that got to do with the fellow breaking his leg? What are you driving at?' Burgrave broke in, staring at his agent.

'I'll come to that in a minyute, Sir Har'ld, if you will permit me to explain,' said Mr Weldon, anxiously and impressively. 'I should tell you that when, acting for me late fawther, I bought the Demesne—that's now me daughter's—I was met with violent opposition on the part of Miss Pindy. In point of fact, I thought she'd attack me personally; but the Captain took my part——' He paused to draw breath.

'Well?' said Burgrave, rather bored. He thought, 'These Irish chaps have the gift of the gab! and all about nothing!'

'Well, Sir Har'ld, I would only suggest to you that it might save what I might call a *fracaw*, if we could arrange for the purchase of the house during Miss Pindy's—what I can only call providential—absence.'

'By Jove!——' said Burgrave, thoughtfully.

Young Johnny watched him. Presently, as a good cook will drop a seasoning into a simmering saucepan, he let fall a word.

'I hold the Prendevilles' reply to my letter making the original proposition. There was nothing said objecting to the transaction, merely a suggestion that the price we offered was insufficient. It was Kit who wrote. He said the fawther would consider it, and for himself he thought the price was not enough, but he'd be glad if we'd keep the offer open. 'Tis plain to me he wants to accept.'

'But we can't get at him if he's down with a broken leg——' said Burgrave, argumentatively.

('He's considering it!' thought Young Johnny.)

They were standing at the wrought-iron gates, and Burgrave's eyes, during Mr Weldon's harangue, had not ceased from absorbing, and appreciating anew, the stately charm of the Big House. A tingling anxiety began to possess him. What if this broken-legged fellow turned nasty and refused to sell? He felt that he had never wanted anything in his life more than this house—it and Peggy and the demesne—they all seemed to go together—if he lost one, he lost all! What was this old bore saying now? He forced himself to listen.

'——It's not in Kit's hands at all, Sir, but as I was saying just now,' went on Mr Weldon in his sing-song voice 'we'd find the Captain a deal easier dealt with in the absence of Miss Pindy—and there can be no question as to the Captain's competence to make and ratify an agreement of the kind,' he paused; 'you see, Sir Har'ld, Miss Pindy may be back tomorrow afternoon!'

'Yes, I see,' replied Sir Harold, still thoughtfully.

Burgrave's first inspection of the Big House had been made with all the disparaging arrogance of the amateur, prepared rather to criticise than to praise. Now it was with the hungry eye of the determined purchaser that he took stock of its attractions. It was a dull day, with slow rain dimming the windows and spoiling the view from them, to the voluble disappointment of Mr Weldon, who rushed from room to room in advance of his patron, to open the shutters in his honour. The spirit of the action was that of Sir Walter Raleigh, when he spread his cloak before his Queen. Young Johnny would cheerfully have devoted his frock-coat to make a door-mat for Sir Harold to wipe his boots on, but since Sir Harold was obviously undisturbed by the mud that his boots were distributing, Young Johnny's zeal was obliged to concentrate itself on the window shutters.

At the high window at the end of the corridor on the first floor, Burgrave stopped.

'What did you exactly offer the fellow in that letter, Weldon?'

'Three thousand, Sir Har'ld,' replied Mr Weldon eagerly. 'If you remember, it was yourself suggested that figure.'

'D'you think he'll take it?'

'Well, as I told you just now, Sir, some objection was made about the price——' said Mr Weldon, pulling nervously at his grey beard. If his hopes had been somewhat dashed by the fact that Burgrave had so far made no allusion to the letter that had so shaken him and Mrs Weldon, he was now drawing encouragement from the intention to buy the house that the young man was certainly showing.

'Well,' said Burgrave, slowly, standing with his back to Mr Weldon, and looking out of the window at the misty view of sea and land that lay below. 'Er—you got my letter?'

'Yes, yes, Sir Har'ld!' panted Mr Weldon.

'Well, if—if other things are—er—are likely to go right——'

'If you will forgive me for interrupting you, Sir Har'ld,' Mr Weldon burst in, irrepressibly, 'I may say I'm quite sure they will!'

(Which was rash on Mr Weldon's part; but it may be presumed that, like most parents of his period, he believed that his authority, fortified as it was by that of St Paul, could not be questioned.)

On either side of Sir Harold's closely-cropped black head two scarlet crescents became evident, which Mr Weldon rightly judged to be his ears, suffused by a blush, and the heart of Mr Weldon, elderly though it was, beat with youthful violence against his tidy black waistcoat.

'Well, er——' continued Burgrave, 'I don't want to let the chance of the house go, for the sake of another four or five hundred—or—er—even more——'

'I quite understand, I quite understand!' said Young Johnny, with enthusiasm, 'and I strongly advocate our approaching the Captain at once, and putting the thing through to-morrow morning, if possible. Miss Pindy, you know——'

A door banged at the far end of the corridor. The Lady Isabella's door.

'Dear me, I thought I'd closed that door,' said Mr Weldon.

Chapter 35

Almost the first thought in Miss Pindy's mind, when she heard of Kit's disaster, had been that, strategically, it was not as unfortunate as it might seem to be. And to Peggy, although her point of view was far from coinciding with Shibby's, the same had occurred. If Kit were away from her, she told herself that she could see him steadily and see him whole; not trembling at his touch, nor blinded by his charm.

Her old granddad used to say to her, chuckling, that Kit was a lad, and an arch boy, and was wont to quote what his old mother, God rest her soul, used to say: 'What was the use of having children if they weren't arch?' And then Old John, having dilated on the satisfaction that in this respect he had given his mother, would proceed to a panegyric of the Prendeville family, 'arch', and 'lads' as they had, undoubtedly, ever been.

But Peggy had other blood, beside that of Old John in her. She was not sure that archness was as desirable a quality as her grandfather considered it. Wasn't it what granddad called 'archness' that had brought about all this misery? She said to herself that even if these accusations were false, they were made plausible by the undisputed facts that the Prendevilles were 'lads', and were 'arch'.

Mrs Weldon had talked to Peggy on the night following on that of Burgrave's arrival. She had gone to her room when certain that her child was in bed, and could not escape her, and had reopened the very distasteful subject of Kit and his misdoings.

'But he denies it, Mother. He says it isn't true, and that she's mad.'

Peggy's face was in her pillow; she would not look at her mother.

A pang that was almost physical silenced little Mrs Johnny for a moment. Her Peggy turned against her! But for all her pain, she knew that the time had come when she must throw that last stone that was still in her sling. She felt, intuitively, that it would make for disillusionment in a very special and humiliating way, a way that would touch Peggy's pride, her sense of honour.

'I'm afraid Kit's word cannot be relied on,' she said, steadily, 'he is said to have behaved disgracefully, even swindled, to win a prize at those races you went to!'

In an instant Peggy was sitting erect, her grey eyes bright with anger, her thick hair about her face like a black storm-cloud.

'All I know is that I saw him ride the most splendid finish——!'

In her mother's mind was the thought, 'My darling! How lovely she is! Must I hurt her?' Aloud, she said, coldly:

'He won by a trick!'

While to Mrs Weldon had befallen the painful task of preaching down a daughter's heart, Mr Weldon's part in the crisis was one from which he derived the most profound enjoyment. He had returned from the morning visit with Burgrave to the Big House, with a heart like a singing bird, and had immediately proceeded to prepare a deed of sale, as between Captain Jasper Prendeville and Sir Harold Burgrave, of Inver House, its gardens, yards, and premises, great and small.

He had gone further into the matter with old Jas when he restored to him the key to the hall door, and had found him well disposed to listen to what his friend and legal adviser put to him as but reasonable, and to his and his children's advantage.

'Three thousand five hundred pounds, Captain!' Mr Weldon had said ('I'll throw in the extra five hundred for him!' he thought. 'The purchaser is agreeable, and it shows good feeling.' Young Johnny was, as has been said before, a kindly little man, especially in vicarious dealings.) 'That's a big lot o' money, and a fine price for a place out o' repair and all that, y'know! But I'd like to knock the best price I could out of an Englishman for an old friend like you!'

'Good boy, Johnny!' said the Captain, winking at the good boy over the bowl of the pipe to which, with a tremulous hand, he was applying a match.

'But maybe, Sir, you'd like to wait for Miss Shibby's return, before doing anything definite?' went on Mr Weldon, deferentially. 'I always hear people saying she's your right-hand man and manages everything for you? And there's Kit?—though, indeed, I know by his letter Kit's only anxious to sell if you got a good price——'

'Damn it all, Johnny!' said the responsive Captain, 'can't I manage my own affairs at my time o' life, without women and boys being brought in to bother me!'

'Well then, sir, if I came up with Sir Harold and bring up a paper, and witnesses, to-morrow morning, will that be all right?' said Mr Weldon, crushing the excitement out of his voice.

'Right as rain, Johnny, right as rain!' replied Jas, with a brave touch of his ancient swagger as a light dragoon. 'I always said the place was a d——d barracks! I'm well pleased to get it off my hands at last!'

Thus it was that on a wet and wild Saturday morning in the middle of September, in the year 1912, Jasper Christopher Prendeville, late Captain — Dragoons, signed the deed that conveyed to Harold Charles Burgrave, Bart., of Loxley Hall, in the County of Durham, England, the house and premises, yards and gardens, commonly known as the Big House of Inver, with right to enter into free and full possession on the first day of October, prox. And thereto were affixed the signatures, sinister in their appropriateness (as the watching spirit of Lady Isabella probably considered them), of John Weldon, solicitor, and George Pindy, stableman and gardener.

Old Jas's hand, always shaky, was shakier than usual as he wrote his name. The three younger men stood by in silence, while the grey, swollen fingers tried to master the unfamiliar fountain-pen, and to force it to carry it out their will. The tip of the old Captain's tongue showed in the corner of his mouth, under the tobacco-stained, drooping, white moustache, forced there by mental as well as merely physical strain.

'By God!' Jas said, blowing a whistling breath, 'that was a job for me! I don't know how long it is since I wrote my name!'

'It's a very stylish signature, Captain!' said Young Johnny, carefully shaking the paper to and fro to dry the ink.

George Pindy thought: 'If me wife's old cock had a pen in his paws he'd write as good as him!' But he said nothing. Nor did Burgrave, whose signature, large and black, and quite illegible, would have done honour to an autographed portrait.

'There's a certain amount of furniture I saw in the house, Cap-

233

tain,' went on Mr Weldon.

'That's Shibby's, that's Shibby's,' said the Captain, who was now looking agitated, as if reaction, after the excitement of the effort of signing, had come upon him. 'By Jove, I don't know what Shibby will say! She's coming back this afternoon—I clean forgot all about her furniture.' He looked from one face to the other, in increasing agitation. 'I'm afraid there'll be the very devil to pay——'

Young Johnny was folding up the deed of sale. He put it in an inner pocket and buttoned his coat over it.

Old Jas's bloodshot eyes sought his face. Tears were in them, terror was waking.

'Johnny! Couldn't it be kept quiet—kept from her—just for a while—just till Kit's back again?'

'Surely, Captain, surely! I'll put the cheque into the bank to your account and I'll keep the receipt for you. That'll be all right. There's no hurry to talk about it at all, is there, Sir Har'ld?' A kinder and more sympathetic voice than Mr Weldon's it would be hard to find—(and, as a matter of fact, he was really distressed to see the old Captain so upset). 'And you, George,' Mr Weldon continued, 'not a word out o' you, bad or good, till I tell you! Mind that!' Some of the kindness was gone, and a quality to which George Pindy was fully alive, had taken its place.

'I will so, Sir,' said George Pindy, earnestly. 'There's no fear but I'll mind it!'

Burgrave said nothing. He had paid no attention to the piteous mumblings of the old Captain. Not because he was unsympathetic, but because he was entirely absorbed in ardent thought of Peggy, and of the demesne. In justice to him it should be noted that in the order of his thoughts, Peggy came first, by quite a very long way.

234

Chapter 36

The morning had been wet and wild, and the afternoon made no attempt at amendment. The entertainment of the guest weighed heavy on Mrs Weldon. Mr Weldon, whose heart was still like a singing bird, declined responsibility.

'Let you leave the young people together, Louisa. You'll find that'll be entertainment enough for him! You've not forgotten what I told you last night he said to me above at the Big House? Very well, then!'

'I can light the fire in the drorn-room,' said Mrs Weldon, despondently. 'There's always the piano—he said he was fond of music—— But I don't know what Peggy——'

The primitive male parent asserted himself in Young Johnny.

'I declare it's a good whipping she should have!' he said, vindictively. 'What more does she want I'd like to know?' (Young Johnny as yet knew nothing of the episode of the ring that had gone back to Kit. The duties of wives are not always compatible with the shielding of offspring.) 'Turning her nose up,' went on Mr Weldon, 'at a wealthy Bar'net, and a fine young man into the bargain! You've spoilt her, Louisa! A girl has a right to do as she's told, and not to be setting up her opingens against her father and mother, especially when they have a fine match as good as made for her!' With which assertion of the authority of fatherhood Mr Weldon walked off to his office, and, as many male parents, however primitive, have done before him, left it to his wife to enforce his commands.

On a soaking afternoon of chilly rain in the west of Ireland—or, indeed, anywhere else—a bright turf and wood fire has a centripedal force that can seldom be resisted. It was not long before the glittering brass fender in Mrs Weldon's 'drorn-room' bore the burden of three pairs of feet, those of Peggy, her mother, and Sir Harold Burgrave.

'Pray smoke, Sir Harold,' Mrs Weldon said, and Peggy who had yielded as much to the desire to escape from herself as to her moth-

235

er's compulsion, realised how tremendous was the importance of a guest for whom such a relaxation of rule had been made.

During that bedroom séance which had lasted long, and from which there had been no escape, her mother had not spared her. Kit's evil deeds had been set forth with the exactness and tenacity of aim that Peggy had known from her babyhood. Her mother never lied, never exaggerated. She had concluded with an entreaty to Peggy to think it all over carefully, when she would surely see how worthless a youth Kit was, 'and then, my darling child, dismiss him from your thoughts. Try and forget all this, try and think of someone——' Mrs Weldon corrected herself quickly—'something else, and forget all this painful story. Look upon it all as something that, as the hymn says, will "fly forgotten, as a dream flies at the opening day"!'

Peggy quite agreed. The only trouble was that Kit's face, his touch, his soft western voice, refused to fly or be forgotten. Supposing he was being slandered by that girl—what then? Was she to throw him over because of that race, when she, herself, had seen his courage and resourcefulness. He had won by pluck—there was no 'trick' about it! Of course she had sent him back the ring. But that was not irrevocable. Everything might yet be cleared up . . .

Peggy was on her way to take up the position by the drawing-room fire that has been mentioned, when Bridget handed her a note. It was from Miss Isabella, and asked, in the fewest possible words, that she would come to the Tower that evening, at about six o'clock.

'Say "Yes," Bridget,' said Peggy, opening the drawing-room door, prepared, honourably, to support her mother in the entertainment of the guest.

Too soon she found that this duty was to devolve on herself alone.

'I made Peggy try over some of your songs while you were out this morning, Sir Harold; it is so long since I have heard any of those lovely songs of Schumann! Don't you think . . . ?'

Sir Harold thought, certainly—if Miss Peggy would be so very kind?——

At the end of the second song, Mrs Weldon, despite its loveliness, slipped from the room, murmuring regrets. The music continued.

Peggy read music easily and liked accompanying. It was certainly pleasanter than talking. The guest had a good voice, and enjoyed singing.

Mrs Weldon, pausing occasionally outside the drawing-room door, said to herself that he sang beautifully, and nothing could be better, and oh, if only!—an aspiration that merged into a prayer, wordless, that she was too humble, too diffident to transmute into words, but none the less intense.

Burgrave sang his way half through his collection of Schumann's songs, delivering the more impassioned numbers with an ardour that woke an answering ring from the old-fashioned, dangling glass lustres on the mantelpiece; shouting:

'Sie ist deine! Sie ist dein'!'

so triumphantly that Mrs Weldon, in the pantry, seeing about tea, wondered, for an instant, if he could have already proposed and been accepted.

Although this was still far from being the case, Burgrave, after each song, found himself more delighted with his accompanist. This, he thought, was all that was wanting to her, that she should be fond of music, and able to accompany him.

'By Jove,' he said to himself, 'she *shall* accompany me! and not only on the piano!'

He was immensely pleased with this conceit, and only with difficulty refrained from repeating it to the accompanist. He contented himself with telling her how perfectly she accompanied, how wonderfully she read music, how delightful it was for a singer to meet with anyone so sympathetic——

This was far from being the suitable attitude for King Cophetua, but there was something about the beggar-maid, something pale and remote, unmoved by the approbation of the monarch, that seemed to call for methods less of condescension than of supplication.

'I should like to hear you on my Bechstein at Loxley,' he went on. 'It's a topper! What a time we should have! I should keep you hard at it all day! No, I won't say that——' the monarch's tone became what the beggar-maid mentally characterised as drivelling—'you should do exactly as you liked best! You would give the word, and I

237

should do as you told me!' He bent down over Peggy's dark head, and murmured, almost at her ear, 'I should like nothing better than that—Peggy! Just to do whatever you wished——'

Peggy felt his breath on her cheek, and knew, without seeing it, how fatuous was his smile. She stood up quickly.

'I'm afraid you'd find that rather poor fun,' she said coolly. 'I wouldn't make rash promises if I were you.'

'There's nothing rash about it,' said Burgrave, hurriedly. 'If you'll only listen to me for a moment—I want to tell you—to ask you—' He took her hand.

'But I don't want to listen,' said Peggy, trying to withdraw her hand and to escape from behind the piano. 'I want to go and help Mother to get tea——'

Burgrave blocked her way. Even if the beggar-maid were discouraging, he did not quite forget that, after all, he was Cophetua.

'You needn't give me an answer at once,' he said, still holding her hand tightly. 'I'll let you off now, but I'll have it out with you next time! No! I *will* hold your hand—it's going to be mine some day, I don't care what you say—it's no use trying to pull it away from me!'

A hand can sometimes act as a battery, charged with a force that thrills and agitates. So it was with Burgrave. His rôle as Cophetua was forgotten. He became, simply, a young man very much in love, and in torturing anxiety as to the views of the loved one. He raised the hand that he was holding to his lips, and began to kiss it. He was big and strong, and Peggy stood, passive, too proud to struggle unavailingly. Just then the sound of her father's step in the hall came to her help. It was strange for Peggy, in this time of antagonism, to welcome her father's step, as it might be that of a deliverer, but at this moment it came for her as the tread of an army with banners.

'My Father is coming! Let me go!' she said in a low voice, tense with indignation.

Burgrave lifted his head and gazed into her eyes.

'You darling!' he said, idiotically.

Peggy snatched her hand from him, and came near to knocking her deliverer down as she swung out of the room with a violence quite unbefitting a beggar-maid.

Chapter 37

Shibby's interview with Peggy, that same dark and wet evening, was brief, but was so far satisfactory that she had, by sheer force of personality, and the unconscious hypnotic power that was hers, succeeded in re-establishing, to some extent, Peggy's wavering belief in Kit. The arguments that he, in his letter, had so deplorably mishandled, became in Shibby's hands flaming swords, which turned every way, slaying and consuming. Before she let Peggy go, she had almost recreated Kit, peerless and stainless, the victim of a mad woman's ravings, and of a slanderer's false witness.

'Them Connors,' she told Peggy, liars and rogues that they were, would be away for America on Monday morning, taking their lies with them, and 'that poor boy,' lying there with his leg broken, and his heart broken, too, would be cleared and justified, and Shibby would, if it pleased God, live to see him rise up out of his bed to reign in glory (with Peggy, was implicit in the prophecy) in the house his ancestors had built. And with the peroration, Peggy, shaken and impressed, had looked at her watch, and found that it was dangerously near dinner-time, and with a hasty farewell, had run home through the rain and slipped in at the back-door.

From which it will be gathered that Captain Jas, old as he was, had known how to keep his own counsel, and no whisper of what the late Mrs Nicholas Prendeville (who had been, it may be remembered, a D'Arcy) might have called 'a hole-and-corner sale,' had reached the ears of the Captain's eldest daughter.

If, for a moment, it had occurred to Shibby, after her arrival that afternoon, that the Captain had seemed to her 'queer', a little more excited than was his wont, eyeing her furtively now and again, then, as it were, pulling himself together, and talking to the dogs, or asking Delia for a light to his pipe, Shibby set it down to his having been left alone for a time, and the dislocation of his daily routine consequent on Nessie's absence.

Nessie had stayed at Cahirbwee to look after Kit. Her passion for service was finding fulfilment in the onerous task of nursing a singularly impatient patient, and Shibby had not taken long to perceive that the highly competent young doctor, who, in the fair field, had so immediately used the wrong thing in the right place, was exhibiting an interest in the nurse as well as the patient, that seemed to her, as she thought, 'no harm at all'. Things might be worse, Shibby said to herself, and Peggy Weldon, on whom so much depended, had appeared to be amenable. If once the Connors were gone, there would be a clear course before her boy—her heart rose.

'If I could once see him settled in the place where he has the right to be, I'd be well pleased enough to die!' she said to herself, lying awake in her bed in the Tower of Inver.

She had been awake for a long time, possessed by a succession of thoughts that came, and turned, and changed, and began again, as though her mind was bound, like Ixion, to a wheel.

The south-west gale that had threatened for the past week, had come in earnest. The wind howled round the Tower; the rain slashed against the little panes of the window, set flat in the deep masonry of the curved wall. Despairing of sleep, Shibby had relit her candle, and its desolate flame flickered in the draughts that beset it, and only served to make darkness visible. On the rounded wall Shibby's few pictures, in their cheap, light frames, were lifted, clatteringly, when the draught from the window met the draught from under the door, and together concentrated in attack on the humble things that they could intimidate. A gust fiercer than its predecessors came; the window fastening yielded, and the casement blew in. Something fell, and there was tinkle of falling glass. Shibby leaped from her bed and slammed the window, jamming down the catch that had failed of its duty. One of her pictures was on the floor, its glass broken. It was a photograph of Kit, taken when he was sixteen.

'I'd rather it was any one o' them than that!' Shibby said, picking it up, and putting it on the narrow shelf over the fireplace. 'It's a nasty thing for a picture to fall.'

She got back into bed and blew out the candle, but sleep would not come to her. When first she had lain down she had seen, with the inner eyes of the spirit, the future as a formless brightness, a sunshiny mist in which the one definite thing was her boy's beloved face. Now, as she lay with open eyes, looking at the pale patch where the window was, Kit felt lost to her. She seemed to see grey, smoky vapours rising from the darkness of the room, twisting and coiling, sometimes almost taking definite shape. Once a dim blur of light, like phosphorus, grew and faded, and grew again, high up on the rounded wall of the old Tower-room.

'It's on me eyes it is!' said Shibby to herself, closing her eyes; yet through the closed lids the vaporous circlings forced themselves on her inner sight. Then, almost suddenly, a flood of hatred of Maggie Connor rose in her. It was as though it had swept in on her from without, storm-driven. She lay on her back, rigid, like a dead woman, her arms by her sides, her fists clenched, 'ill-wishing' Maggie Connor. Nothing else seemed to her to have any importance. She felt like a horse straining with all his force to move some tremendous load, whipped on by a pitiless driver. Never before had such a passion of hatred held her in its grasp. At last, with a long sigh, she turned over on her side, and exhaustion came on her. She fell into sleep.

First Mass at Cloon Chapel was at half-past eight o'clock. Whatever might be the weather Miss Pindy's tall figure was one of the first to arrive of the morning congregation. On this Sunday morning, even though the fierce continuance of the storm might have given her reason good for staying indoors, she was as early as usual in her accustomed place. At the end of the service, she was on her way home up the village street, when old Judy Davin, standing at the door of her little house, intercepted her.

'I wasn't rightly sure were ye back in it,' Judy said. 'I heard ye were from home. Come inside, asthore, for a minyute——'

Half-an-hour later Shibby was on her way home. Up the narrow street, sheeted and shining with rain, she strode, over the Crooked Bridge, through whose low arches the Fiddaun was rushing with unaccustomed speed, swirling high round the piers, trailing ropes of yellow foam with it down to the harbour, on through the sombre trees of the demesne, under whose branches she found at least shelter from the wind, though the relentless rain beat through the leaves and gave to the avenue the semblance of a running stream.

Upon Shibby the wind and rain spent themselves in vain. How should she, a strong daughter of the West, give heed to forces so familiar that they could seem to her almost like friends, when that wheel of maddening thought was turning again in her head, set spinning faster than ever by the hand of old Judy Davin?

'Jimmy's all in a glee to go!' Judy said, 'and very wishful entirely to take the sisther with himself, the way the neighbours'd never know what way she is, but sure, without he had ropes and men to dhrag her, she wouldn't stir for him! 'Tis what he said to me last night, "Would Miss Pindy come and spake to her? There's ne'er a one," says he, "not the praist, nor meself," says he, "nor any person at all," says he, "that she'd be in dread of the way she is of Miss Pindy!"'

'I'll go see her to-night,' Shibby had answered, 'but God knows what good I'll do!'

'Why then,' Judy said, ''tis what Jimmy said if yourself'd coax her to the Tower to-night, she might be in dread to refuse ye, and he'd get her away unbeknownst in the morning airly, and when he had her in the thrain she might be satisfied to go quite. There was no other way at all, says he to me, that he could see. "Honest to God!" says he, "let you tell herself," says he, "that I done my share the way I said I would, and kep' her mouth shut, and me own, too!" says he.'

All through the lonely, stormy day Shibby's mind wrought in labour with the problem of Maggie Connor. It was not usual with her to fail of an expedient when she had a point to gain, but little as she expected success to attend Jimmy Connor's scheme, nothing more feasible presented itself to her.

After her late Sunday breakfast she went up to the Big House and shut herself in there. The trouble in her mind would not let her rest. Back and forth she went through the great empty house, opening the shutters in its half-furnished rooms, her eyes telling her what was still lacking to them, her heart threatening her that labour was in vain. She tramped up and down the long corridor from Lady Isabella's room to the west window, her mood black as the sky, fierce as the wind from the Atlantic that was clouding the windows with the salt scum with which it was laden. To be thwarted, beaten in the plan to which she had given her life—to be set at naught by the senseless opposition of such a one as Maggie Connor! Who shall say that the inveterate spirit of that ancestress from whom she had inherited so much, did not follow her, as she paced the corridor, darkening counsel, deepening hatred?

When she went into the drawing-room she averted her eyes from the smiling boy in blue velvet. His beauty had come down the centuries to Kit. Why had he not kept it to himself, if with it had to be linked his weakness?

'You were well quit of him before he broke your heart for ye!' said Shibby to the picture of his wife.

'His children did that for me!' the Lady Isabella's ice-cold blue eyes seemed to reply, with the smile that mocked the knife in her heart.

Shibby could not smile with that steely contempt for the wounds that fate had dealt her. She could fight, and could endure, but to smile with that heart-wound was beyond the power of her breeding.

At the midday meal old Jas seemed more alert than was usual with him. He made inquiries about Kit, and told, at great length and for the hundredth time, the story of how he had broken his wrist at a dance in Calcutta, and brought down the Colonel's wife with him—and a dooce of a big woman she was, too. 'Of course it was after supper, y'know, and I wouldn't like to say that what we used to call "brandy-pawnee" hadn't a hand in it!' the old Captain was accustomed to add, with the satisfaction that is often afforded to old men by the memory of their past excesses. 'I'm afraid Kit can't carry his liquor as I could!' Jas went on. 'They used to say of me in the Regiment that "no man ever saw Jas blind, but if you boiled down his bones, a fellow would get drunk on the broth!" That was a dam' funny character to have! Eh, Shibby? You couldn't say that of Kit, eh?'

'God knows he's the kind son for ye!' said Shibby, with sudden bitterness. 'I can say enough for him without wanting that!'

Old Jas looked at her apprehensively. Telling his story had raised his spirits and restored him for the moment some of his old self-confidence. But it was for the moment only. He was unused to sharpness of manner from Shibby. It scared him, and he hastened to make the amends that he believed would please her.

'Kit's a good boy. I'm finding no fault with him! No, no, Shibby, none at all. He's not had the chances I had. But he's young yet. A

243

better time might be coming for him and for me, too! There might be life in the old dog yet!'

Shibby stared at the Captain. She thought of him as incapable of an act or a thought unauthorised by her, as held in the hollow of her hand. Yet now, even through her preoccupation, she felt some stir, some excitement moving him to which she had no clue.

'Ah, it might be a new pipe he got Delia to buy for him unknown to me!' she thought, 'or it might be someone that gave him a drop. A small taste of potteen that he might put to hide from me. Little enough'd be too much for him now, for all his boasting!'

At another time she would have made instant inquisition into the matter. But not to-day, she thought, not till the Connors were away, out of sight—— Oh, God! —out of mind forever.

Chapter 38

Shibby waited for twilight to come before she went down again to the village. The wind and rain had abated no share of their violence. Rather, as the light failed, their force increased. Shibby put on the long hooded cloak that the peasant women of the south wear, and went out into the storm. No creature was abroad in the village street. The doors of the houses were shut; the pale and dying light in the sky shone under her feet on the wet flag-stones of the pathway. A plaited yellow stream ran in the gutters; it was the top of high-water, and the road outside Connor's house, at the end of the street, was flooded with the gutter-water that was backed up by the sea. The day being Sunday, shutters hid the usual attractions of Connor's public house, but lamplight showed through them.

Shibby knocked, and, after some delay, the door was opened by the old father of those with whom her business lay. The storm rushed in, flinging back the door, with the old and tottering man behind it. Shibby caught it quickly, and the wind could not prevail against her strong arm. She went into the house, and bolted the door, and, standing with her back against it, looking, with her blown white hair and long dark cloak, herself an embodiment of storm, she asked the old man where were his son and daughter.

'Jimmy's gone to the station with the boxes for the train in the morning. I d'no where is Maggie. She's not inside at all. She went out' the house this long while,' said the old man, beginning to cry. 'What'll I do at all with no one to my care!'

'Never mind yourself, now,' said Shibby, roughly, 'only tell me where would I find Maggie?'

From her great height she looked down on the small, bent, old creature, snuffling and moaning; pity for him that at another time she might have felt, now had no power to move her.

'Can't ye answer me?' she shouted at him. 'Where is Maggie? Ye can have yer fill o' crying if ye'll tell me where can I find her?' She caught him by his thin shoulder, willing to answer her.

245

'God alone knows where is she!' lamented the old man. 'Gone with Jimmy, maybe—— All I have is going from me! Sorrow is on me! Sorrow only is my companion!' He fell on his knees, and in Irish began loudly to invoke the help of Heaven and the Saints.

Shibby looked at him, the look that a hound, baffled on the line, flings at a yelping cur-dog. Then she said to the crumpled figure at her feet:

'There's more in trouble beside yourself, as little as ye think it!' and went out of the house again into the storm. She heard the bolt shot in the door behind her.

'His prayers didn't hold him long!' she said, contemptuously. 'And now what'll I do? In God's name what way can I turn?'

She stood and thought hard, unaware of the wind and rain, thwarted and furious. To follow Jimmy to the station was her first impulse, and then she remembered Judy Davin, and how she had said that Maggie would often go into her little house. A few steps brought her to the door. She found it on the latch, and opened it and went in. Old Judy was sitting on a low stool by the fire, drinking a cup of tea. Her cat was beside her, her hens were perched on a bar that spanned the end of the little earth-floored cabin.

'For God's sake! Shibby, is it yourself? Sure ye're dhrownded ! Sit down to the fire——'

Shibby cut her short.

'D'ye know where is Maggie Connor?'

'Fegs I do not! Only I seen her going east the road this good while back. The way she's goin' always. Sure I called to her to come in to me here out o' the rain. But all the answer she had was how that she couldn't wait, and she was late enough as it was, and away with her! It's likely it might be for Carrig-a-breac she was going, or maybe the Bridge. Oh, she's past all bounds now, the crathur! Sure Jimmy'll never stir her!'

'I'll stir her!' said Shibby, turning to go. 'If it's with my hands I have to drag her——'

The door slammed behind her.

'The Lord save us!' said old Judy, beginning again on her cup of tea, and throwing a crumb to the cat. 'Shibby's a fright altogether! Sich a night to be walkin' the roads! Eat that for yourself now,

Pishkin, me and you'll mind the fire and be aisy!'

Shibby tramped on through the gloom. It was an hour past sunset, and the rain clouds had brought night before its time. As she crossed the Crooked Bridge, that her great-grandfather had built, she stood for a moment and looked up and down the river. The tide had just turned, and the river was rushing down with it to the ocean in whirling eddies of black oil, patterned with grey foam, and bearing with it, here and there, nets of broken branches, spoils of the wind. Above the bridge the shadow of the Inver trees made a profound blackness. Shibby's eyes tried in vain to pierce it as far as where the Rock of the Trout hung over the water, but the spears of the rain slanted impenetrably between her and that which she strained her sight to see. Below the bridge the lights in the houses had come out. The windows of the small Protestant Church, down at the lower end of the village, by the road to the Long Strand, were lighted, and showed dimly through the rain. Muffled by the wind, the slow, recurring note of the bell, summoning the scant congregation to evening prayer, came to her. The sound gave an instant of pause to her racing thoughts. It was so remote and self-engrossed. Its implication of peace affected her.

'I might be in it myself! I have Protestant seed and breed in me,' she said, 'and look at me now!' The religious aspect was not in her mind, it was the enfolded peace of those lit windows, and the bell's quiet voice that she yearned to; she, alone, out in the fierce weather, with the knife in her heart.

She went on over the bridge and down into the heavy darkness of the wood. At the track that led to Carrig-a-breac she left the road. In the shelter of the hazel bushes that walled the narrow path to the rock, she waited and listened. It had seemed to her that a sound that was not the wind's sound had come to her. She pressed on, and a long cry, as it were a string of sobs, came wailing down the tunnel of the hazels. The hound had hit the line.

Beyond the bushes, on the great rock above the river, Maggie Connor was sitting, crouched, with her arms encircling her knees, and her chin on them. Her face was to the river. Shibby stood for a moment, thinking what she should do. Then she went forward, and said, quietly:

247

'Maggie, is that yourself?'

Maggie Connor sprang to her feet, with a single supple movement, and faced the intruder.

'Who is it? What is it ye want? This is my place! mine, and Mr Kit Prendeville's!' her voice rose, 'I tell ye it's mine! There's no other shall set foot in it!'

Shibby came nearer. Out in the open space over the water there was still light enough for the two to see each other's faces. Consciously and deliberately Shibby concentrated the forces of her will on the little, dimly-seen figure, so small an adversary, but so potent; another link in the chain of ruin that the Prendevilles had forged for themselves.

'You're coming with me now,' said Shibby, her eyes on Maggie's pale face, her voice relentless in determination. 'This is no place for ye. Come away!'

She moved a step nearer, and put her hand out from under her cloak and took a gentle hold of Maggie's arm.

'Come away gerr'l,' she repeated, firmly and quietly. 'Ye'll come to the Tower with me out o' the rain.' Her hand tightened its grip.

Maggie gazed up into the eyes that were compelling her to their will. She was trembling so much that Shibby braced herself to support her in case she should fall.

'She'll come!' she thought, with triumph, and the thought deepened the intensity of her will.

'What'll I do at the Tower?' Maggie whispered. 'Why would I go there?'

Shibby thought, 'Will I tell her she'll see Kit?'

Perhaps the instant of hesitation, the strain of indecision, loosed the hold she was gaining. In a second the quiet mood was gone, and Shibby knew that she had failed.

The muttered, timid questions ceased; Maggie's voice rose suddenly to a shriek, as swift, as fierce as the wind, and the words came rushing so fast as to be almost unintelligible.

'I'll not go to the Tower! It's Kit I want and he's not there! Tell me no lies! Jimmy went looking for him and he wasn't in it! He's lost! He's gone! He went galloping away, away down the Long Strand— sure I seen him meself! He's gone away over the sea to Ameriky with

248

Weldon's daughter—— Let me go!—— I'll go after him! By water he went, it's by water I'll go!——' She tore, shrieking, at Shibby's hand. Slight, wisp of a creature though she was, the strength that madness gives was in her and the strain was hard.

Shibby stood like a great rock, every muscle braced. Her tremendous figure, in the long cloak, was like a tower from which a captive bird was trying in vain to escape.

'Let me go! Let me go!'

Shibby's two strong hands held her captive implacably. Thought ceased for her; every faculty was concentrated in struggle, nightmare struggle, to which only the wind and the rain gave reality. Then in the chaos of her mind words blazed like a fire, shouted themselves in her ears above the voices of the storm, above Maggie Connor's horrible outcries . . .

'Let her go!' the voice said to Shibby, dinned the words into her brain, as it were from without.

Did those strong hands voluntarily loose their hold, or had the strain mastered them? Shibby found herself standing alone upon the rock, shaking in every limb, all faculties suspended, all sensation, save only horror, stupefied. Through the wind there came again to her the note of the church bell; it came like a gentle hand that touched her, recalling her to a sense of the present, from the nightmare in which time was not.

She fell on her knees on Carrig-a-breac and tried to say a prayer. . . .

'Merciful God, Thou knowest . . . Thou knowest——' What did he know? The prayer was checked.

She rose to her feet.

'I'll tell God no lies! Let the truth stand before Him, I'll take what's owing to me!'

Chapter 39

The storm passed, as storms do on that western seaboard, rushing upon it like a devastating army, ravaging, and passing on, sated, yet only half-spent. But on Monday morning the sun was shining again, and on the demesne avenue the elms and beeches stretched their tired arms gratefully in the sunshine, and thought no more of the leafy twigs that lay thick on the ground at their feet.

Burgrave and Peggy were walking together towards the Big House. Burgrave, rejected (yet sorrowing not as one without hope), was a preferable companion to the enamoured monarch, extending the sceptre in supreme confidence. He had passed with success through the social ordeal of a wet Sunday. He had accompanied Mr and Mrs Weldon to Church, unmurmuring, even though Peggy had refused to be of the party. The afternoon had been a chastened edition of its forerunner. The fire in the 'drorn-room,' the music, the excellent tea, Mrs Weldon's discreet self-effacement—all these precedents had been observed, but the Cophetuan interlude was omitted. The songs selected had been of a passionate type indeed, yet mournful. No more triumphant bellowings, announcing the possession of the loved one, awoke response in the candle-lustres. Peggy, well aware to what the changed selection was to be attributed, found herself not unmoved by it.

'He's not so bad when he's taken down a peg or two. He's really got a very fine voice——'

It pleased her to reflect how very different was her attitude to that of her parents.

'——Very good for him to find someone who doesn't grovel to him!' She said to her mother, with serene patronage, and Mrs Johnny, who was rather shocked, fell into meditation on the difference between girls of her day and those of the present—a not infrequent subject of reflection with successive generations of mothers.

The delicious sunshine after three days of rain would have predisposed a more severe person than Peggy to friendliness. Burgrave had, after all, she thought, in the time-honoured, bromidic formula, paid her the highest compliment in his power. He wasn't Kit of course—— Poor Kit, with his broken leg! Her thoughts diverged to him. She had been rather violent in sending him back his ring (such a lovely ring, too)—supposing all those stories were lies? But then, supposing they weren't, what then? Her temper flared. If he had a fancy for that red-haired village girl—why then . . . And that story about the races . . . It was all very uncomfortable . . . and this being the conclusion to which she had come after nearly a week of—as her Mother said—'thinking it all over, prayerfully and carefully', it will be understood that absence was not having its traditional effect upon Peggy's heart.

The first hint of autumn was in the air; the exquisite blue of the sky was all the bluer for the few yellow leaves that flecked the topmost branches of the elms; the bracken beneath them showed here and there a golden plume among its heavy green fronds. Young Johnny's black bullocks were grazing in the sunny spaces beyond the trees, rich accents of darkness, that made the grass look all the more brilliant a green. Peggy thought of how her father had that morning asked her to let him continue to have the grazing! *Asked* her! How incredible! All this beauty hers! Her very own! Old John's blood sang in her. That deep passion of possession, the desire for her tangible, living land, that had been his, had been latent in Peggy until now. Now, more fortunate than most, the desire had only awakened with its fulfilment.

The thought of Kit was inevitably bound up with the demesne. How delightful it would be to go to him with this in her hand! To join together again the demesne and the house! But not if——

She frowned, and unconsciously quickened her step. Burgrave, walking at her side, wondered what were her thoughts. In his subjugated mind was no room for any thought save thought of her. How well she moved. How perfectly she adapted her step to his—from, no doubt, an unconscious wish for harmony. That was what he liked in a girl, to hold her own, and yet to mould herself on him . . . to accept him as the one that gave the time . . . But, dash it all, she had to accept him in another way first! . . .

They had come to the foot of the rise in the avenue, at the

summit of which the Big House stood. The morning sun shone on its long, grave façade, and in Burgrave, as in Peggy, the intimate joy of proprietorship stirred.

'It knocks Loxley all to fits!' he thought. All it wanted was the demesne, and all he wanted was Peggy, in whose hand—the hand that he had kissed, but might not keep—the demesne was. Instinctively he put his finger and thumb into his waistcoat pocket, and felt for the ring on his watch-chain, that he had brought with him.

'In case of emergencies,' he had said to himself, with a Cophetuan smile. Such a jolly ring, too! He would bet she hadn't often seen such diamonds. But now, what good was it? He heaved an ingenuous sigh.

Together they stood, and looked at the Big House.

'Stunning old house, isn't it?' he said, and thought, 'Shall I tell her it's mine?'

Peggy did not reply. On her had rushed the remembrance of the first day she had been in the house, and seen the picture of the earlier Kit, and what had followed, and then of the later day, that now seemed so long ago, when she and Kit had sat together in the great drawing-room, and she had told him that Beauty Kit was like him, 'but not so pretty'! With the memory of that foolish speech her expression changed and softened, and she too sighed, and let memory have its way with her.

Burgrave, gazing at her, still fingering the ring, said to himself that he couldn't stand it, and he'd have another try—but before the impulse could be yielded to, a young man came into view, coming as if from the Tower, and hurrying down the avenue towards them. He had no hat on his head, and his rough red hair glowed in the sun like a halo of fire. His face was crimson, his open mouth showed white teeth under a bristling red moustache. Before he had reached them he had begun to speak. He stopped in front of Peggy, and addressed himself breathlessly to her.

'D'ye know where is me sisther? She was up with ye last week— did ye see her to-day?'

Peggy recognised Jimmy Connor, and instantly she was back in the present, with all its hateful warnings, accusations, threats.

'No, I know nothing about her——'

252

'She's lost since last night! She was to be going to Ameriky with me this day! I'm searching the wide world for her since before the dawn—distracted I am!'

He shrieked the words at Peggy in a high, penetrating tenor, and at a speed that was bewildering and made them almost unintelligible.

'What's he yelling about?' said Burgrave angrily.

'I know nothing about your sister,' Peggy repeated. She felt glad that she was not alone. She thought, 'He looks like a madman!'

'She's gone away with Kit Prendeville! It's with him she's gone, and you know it!' He dashed out a fist, almost in Peggy's face, foam was on his coarse mouth: 'That God Almighty may——'

'Come, none o' that!' shouted Burgrave, quickly placing himself in front of Peggy. 'You clear out! The lady knows nothing about your sister! It's no affair of hers who she's gone away with!'

Jimmy Connor, startled, silenced for a second, glared at Burgrave with desperate eyes. Then he stepped to one side, trying to confront Peggy again. As he did so he spat at her such an epithet as he and his like employ in a last resort of hatred and rage. Contrary to his intention, it had no successors. Burgrave's big fist stemmed the outflow with so instant a response that Jimmy Connor was on his back on the avenue before he knew what had happened to him.

Burgrave took Peggy by the arm.

'Come away, Miss Peggy. 'The fellow's mad or drunk, or both! That'll quiet him for a bit!' He was well pleased with the chance that had come of showing her how he could defend her.

Pity might be given to Jimmy Connor, can hardly in fairness be withheld. He was justified, according to his lights, in all he had done. He had observed his contract with Miss Pindy in every particular, only to find himself on his back on the Inver avenue, with a cut lip, his sister lost, and his plans shattered. Small wonder that, as he got on to his feet, dizzy and shaken, and hurried as fast as he could on his way to the village to continue his search for Maggie, thoughts of the injustice of all things earthly filled his wounded mouth with curses.

Burgrave and Peggy stood at the wrought-iron gates. They were silent, both their minds full of the thoughts that the encounter with

253

Connor had quickened and intensified. The words 'gone away with Kit Prendeville', in Jimmy Connor's hideous falsetto, rang in Peggy's ears. That such a thing could be said of Kit! that such a thing might even be true—perhaps *was* true! The man who had shrieked it at her was not lying, the very sweat that streamed from his wild face told of his sincerity. He might, as Burgrave had said, be mad or drunk, but he spoke what he believed when he said his sister had gone away with Kit Prendeville! Kit, who had told her he loved her, and she had believed him!—— Kit, whose lips had clung to hers, eloquent in silence! Oh, that she had never met him! Oh, that she had not been persuaded by him to—her anger gathered force and bitterness—to take the place of Maggie Connor! To compete with such a rival for his affection! Well, it seemed that, after all, Maggie had won! She had secured him—she had 'gone away with Kit Prendeville!'

Peggy's responses to Burgrave's rather perfunctory conversation failed. She had forgotten him, lost in the torture of her thoughts. He looked at her covertly. She was pale, her eyes, strained and fixed, were as though they saw nothing. Perception and intuition were not among Burgrave's gifts, but he was very much in love, a condition that will sometimes develop these useful qualities. Mr Weldon had not failed to enlighten him as to every unpleasant episode of Kit's career, and though he had not thought it necessary to allude to the ring that had been given and returned, Burgrave had felt that Mr Weldon must have had some personal reason for so rancorous a biography. Now, as he looked at Peggy, he knew, with sudden hot certainty, her part in Kit Prendeville's story. He saw her in distress, and knew, in this moment of enlightenment, what caused it. The thought that it was another man who had hurt her, and that it was he who stood between him and what he was resolved should be his, lashed Burgrave's stolid soul into action, and as a heavy horse if whipped into violence may become uncontrollable, so it was with Burgrave and his emotions. Hardly knowing what he did, with a galloping heart forcing him beyond his natural pace, he put his arms round Peggy. He pressed her to him, muttering her name, whispering that he loved her, that he would keep her safe, that no one should ever harm or frighten her again, if only she would trust herself to him—'No one could love you as I do, Peggy—— You can trust me—I promise you that! Can't you love me a little? . . . '

Thus did King Cophetua make his humble confession to the beggar-maid, laying aside his crown and sceptre, his arrogance, and self-satisfaction, at the imperious bidding of a King greater than he.

Miss Isabella Pindy, looking out of an upper window of the Big House, the window, as it happened, of the room that had been the Lady Isabella Prendeville's, saw, and stiffened as she saw, the girl whom, in this moment of swift revulsion, she again called 'The Grabber's daughter', in the arms of the Englishman. And as she watched, with wide blue eyes, that, but for their colour, might have brought to mind those of an angry lioness, she saw the Englishman take from a gold chain a ring that flashed in the sunshine, and put it on the finger of the Grabber's daughter.

Chapter 40

It was Tuesday morning. Shibby was seated in a first-class carriage of the train that was conveying her from Clytagh to Cahirbwee. The first-class carriages were generally empty, and she had indulged in this, for her, unusual extravagance, in order to be alone.

The moment of departure had come; the guard was waving his green flag, when a porter snatched open Shibby's carriage-door, and, as the train began to move, Dr Magner scrambled in.

'Why, Shibby! Is it yourself? This is a surprise to find you here! I'm delighted to see you!' he began. 'I didn't see you this long time—since old John Weldon's funeral I think it was?—and how are you?'

'I'm well, thank you,' Shibby said, briefly. Well as she liked Willy Magner, she was not disposed for company.

'That's right!' said the Doctor. He paused, and put on his eye-glasses the better to observe her. 'But I may tell you I've seen you looking better.'

'I'm well enough,' Shibby repeated.

'I suppose you heard the news?' said the Doctor.

'What news?'

'This about Maggie Connor——'

'I was told it at the station just now,' said Shibby, steadily, 'drowned, they were saying, she was. But I heard no more.'

'She wasn't seen since Sunday,' said the Doctor. 'She was lost. No one knew where she was. The brother was searching the country for her all yesterday——'

'He was up with us, too—' Shibby threw in.

'It was fishermen that found her body in their nets this morning—the unfortunate creature! They think she might have fallen into the river off the big rock—Carrig-a-breac, as they call it. She was there constantly. They think she might have been there Sunday night—the night it blew so hard.'

'She was mad,' said Shibby, in a voice of iron. 'She's no loss!'

The Doctor looked at her, and thought: 'Then it must have been

Kit!' He said aloud:

''Tis a sad affair to be sure. There'll be an inquest to-morrow. Between you and me, Shibby—though I wouldn't say it to everyone—it looks like suicide, but of course they'll bring it in "Death by misadventure."'I'm told Jimmy was taking her to America, and they were to have started yesterday———'

Shibby was sitting in a corner of the carriage with her back to the light. The sun shone in, and the Doctor, though he looked hard at her, could not see her face clearly.

'I wonder where did Jimmy get the money?' He leaned forward and met her eyes.

'He got it from me, if you want to know, Willy,' said Shibby, with her head up. 'It was I paid their way there!'

'Then it *was* Kit!' thought Doctor Magner, regarding her with the look of comprehending compassion that comes not seldom on a doctor's face.

Shibby met the look in silence. For one instant the thought came to her, should she tell Willy Magner all that there was to tell? Would it stop the gnawing of the wolf at her soul if she dragged it out, for an instant even? Willy was her friend. He would understand.

Then the long habit of secrecy mastered what she felt to be weakness. She told herself that there was no good in talking now. She repented of nothing. If the girl wanted to drown herself, it was no business of hers to stop her. Kit was free—that was the main thing—and Kit had the Big House! She would find a good match for him yet! Yes, she had done well! She folded her cloak over the wolf.

They talked on of Kit, and his accident.

'That Handcock that's attending him is a clever chap, I know him well,' said the Doctor, 'and he comes of nice people—warm people, too, begad!'

'Nessie says he's minding Kit well. He's doing grand, she says.'

'Well, that's good, anyhow,' said the Doctor, smiling at her, wondering what was wrong with her. 'You'll have to be looking about for an heiress for him. I hope we'll live to see him reigning at the Big House yet! Here's my station———' He stood up and collected his newspaper and his umbrella and black bag. He took her hand. 'Well,

257

good-bye, Shibby, my dear. Be taking care of yourself now! Remember good people are scarce, and the bad ones are afraid to die! And we're not as young as we used to be, worse luck!'

Miss Pindy arrived at Cahirbwee early in the afternoon. She had to cross the line by a bridge in the station, and in doing so she cast an eye down on to the departure platform. Two or three men were standing there, waiting for the uptrain to Clytagh, and among them it seemed to her that the aspect of one figure was familiar. She stood still and looked down attentively. At the same moment the man looked up, and she recognised Mr John Weldon.

'Now what is that one doing here?' she thought.

A presentiment of evil came upon her. 'Johnny Weldon never brought me anything but what was bad!'

As she walked through the town the people looked at her, wondering who was the big woman with the face of trouble on her.

There was a bright little space of garden between the McKnight's house and the road. Dahlias and marigolds and Michaelmas daisies filled it full of vivid colour, and a bed of phloxes of every delicate shade, were like a box of French *fondants*. A pergola hung with climbing roses went from the gate to the tidy little hall-door. Standing on the path, under the trellis, with a few red roses in her hand, was Nessie. A young man was standing beside her, whom Nessie introduced as Doctor Handcock. Shibby noticed that he had a red rose in his buttonhole.

'He's doing first-rate,' Dr Handcock said of his patient. 'I never knew a fracture to do better. He's being well nursed,' he added, looking at Nessie, and seeming to find it difficult to withdraw his eyes from her face.

Shibby went into the house saying to herself, 'Faith, he's taken with her!' The blackness lifted for a moment from her spirit and the tooth of the wolf gave her a respite. She even smiled a little.

Kit's greetings were brief. His eyes were very bright and his face was flushed.

'Is there fever on him?' thought Shibby, anxiously—'whatever way he is, he must hear what I have to tell him——' But not at once; she might give him a few minutes of peace. She entered upon minute inquiries as to his health. Kit answered them briefly and with impatience. Then he broke in on them.

'I had a visitor here already this morning! who d'ye think?' He did not wait for her to reply. 'Young Johnny! And what d'ye think he came about?'

'No good!' said Shibby, and felt the formless dread gripping her more tightly.

'Maybe that's what you'll think!' said Kit, with excitement. 'I'm hardly sure myself what I think—I told Nessie not to tell you—she says she's sorry—but *I* think, maybe——'

'For God's sake, child, what is it?' broke in Shibby.

'Well, it's the Captain that's done it!' said Kit, his excitement growing, even though into his eyes, that were fixed on Shibby's face, something like fear was coming. 'When the cat's away, y'know, Shibby——' he went on, with a wild snatch of excited laughter.

'For God's sake, child what is it?' broke in Shibby.

'He's sold the Big House to the Englishman for three thousand five hundred! Think o' that! By Jove, it's a big lot o' money!' Kit gabbled on, the hot colour deepening in his face. 'It might be worse! I'll start a training-stable!—or I might go to America——' He caught sight of Shibby's face, and at the look in it his heart quailed.

She was standing at the foot of the bed, clutching the rail with both hands.

'The curse of God is on me!' she said in a low voice, 'what use is there to strive? Laugh away, boy! You're easy pleased! Your sweetheart has left you for another man, and your fancy-girl is drowned, and now your house is sold!'

Her hands released their grip of the rail. She looked round her, vaguely. There was a chair by the door, placed with its back to the wall, without relation to the life of the room. She began to move towards it. A small table, with bottles on it, was by the foot of the bed. She stumbled against it and some of the bottles, and a glass of water that was on it, fell with a crash, and the water streamed on to the floor. She took no notice, but went on with an uncertain step, and sat down heavily on the chair.

Kit raised himself as well as he could, twisting his head and shoulders round towards Shibby.

'What on earth are you saying? What man? Who's drowned?

259

Johnny Weldon told me nothing——'

Shibby made no answer. She sat in a terrible silence, looking straight in front of her, her face fixed in iron stillness, like a stone guardian of an Egyptian tomb. She was like a huge blot in the clean little room, an immense embodiment of the spirit of Tragedy.

'Why won't you answer me?' Kit yelled at her in his high voice, made shrill by fear. He caught at a handbell that was beside him and rang it furiously.

Nessie came flying upstairs at the summons.

'What is it, Kit? What's the matter?'

'She won't speak,' Kit gasped. 'She's gone mad! She's saying—I don't know what—lies—I don't believe her——' He wrenched himself farther round, in order to see Shibby, and fell backwards with a cry:

'Damnation! My leg——'

He lay still on his pillows, fainting.

Nessie sprang to the open window, calling to the Doctor to come back, and then addressed herself to Kit. In a moment the young Doctor was there beside her, helping to take the pillows from under Kit's head, telling her he'd be all right directly.

Shibby had risen to her feet and was watching them. The colour began to return to Kit's face.

'Ah, he'll be all right now in a minute,' said the Doctor. 'We'll have a look at the leg, presently. He must have given it a twist.'

'Nessie,' said Shibby, quietly, 'come here a minute.' She put a hand on Nessie's shoulder, as if to steady herself. 'I'm going back now. Tell him Peggy's thrown him over for the Englishman. That's the first of it. And Maggie Connor's after drowning herself. That's the next of it. No, let me go, child—' Nessie had caught at her arm. 'Yourself and himself know the rest of it. The Big House is gone. He's after telling me that. There's no more to say——'

As Shibby went along the streets of Cahirbwee one woman said to another:

'There goes that big woman agin!'

The other said:

'God! As bad as she was before, she looks dead altogether now!'

Chapter 41

Old Jas, after his brief efflorescence of independence, relapsed into so deep a condition of apathetic torpor that it seemed as though the effort had exhausted his remnant of vitality. When, at half-past eight o'clock, Shibby arrived from Cahirbwee, he took no notice of her entrance, and remained humped over the fire in the Tower sitting-room, with a dog on his knees.

The dog, who was Fly, was watching, with eyes of profound and jealous indignation, Tinker, crouched under a table in a corner of the room. The third dog, Sailor, sat at a short distance, also watching Tinker.

Shibby was very tired.

'Where's Delia?' she said, 'I told her to have things ready for me.'

Jas roused himself.

'She left the supper on the table,' he said, blinking at his daughter, 'she said you'd find the kettle on the boil—She's gone to the village—she said there was no—something—I forget——' his voice was lost in a fit of coughing.

'It's a funny way she left the table!' said Shibby, grimly, 'or was it yourself threw all, hither and over? There was a cold chicken. Surely you didn't eat the whole of it?'

It was of the strength of her character that above the fatigue of her body, and the despair that was crushing her soul, she could force an attention that was active, even though superficial, to the household affairs to which she had given her life.

While she was speaking, a crunching sound, that had ceased at her entrance, came again from beneath the table in the corner. Fly's attention became more strained. Sailor whined. Shibby stooped and looked under the table.

'I see the dog has it,' she said in an expressionless voice. 'It's a wonder to me that you could sit there and leave them dogs destroy everything.'

'I didn't know—I might have been asleep——' the Captain said,

261

guiltily; 'I know I didn't have my smoke. I couldn't find the matches—I must have gone asleep—that was how it was——' He mumbled apologies, repeating the same words over and over again in his alarm and confusion.

'No matter,' said Shibby, 'let the dog finish all now. I want nothing. I'll go to my bed.' She had opened the door, when she stopped. 'How well you wouldn't tell me you had the house sold behind my back!'

She had said to herself that she would say nothing to the old man, but fatigue, and the irritation that the dogs had aroused in her, broke down her resolve. She shut the door without waiting for a reply.

Delia Cloherty, who was Miss Pindy's servant, thought the time too long till the next morning, when she would see her mistress and could tell her the news that she had gathered in the village. The riches of her budget were almost an embarrassment. Delia Cloherty could gladly have devoted the entire morning to discussing Maggie Connor's disastrous end, with particulars of her appearance when the fishermen brought her body home, coupled with her own regret that the priest had had Maggie carried to the chapel, and had forbidden a wake, and Miss Pindy would therefore be unable to see her. But this topic, entrancing though it was, was not encouraged by Delia's mistress, and was soon elbowed aside in order to permit of the detailed setting-forth of Miss Peggy Weldon's 'Uprise.'

Thus did Cloon regard the engagement of Young Johnny's daughter. Mr Weldon, it will be seen, had not delayed the announcement of the blossoming of the thorn which, on its first appearance, he had received with so much disappointment. Joy had indeed budded from it, and Mr Weldon's origin was not so remote from the village as to deprive him of the satisfaction of realising how little his less successful acquaintances there would enjoy his triumph.

'Sir Har'ld has bought the Big House from the poor old Captain, and a nice sum he paid for it, too . . . me daughter's the owner of the demesne now . . . Isn't it a nice thing to think me daughter and her intended will be joining the two together in Holy Matrimony!' In such manner as this did Young Johnny triumph through his native place, and even as far as to Clytagh and Monarde went the sound of his triumphing.

The various groups of Pindys, received the intelligence with contempt that deepened in direct ratio with their nearness to the family tree. But Weldons, of differing degrees of consanguinity, went more proudly to church, and one family of second-cousins, generously overlooking past affronts, went so far in their pride and family feeling, as to send the bride-elect two gifts, which were described in the letter that accompanied them as 'a poll-glass and a biscuiteer'—the former, it should, perhaps, be explained, being a hand-mirror for the dressing-table—that in their sending as in their reception, exemplified very strikingly the truth that it is more blessed to give than to receive.

'Mrs Weldon's going to England with the daughter to buy clothes, and it's in London the wedding'll be!' Delia Cloherty reported, and Shibby could not choose but hear.

Some few days later Dr Magner came to see Shibby. Not to condole, or to attempt to comfort. He knew her too well to indulge in methods so crude. He told her that the people were laughing at Young Johnny and his boastings, and were saying that the place was like dead without Master Kit riding his horses out through the village, and that Jimmy Connor had gone to America, and the old man was back in the workhouse at Clytagh; and the Doctor even chased, for a moment, the darkness from Shibby's brow, by telling her how he had met Dr Handcock, and that there was no doubt but that Nessie had hit him hard, and there were more beside Peggy Weldon that would be getting married soon. Then, encouraged by his success, Willy Magner adventured nearer to the seat of trouble, and told Shibby that he had seen Kit, and his leg was doing nicely, and there was no doubt but a handy sum of money in the heel of a young man's fist, was a more useful thing for him than a big empty house—and for his part, he didn't hold with a boy getting married too young——

'Thank ye, Willy,' Shibby said, interrupting him, 'I'm obliged to ye——'

She stopped speaking. Willy Magner, for the second time in his life, saw tears in her eyes, and knew that he had gone too deep.

She stood up and turned away from him.

The tears brought with them remembrance of the day that she had wept on Willy Magner's shoulder. She had chosen loneliness then. She asked no better now.

She turned to him again, looking straight into his eyes through the unshed tears, too proud to hide them, defying his pity. Her voice was steady when she spoke.

'I've settled to have an oxtion of the things I have above in the Big House. There's some nice things there——'

'Furniture and the like are going dear now, I'm told,' said the Doctor, accepting the closure. 'You should do well with them.'

'The things are good!' said Shibby, nodding her head.

Miss Pindy and Delia Cloherty and Judy Davin spent, during the following week, long hours in assembling, and arranging for sale, the furniture that was in the Big House. The Lady Isabella's room was untouched. Burgrave had not forgotten the carved mirror and the old mahogany wardrobes, and had made so generous a bid for the contents of the room (excepting only the brazen bedstead) that Shibby accepted it, being accustomed to subordinate sentiment, even hostilities, to financial considerations, and was well satisfied that what she regarded as her greatest success, the brass bedstead, should be left out of the bargain.

Old Jas doddered up and down stairs and round the house after them, much as a very old dog will simulate independence, and refuse to come when called, yet will always keep somewhere in the owner's neighbourhood. Shibby went about the business with steady purpose, hearing not half the incessant conversation of her two helpers, heeding not at all that which she heard. She had enough to think of, she told herself, without to be minding them and their chat. Uppermost in her thought was the practical matter of the sale. She could have told to a penny the price that she had given for each of these things, but she had not the self-consciousness that might have summed up for her the uncertainties, the plots, the sacrifices that each one of them had involved. All details such as these were massed into a single oppression. Her immense common-sense alone upheld her. Without it she must have sunk under the growing weight of foreboding that lay on her soul. Ever, as she went about her work in the Big House, she felt herself not alone. Her nerve was like a rock, yet there were moments when she feared to look behind her, so near and tangible was the brooding influence.

'Is it Maggie Connor that's following me?' she asked herself; 'let her follow me if she likes! I'd do the same again to-morrow!'

Much might be lost, but Kit was free. She need no longer school her spirit to accept an alliance with 'The Grabber's daughter'. The bitterness was now concentrated in the prospect of the usurper reigning in the Big House. Always as this thought forced itself upon her—and it was seldom far away—a cloud would envelope her, a cloud charged with lightnings and rumbling with thunder.

All the morning the auctioneer's man had been there, pasteing sale-numbers on the hard-won fruit of her economies. The dinner service, that she had bought after Kit had told her that Peggy was 'his to do what he liked with,' had been unpacked and was displayed in the drawing-room; the straw littered the floor that she had kept so clean and swept. The curtains that she had made were spread forth on the prized Chesterfield sofa. It maddened her to think of the village people, the farmers' wives from the country round, the second-hand dealers from Clytagh, coming and prying, appraising, despising, gloating over their bargains . . .

It was past five o'clock. Shibby had gone upstairs to lock up the Lady Isabella's room. The brass bedstead had been withdrawn, and she was locking the door in order to prevent the crowd, the hated crowd, that on the morrow would surge through the house, from surging in there. She stood at the heavy teak door, leaning against it, the twisted ring of brass that was the handle, in her hand, and looked down the long, familiar corridor, and, at last, her self-control failed her.

'I'm done!' she said aloud, 'I'm beat. I done my best. There never was luck in it! There was too much pride and wickedness long ago, destroying the ones that came after—Pride and badness, all sorts . . . God knows I had the pride, but it's broke in me now——'

Stung by the thought of the irrevocable, overmastering past she jerked her head sideways, as a horse will jerk his head, stung by a fly. It struck the door violently, and she welcomed the pain that shut out thought. She pressed her forehead against the panel, her head dizzy and ringing with the blow, and as she stood there, quiet, she heard what seemed to her was the sound of footsteps in the room. Then, in her hand, she thought she felt the old brass handle move, and with that strange stir of the handle in her hand a run of chill went up her spine and spread like a wind over her face.

She swung round and locked the door. 'I'm a fool. I'll go home and have me tea—I can come back again——'

She looked into the drawing-room as she passed, and saw that the auctioneers' men had put sale numbers on the portraits that still hung on the walls.

'Ha! then! Them'll not stay there long!' she said fiercely, 'what a notion he had that the family pictures would be sold!'

The man had gone. She said to herself that she would take the numbers off when she came back after her tea, and she called to the other women to come with her.

'Where is the Captain?'

'I think he went home awhile ago, Miss,' said Delia Cloherty.

'I'll lock the door, so,' said Shibby.

The three dogs were awaiting her, ready for tea, indignant that it should be so much later than usual. But the Captain was not there. 'It must be he was in it after all,' said Shibby. 'Well, no matter. He'll come out the back door when he wants his tea. Anyway I'm going back meself just now——'

The end of September was near, and the sun had set when Shibby went back to the Big House. She was deadly tired; her head ached from the blow she had given it, and the black cloud was over her, wrapping her about. She walked heavily up the high flight of limestone steps. The Devannes marriage-stone, with the Lady Isabella's initials in the corner caught her eye.

''Twas little but the Weldon arms were there to face it!' she said, with a bitter smile, 'though it might fail them all to say what they were!'

She unlocked the great door and pushed it in. A rush of smoke met her. She staggered back.

'Good God! Fire!'

The smoke swirled out, making her cough and choke. Then she remembered the Captain.

'Captain!' she shouted, and rushed in through the smoke. 'Captain! Are ye there! Come out!'

She could see nothing, but the horrible crackling hurry of fire seemed to come from the drawing-room. Half-way across the hall she stumbled heavily, almost fell, over some large, solid object. Instantly she knew that she need go no further, old Jas was at her feet. She groped at his body, and found his shoulders, and catching him under both arms, she began to drag his great frame towards the open door. Whether he were dead or alive she knew not, his body was entirely inert. Big and strong as she was, and endowed with the frantic strength that can be given in crises, it was all that she could do to move him. The smoke stormed through the hall, bursting in whirling masses, that seemed almost solid, through the door that she had left open.

'Can I do it?—Can I do it?' She panted, choking and smothering, feeling her strength failing her, wondering how soon she, too, must yield and fall beside the old man, the father who had never owned her as his daughter.

She was but half-way across the great hall when she heard voices outside.

'Help!' she shrieked, her voice half-stifled, 'Come and help me!'

Then she found that a man was at her side. She could see nothing, her eyes were streaming, blinded by the smoke, but she felt her load suddenly lightened. The unseen helper had laid hold of the Captain, and was straining with her at the task. At last they were on the steps, and in the smoke Shibby was aware of Delia Cloherty beside her, grasping one of the Captain's arms, and sharing her effort. The man who had come to her aid had taken the Captain's feet, and was drawing his body down the steps.

Half carrying, half dragging, they brought the old man out through the gates, and laid him on the grass beyond the eddying smoke.

The rescuers stood, panting, coughing, trembling with shock and effort.

'He's gone,' said the man, looking down on old Jas, 'we were too late!'

Then it was that Shibby saw who had helped her—her enemy, Young Johnny.

The story of the Big House of Inver is finished. The only noteworthy observation that need still be told is that of Mr John Weldon.

'Sure I had it insured, to be sure! On the same day we paid the money—and all that's in it, too, thank God!'

'I'm an insurance agent, don't ye know!'

THE END

Notes

Publishing history

The Big House of Inver was finished in June 1925, and published a few months later by William Heinemann Ltd. It was well received by the reviewers, although it disappointed readers who persisted in thinking of Somerville and Ross as writers of jolly hunting tales. 10,000 copies were printed of the first edition, of which 8,000 had been sold a year later.

The themes Edith Somerville had in mind can be seen in the two other titles considered for the novel, *A Victim of the Past*, and *Restoration*. (Hilary Robinson *Somerville and Ross p 179.)*

Critical opinion now regards *The Big House of Inver* as second only to *The Real Charlotte* as an achievement, and for many its theme of the decay of the old colonising power gives it a special contemporary interest. As Hilary Robinson wrote: '*The Real Charlotte* and *The Big House of Inver* deserve to take their place beside *Mansfield Park* as well as beside Maria Edgeworth's *Castle Rackrent* and Yeats' *Purgatory*. They are among the great novels of passion in English, necessarily Irish, but no more provincial than Dean Swift or Yeats. Somerville and Ross' achievement is to show their Irish lives as deeply and eternally significant' (*Somerville and Ross: A Critical Appreciation* pp 203–4).

General notes

1 *claret from Bordeaux* Throughout the 18th century great quantities of wool was smuggled out and wine in to the West of Ireland.
1 *Queen Anne* (1702–14) the immediate successor of William of Orange.
2 *a newish King* George I, the king of Hanover in Germany, inherited the throne in 1714. He spoke no English and was widely disliked for his rudeness and the greed of his favourites (not only by the Jacobites, who saw him as a usurper).

2 *Barony of Iveragh* A barony was a subdivision of a county. There were seventeen baronies in Galway. Iveragh is actually the name of a barony in south Kerry.

3 *Je Prends* French—I take.

3 *season at the Vice-regal court* 'People used still to come up and take houses for the season, and wealthy and poor of good family mingled for a few weeks at dinners, dances, Court functions and all sorts of miscellaneous sports and games,' P. L. Dickinson *The Dublin of Yesterday*. The Castle Season ran for six weeks in February and March.

3 *Italian workmen* The best-known such stuccadores (plasterwork specialists capable of producing the fashionable 'gorgeous deep-moulded ceilings' p 38), were the Lafranchini brothers, who were responsible for ceilings in Carton, Russborough and numerous Dublin houses. They were in fact Swiss.

3 *High Sheriff* An influential but potentially expensive post. The sheriff was responsible for conducting elections, selecting the grand jury and other local government functions. The normal term of office was one year.

4 *duel* About one Irish duel in four ended in death. However, by 1824 duelling had declined sharply from its mid 18th-century peak and was actively discouraged by many magistrates. 18th-century duels used to be conducted in private, well away from prying eyes. The attendance of crowds, as described here, was a 19th-century innovation. (See J. Kelly *'That Damn'd Thing called Honour' Duelling in Ireland 1570–1860* Cork 1995)

6 *coragh* Irish *curragh*—the traditional canvas or hide covered rowing boat.

6 *caioneing* Irish *caoineadh* (keening)—traditional women's mourning cry. See also the note to p 191.

6 *Peelers* The non-sectarian police force established by Sir Robert Peel in 1814 to replace the 'Barnies', the feeble (and exclusively Protestant) baronial police. Reorganised by province in 1822, and finally centralised as the Royal Irish Constabulary in 1836.

8 *tithe riots* In the 1830s resistance to tithes (a tax paid by Catholic and Presbyterian as well as Church of Ireland farmers to support

the Church of Ireland clergy) rose to a new height of bitterness and violence. As early as 1832, 242 murders, and numerous robberies, cattle-maimings and attacks on houses had been attributed to tithe rioters.

10 *Sir Charles Napier* In an outrageous piece of British 19th-century imperialism, Napier (1782–1853) invaded the wealthy north Indian state of Scind in 1843. He was supposed to have announced the victory by a cable consisting of the Latin word *peccavi* (meaning 'I have sinned') as a coded despatch. Until the reforms of 1871 virtually all commissions in the British Army were bought from the current holder by his successor.

11 *famine of 1845* The fatal effects of the potato blight were first reported on 5 September 1845. The crop failures continued until 1850, by which time at least one million people had died and as many had emigrated.

12 *Stephen Gwynn* (1864–1950) Author and Redmondite nationalist MP for Galway 1906–18. Enlisting at the age of 50, he fought in the British Army in the First World War from 1914 to 1917. His *History of Ireland* was published in Dublin and London in 1923.

13 *famine-fever* The two most prevalent diseases during the famine years were typhus and relapsing fever, both of which are carried by lice. Edith Somerville's optimistic relegation of typhus to 'backward places' was ill-founded. In fact, 'Ireland was the last country in Western Europe with louse-born typhus, and the Anglo-Irish health administration never mastered the disease' (James Deeny *The End of the Epidemic* Dublin 1995 p 53). Typhus was finally eradicated in the 1940s.

14 *Nunc Dimittis* 'Lord, now lettest Thou thy servant depart according to Thy word, in peace' Luke 2:29. Edith Somerville was for decades organist at her local church; *The Big House of Inver,* her last substantial book, contains at least a dozen references to passages in the King James version of the Bible or the Book of Common Prayer, considerably more than, for instance, in *The Real Charlotte.*

15 *pony-phaeton* Light four-wheeled open carriage.

271

15 *bar sinister* A marking on a coat of arms popularly, but mistakenly, believed to signify illegitimacy.

15 *Droit de Seigneur* The legend that a feudal lord was entitled to sleep with any newly-married bride from his manor. Imaginative nationalists accused Irish landlords of exercising this right, even stipulating it in leases.

16 *Mr Wordsworth's authority* 'The good old rule/sufficeth them, the simple plan,/That they should take, who have the power,/And they should keep who can.' From William Wordsworth's *Memorials of a Tour in Scotland 1803: Rob Roy's Grave.* The reference to the Prendeville motto, 'I take', is clear, and for readers who recognised the quotation, the author foreshadows her story with the last line.

16 *the Cape* In 1848 Sir Harry Smith claimed sovereignity over all Boer territory and defeated a Boer army; fighting rumbled on until 1852.

16 *lucky hand* Untrained midwives were common in the west of Ireland until the 1930s. In the 1850s both trained and untrained attendants were guilty of cross-infecting patients with the often fatal puerperal fever.

20 *Grand Jury list* The list of the county's eligible property owners from which the Grand Jury was picked.

21 *nice tourney rules* A tourney is a mock battle, especially one mimicking medieval combat.

23 *turning up his little finger* Familiar figure of speech (technically metonymy) for drinking.

24 *Plan of Campaign* The depressed farming conditions of the 1870s put pressure on tenants, and the Land League was established in 1879 to protect them. In 1886, with conditions not improving, a stratagem, called the 'Plan of Campaign', was proposed whereby tenants offered what they considered a fair rent, and if this was refused paid none.

25 *demesne land* The land attached to the big house, usually including woods, parkland and the home farm.

26 *Half-seas-over* Half way through a sea journey, hence half drunk.

26 *grauver* Irish *grámhar*–affectionate, kind, tender.

27 *King Ahasuerus* Quotation not quite accurate, see the Old Testa-

ment Book of Esther especially 2:10 onwards (King James version).

30 *the Preacher* Old Testament Ecclesiastes 11:7. The Preacher's normal view of life is certainly gloomy: 'he that increaseth knowledge, increaseth sorrow' (1:18), 'he that diggeth a pit shall fall into it' (10:8) or 'of making of books there is no end; and much study is a weariness of the flesh' (12:12).

30 *young Kit* The date is now 1912 (the year in which Martin Ross sent Edith the letter about Tyrone House). Kit is 24. The whole of the rest of the story takes no more than a few months.

31 *National School* The state-backed primary school system established in 1831.

32 *Queen's Colleges* Queen's Colleges were established in Galway, Cork and Belfast in 1845 in an attempt to provide university education that did not offend religious sensitivities. In 1908 the National University of Ireland absorbed the Cork and Galway Queen's Colleges.

32 *seventy times seven* The number of times a Christian is enjoined to forgive, see Matthew 18:22.

34 *John Gilpin* From a poem of that name by William Cowper (1731–1800): 'His horse, who never in that sort/had handled been before/what thing upon his back had got/did wonder more and more.'

40 *Flora Macdonald* During Bonnie Prince Charlie's escape from the Battle of Culloden (1746) she aided his escape supposedly by using her own arm to bolt a door.

40 *Shibby's furniture* A Chesterfield was a large over-stuffed sofa, not in keeping with the elegant 18th-century house; a prie-Dieu chair had a long sloping back and doubled as a prayer-stool.

41 *£8* Equivalent to £500 in 1999.

42 *the Grabber* 'Grabber', one who took the land of an evicted tenant, a term nearly as opprobrious as 'informer'.

42 *a warm man* An old usage, meaning well-off, comfortably secure in possessions, rather than seriously rich.

45 *Burke's Landed Gentry* Originally published in 1832, and regularly updated since, *Burke's* was a reference book detailing the legitimate families of all untitled but land-owning gentlemen. By

1912 however, Edith Somerville points out, the title had become a pious fraud, since many of the families listed no longer held any more 'than such lands as were comprised in their flower-gardens' (p 58).

45 *Norn* Three maidens in Scandinavian myth who spun or wove the fates of men.

45 *Droic h'uil* Irish *droch shúil* the evil eye. On p 81 we learn that the village people referred to Shibby as 'the Big Woman with the Bad Eye'. On p 128 it is made clear that Maggie certainly has something to fear, and on p 241 Shibby powerfully 'ill-wishes' her.

46 *Shrove after Shrove* Shrove Tuesday was a popular time for getting married since no weddings were allowed during Lent.

46 *Commy-tee* Traditional pronunciation of committee. The appoint-ment of the local dispensary (welfare) doctor was in the hands of the Board of Guardians of the local Poor House, whose vulner-ability to corruption—what Edith Somerville calls 'material ar-guments'—was widely known.

50 *the gods* '"Whom the gods love die young" was said of yore' Lord Byron *Don Juan* canto 4.12.

51 *valance* Cloth border hanging down below the chair.

53 *Land Purchase Act of 1903* The culmination of a long series of Acts which transformed Irish landholding from domination by landlords (who often owned thousands of acres divided into many farms) to ownership of their farms by individual farmers. The Act gave landlords an immediate bonus if they sold their entire estate to the tenants. Most landlords seized the chance to escape from the long struggle over rents, and over 7 million acres changed hands under its provisions.

55 *Pope Julius* As well as building St Peter's, Julius II (1503–13) sponsored Michelangelo (especially the Sistine Chapel) and Raphael.

55 *John's religion* Long before the *Ne Temere* papal decree (1908), it was Catholic teaching that all children of a Catholic should be baptised Catholic. In practice in a mixed marriage boys often took their father's religion and girls their mother's.

58 *Bench of Tuppennies* Tuppenny = two-pence. In his second term

as Chief Secretary (1892–5) Lord Morley attacked some of the privileges of the Ascendancy and in particular removed some of the more politically objectionable magistrates from the bench, replacing them with local, less flashy, men.

60 *brown habit* Pious Catholics often donned the dark brown robes of the (lay) Third Order of St Francis on their deathbeds.

62 *Fifth Commandment* In Church of Ireland and Church of England usage, the Fifth Commandment is: 'Honour thy father and thy mother; that thy days may be long in the land which the Lord thy God giveth thee.' For Catholics and Lutherans, the Fifth Commandment is 'Thou shalt not kill.' The author clearly has the former audience in mind.

63 *Mahomet's coffin* Legend had it that Mohammed's body had been enclosed in an iron coffin which was suspended in the air between two natural magnets.

69 *like St Paul talks about* 'Salute one another with an holy kiss' says St Paul in his letter to the Romans 16:16

73 *"chimes at midnight"* *Henry IV Part II*, Act 3 Scene 2: *Falstaff* 'we have heard the chimes at midnight, Master Shallow'—educated cliché for a life of debauch.

79 *whose mother had died* Dr Magner, Kit and Shibby all believe that Maggie's mother is still alive in the Asylum (pp 153, 169, 176).

80 *Foxy Mag* Foxy meant redheaded.

80 *dolman* A close-fitting jacket which had its sleeves cut in one piece with the back.

81 *Royal Irish Constabulary* Originally an armed semi-military force, by 1900 the RIC had become 'domesticated'. It was disbanded in 1921.

84 *weight* To ensure an even race, the committee handicapped the better horses by making sure they carried a particular total burden (made up of jockey plus saddle plus special extra lead weights in a belt). We later (p 106–7) learn that Nora has to carry 11 stone as opposed to 10 st 3 lbs for the rival Lively Lad, a handicap of 11 lbs.

90 *shilling* Also called a 'bob'; 12 old pence (1/20th of a pound) is equivalent to £3 in 1999 values.

93 *one-day licence* A special licence to sell alcoholic drink on the

race course granted by the magistrates (see 'Occasional Licences' in *Experiences of an Irish RM).*

95 *tossed Kit's cup* Shibby has dark powers, this time telling fortunes by examining the tea leaves left in Kit's cup. (See also p 97 where Shibby brushes her hair over her eyes and peers into a mirror to see the future.) On p 121 she is described as living near the border between this world 'sense' and the spirit world 'sensibility'.

101 *a good price* The key to the fraud is that no one believed that Nora could win given the handicap, so happily gave high odds.

103 *George Meredith* 'A foolish consistency is the hobgoblin of little minds' is from Ralph Waldo Emerson's essay 'Self-Reliance'.

111 *crooked bridge* The High Sheriff was the convenor of the Grand Jury, among whose responsibilities was the allocation of funds for roads and bridges.

114 *weasel* Technically, weasels do not occur in Ireland. The somewhat larger stoat is often called a weasel and fills the same position of ill-omen, it being considered bad luck to meet one, especially in the morning.

120 *Love's young dream* 'No, there's nothing half so sweet in life/As love's young dream' is from a ballad by Ireland's most popular songwriter, Thomas Moore (1779–1852).

121 *a figure* It is clear from p 122 that this is Lady Isabella—even the prosaic Sir Harold sees her (p 149), though her appearances are generally associated with Jas being in the Big House. The presence, however interpreted, of Lady Isabella is crucial to the action. For instance, on p 242 'her inveterate spirit' darkens counsel, deepens hatred.

123 *fast day* Until after the Second Vatican Council, Catholics were obliged to abstain from meat on Fridays. Kit, being a Protestant, is allowed chicken.

124 *smelleth the battle* 'He says among the trumpets, Ha ha; and he smelleth the battle afar off, the thunder of the captains, and the shouting.' Job 39:24.

131 *a car* An outside or jaunting car, took four passengers facing outwards.

133 *habit-skirt* A tight-fitting skirt designed for side-saddle riding.

134 *King Cophetua* Legendary king who fell in love with a 'perni-

cious and undubiate beggar' (*Love's Labour's Lost* Act 4 Scene 1) and made her his queen.

139 *status quo ante* Latin—situation as before.

139 *render unto Caesar* Matthew 19:21.

140 *Jabot* An elaborate bow or cravat tied at the neck.

140 *went Nap* In the nursery card game based on whist, the player who calls Nap undertakes to win all the tricks in the game.

142 *white man* An American expression, with obviously insensitive, racist, overtones. Earlier used as a commendation of Peggy's dress-sense (p 103).

146 *£15,000 a year* Equivalent to £900,000 in 1999 values.

148 *Nehushtan* A derisive expression, meaning made of brass; 2 Kings 18:4 'and [he] brake in pieces the brasen serpent that Moses had made, for unto those days the children of Israel did burn incense to it: and he called it Nehushtan'.

149 *Appollyon* Described as 'the angel of the bottomless pit' in Revelations 9:11.

150 *a Sahib* A 'sir' in Anglo-Indian. Jas, who had at least been to India, has considerably more right to use this jargon than Sir Harold.

153 *marrying and intermarrying* Medical opinion firmly believed that insanity and tuberculosis were hereditary and aggravated by marriage of close relatives.

155 *old John's will* To prevent fraud, beneficiaries were not allowed to act as witnesses to the signature of the will-maker.

158 *Juggernaut* Literally, 'Lord of the world'—during a festival in Orissa, India, an enormous statue of Vishnu on a huge carriage was dragged by hundreds of pilgrims to a nearby shrine. The journey took days. Legend had it that in a kind of holy suicide men threw themselves under the car and were crushed, but the statue continued remorselessly on.

159 *What a country!* In 'Children of the Captivity' Somerville and Ross wrote: 'The very wind that blows softly over brown acres of bog carries perfumes and sounds that England does not know: the women digging the potato-land are talking of things that England does not understand. The question that remains is whether England will ever understand.' (*Some Irish Yesterdays* 1906)

159 *Andromeda* In Greek myth, she was chained naked to a rock as a sacrifice to a (female) sea-monster, and rescued by Perseus. This was a favourite subject for Victorian painters.

160 *Clerk of the Weather* A typically ponderous, late-Victorian joke, implying that Sir Harold had bribed God to make the weather good.

163 *Quarter Sessions* Four times a year the magistrates of a county gathered to try the more serious cases arising in the area. This would of course be a busy time for a solicitor.

173 *£3,000* Equivalent to £200,000 in 1999.

176 *County asylum* Although strictly intended for mental patients, it was relatively easy to get someone admitted, and inspectors constantly complained that the aged, the infirm, the bedridden, even those in extreme want or dying were committed on the strength of magisterial warrants (Joseph Robins *Fools and Mad* Dublin 1986 p 111).

178 *Bail ó Dhia ort* Irish—the blessing of God be with you. Shibby's use of the expression 'God bless the work!' underlines the financial importance of Kit's task.

183 *in bonds* A binding verbal agreement.

187 *bosthoon* Irish *bastún*—fool, blockhead.

191 *Irish Cry* 'I had often been told of the Irish custom of "keening" at funerals, but I was not prepared for anything so barbaric and so despairing. It broke out with increasing volume and intensity while the coffin was being lifted . . . the women clapping their hands and beating their breasts, their chant rising and swelling like the howl of the wind on a wild night.' (from Somerville and Ross's first novel *An Irish Cousin*)

192 *£50* £3,250 in 1999 values.

201 *Kingstown* Dunleary was named Kingstown in honour of the visit of George IV in 1821; it was renamed Dún Laoghaire in 1922.

202 *mourning* Mrs Weldon would wear special dark garments for at least six months after the death of her father-in-law.

203 *convenances* Conventions, suitable behaviour.

212 *clean forgotten* 'I am clean forgotten, as a dead man out of mind' Psalms 31:14.

217 *No John!* In *Somerville and Ross—A Critical Appreciation* Hilary
Robinson points out that most of the 'dialect' speech in this novel
can be directly traced to Edith Somerville's notebook recordings
of things she had actually heard.

218 *snaffle* The oldest and simplest form of bit, lacking a curb, so
requiring greater riding skill.

221 *asthoreen* Irish *a stór*—treasure, with diminutive, my little darling.

226 *half sovereign* A sovereign was a £1 gold coin, worth over £50 in
1999 terms.

226 *Esau* A reference to Genesis 33:6.

228 *entail* Legal term denoting the inheritance of land under conditions that prevented the present owner from selling it.

228 *fracaw* Fracas, disturbance.

230 *St Paul* 'Children, obey your parents in the Lord: for this is
right' St Paul's letter to the Ephesians 6:1.

231 *arch* An old usage meaning saucy, pleasantly mischievous, bold.

234 *Peggy came first* Kit, presented with the same choice, decided
'on the whole, horses were safest' (p 214).

240 *Ixion* Greek legend—after attempting to seduce Zeus' wife Hera,
Ixion was bound to a perpetually fiery wheel that rolled endlessly
across the heavens.

243 *brandy pawnee* Brandy and water—the remark about the broth
was recorded in Edith Somerville's notebooks.

Chronology of the story

As usual, the dating of the story is precise. It was Somerville and Ross's custom to plan out in great detail not only the dates of events, but genealogical tables and maps of the fictional area about which they were writing. Note that the events of the novel occur exactly two hundred years after the building of the Big House.

1712 Big House completed
1824   (June) Jas born.
         (July) His father dies in a duel.
1830–33 Tithe Wars.
1839 Jas and his mother resume ownership of the Big House.
1842–3 Jas takes part in the annexation of Sind.
1845–9 Great Famine.
1849 Jas returns from India; goes with his regiment to South Africa.
1850 Shibby born; John Weldon born.
1852 Jas returns from South Africa.
1870 John Weldon proposes to Shibby. He is rejected and goes to Dublin, where he becomes a solicitor.
1880 'thirty years and more ago'—Willy Magner proposes to Shibby. She refuses.
1887 'Half-seas-over' lease. Jas marries.
1888 Kit born.
1890 Peggy Weldon born.
1899 Shibby recaptures the drawing-room of the Big House from Mrs Bob Pindy.
1903 Weldon acquires the demesne land 'under the Act' (Land Acts).
1912   (April) Maggie Connor becomes pregnant.
         (May) Kit meets Peggy again. He is now aged 24.
         (July) Peggy goes to the Big House; Old John visits the Captain; Clytagh Races; Maggie and Kit row; Kit fights Jim O'Connor; Sir Harold arrives by yacht.
         (August) Kit proposes to Peggy; Shibby visits Old John who has been in bed three weeks.
         (August) Old John dies.
         (September) Jas sells the Big House.

Lightning Source UK Ltd.
Milton Keynes UK
UKHW020929271220
375968UK00010B/502